The Oysterville Sewing Circle

ALSO BY SUSAN WIGGS

CONTEMPORARY NOVELS

Between You & Me

Map of the Heart

Family Tree

Home Before Dark

The Ocean Between Us

Summer by the Sea

Table for Five

Lakeside Cottage

Just Breathe

The Goodbye Quilt

THE BELLA VISTA CHRONICLES

The Apple Orchard

The Beekeeper's Ball

THE LAKESHORE CHRONICLES

Summer at Willow Lake

The Winter Lodge

Dockside

Snowfall at Willow Lake

Fireside

Lakeshore Christmas

The Summer Hideaway

Marrying Daisy Bellamy

Return to Willow Lake

Candlelight Christmas

Starlight on Willow Lake

HISTORICAL NOVELS

The Lightkeeper

The Drifter

The Mistress of Normandy

The Maiden of Ireland

The Tudor Rose Trilogy

At the King's Command

The Maiden's Hand

At the Queen's Summons

The Chicago Fire Trilogy

The Hostage

The Mistress

The Firebrand

The Calhoun Chronicles

The Charm School

The Horsemaster's Daughter

Halfway to Heaven

Enchanted Afternoon

A Summer Affair

The Oysterville Sewing Circle

A Novel

Susan Wiggs

This is a work of fiction. Names, characters, places, and incidents are products of the author's imagination or are used fictitiously and are not to be construed as real. Any resemblance to actual events, locales, organizations, or persons, living or dead, is entirely coincidental.

HarperCollins books may be purchased for educational, business, or sales promotional use. For information, please e-mail the Special Markets Department at SPsales@harpercollins.com.

FIRST HARPERLUXE EDITION

ISBN: 978-0-06-291232-9

HarperLuxe™ is a trademark of HarperCollins Publishers.

Library of Congress Cataloging-in-Publication Data is available upon request.

19 20 21 22 23 LSC 10 9 8 7 6 5 4 3 2 1

For the survivors

The Oysterville Sewing Circle

Prologue

In the darkest hour before the breaking dawn, Caroline Shelby rolled into Oysterville, a town perched at the farthest corner of Washington State. The tiny hamlet hung at the very tip of a narrow peninsula, crooked like a beckoning finger between the placid bay and the raging Pacific.

She was home.

Home to a place she'd left behind forever. To a place that held her heart and memories, but not her future—or so she'd thought, until this moment. The chaotic, unplanned journey that had brought her here had frayed her nerves and blurred her vision, and she nearly missed seeing a vague shadow stir at the side of the road, then dart in front of her.

She swerved just in time to miss the scuttling possum, hoping the lurching motion of the car wouldn't wake the kids. A glance in the rearview mirror reassured her that they slept on. Keep dreaming, she silently told them. Just a little while longer.

Familiar sights sprang up along the watery-edged roadway as she passed through the peninsula's largest town of Long Beach. Unlike its better-known namesake in California, Washington's Long Beach had a boardwalk, carnival rides, a freak show museum, and a collection of oddities like the world's largest frying pan and a carved razor clam the size of a surfboard.

Beyond the main drag lay a scattering of small settlements and church camps, leading toward Oysterville, a town forgotten by time. The settlement at the end of the earth.

She and her friends used to call it that, only half joking. This was the last place she thought she'd end up.

And the last person she expected to see was the first guy she'd ever loved.

Will Jensen. Willem Karl Jensen.

At first she thought he was an apparition, bathed in the misty glow of the sodium-vapor lights that illuminated the intersection of the coast road and the town center. No one was supposed to be out at this hour, were they? No one but sneaky otters slithering around the oystering fleet, or families of raccoons and possum feasting from upended trash cans.

Yet there he was in all his six-foot-two, sweaty glory, with *Jensen* spelled out in reflective block letters across his broad shoulders. He was jogging along at the head of a gaggle of teenage boys in Peninsula Mariners jerseys and loose running shorts. She drove slowly past the peloton of runners, veering into the oncoming lane to give them a wide berth.

Will Jensen.

He wouldn't recognize the car, of course, but he might wonder at the New York license plates. In a town this small and this far from the East Coast, locals tended to notice things like that. In general, people from New York didn't come here. She'd been gone so long, she felt like a fish out of water.

How ironic that after ten years of silence, they would both wind up here again, where it had all started—and ended.

The town's only stoplight turned red, and as she stopped, an angry roar erupted from the back seat. The sound jerked her away from her meandering thoughts. Flick and Addie had endured the tense cross-country drive with aplomb, probably born of shock, confusion, and grief. Now, as they reached the end, the children's patience had run out.

"Hungry," Flick wailed, having been stirred awake by the change in speed.

I should have run that damn light, Caroline thought. No one but the early-morning joggers would have seen. She steeled herself against a fresh onslaught of worry, then reminded herself that she and the children were safe. *Safe.*

"I have to pee," Addie said. "*Now.*"

Caroline gritted her teeth. In the rearview mirror, she saw Will and his team coming toward her. Ahead on the right was the Bait & Switch Fuel Stop, its neon sign flickering weakly against the bruised-looking sky. OPEN 24 HRS, same as it had always been, back in the days when she and her friends would come here for penny candy and kite string. Mr. Espy, the owner of the shop, used to claim he was part vampire, manning the register every night for decades.

She turned into the lot and parked in front of the shop. A bound stack of morning papers lay on the mat in front of the door. "I'll get you something here," she said to Flick. "And you can use the restroom," she told Addie.

"Too late," came the reply in a small, chastened voice. "I peed." Then she burst into tears.

"Gross," Flick burst out. "I can smell it." And then he, too, started to cry.

Pressing her lips together to hold in her exasperation, Caroline unbuckled the now-howling Addie from her booster seat. "We'll get you cleaned up, sweetie," she said, then went around to the back of the dilapidated station wagon and fished a clean pair of undies and some leggings from a bag.

"I want Mama," Addie sobbed.

"Mama's not here," Flick stated. "Mama's dead."

Addie's cries kicked into high gear.

"I'm sorry, honey," Caroline said, knowing the soothing, overused phrase could never penetrate the five-year-old's uncomprehending grief. With a scowl at Flick, she said, "That's not helpful." Then she took the little girl's grubby hand. "Let's go."

A small bell chimed as she opened the door. She turned in time to see Flick heading the opposite way at a blind, angry run toward the road. "Flick," she called. "Get back here."

"I want Mama," Addie sobbed again.

Caroline let go of her hand. "Wait right here and don't move. I need to get your brother."

He was quicker than any six-year-old should be, darting through the half dark across the damp asphalt parking lot. Within seconds, he was shrouded in mist as he headed toward the cranberry bog behind the store. "Flick, get back here," Caroline yelled, breaking into a run. "I swear . . ."

"Whoa there," came a deep voice. A large shadow moved into view, blocking the little boy's path.

Caroline rushed over, engulfed in a sweet flood of relief. "Thank you," she said, grabbing for Flick's hand.

The kid wrenched his fingers from her grip. "Lemme go!"

"Flick—"

Will Jensen hunkered down, blocking his path. He positioned his large frame close in front of the boy and looked him in the eye. "Your name's Flick?"

The boy stood still, his chest heaving with heavy breaths. He glowered at Will, giving the stranger a suspicious side-eye.

"I'm Coach Jensen," Will said, showing a sort of practiced ease with the kid. "You're a fast runner, Flick," he said. "Maybe you'll join my team one day. I coach football and cross-country. We train every morning."

Flick gave the briefest of nods. "Okay," he said.

"Cool, keep us in mind. The team can always use a fast runner."

Caroline forgot how to speak as she stared at Will. There had been a time when she'd known the precise set of his shoulders, the shape of his hands, the timbre of his voice.

Will straightened up. She sensed the moment he recognized her. His entire body stiffened, and the friendly expression on his face shifted to astonishment. Nordic blue eyes narrowed as he said, "Hey, stranger. You're back."

Hey, stranger.

This was the way she used to greet him at the start of every summer of their youth. She had grown up on the peninsula, with salt water running through her veins and sand dusting her feet like a cinnamon doughnut from her parents' beachside restaurant. Will Jensen had been one of the summer visitors from the city, polished and privileged, who came to the shore each June.

You're back.

Now the decades-old greeting wasn't accompanied by the grins of anticipatory delight they'd shared each year as they met again. When they were kids, they used to imagine the adventures that awaited them—racing along the endless beaches with their kites, digging for razor clams while the surf eddied around their sun-browned bare feet, feeling the shy prodding of youthful attraction, watching for the mythic green flash as the sun went down over the ocean, telling stories around a beach fire made of driftwood bones.

Now she merely said, “Yep. I am.” Then she took Flick’s hand and turned toward the Bait & Switch. “Come on, let’s go find your sister.”

The entrance to the shop, where she’d left the little girl, was deserted.

Addie was missing.

“Where’d she go?” Caroline demanded, looking from side to side, then lengthening her strides as she towed Flick along with her. “Addie?” she called, ducking into the shop. A quick scan of the aisles yielded nothing. No movement was reflected in the convex security mirrors. “Have you seen a little girl?” she asked the sleepy-looking clerk at the counter. Not Mr. Espy, but an overweight youth with a game going on his phone. “She’s five years old, mixed race, like her brother.” She indicated Flick.

“Is Addie lost?” Flick asked, his gaze darting around the aisles and display racks.

The clerk shrugged his shoulders and palmed his hair out of his face. “Didn’t see nobody.”

“I left her right here by the door, like thirty seconds ago.” Caroline’s heart iced with fear. “Addie,” she called. "Adeline Maria, where are you? Help me look," she said to the kid. "She can't have gone far."

Will, who had followed her into the shop, turned to his team of sweaty athletes. "Go look for her," he ordered. "Little girl named Addie. She was here just a minute ago. Come on, look lively."

The boys—there were about a half dozen of them—fanned out across the parking lot, calling her name.

Caroline found the clean leggings and undies in a small heap by the door. "She needed the restroom. I told her to wait. I was only gone a minute." Her voice wavered with terror. "Oh, God—"

"We'll find her. You check inside the store," Will said.

She grabbed the clothes and stuffed them in her jacket pocket. "Stay with me, Flick," she ordered. "Do not let go of my hand, you hear me?"

His sweet round face was stony, his eyes shadowed by fear. "Addie's lost," he said. "I didn't mean for her to get lost."

"She was here a minute ago," Caroline said. "Addie! Where'd you go, sweetheart?" They went up and down the aisles, looking high and low among the stocked shelves. The store seemed no different from decades ago. They passed bins of candy and bags of marshmallows for s'mores. There were fishing supplies in abundance and a noisy chest freezer filled with bait and ice cream treats. Boxes of soup mix and Willapa Bay oyster breading and fish fry. A sign designating goods from local vendors—kettle corn, bread, eggs from Seaside Farm, milk from Smith's Dairy. Caroline's mother used to send her or one of her siblings to the Bait & Switch for supplies—bread, peanut butter, toilet paper, cupcake tins . . . With five kids in the house, they were always running out of something.

She made her way methodically along each aisle. She checked the restroom—twice. The indolent clerk pitched in, poking around the supply room in the back, to no avail.

Good God. Good fucking God, she'd only been in charge of these kids for a week and she'd already lost one of them. They had come from the urban pile of Hell's Kitchen back in New York City, yet here in what had to be the smallest town in America, Addie had gone missing.

Caroline unzipped her pocket and fumbled for her phone. No signal. No goddamn signal.

"I need your phone," she said, grabbing the clerk's from the counter. "I'm calling 911."

The guy shrugged. At the same time, Will stuck his head in the door. "Found her."

Caroline's legs nearly gave out. She set down the phone. "Where is she? Is she all right?"

He nodded and crooked his finger. Feeling weak with relief, she grabbed Flick and followed Will outside to Angelique's car—her car now, Caroline supposed.

She leaned down and peered into the window. There, curled up on the back seat, was Addie, sound asleep, clutching her favorite toy, a Wonder Woman doll with long black hair. Caroline took a deep breath. "Oh, thank God. *Addie.*"

"One of the guys spotted her," Will said.

Flick climbed in through the opposite door, his face stolid with contrition.

Caroline collapsed momentarily against the car, trying to remember how to breathe normally. The panicked departure, the jumbled, seemingly endless days of the drive, her terrible fears and confusion, the careening sense that her life was reeling out of control, rolled over her in a giant wave of exhaustion.

"You all right now?" asked Will.

Another echo sounded in Caroline's head. He'd asked her that question ten years before, the night everything had fallen apart. *You all right?*

No, she thought. Not even close to all right. Had she done the right thing, coming here? She nodded. "Thanks for helping. Tell your guys thanks, too."

"I will."

After so many years, he didn't look so very different. Just . . . more solid, maybe. Grounded by life. Big and athletic, a square-jawed all-American, he had kind eyes and a ready smile. The smile was fleeting now.

"I guess . . . you're headed to your folks' place?"

"They're expecting me." She felt a sense of dread, anticipating a barrage of welcome. Yet it was nothing compared to the situation she'd fled.

"That's good." He cleared his throat, his gaze moving over her, the crappy car stuffed with hastily packed belongings, the little kids in the back seat. Then he studied her face with a probing gaze. His eyes were filled with questions she was too exhausted to answer.

She remembered the way he used to know her every thought, could read her every mood. That was all so long ago, in an era that belonged to different people in a different life. He was a stranger now. A stranger she had never forgotten.

He went around to the rear of the car, where she'd left the hatchback wide open. His gaze flicked over the crammed interior—hastily stuffed luggage and gear, her prized single-needle sewing machine broken down in pieces to fit, her serger, boxes of belongings. He shut the door and turned to her.

"So you're back," he stated.

"I'm back."

He looked in the car window. "The kids . . . ?"

Not now, she thought. The explanation was far too complicated to explain to someone she barely knew anymore. Right now she just needed to get home.

"They're mine," she said simply, and got back in the car.

PART ONE

The cure for anything is salt water:
sweat, tears or the sea.

—Isak Dinesen

Chapter 1

New York City
Fashion Week

A plume of vapor from a garment steamer clouded the backstage section where Caroline was working. She and a couple of others from the Mick Taylor design team inspected, tagged, and hung each item in readiness for the show. The area was overheated with makeup lights, klieg lights, and too many bodies crammed into the space.

When an elite designer was about to unveil his work to the public, the bustling pre-show energy was palpable. Caroline loved it, even the stress and drama. Today's event was particularly exciting for her, because several of the designs she'd created for Mick's label would be featured. It wasn't quite the same as having her own line, but it was definitely a step in that direction. Although she labored long hours for Mick, she used every spare moment to work on her own collection. She gave up lunch hours, social time, sleep. She was a striver. She did what it took.

This was a key show for Mick Taylor, too. The past couple of seasons had failed to impress the fashion critics and influencers. Investors were getting nervous. Buyers for high-end stores wanted to be blown away. Mick and his design director were on edge. The whole industry was watching to see if he would climb back to the top of the food chain.

Everyone on the design team had been told to focus on the wow factor that would carry the designer to even greater heights. Rilla Stein, the design director, was dogged and demanding of her staff, and her loyalty to Mick was absolutely ferocious. Most of the team members were terrified of her. Though she favored pointy glasses and Peter Pan collars and looked like a cartoon librarian, she breathed fire in the design studio and had the personality of a pit viper.

"Hey, Caroline, can you give me a hand over here?" called Daria. She was a model on hiatus due to pregnancy, and was now working as a stylist. Her girl-next-door looks and growing baby bump contrasted dramatically with Angelique, Mick's longtime favorite model, who stood on an upended crate. Angelique had become the hottest runway model in the city. She hadn't even gone through casting. Mick had anointed her as his muse.

She was sought after for her innate sense of drama and her ability to switch looks at lightning speed, sometimes in as little as thirty seconds flat. She had dramatic chiseled cheekbones, bee-stung lips, and the slightest gap between her teeth. Her wide-set eyes held a shadow of mystery. Daria had styled her with a bold palette of makeup and a swirling updo, bringing the model's features into sharp relief. To those who didn't know Angelique, there was something vaguely frightening about her, a trait that commanded attention. She was one of Caroline's best friends in the city, though, and rather than being scared of her, Caroline was inspired by her.

Orson Maynard, a Page Six reporter and fashion blogger, introduced his newest intern, Becky Barrow, to Angelique. "She's working on a blog post for me, and she's been wanting to meet you," Orson said.

"And now you have." Angelique's expression softened as she shook hands with Becky, who regarded her with worshipful eyes. Angelique had avid fans in the fashion world. She'd been discovered in her native

Haiti by Mick himself, who had been on a shoot on one of the island's dramatic beaches. The cutting-edge designer was known for going to third world countries and using local talent in his fashion shoots. He'd even won humanitarian awards for his contributions to the places he'd visited.

"You must have been so excited when Mick discovered you," Becky said. "I'd love to hear how it came about. And is it okay to record?"

Angelique nodded. A mention on the right blog was good business. "Ah, that. It is not such a big story. I was just sixteen and as green as saw grass. I thought I was prepared, of course, because I was so keen. Haiti has some of the most beautiful beaches in the world. Every time I heard of a shoot going on near Port-au-Prince, I made myself useful, doing odd jobs and absorbing everything like a sponge. I learned to walk, to pose. I learned styling and makeup. I started asking for work. Any kind of work—fetching and carrying, running errands, translating because the people who came from the U.S. always needed an interpreter."

"And that's when Mick Taylor discovered you." Becky was starstruck.

"*Discover* is not quite the right word. He noticed me on a shoot when I was too young to work. Then on another shoot a year later. By that time, I had my son, Francis—he's six now. Yes, I was a teen mom," Angelique said.

"You're a fabulous mom, and Flick is amazing," Daria said.

"A year after that, I had Addie and we were able to come to New York."

"He changed your life."

"Speaking of change," Orson said, giving Caroline a nudge, "I hear you're exhibiting your original designs for the Emerging Talent program."

"I am indeed," Caroline said, aiming for a casual tone. Deep down, she was wildly excited about the opportunity. She turned to Becky. "Don't put that in your blog post, though. It's not my first rodeo, and I'm a dark horse."

"So you've exhibited before?"

"Several times."

The Emerging Talent program, funded by a consortium of established designers who had formed a nonprofit in order to nurture new artists, was the most prestigious in the New York fashion world. A panel of industry experts would view the work of several designers. The chosen one would be given a chance to exhibit their collection at the biggest runway show of the season.

If the featured designs impressed the right people, it could be the start of a successful career.

"Five minutes, everyone," called a production assistant.

"We'll find you after the show," Orson said. "Get the rest of the story."

The energy in the room heightened a notch. With a critical eye, Caroline studied a cutout jersey dress she had designed. The look featured an experimental serape made of yarn from recycled sari silk. Rilla had raised objections to the woven pieces, but Caroline had held her ground. Regarding Angelique in her show-ready hair and makeup, she was glad she had. The look was arresting, otherworldly, a stunning way to lead off the show.

"You're a fantasy woman," Caroline said. "People are going to be picking themselves up off the floor when they see you."

Angelique laughed softly. "I wouldn't want to cause an accident, *chère*." She tilted her head at a haughty angle, then stepped down and took a few practice strides.

"Amazing," Caroline said. "You're like a master class on how to walk past your ex in public." She hesitated, then said, "Speaking of your ex, what's going on with Roman?"

A few weeks before, Angelique had fallen in love. Roman Blake, a fit model for a big athletic brand, had seemed like her perfect match. He was stunningly handsome, with tattoos in all the right places, a shaved head that somehow made him even better looking, and—according to Angelique—mad skills in the sack. The few times Caroline had met him, she'd found him intimidating, with a flinty gaze and not much to say. He and Angelique had broken up the week before.

Angelique muttered a phrase in Kreyòl, her native patois, that needed no translation. "He is someone else's problem now, I imagine," she added.

"And you?" Caroline asked. "Are you doing all right?"

"I am doing fantastic," she said, turning so the serape wafted like wings, "and I think it might have something to do with this fantastic look I'm wearing."

Caroline backed off. She and Angelique and Daria were close, but Angelique had always been intensely private. "Thanks," she said. "So you like it? Really?" Caroline was constantly second-guessing herself.

"Really, *copine*." Angelique's face lit with a smile, breaking through her signature coolness.

"I owe you big-time for this gig," Caroline said. It had been Angelique who had introduced Caroline to

Rilla, which had led to her getting the contract job. "If there's ever anything I can do for you . . ."

"Let's see . . . balance my checking account? Finish raising my kids? Find me a bigger apartment?" Angelique stuck out her tongue. "Just a few small favors."

"I'll get right on that." Caroline thought of her own tiny checking account and apartment to match. Even if she wanted kids, she couldn't afford them.

Angelique stepped back up on the riser and used a hand mirror to check her makeup. "Wearing your clothes is reward enough," she said, and Caroline felt a rush of gratitude.

"I love everything about this look," Daria said. "It's going to stop the show, just you watch."

"Thanks, Dar." Caroline looked at them both—twin towers of excessive beauty. "There's a special place in heaven for loyal friends." She had enormous respect for what they did as runway models. But she never felt the urge—nor did she have the looks or skills—to join their ranks.

The industry could be hard, sometimes brutal. Up close and firsthand, she'd witnessed young women who barely made a living, crammed together in over-crowded apartments and struggling to make ends meet. Too many of them—even some of the most successful models in the business—suffered from eating disorders, financial manipulation by agencies, sexual predation, and loneliness.

As a designer, she struggled with her conscience. She was part of an industry that set up the models for a hard, even dangerous road. Early on, she'd made a promise that she wouldn't fall prey to the industry's worst practices. Her own designs were meant to be beautiful on any woman, not just a size 2 supermodel.

A flurry and buzz erupted as Mick himself swept through the staging area, leaving a ripple of excitement in his wake. Despite his stature in the design world, he looked unremarkable—modest, even. He was middle-aged and paunchy in jeans and a plain polo, and he had the affable mien of everyone's favorite uncle. Those eyes, though. They were the clearest, brightest blue, the heart of a flame, and so intensely sharp they didn't seem to belong in his ordinary face.

When he'd burst onto the scene, the press had described him as an everyman whose cutting-edge designs translated seamlessly into ready-to-wear looks. Emerging designers like Caroline regarded him as the perfect mentor—encouraging without demanding, critiquing without disparaging. She liked working for him because she'd learned so much. Looking at him now, you would never know his brand was on shaky ground and that he was just back from a stint in rehab.

He moved through the crowded space, pausing to make a comment or adjustment, greeting models and designers with an affable grin. Rilla, his shadow, followed behind, making more adjustments, though not looking at all affable.

"Well, well, well," Mick said when he got to Angelique, who was still on the pedestal. She stood like a statue of a goddess, gazing straight ahead as if barely acknowledging his existence. "So this is our lead look today."

Caroline held her breath while he inspected the garment. When he turned to her, she nearly passed out.

"This is your work?" he asked.

"I . . . Yes. It is." Don't stammer, Caroline, she told herself. Own it.

At his side, Rilla held up her clipboard and said something to him, sotto voce.

He nodded.

Caroline was half-dead by the time he spoke to her again. Had she done something wrong? Did he hate it? Was the upcycled sari too ambiguous? Would he insist on leading with a different look?

He paused, studied the outfit. She'd worked for hours to perfect it. He walked in a circle around Angelique, then turned once again to Caroline. "It's brilliant," he said. "What's your name again?"

"Caroline Shelby." Her reply came on a gust of relief.

"Good work, Ms. Shelby." He gave her a thumbs-up sign, and then he strode away.

"Fix the armhole," Rilla said in a clipped imperative.

Caroline slumped against Daria. "He likes it."

Daria high-fived her. "He likes it."

"Help me figure out what's up with the armhole." Caroline lifted Angelique's elbow.

Angelique flinched and sucked in her breath with a hiss.

"Oh, sorry! Did I hurt you? Is there a pin stuck somewhere?" Caroline brushed aside the draped fabric. Then she noticed a smudge of concealer makeup along the edge of the garment. She grabbed a pad and scrubbed at it. That was when she noticed a livid bruise coloring Angelique's side from rib cage to armpit. "Hey, what happened here? Oh my God, Daria, did you see this?"

"*No.*" Daria frowned. "Looks painful. Ange, how did you hurt yourself?"

"That." Angelique pulled away and waved a dismissive hand. "I did hurt myself—I tripped and fell on the stairs. I'm so clumsy sometimes."

Caroline felt a nudge of concern. "You're not clumsy," she said, exchanging a glance with Daria, who looked on, wide-eyed. "You're one of the most graceful models in the business. Did someone hurt you?"

A production assistant with a headset and clipboard brushed past. "Two minutes," she said to the group.

"I told you, I fell," murmured Angelique.

Caroline was at a loss. Her hands worked independently of her mind, quickly altering the armhole even as she studied her friend's bruises. "That's not what this looks like. Talk to me."

"Finish the draping," said Angelique. "Do not make this into something that it's not."

Maybe it *was* nothing, Caroline told herself. Extremely thin models tended to bruise easily, which was another thing to worry about. But maybe she should heed what the subtle quiver of instinct was telling her—Angelique was in trouble.

"If you ever need anything . . . maybe just to talk—"

"I hate talking."

"I know. I talk all the time, though."

"I know," Angelique echoed.

"Just . . . I'll help, whenever you need me. I mean that. Any hour of the day or night. You can come to me anytime."

Angelique offered a swift eye roll. "Listen, I've been on my own since I was sixteen. Taking a fall down the stairs is the least of my worries."

"Places, everyone," someone said. "Line up over here." An assistant organized the models at the side entrance.

"Remember what I told you," Caroline said. "If you ever need anything, if I can help—"

"*Nom de Dieu,* just stop." Angelique's face froze into a regal mask as she prepared to walk. A pro to the last inch of her shadow, she squared her posture, getting into character for the show. "We have work to do."

"We're not done with this conversation," Caroline said.

"Yes, we are." Angelique stepped down and followed a PA to the runway, gliding effortlessly to her place at the head of the line.

Music floated in from the runway area, and the backstage monitors showed a packed house. Caroline's gaze was glued to a monitor.

"I'm worried about her," she said to Daria as she tracked Angelique's progress through the shifting sea of people to the head of the line.

"Me too. Was she in a fight? Did someone hit her?"

"I immediately thought of Roman Blake," Caroline said. "They broke up, but what if he didn't take it so well?"

"In that case, it's good they're history, then," Daria said.

Caroline flashed on a memory from a few weeks back. A group of friends had met at Terminus, a club favored by actors and models. She'd spotted Angelique and Roman on the rooftop terrace, their postures tense as they spoke heatedly. Roman had grabbed her arm and she'd flung him off and walked away. Caroline hadn't said anything that night. Now she wished she had.

"Guess so," she said.

"And we could be totally wrong," Daria pointed out, organizing a suitcase-size makeup box. "One time, I fell off a horse during a shoot and I looked like the walking dead for days. What are the chances that it might be exactly what she said, that she fell down the stairs?"

"When was the last time you fell down the stairs?" Caroline stepped back as more models made their way to the lineup. Another of her designs drifted past, but she was too distracted to inspect it. "I hope we've seen the last of Roman."

Daria nodded. "Could it be someone else? A new guy? Someone from her past? What do you know about the father of her kids?"

"She once said he's not in the picture and never mentioned him again."

Daria gestured at the backstage monitor. "Look at her now. My God, Caroline."

The screen displaying the action on the runway showed Angelique at the height of her powers, leading off one of the most important collections of the season. The dramatic lighting and the haunting music by Sade surrounded her angular, gliding form as she conquered the runway. Onlookers held still, leaning forward, their gazes devouring her.

"She looks like a fucking queen," Daria whispered. "And that outfit . . ."

Caroline couldn't suppress a smile as the look she'd designed created a stir in the audience. The top fashion critics and bloggers furiously scribbled or tapped out their notes as the camera flashes detonated.

Angelique did look like a queen, the controversial serape floating behind her like a royal robe. The last thing she looked like was a victim.

Chapter 2

On the day she was set to exhibit her original line for adjudication, Caroline stepped outside her apartment in the Meatpacking District. The crisp air had the kind of brilliant clarity that caused even the most jaded New Yorkers to lift their eyes to the diamond-sharp blue sky.

The light of late afternoon painted the entire landscape with layers of rare and shimmering gold. The temperature was exactly right for jeans and boots and a cozy sweater. Under such conditions, it was impossible not to appreciate the world's most exciting city. She took the weather as a sign from above. People tended to romanticize New York City in autumn for good reason. When the weather gave the city a gift, it was spectacular.

Rolling her shrouded garment rack down the sidewalk, she buzzed and hummed with anticipation. Beside her—dwarfing her—were two towers of runway expertise: Daria and Angelique. Her friends were going to help showcase her designs for the panel of judges tasked with selecting the next candidate for the Emerging Talent program. As they passed the flagship store of Diane von Furstenberg, with spotless windows framing her iconic designs, Caroline felt a wave of nerves.

"I'm dying," she said. "What if they hate my stuff?"

"They will love it," said Angelique. Without the artifice of hair and makeup, she was still striking, long-necked and graceful, her bold features intense. "These people have taste."

Caroline sent her a grateful smile. "I couldn't do this without you," she said.

"You could, but I am happy to help."

"How are you doing?" Caroline asked. Tentative, not wanting to pry, but unable to forget the day she'd seen her friend's body ripe with bruises.

"I'm brilliant," Angelique said with a breezy smile. "I am ready to watch you blow the panel away today with this collection."

"They've never seen anything like it," said Daria. She was eight months pregnant now, and until today had been sidelined by the pregnancy. But with her full-moon belly and soft features, she was exactly what Caroline needed.

She was too broke to pay her models, but they had made a swap. She'd made school clothes for Angelique's kids, Flick and little Addie. For Daria, she'd created a six-piece maternity wardrobe, and Daria swore that every time she wore something from the collection, people asked where she'd bought it.

"Did you get leg cramps?" Daria asked Angelique as they walked along. "When you were pregnant, I mean."

"I did, yes, with Flick especially. When I was carrying my little boy, the cramps would keep me up at night. Try eating a banana at bedtime. The potassium might help."

Caroline tried to picture her friend pregnant. Angelique would have been just sixteen or seventeen, already on her own in Haiti. Flick came along, and less than a year later, Addie—no partner to help. It almost made Caroline feel guilty about her freakishly normal family back in Washington State.

"Did you find yourself getting up every couple of hours to pee?" Daria asked. "That's all I've been doing lately."

"Welcome to the third trimester," said Angelique. "Consider it training for getting up for night feedings."

"You both make childbearing sound so pleasant," Caroline said.

"What hospital did you use?" Daria asked.

"It was in Port-au-Prince." Angelique cut her glance away, stepping around a crack in the sidewalk. "We came to New York when they were babies. Addie was still nursing. I remember that, because of leaks during one of my agency interviews."

"Oh, man."

"You should have seen their faces. They signed me, though, and because of Mick I didn't have to go through casting."

"They would have been crazy not to," Caroline said. "You're incredible."

The venue for the design challenge event was a cavernous, light-filled old building that had once been a meat warehouse. Now it was at the center of the design district, a gathering place exploding with creativity. Caroline slowed her pace as they approached the big double doors.

"You seem nervous," Daria observed, helping to navigate the rolling rack past a busy food cart and angling it into the staging area.

"What if they love something else more?" Caroline said, eyeing the other hopeful designers waiting to present their styles. She knew most of them, at least in passing. The world of design was a small one, and the pool of talent made for intense competition.

"You can't think that way," Daria said.

"Am I awful for wanting this so much?" asked Caroline. The event was renowned in the fashion world, and the stakes couldn't be higher. She had entered the competition before but had never made the cut. Her collection was not edgy enough. Not tasteful enough. Not bold enough. Too bold. Incoherent. Unmanageable. She'd heard it all.

"Just awful, *chérie,*" said Angelique.

"This is my sixth attempt," she said. "If I fail this time . . ."

"You'll what?" Daria demanded.

Caroline took a deep breath. She remembered advice she'd read somewhere: *Don't ask who is going to let you. Ask who is going to stop you.* "I'll try again."

"You never give up," Daria said. "I like that. This is it for you. Sixth time is the charm." She patted her pregnant belly. "This is our shot, and you've worked your ass off. It's a can't-miss. What's this fabric?"

"It's a silk jersey. Gets its shimmer from copper thread." Caroline busied herself with the chosen looks on the rolling rack. The samples had to be flawless and pristine. Not a stray thread or fleck of lint. She had poured hours into these designs, and she wanted them to shine on the runway.

While she styled her models in the staging area, she couldn't help having her doubts. There was so much talent crammed into the space, it was ridiculous. Several of the designers had attended the Fashion Institute of Technology, same as her. Others she knew from jobs at the big design houses. And they were good. She saw spectacular gowns, palazzo pants, dramatic sheaths, hand-painted fabrics, and shapes that draped the models like living sculpture.

She could feel the attention on her as well—for good reason. It wasn't every day a designer showed up with a pregnant model and someone as well-known as Angelique. But Daria's pregnancy was key to Caroline's exhibit. Creating a collection like this was a huge risk. She knew that. She also knew that the biggest achievements of her career so far had resulted from risk-taking. Two years before, she'd landed the contract job with Mick Taylor by showing a collection of rainwear that changed color when it got wet.

Daria and Angelique were behind a folding screen, putting the finishing touches on their looks. Angelique stepped aside for a moment. "I want you to have a token—for luck." She held out a triple-strand bracelet of small shells expertly strung together. "When I was a girl, I gathered cowrie shells on the beach and made bracelets to sell to tourists. The shell is a symbol of the ocean spirit of wealth and earth, and it offers goddess protection—very powerful, because it is connected with the strength of the ocean."

Caroline held out her arm so Angelique could tie on the three strands. "You're going to make me cry," she said. "What did I do to deserve a friend like you?"

Angelique didn't answer. Instead, she stepped back and said, "There, you're fully protected. Now go and show off your hard work."

Caroline rolled the garment rack into the showroom. The five-judge panel sat at a draped table littered with papers, cameras, smartphones, and coffee cups. The adjudicators were bright lights of the fashion world—a magazine editor, a fashion critic, and three top designers, all eager to find new talent. So many ways to fail, thought Caroline, hoping they couldn't see her sweat.

She stood in front of her garment rack and unzipped the covering. Maisie Trellis, the critic, perched a pair of reading glasses on her nose and consulted the screen of her tablet. "You're Caroline Shelby, from Oysterville, Washington."

Caroline nodded. "That's where I grew up, yes. It's about as far west as you can get before falling into the ocean."

"Tell us a bit about your career so far."

"I went to the Fashion Institute of Technology and I've been doing contract work. My first job out of school was refurbishing vintage couture. I did alterations, piecework, anything that would help me pay the rent."

"And now you're designing for Mick Taylor."

"Just finished working on a ready-to-wear collection."

"Tell us about this." Maisie peered over her glasses at the rack.

Caroline paused. Drew a breath. This was her moment. "I call this line Chrysalis." She unveiled the rack. Fabrics in a palette of earth and sky tones shimmered in the autumn light through the windows. Daria emerged from behind the folding screen, her pregnancy eliciting murmurs from the panel. The fabric draped her ripe belly like a cocoon of gossamer, floating with every step she took. Next, Angelique stepped out, a willow-slim goddess, wearing a similar look.

"My garments won't be obsolete after the baby comes," Caroline said, encouraged by the expressions on the people's faces. "Like a chrysalis, the top transforms."

With a sweep of drama, Angelique demonstrated the conversion. The gorgeous tunic draped upward, fastening at the shoulders. "It creates a sling for the baby, and a modesty shroud for the nursing mother," Caroline said. "It's a piece that will last beyond the pregnancy, and even beyond nursing."

She showed the rest of the collection, piece by piece. Each garment had a secret conversion achieved by different ways of draping and fastening. The fabrics were all sustainable and organic, with bright accents shot through with mother-of-pearl, a nod to her childhood home by the sea. She had created a signature grace note at the shoulder of each piece, a stylized nautilus shell highlighted with shimmering thread.

"What was your inspiration?" asked one of the judges. "Do you have children?"

"Oh my gosh, no." In a moment of stark honesty, she added, "I doubt I'll ever have kids. I'm the middle child of five, and I kind of got lost in my busy family. I do like other people's kids, but I love my independence. My inspiration comes from people like Angelique and Daria. They're working moms, and they deserve to wear beautiful things every day, through pregnancy, nursing, and beyond. And it's also my commitment to sustainable practices. I imagine you hear that a lot. It's a buzzword—what to do about textile waste created by discarded garments. My maternity tunic can live on as a nursing top and carrier sling, and the fabric source I used was CycleUp for most of the pieces." It was the industry standard for recycled fabrics.

The panel inspected each garment while she watched, her heart in her mouth. Her craftsmanship was impeccable, every stitch in place, every edge and pleat knife-sharp. She knew this was her finest work. And when the demonstration ended, she felt a wave of pride. "This is the best I've got. I hope you like it. Thank you for the opportunity."

The judges consulted one another, asked more questions, made more notes. Then Maisie dismissed her with an impenetrable look. "We're intrigued, Caroline Shelby. But we have a long way to go today. We'll let you know."

Chapter 3

Caroline bumped her way down the stairs of her apartment, lugging an overstuffed suitcase. She always brought extra supplies to a show—fabric and thread, pins, scissors, touch-up for makeup, towels, a flashlight and double-sided tape, and wipes in case of model meltdowns . . . or designer meltdowns.

She was not going to have a meltdown today. Totally the opposite. Today was going to be a huge leap forward in her career. Finally, after so many abject failures and near misses, her Chrysalis line had been selected for the Emerging Talent program. The collection bearing her name would be showcased on the runway in front of all the fashion elite in the city.

If she impressed the right people, she would get her shot at creating apparel under her own name.

That, she knew, would be life-changing. People back home had never quite understood her aspirations. They had been kind enough. They were quick to say they appreciated her creativity. Yet they'd always been mystified by her life and work. Her entry-level jobs, most of them involving long hours and low pay, had struck them as thankless and unrewarding. Which was quite an indictment, coming from her family of restaurateurs.

But a line of apparel—that would be concrete proof that she'd set out on the right path. A ready-to-wear collection was a tangible achievement, something everyone could see. That alone was thrilling. It also gave Caroline the kind of fulfillment she'd always sought—the satisfaction of a particular creative hunger.

She had been focused on this goal for eight seasons of working for Mick Taylor. She'd learned a lot, but it wasn't her dream. The dream was what she did after she went home, after she'd spent uncounted hours designing season after season of cutting-edge fashions under the keen eye of Rilla Stein. She'd learned to subsist on microwave burritos and too much caffeine, staying up long into the night to create something wholly her own, an exuberant expression of her unique aesthetic.

She pulled her gear along the sidewalk toward Illumination, dreaming of a day when she'd have assistants and stylists to help. Today's show venue had a long runway and brilliant lighting, a waterfall backdrop, and tons of backstage monitors so she wouldn't miss a moment. Every time she pictured her collection on display, she had to pinch herself.

She hoped her outfit was okay. She had opted for stark black and white, her usual work attire. The skinny black pants and boxy white top, chunky jewelry and flat shoes were well suited for rushing around the city.

The backstage was divided into two wings, east and west, separated by a folding wall. Caroline was assigned to the east side. In the staging area, a buzz of excitement vibrated through the air, which smelled of hair spray and aniline. She joined the flow of rushing designers, dressers, assistants, models, producers, photographers and their entourages, bloggers, and reporters. It was a ballet of barely controlled chaos as showtime approached. The established designers would show their collections, and Caroline's debut would come at the very end.

She wove a path through the racks and found her station. She checked her notes and spotted Angelique standing on a riser and chatting with Orson Maynard, who was furiously taking notes.

"I heard a rumor that you're responsible for all this lovely," Orson said, regarding the fantasy ball gown Caroline had designed for Mick Taylor's line.

"The garment's my design, but all the lovely comes from Angelique." Caroline noticed a raw edge peeking out of the bodice. "Hold still," she said, swiftly threading a needle to tack it into place.

Daria arrived, huffing and puffing as she set down a box of accessories. She stepped back to admire Angelique. "Wow."

"How are you feeling?" Caroline took a chunky cocktail ring from the box and tried it on Angelique.

"I'm good," said Daria. "I'd rather be out on the runway, but you're the only designer in need of a massively pregnant model." She selected a makeup brush and touched up Angelique's cheekbones.

"You both looked incredible at my presentation," said Caroline.

Orson bustled forward with his notepad. "And . . . ?" he asked.

Caroline had forgotten he was there. She ducked her head and busied herself by sorting through the accessories.

"You're not supposed to have heard anything." Caroline suppressed a riff of excitement.

"You know how the rumors fly," he told her.

"What did you hear?"

"That your originals have been selected for the Emerging Talent program."

She tried not to react. Tried not to hyperventilate. "Oh?"

"Stomp your foot once if it's true, twice if it's not."

"It is true," Angelique murmured between strokes of Daria's makeup brush. "But you cannot say anything about it yet."

"She's right," said Caroline. "This whole conversation has to be off the record."

"Of course." Orson put away his notes. "So I take it you're stomping once."

Caroline couldn't keep the grin from her face. "The whole world will see at the end of today's show."

"It's so awesome," Daria said. "When I saw the work she submitted to the panel, I knew they'd pick her."

"Now I'm salivating," said Orson.

"I've barely been able to sleep or eat since I got the call." Caroline was bursting. The moment she'd heard the news, her entire world had shifted on its axis.

"Can you set my phone by me?" Angelique asked. "I need to call my kids."

Caroline propped the phone on a rack close by, and Angelique made a video call. Her daughter picked up, poking her face in close. "*Maman,*" she said in her little Minnie Mouse voice, and then asked something in Haitian Kreyòl.

"At the show, *ti cheri mwen.* Tell your brother to come."

The picture tilted as Addie called for Flick. The two of them leaned in close, chattering to their mother in a rapid patois of French and English.

"Her kids are so danged cute," Daria said.

Caroline poked her face next to Angelique's. "Hi, guys! Remember me?"

"Caroline!" Addie clapped her hands. "You made me a hood with a mask."

"That's right. For when you need to hide from the paparazzi."

"What's paparazzi?" asked Flick.

"All the people who want to take your picture when you're getting coffee," said Caroline.

"I don't like coffee," Flick said.

"Then you probably don't have to worry about the paparazzi," said Angelique.

"When are you coming home, *Maman*?" asked Addie.

"After the show. After you're asleep. Be good for Nila, okay?" She added something in French and blew them a kiss.

"They're wonderful," Caroline said.

Angelique smiled. "They're my life."

"I don't know how you do it all, being a single mom and having this amazing career."

Daria nodded. "It must be really hard. No idea how I could make it work if I didn't have Layton."

"I don't wonder about these things," said Angelique. "I do what must be done."

Daria's hand drifted to her distended belly. She gasped and moved her hand lower.

"Are you all right?" asked Caroline.

She nodded. "Braxton-Hicks contractions."

"You're sure?"

"Yep. Saw the doctor this morning."

"Here we go," a production manager called. "Five-minute warning!"

Caroline had to set aside her worry through the backstage frenzy of the show. Everyone pitched in to style the models and send them out to the percussive soundtrack that flowed through the speakers. Between hurried wardrobe changes, Caroline and Daria watched on the live-feed monitors set backstage. The buzziest stars and media types sat in the front rows along the runway. Plugged-in bloggers commented on the show in a constant stream, and the feed scrolled along the bottom of the monitors.

Even on the screens, the scene looked incredible. The theme of water and light worked beautifully. The models appeared to float along with the current projected on the surface of the runway.

"God, I love my job," she murmured, watching a gaucho pants and midriff blouse ensemble she'd designed for Mick Taylor shimmer past the admiring crowd.

The accolades for the entire collection were enthusiastic, judging by the popping of cameras, the eruptions of applause, and the sight of critics and bloggers madly live-tweeting and broadcasting the show. She checked her phone's live feed. The list that scrolled up the screen was filled with words of praise.

Daria high-fived her. "That was incredible. And we're done here. The finale is coming from the other side of the stage. After that, it's your moment."

She shuddered with pleasure and nerves. "Cool. Let's watch."

Jostled by models hurrying to and fro to change, they found a spot by a large screen just as the final collection came from the opposite side of the stage. The soundtrack shifted to a haunting electronic version of Handel's *Water Music.*

The lead model emerged, and a collective gasp issued from the audience. The live feed at the bottom of the screen immediately lit with comments. Caroline tilted her head up to watch. She blinked, then frowned in confusion. What the hell . . . ?

The model, visibly and dramatically pregnant, was

wearing a tunic. And not just any tunic. It was a piece Caroline had designed for her original line.

She grabbed Daria's arm and dug her fingers in deep.

"Ouch! Hey—"

"Look at the runway," Caroline said in a strangled whisper. At the far end, the model demonstrated the garment's conversion from maternity tunic to nursing top, and the audience went crazy.

"Holy crap," Daria said. "Is that . . . ? Oh, God."

"It's my collection." Caroline felt nauseous as her clothes paraded down the runway, garnering looks of admiration and bursts of applause. The garments were virtually indistinguishable from her designs. Her original designs. The samples were made from slightly different fabrics. More expensive headwear and footwear. Models she'd never seen before.

But the unique aspects of the clothing—the conversion from maternity to nursing to fashion, and even the stylized nautilus motif at the shoulder—had been lifted straight from Caroline's own designs. A blatant, outright theft.

The collection was touted as Mick Taylor's innovative new line called Cocoon.

Caroline crossed her arms in front of her middle as a wave of nausea reared up inside her. The sense of violation was as overwhelming as a physical assault, invasive and shocking. The live tweet feed at the bottom of the screen lit with more praise: *Mick Taylor is back with a stunner of a collection.*

Daria was saying something, but Caroline couldn't hear through the roar of outrage in her ears. Her gaze stayed glued to the monitor, which now showed Mick Taylor at center stage, accepting accolades like a conquering hero.

All through the backstage area, the post-show rush continued to swirl like a tornado, but still she didn't move. Yet her thoughts whirled around and around. Mick Taylor had copied her original collection, the one that was meant to launch her own career. The man she worked for, the man to whom she'd given her loyalty and hard work, had stolen her designs.

She staggered, dizzy with outrage. Angelique appeared at her side, bringing her to a stool. "Did you see?" Caroline asked, still too shocked to feel anything but numb disbelief.

"I'm so sorry. Come sit," Angelique said.

"How completely shitty," Daria said. "What an underhanded thing to do."

Caroline took a deep breath. The numbness was wearing off and giving way to something more awful. Everyone knew what stealing looked like, but nothing could have prepared her for the shock of it. "I'm shaking. God, I feel so violated."

"He is terrible," said Angelique. "I'm ashamed to even know him."

Caroline had to remind herself to breathe. This was a common occurrence in the fashion industry, happening at all levels. No one was safe. This particular situation was a virtual case study of a major label appropriating designs from an independent artist. Students in design school were told to expect it, and maybe on some level she had. The practice went by different names—"referencing," "inspired by," "an homage."

Trying not to puke, she rocked back and forth on the stool. "No one is dead or injured," she muttered. "No one has been given a cancer diagnosis. It's not the end of the world."

"That is right," Angelique said. "You're strong. You'll get through this. You will go on to do great things."

She tried to shake off the nausea. Tried to pull herself together. Her phone vibrated, the screen crowded with messages and notifications. After a few minutes, a new sensation coursed through her—a slow burn of anger. "Right," she said. "I never got into this field because it was easy, did I?"

"Exactly," said Daria.

"I'm going to go find him."

"No," said Angelique, her eyes widening. "Don't do it, Caroline. Mick will—"

"He'll what?" Caroline stood. The anger simmered like a fever, heightening her senses. "What will he do? Destroy my career? He's already done that." The reality shuddered through her: "I can't show my collection now. I literally have nothing to lose."

Daria and Angelique looked at each other. "I'm sorry," Daria whispered.

Mick had planned the theft just right, Caroline realized. He had preempted her debut and sabotaged any attempt she might make to launch her line—with these designs, anyway. "I'll survive," she said with quiet conviction. "But that doesn't mean I'll go without a fight."

To her utter mortification, an announcement was made, and her collection was sent out on the runway. The audience was expecting a big reveal of the Emerging Talent recipient. Caroline couldn't bring herself to look at the monitors. She didn't want to see the expressions on the faces of the attendees. Didn't want to see them pointing and whispering, speculating about the rampant similarities between her designs and those of Mick Taylor. As far as the audience knew, she was the thief, not him.

It was the ultimate betrayal by a man she had trusted. She had a complicated relationship with him; for the past couple of years it had been the biggest relationship of her life, leaving little room for anything else. She owed her career to him. Yet today he'd stolen that and destroyed her in public. She felt duped and naive. How could she have trusted him? How had she not seen this coming?

Maybe she'd been dazzled by his fame, drawn in by his aw-shucks charm and charisma. Maybe she'd missed the signs.

Someone—a production assistant or intern—gave her a shove to follow the final model out onto the runway. What should have been a march of triumph had turned into a walk of shame. The applause was subdued, and instead of her prepared remarks about her inspiration and her expressed gratitude to Mick Taylor, she managed to choke out, "Thank you for the opportunity."

There was a collective hush, followed by a scramble as the audience made for the exits. Caroline rushed backstage, on fire with a sense of betrayal.

"Caroline, wait." Angelique reached for her.

Caroline shook her head, then wove a path through the crowd and made her way into the auditorium. It was emptying out slowly. The star designers were clustered near the runway, surrounded by their entourages, accepting congratulations, getting invited to after-parties, posing for photos, answering questions from the press.

Mick was easy enough to find, the center of an undulating cluster of reporters and photographers. He and Rilla were all smiles as they basked in the afterglow of the successful show.

Caroline jostled a path through the crowd. Rilla noticed her first. "Good show, Caroline," she said. "The looks you worked on were so great."

Caroline ignored her, even though Rilla was her mentor at work, the one who'd hired her and the supervisor she reported to. Rilla was supposed to protect her designers. But of course the design director's first loyalty was to Mick.

Squeezing through an opening in the crowd, she planted herself directly in front of him. "You stole my designs," she stated, speaking slowly and clearly.

He looked down at her, his brow quirked in a small frown. "Sorry, what?"

Several cameras snapped their picture.

She went up on tiptoe and said into his ear, "You copied my designs—your so-called Cocoon line."

The frown deepened. His gaze flicked briefly to Rilla. Then he reacted with a patronizing smile. A few more camera flashes went off. "And what was your name again?"

Caroline knew the deliberate, direct cut was meant to put her in her place. Standing on tiptoe again, she cupped her hands and said with perfect articulation, "I'm about to be your worst nightmare. That's who I am."

His easy smile never wavered. Her bravado now felt like a curl of dread in her gut. Deep down, she knew what he was doing. "And five minutes from now," Mick said, "no one will remember your name."

Chapter 4

The door buzzer sounded in the middle of the night. Caroline scrambled out of bed in confusion and went to stand in front of the receiver by the door. All the locks were done up.

The buzzer went off again.

Still she hesitated. Nobody came to see her in the middle of the night. Nobody came to see her at all anymore. Not since she had declared war on Mick Taylor—and lost. She'd gone down in flames of glory. No, not even glory. All the righteous anger in the world was no foil for reality in the fashion business—designers stole from one another, shamelessly and blatantly, all the time. And the victims had almost no recourse. Mick held all the cards. He had the power to get someone fired and blackballed with a single swipe on his phone.

Shrugging into a hoodie, she went to the front window and looked out. Angelique's car was parked on the street in front of the downstairs deli. What the hell? She buzzed her in, then clumped down the stairs.

"We need a place to stay," Angelique said. "Me and my kids." Addie and Flick clung to her legs.

"Did something happen?"

Angelique ducked her head, indicating the children. "Can you help?"

Caroline was not mystified. She knew this had something to do with the bruises she had observed on Angelique at the fashion show a while back. She nodded. Within minutes, they had brought the children up to her place. Her impossibly tiny place. Flick and Addie whined in sleepy protest. Caroline and Angelique managed to get them settled on the foldout sofa. After they were asleep, Angelique collapsed into a chair. Even in the dim light, Caroline could see that the model's lip was swollen and crusted with dried blood.

"Who did this?" She got a damp cloth and some ice for her friend's lip. "Was it Roman?"

"Roman? No. He's . . . we're . . . no." She seemed confused, agitated. "I told you, I broke up with Roman. He's not—"

"Is he pissed about the breakup? Will he be a problem?"

"Roman? No," she said again.

"Then who hurt you? We need to get you to a doctor. Or the police."

Angelique shook her head. "And be up all night answering questions? What do I do with my kids? Listen, I don't need either. I'm . . . I just need to get away. I was behind on the rent. There was an eviction notice. Everything I own is in the car."

"Ange, I had no idea. I thought you were doing so well."

"My agency was deducting rent money from my pay—but not paying the rent. And that is only the start."

Caroline knew some agencies were notorious for taking advantage of models. She didn't want to press Angelique tonight. "Tell me who did this. This is serious. You need help. More help than I know how to give."

"No," she said again. "I can't—I'll be all right. It's complicated."

"It's not complicated. You've been assaulted—and not for the first time. I'm calling the police."

"You can't. You must not. I'll be deported."

Caroline frowned. "Are you undocumented?"

Angelique nodded. "My work visa expired. If you call the authorities, I could lose my kids. I'm just so tired. I need to rest. Can we talk about it tomorrow?"

"Are you safe?" Caroline asked. "Were you followed?"

"No. I wouldn't put you in danger."

"Listen, you and your kids can stay as long as you need to," said Caroline. "But if you don't report this, there's no guarantee that you'll be safe."

"I can't risk being deported," she repeated with a shudder.

"Then could you claim asylum or something? I know it's probably not a simple process, but it would be a start."

"I'm not starting anything tonight." Angelique gave a weary sigh and dabbed gingerly at her lip. "It was a mistake to come here. I should go."

"Don't you dare. I want to help. But I have to know how. We need to figure out what to do in a situation like this."

Angelique steadfastly refused to name her attacker. She refused to press charges. "My visa's expired," she explained again. "That means I'm here illegally. My kids are here illegally. I can't risk it."

"What happened to you is illegal, regardless of your status."

"Perhaps, but I still won't risk it."

"What would happen if you did go back to Haiti?" Caroline asked. "Would it be the end of the world?"

"As a matter of fact, it would."

"It would be worse than being battered by a man you're scared to name?" She still suspected Roman, the jilted boyfriend, but for some reason, Angelique was protecting him.

"Haiti is much worse, and I do not say that lightly."

"Seriously? Don't you have family back home? Friends?"

Angelique looked at her for several seconds. "Let me tell you about life in Haiti. What I would go back to. We lived in the Cité Soleil slum—that's in Port-au-Prince—in a shack made from sheets of corrugated tin. I was three years old when I lost my mother. I'm told she died of the cholera along with my baby brother. There is always a cholera outbreak in Cité Soleil."

"I'm sorry. I didn't know."

"My father had no education because his family turned him out to work when he was ten years old. He survived by working as a *bayakou.*" She paused. "Do you know what that is?"

"No, sorry, I don't."

"Consider yourself fortunate that you don't. You see, in Haiti, in many parts of the city, there is no sewage system. Families that can't afford them have latrines instead. And these latrines need to be emptied. That is the job of the *bayakou.* My father earned the equivalent of four dollars a night doing this work. It was barely enough to keep us alive. He went out at night while I slept." She paused. "Are you sure you want to hear this?"

"You lived it. I can handle hearing it."

"He worked his job naked, because there was no way to clean clothes tainted by the filth. When I was very small, I was proud to have such a hardworking papa. By the time I reached school age, that all changed. The other children shunned me because of the labor my father did. You can imagine the names they called me."

"Jesus, Angelique. I had no idea."

"Most of the world does not. I was fifteen when Papa died. It was an infection. He was always getting something from the work he did—infections, sores that wouldn't heal. He kept me away from him. I have no memory of ever touching him. When he died, I had nothing. I sold bracelets made from cowrie shells I found on the beach, and sometimes relied on the charity of strangers."

Caroline gently covered Angelique's slim, elegant hand with her own. Angelique's nails were bitten and ragged. "You had it so rough. I can't even imagine. Now I know you're even more awesome because you found a way to survive."

Angelique was silent for several seconds. Then at last she cried. Her tears were fierce and regal, and she looked like a queen sitting there, her life in tatters. "I came here to give my children a chance at a better life. What a terrible failure I am now."

Caroline tried to sound confident and decisive. "None of this is your fault. And you're not alone. I want you to try getting some sleep. Tomorrow we'll figure out a way through this."

Caroline didn't sleep at all that night. She couldn't. It was too upsetting to think about some monster hitting her friend. It was the height of frustration that she was at such a loss. She was angry—at her friend for not leveling with her. At the assailant Angelique refused to name. At the agency that exploited a vulnerable model. At herself for not knowing how to support her friend.

She spent hours online, researching shelters and aid organizations for both immigrants and victims of domestic violence. She stalked Roman Blake online. She stalked Angelique, too, culling through her list of friends and associates, trying to determine who else in her life might have attacked her.

In the morning, they went together to the kids' school. Despite what had occurred the night before,

Angelique looked incredible—her damaged lip concealed, fingernails trimmed, hair done, boxy top over skinny jeans with half boots. It made Caroline wonder how many times her friend had hidden the horrors she'd endured.

The children seemed unaware of the drama. They knew only that they were moving, a frequent occurrence in their lives. At the school, Caroline filled out a form designating herself as the children's guardian and emergency contact. Then she convinced Angelique to go with her to the Lower East Side Haven, a place that provided services to victims. The staff there was discreet and moved with incredible swiftness, offering ways to keep her and her children safe. To Caroline's surprise, no one pressured Angelique to name her abuser or to turn him in. One of the counselors explained that in the midst of a volatile situation, the priority was safety before justice.

After an exhaustive round of questions, the counselor said, "I wish I had better news. But I have to tell you, there's a waiting list for accommodations. It's a sad fact that the need is greater than what we can provide."

Seeing the anguish on her friend's face, Caroline took Angelique's hand. "You and the kids will stay with me." She turned to the counselor. "We'll make it work."

"Coming here was the right thing to do." The counselor leveled her gaze at Angelique. "It's incredibly important to have a plan." She went through it step by step. Gas in the car. A prepaid phone, bought with cash. An emergency fund.

Angelique tensed up when the counselor asked about personal documents—ID, birth certificates for herself and the kids, insurance policies and papers, financial documents. She was caught in the horrible bind that so many undocumented workers with children faced. She could be deported at any time. She might be separated from her children. The prospect made her physically ill; Caroline could see her shaking.

"I'm sorry to have to ask this," the counselor went on. "Do you have a plan for your children in case something happens to you?"

"The plan is that I'll be the guardian. I know your kids, Ange. And it's just a backup, after all." Caroline tried to sound reassuring.

Angelique stared down at the stack of papers. She held herself very still.

"Every parent is obligated to have a plan, no matter what the circumstances. I know you love your children," the counselor pointed out. "Have you made a will?"

Chapter 5

Caroline's phone vibrated like a trapped bee against her chest. She ignored it. She was on a city bus, swaying under the weight of a duffel bag stuffed with vintage leather jackets that needed re-furbishing. Thanks to Mick Taylor, she had been blacklisted. She had tried to defend herself, blasting Mick on social media, contacting bloggers and reporters. But the situation was all too common, and she was ignored. None of the design houses in the city would hire her, so in order to make the rent, she had to take in piecework the way she used to do when she was in design school.

It was a huge step backward. Many steps, in fact. After crawling forward for years, she'd been knocked all the way back to square one. Thinking about all the time and effort she'd poured into getting this far in her career, she wondered what the point was now. There were moments when she wanted to give up, to curl into a ball and wail about the injustice of it all.

And then, with the same dogged determination that had driven her to New York, she forced herself through those moments. Sometimes it felt like she was dragging herself from one side of the moment to the other through a pit of mud.

Then she would picture Mick's smug, patronizing face, and the image would help her find the fire once again. How could she ever have thought he was her mentor, her mild-mannered surrogate uncle? He might have copied her designs, but she refused to allow him to steal her dream. And despite his status in the fashion world, he and his design director knew what they had done, whether they admitted it or not.

The trouble with being a design thief was that he would forever be in the trap of having to steal. Caroline knew she had an infinite variety of designs inside her. A thief was limited to those he could appropriate from others.

"You are an empty soul, Mick Taylor," she muttered under her breath. "As empty as—"

The phone vibrated again. She wrenched it out of her pocket, but missed the call. As empty as my bank account. Christ.

She exited the bus as the phone vibrated yet again—another notification of an incoming call and a voice mail. She didn't recognize the number. Maybe for once it would be good news. God, wouldn't it be nice if she found a gig?

She ducked inside her apartment building to escape the street noise. The usual pile of junk mail had escaped the too-small boxes and littered the foyer of the building, which always seemed to smell like soup. Nothing of note. Coupons, credit card offers, her Con Ed bill with a U-shaped heel mark where someone had stepped on it, stamping it with the honeycomb tread of a high-end Apiary shoe.

She threw the mail on top of her duffel and lugged it upstairs, then set it down to let herself in. The door wasn't locked, which rankled her. Since Angelique and her kids had come to stay, Caroline's tiny space was even more crowded than ever. "Hello?" she called.

The apartment was quiet. There was . . . something. Something was off. Caroline couldn't quite place the niggling sensation that prickled across her skin. It was subtle, just a peculiar heaviness in the air. An unfamiliar scent.

"Oh, hey, Angelique," she said, shaking off the feeling.

Her friend was napping on the overstuffed sofa. She didn't stir. Her routine was erratic sometimes, although each day after getting the kids off to school, Angelique went to church at Saint Kilda's. It was just something she did, and she seemed private about it, so Caroline didn't ask questions.

"Ange." Caroline dragged the duffel into the room. "Hey, girl," she said. "You left the door unlocked. Bad idea to—" Her phone buzzed again, and this time she picked up. "Hello?"

"This is the attendance clerk at Sunrise Academy," said a voice. "We haven't been able to get hold of Ms. Baptiste, and her children are waiting to be picked up. Your number is listed as an alternate contact. Would you have any idea where she is?"

"As a matter of fact, I just walked in the door, and she's here."

"Oh, good. Can you tell her to come right away? Unfortunately, it's late and no one can stay with Ms. Baptiste's children."

"I'll tell her," Caroline said, feeling a twinge of annoyance as she rang off. How could Angelique forget her kids? "Hey, girl," she said. "You need to get over to the school, stat. Your kids are waiting."

Angelique still didn't wake up. She didn't move.

Caroline felt a weird knot of apprehension in her gut. Crossing the cluttered room, she swept aside the window drape and looked at her friend.

"No." Her voice was a low plea of disbelief. "Dear God, no." She froze for three beats of her heart. One—the angle of Angelique's head. Two—the ashy pallor of her skin. Three—some kind of drug paraphernalia on the floor.

Caroline didn't scream. Not out loud, anyway.

Then she stumbled back and dove for her phone.

While law enforcement people and paramedics swarmed the place, Caroline shook with unbearable fright. She answered the first round of questions with wooden, disjointed replies. Then she rushed to the bathroom and threw up.

Someone from the medical examiner's office came. More questions. All signs pointed to an accidental drug overdose, to be verified by a toxicology report. Overdose? How could there be an overdose when Angelique didn't use drugs?

"It happens," a guy said, standing over Caroline as she hyperventilated. "Addicts know how to hide things." He said the body would be removed by the ME and an investigative report would be prepared.

She couldn't take it all in. Words like *the body* and *the deceased* had never been uttered before in her presence. Angelique, an addict? How could that be?

She managed to call the school again. Tried to choke out an explanation of the inexplicable. She arrived at the school just as darkness was settling over the city. The principal was there, along with a social worker. Flick and Addie, in their little tartan and navy uniforms, were in the main office, eating Goldfish crackers and watching a kids' show on a laptop.

Caroline forced herself to stop shaking. She went into the office and sat on the floor next to them. "Hey, you two," she said, her voice a bit too bright.

"Want some Goldfish?" Flick held out the container.

"No, thank you." She closed the laptop. Looked at the principal and social worker, who stood by. "I'm here because something happened to your mama," she said. Good God. "It's terrible news. Addie, Flick." She drew them close, their tiny warm bodies feeling so fragile. "The worst possible thing happened. Your mama died today."

Addie tilted her head to one side. Then her sweet face crumpled. "She can't be dead. I don't want her to be dead."

"Nobody does. She would never leave you on purpose. It was an accident. She took a bad drug and it caused her to die. You won't be able to see her anymore, but you're safe with me." Every word felt wrenched from her. "I'm so sorry it happened. So very sorry. We're going to be sad for a long time, but I'll take care of you."

Flick pounded the Goldfish into crumbs. His face was blank with bewilderment. "Where's Mama now?"

"They took her to a special place," Caroline said. "They have to check and see exactly what caused her to die. And then . . . I'm not sure." She sent a helpless look at the social worker. Addie dissolved into tears. Flick, just a year older, scooted over next to his sister and put both his arms around her.

"Where are we going?" asked Flick. "Are we going home?"

According to the emergency caseworker, the child protective services system would take them in if there were no other alternatives. The caseworker also said the system was beyond overburdened. There were more children in need than the department could handle. There were emergency foster homes, but that was a temporary measure. The caseworker told Caroline that lacking a guardian, Flick and Addie would be placed among strangers, possibly separated.

It took Caroline about two seconds to nix that idea. She absolutely could not abide the thought of these poor kids thrust into the unknown, their already traumatized hearts shredded, possibly beyond repair. "They're staying with me," she declared. "Tell me what I have to do."

A social worker helped her file a petition for emergency guardianship. With both children in tow and no money for a lawyer, she showed up in court for a hearing. The social worker said there would be no need for a lawyer, since there was no one to dispute guardianship. The boxy, high-ceilinged room was crowded and noisy, and the kids huddled close on a bench until it was their turn. A family court advocate explained that it wouldn't be a full formal hearing, and that the orders would be temporary.

The judge looked harried, though not overwhelmed. Just . . . resigned and sympathetic. He regarded her thoughtfully, studied the police report, then each of the children. "I'm very sorry for your loss," he said. "I've read over everything personally in this case. Ms. Shelby, thank you for submitting your information so quickly."

There had been a mad scramble for the school's affidavits, custody evaluations, a notarized will, the police report, and the coroner's findings. A social worker had visited Caroline's apartment—so small, but deemed adequate to accommodate the children. While the judge shuffled through a file of papers, Addie's teacher showed up and escorted the kids out into the hall.

Good, thought Caroline. She didn't want them hearing what was likely to be said about their mother.

"What was your relationship to Ms. Baptiste?"

"She was my friend, Your Honor. We work—worked—in the same industry and . . . we were friends. Close friends." Caroline took a deep breath, trying to ignore the bumping and whispering of other people in the courtroom. "We met as colleagues. Angelique was a model, and I'm a designer. She came to me on the night of March twenty-third with injuries from a fight. She wouldn't call police and she wouldn't say who hurt her. I don't believe the kids know, either. She and the children stayed at my place. I agreed to be designated as guardian in case something happened to Angelique. I never dreamed the situation would arise."

"Were you aware of her drug use?"

"Not at all," Caroline admitted. "I had no idea. I still can't believe it."

"And yet she died in your apartment of an overdose of intravenous drugs."

She looked up at the judge, her chest tight with anguish. "I'm no expert, but I can tell you I never noticed a single sign of that. Angelique was one of the best models in the industry. She worked hard. She loved her kids and they adored her. I wish I'd known. I wish I could have done something. Your Honor, the only thing I can do for my friend now is take care of her children."

She thought again of Roman Blake. He'd been questioned by the police, and it was found that he had a criminal record, but he was released based on the fact that there was nothing to tie him to Angelique. He had no legal claim to the children, but Caroline was fearful of him. She needed to protect Flick and Addie.

"You understand fully that you're making a serious commitment in every way—financially, emotionally—"

"I do understand. It's a lot. But there's no one else. She has no living family. I can do this, Your Honor. I always said I'd be there for her." She snapped her mouth shut, reminding herself not to babble.

"You're currently unemployed. Is that correct?"

"No," she said, her chin lifting in self-defense. "I'm working independently."

"According to your recent bank statements, you're not bringing in enough money to support yourself, let alone two children. We need to know your plan, Ms. Shelby."

She had lain awake half the night, agonizing over her decision. Referring to the documents she'd submitted to the custody evaluator, she said, "My plan is to take Flick—Francis—and Adeline to my home state of Washington. We will be staying at my family home where I grew up in the town of Oysterville."

The judge studied the documents. "I've read the statements you provided from Dorothy and Lyle Shelby. Your parents?"

"Yes, sir. Your Honor." When Caroline had called them in a panic, they had not hesitated, bless them. *Bring those poor children home,* her mother had said. *We'll sort everything out once you get here.*

Assuming the judge would allow it. He looked over more papers, taking his time, making notes. Caroline scarcely dared to breathe. So far no one had asked about Angelique's immigration status or that of the children for fear of introducing even more complications and a new round of bureaucratic horrors. Don't ask, she silently pleaded. Please don't ask.

The judge put aside the file and studied Caroline for a long time. "The reports do say you appear to be providing a safe and supportive situation for these children. I'm going to sign this order. I'm going to grant you emergency custody, and I will allow you to take the children to Washington, provided you commit to certain conditions." He enumerated her duties to provide information through official channels. "I wish you the best, Ms. Shelby. I anticipate that the probate court will honor Ms. Baptiste's will unless you're found to be grossly unfit."

"Thank you, Your Honor. I'll take care of them." Although she tried to infuse her voice with confidence, Caroline was terrified. There were moments—many of them—when she did feel grossly unfit. She was about to change her life forever, heading down a path she'd never foreseen.

PART TWO

You will never be completely at home again,
because part of your heart always will be elsewhere.
That is the price you pay for the richness of loving and
knowing people in more than one place.

—MIRIAM ADENEY

Chapter 6

Running into—literally running into—Caroline Shelby on a random foggy morning threw Will Jensen off his game. Not that he had game, but he had athletes in training. Their morning run had been interrupted so unexpectedly that after the strange chance encounter, Will sent the team to the locker room early that morning. He offered an extra high five to Gil Stanton, the guy who had spotted the lost little girl asleep in the car.

Will tried to get his head around the idea that Caroline "I'm never having kids" Shelby had two kids. How did he not know that? How had he not heard anything through the grapevine?

One thing he did know—though not from experience—was that a missing child was every parent's worst nightmare.

"See you in class, Coach," said Augie Sandoval, the captain of the cross-country team.

Will drained his water bottle and headed back to the athletic compound, where his office was located. He flipped on the coffeemaker and turned on his laptop. There was a small private shower room for the coach, closer and more convenient than going back home to get ready for the day. Besides, Sierra had been up late the night before, and he didn't want to wake her.

These days he took a lot of showers at work.

After the brutally short, not-even-lukewarm showers he'd endured during his service in the navy, a long blast of hot water was a luxury that never got old. While indulging in the morning ritual, he usually thought about his day—algebra, trig, vo-tech, office hours. After school, there would be one or more of the ubiquitous meetings—planning and development, compliance, community outreach—a couple of which he had somehow managed to be appointed to chair.

Then home to work on the house. Another consuming project, but that one was a labor of love. After his discharge following the injury, he had pursued a different dream—restoring the generations-old family home known as Water's Edge. The rambling Carpenter Gothic had been built by his ancestor, Arne

Jensen, an oysterman who made a living shipping fresh oysters to the Bay Area during the years of the Gold Rush.

Will had spent the summers of his boyhood with his grandparents in the old house on the generous green parcel, with its big barn, oyster sheds and docks, and fleet of dinghies and powerboats. Over time, the house had deteriorated, and when his grandparents had retired to Arizona, they'd deeded the place to Will. He'd always dreamed of restoring it to its former glory.

Today he had something else on his mind—Caroline Shelby. He wished he didn't know that it had been ten years since he'd last seen her. He wished he didn't know the exact date he'd watched her drive away, tires spitting crushed oyster shells in their wake—the day he'd married her best friend, Sierra Moore.

But he did know, and that bugged the shit out of him.

He wondered what she was doing back here. She was supposed to be living large in New York City, making her name as a famous designer. He hadn't thought about her in years, and suddenly there she was, clearly exhausted and stressed by her two little kids—damn, two kids—and an old car crammed with baggage. Despite the circumstances, Caroline still looked like the girl he'd known for most of his life—small and intense, her mouth like a red valentine, her movements quick with agitation, her cropped, mussed hair streaked with crazy neon highlights like one of his high school kids.

The town being what it was, local gossip was bound to fill in the answers to the questions buzzing through his mind. Mainly, the kids. A girl named Addie. A boy named Flick. What the hell? Where was their dad?

Apparently, Caroline had been busy with more than her career.

With steam swirling around him, he stepped out of the shower and groped for a towel.

"Here you go." Someone placed it in his hand.

"Jesus." He snatched the towel and jumped back. Then he recovered, leaned forward through the dissipating steam, and kissed his wife—lightly and briefly, so she wouldn't remind him not to muss her makeup. "Hi, babe," he said. "You're up early."

"Heading down to Portland," she said. "I stopped in to say goodbye."

Again?

"The fall catalog shoot," she reminded him, stepping out of the tiny cubicle.

He scrubbed his head to dry his hair. "Fall, huh?"

"In the fashion world, the seasons are reversed, remember?" She wiped the fogged shaving mirror with her sleeve and leaned in to inspect her face. "Miriam Goddard was asking me where I get my hair done. Was that a veiled insult, do you think?"

"I don't get it. Your hair's perfect, like the rest of you."

Her smile was fleeting. "I'll take your word for it. We live in a fishbowl here. I feel like everyone has an opinion about us."

He let the towel drop and reached around behind her. "You're always complaining about the town gossips. Let's give them something to gossip about."

She pushed her hand against his chest. "Very funny. You need to get to class, and I need to get on the road."

"Let's be late."

"Let's not." She patted him lightly on the shoulder, then stepped out into the office. "You can't get away with anything in a town like this."

"I like small-town life," he said, dressing quickly. "I like the slow pace, the sense of community."

"The sense that everyone knows everyone else's business," she said. "Trust me, being Pastor Moore's only daughter was no picnic. You were a navy brat. You have no idea what it's like, having to make sure you don't embarrass your parents."

Sierra sometimes chafed under the scrutiny, but Will was philosophical. "Good thing we're old enough now, and married. Nothing for folks to see here, simple as that."

"It's not so simple," she said. "Some people will always find something to gossip about."

"Could be you're right." He came out of the bathroom with his tie slung around his neck. "Remember that summer your dad caught us making out in the choir loft? I had my hand up your—"

"Knock it off," she said, removing his hand. Then she stepped forward and tied his tie for him in a now-familiar ritual. "You headed back to the city, and I was left to face the consequences."

"Come on, we had fun. Your folks are my biggest fans now."

"Indeed. Sometimes I think they like you better than me." She was all done up as usual, her hair gleaming, makeup airbrushed to perfection over a forehead smoothed by Botox injections she insisted she needed.

"Guess you have a busy day lined up," he said.

"Yep. Interior and exterior shots today." She smoothed his collar and stepped back.

"Sounds good. So you're going to put on pretty clothes and knock 'em dead," he said.

"Right." Her too-smooth brow tried to frown. "The world's oldest model."

"Only my ninth graders think thirty-four is old."

"News flash—the entire fashion industry thinks thirty-four is old."

He knew better than to argue with any female about the fashion world. But damn. Despite the accident that had taken one eye, his good eye could see perfectly well that his wife was gorgeous. The kind of gorgeous that made people do a double take, the way they might when a perfect rainbow appeared in the sky. She had shiny red hair and a tall, slender body, green eyes that gleamed like rare jewels. Her face had graced ads for toothpaste, cat litter, fine perfume—anything that could be marketed alongside a pretty face.

And as incredible as she looked, she had managed to pursue the one career where her looks were not particularly striking—merely commonplace in that world.

Lately—and he knew this frustrated her—the bookings for her high-fashion modeling had tapered off. He was not going to be the one to ask the reason for this. He didn't want to hear her say it was because she was old. He didn't want to hear her say it was because she lived in the world's smallest backwater, where she had to drive for two hours or more to find even a glimmer of civilization.

"Do you have time for a cup of coffee?"

She glanced at the clock over his office door. "Just a bit. Hair and makeup starts at eleven.

"Whose pretty clothes will you be wearing today?"

She hesitated. He could tell she wasn't happy. "McCall's," she said briefly.

A discount store on the lower end of the spectrum, then. Not exactly Nordstrom. "They're lucky to get you."

She took the proffered cup of coffee and sprinkled it with a dusting of stevia, ever mindful of avoiding extra calories. "Right."

He added a generous dollop of cream and real sugar to his cup. After the morning run, he was starving, and he didn't have a break until third period. While loading up his messenger bag for the day, he debated with himself about whether to bring up this morning's encounter with Caroline.

If he didn't, Sierra would hear about the drama of the "lost, not lost" kid from someone else. She'd hear one of his athletes had found the little girl. She might wonder why he hadn't said anything about the encounter. If he did—

"I ran into Caroline Shelby," he said, threading a belt around his pants. "This morning."

She perched one hip on the edge of his desk. Her eyes widened and her lips parted in surprise. "Caroline! You're kidding. She's been a ghost for the past ten years. Where did you see her? Here in town?"

He nodded. "During a training run with the team, super early. She was at the Bait & Switch. Seems like she'd just rolled into town, like maybe she'd been driving all night. That's how it appeared, anyway. Did you know she was coming?"

"No. Why would I? We haven't been in touch in years, other than the occasional wave on Facebook. What's she doing here?"

"I didn't ask. Like I said, it was early, and I was out with the cross-country team." He paused. "She has two kids. Did you know that?"

Her green eyes opened even wider. "Caroline has kids?"

"Little boy and little girl."

"Wow, I had no idea. I guess I'll run into her at some point, then. Is she staying at her folks' place?"

"Didn't ask that, either."

"Caroline Shelby. Two kids. Wow," she said again, slowly shaking her head.

Will had thought he and Sierra would have a kid or two by now. That had always been the plan, anyway. So far no luck. Not for lack of trying, which was admittedly his favorite part of the process. He was ready for kids. He pictured them growing up here, the place where his heart had always belonged. He had been all over the world while serving in the navy. He'd been deployed with his SEAL team to places most people had never heard of. His team had been based in Coronado, and he'd seen places of magic and stunning beauty, but when he thought about where he belonged, his mind always wandered back to Oysterville, where the summers burst over the land like golden blessings, and the winters roared through with torrential abandon.

Sierra had agreed to the plan. Like Caroline, she had grown up here. Her father was still the senior pastor at Seaside Church, and her mother managed the church's newsletter and social calendar.

Sierra glanced at the clock over the office door. "I need to hit the road." Stepping up on tiptoe, she gave him a peck on the cheek. "Don't hold dinner for me. I'll probably be late. I might stay over in the city."

That was a compromise they'd made early on. If they were going to live out on the coast, she wouldn't always make it home after a job. "Okay, let me know. Go be gorgeous."

"Right." Small eye roll.

"Be safe on the road. Love you."

And then she was gone. *Love you.* Of course he loved her. She was his wife. These days, their *love you*s were rote and reflexive, a sign they were in a settled phase of their marriage. Which wasn't a bad thing. Yet sometimes he felt bad about it. He hoped it was his imagination, but more and more lately, his wife was showing signs of discontent. She talked constantly of the city life she'd lived while he was on deployment—L.A., Portland, Seattle. Now there were unsettling signals that their marriage was fraying at the edges. What would make her happy? He made a note to work on the cedar-lined walk-in closet he was building for her at the house. Maybe he'd finish it tonight as a surprise for when she got home.

He organized his things for the day and made his way from the athletic complex, past the administration center to the high school. Colleagues and students greeted him along the way. Although Sierra called it a fishbowl, Will liked the close-knit feel of the community, the sense of permanence of life here. Growing up a navy brat, he'd never lived in one place long enough to truly fit in, and the only place that had ever felt like home was Water's Edge.

When he and Sierra had settled here permanently following his discharge, they were treated like small-town royalty—the preacher's daughter and the wounded hero, a designation he was happy to shed as time went on. Now he was just Coach Jensen, settling into a job and a life that felt like the right fit for him—most of the time.

Because of his coaching duties, he didn't have a homeroom to supervise, so he hit the staff room to check his mailbox, then the math office to log in, view his calendar, and grab some supplies. The school hallway was festooned with notices—an upcoming Tolo dance, college night, club meetings—and after announcements and the Pledge of Allegiance, it was crowded with kids slamming their lockers, talking too loud, hauling their overstuffed backpacks to class.

Will strode into his classroom just as the first period bell rang. He blinked the lights once to signal his arrival, then stood at the front of the class. "All right, you scholars and ne'er-do-wells," he said, his customary greeting. "Let's kick those brains into gear."

There were the usual shuffles and a few groans and yawns. Homework out. Phone check—he took attendance by the phone parking lot, a charging station at the front table. A missing phone meant a missing student—or a forgetful one. Seat 2C was not present. "Ms. Lowry," he said. "You're either absent or you're Snapchatting after first bell . . ."

With an elaborate sigh, May Lowry surrendered her phone to the charging station. "All present and accounted for," he said, then turned to the whiteboard to pose the first problem of the day. "So let's say you're starting a car trip at nine in the morning from a point—"

"What point?" called someone in the back.

"From wherever, moron," said the kid next to him. "It doesn't matter."

"I say it matters."

"Fine," Will interjected. "New York City. Your car trip is starting in New York City."

"And where am I going?" asked May.

"Oysterville," said another kid, "where else? Aren't we the center of the universe?"

"Listen up," Will said. "The plot thickens. You're traveling at forty miles per hour. At ten A.M., another car started traveling from the same point at sixty miles per hour in the same direction. At what time will that car catch up and pass you?" He sketched out the problem on the board.

Jana Lassiter raised her hand. She was a cheeky girl, smart and fun to have in class. "I have a question. If I'm in New York City, why would I ever leave and come back here?"

"Yeah, good question," someone else said.

"We're America's Tidewater Vacationland," Will said, "according to the highway billboard. But that's not the point—"

"Have *you* been to New York City?" Jana asked.

Will was sorry he'd brought it up.

"Mr. Jensen's been all over the world," said another girl, Helen Stokes. Embarrassingly, she was one of several girls who had a crush on him, which he pretended not to notice. "In the navy, right, Mr. Jensen?"

"Again, not the point. This is a rate, time, and distance problem."

"How is this going to help us in the real world?" asked someone.

"You're not even going to get to the real world if you don't pass this class," Will pointed out.

"Did you have to know this stuff to be a Navy SEAL?"

"Math was just the tip of the iceberg," Will said.

"Is it true you got injured saving a life? Is it true you have a glass eye?"

"A prosthetic eye. I'll tell you what's true," Will said, easily skirting the topic. "Detention, that's what. And you're about three seconds from a maximum sentence."

Chastened, the boy slumped in his chair. "Sorry, sir."

"So instead of trying to distract everyone, let's work the problem, people. Let's let *D*1 equal the distance of the first car, and *t* equals time . . ."

Distance, rate, and time, reduced to a neat equation. It wasn't messy. It had one and only one solution, not a hundred possible paths and permutations. *If Caroline Shelby left town at warp speed and traveled a distance of a whole continent and ten years, at what point would he quit wondering what might have been?*

Chapter 7

As Caroline drove the final leg of her journey, the morning marine layer hung like weightless gauze in the salmonberry and bracken that bordered the road. The strange mist made her feel displaced in time and space, as if she were floating through some primordial world.

She was on edge from the adrenaline rush of misplacing Addie at the Bait & Switch. She felt jittery and wide awake, engulfed by a sense of unreality. Yet what had set her on this path was all too real. She had come here because she needed breathing space, a way to sort herself out, a plan for the children. She had no idea if she'd find the answers here, but she was out of options.

"It's kinda spooky out there," Flick said from the back seat.

"You think?" In the early light, the estuaries and forested uplands probably did look vaguely threatening.

"Are we safe?"

He asked her that a lot. No six-year-old should have to ask that question. Finally she felt confident of the answer. "Absolutely."

"I don't see any houses. Just woods and fog."

"And hundreds of thousands of shorebirds," she pointed out. "It's the spring migration, and all kinds of birds come here to rest and feed. I'll take you exploring, and you'll see. We'll get you some binoculars like a professional bird watcher."

Addie awakened with a whimper. "Is it morning?"

"You got lost," Flick said. "You were naughty."

"I'm not naughty."

"She's not naughty." Caroline intervened before the bickering had a chance to take hold. "Addie, even though you didn't mean to do anything wrong, you forgot to stay put when I went after Flick back at the gas station." She glanced in the rearview mirror. The little girl yawned and rubbed her eyes. "It's scary to me when I don't know where you are every moment. So when you climbed back into the car without telling me, I got really worried."

Addie stared out the window, blinking the sleep from her eyes.

"Mama left without telling us," Flick pointed out.

Caroline tried not to flinch at the memory. "That's completely different. She didn't leave you by choice. She wouldn't have done that for the world."

Since the incident—she didn't know what else to call it—she had been speed-reading books on helping young children through crisis. During the week-long drive, she'd had daily videoconferences with a child psychologist she couldn't afford. The counselor and the books offered suggestions—how to speak in terms the children would understand, how to respond honestly and reassuringly. Yet ultimately, there was no script for this, no road map to point her in the right direction. Despite her efforts so far, she knew that in the end, words would never be enough.

Don't lie. But don't overexplain.

"You said we were almost there." Flick switched topics, craning his neck as they passed a billboard welcoming them to YOUR TIDEWATER VACATIONLAND.

"Are we almost there?" Addie asked.

"Well, that depends on what you mean by *almost*. I can tell you, we'll be there in time for breakfast. I sent my sister Virginia a text message, and she said she's making blueberry pancakes with real syrup. Her blueberry pancakes are the best in all the land."

A glance at the rearview mirror told her she had their attention. Good, she thought. Engage them in the "right here, right now" moment. Another thing she'd figured out in her crash course in parenting was to offer the children concrete information on a level they could understand. Tell them things in advance. Not too far in advance, but let them know what to expect and anticipate. They had only ever known the busy, eclectic neighborhood of Hell's Kitchen, where they'd lived with their mother, just a block from their primary school on West Forty-Fourth Street. Now they were about to enter a strange new world, and Caroline could tell from their quiet, wide-eyed expressions that they were worried.

"Let's play the remembering game," she said, hoping to stave off the restlessness that often preceded meltdowns. "What's the name of the town where my family lives?"

"Oysterville," they piped up together.

"Hey, that's great. You got that down. Here's a tricky question. How many brothers and sisters do I have?"

"Five!" Flick said.

"Five kids in my family, so I have four siblings."

"How many is four?" asked Addie.

"Like your fingers," Flick said, holding up his hand. "One, two, three, four."

"You're right about the fingers," Caroline said. "I have two older sisters and two younger brothers. Remember, I told you our family was a sibling sandwich with me in the middle."

Crushed in the middle, she thought.

"Let's play the name game one more time," she said. She wanted to familiarize them with their new circumstances so things wouldn't feel so completely foreign to them. "Can you remember my sisters' names?"

"Virginia," said Flick. "You just said."

"Good. How about my other sister? Remember how I said we're all named after states. Caroline for Carolina, Virginia, and . . . ?"

"Georgia!" Flick said.

"Georgia," Addie repeated.

"That's right. And my two brothers are both younger than me, because I'm in the middle. Our parents named the boys after cities." In the too-much-information department, her parents liked to tell people they named each child after the place where he or she had been conceived. "See if you can remember," she said. "I showed you their pictures on my phone."

"Jackson."

"That's right. Jackson lives on a boat in the harbor at Ilwaco. It was dark when we passed it, but I bet he'd like to show you around. He's the seafood buyer for the restaurant, and he's a fisherman, too."

"How can he live on a boat?" asked Addie.

"Believe me, you're not the first girl to ask that." Jackson was the free spirit of the family, never overly concerned with domestic matters.

"Is it a house, only it's on a boat?"

"Not exactly. It's more like a boat with really small rooms. You'll see one day soon. Now, what about my other brother—the youngest one in the family?"

Hesitation.

"Starts with *Au,*" she hinted. "When you're older, you'll study states and capitals in school, and you'll learn that this is the capital of Texas."

Flick shrugged. "I forgot."

"That's all right. It's hard to remember names before you get to know who they belong to. My brothers are Jackson and Austin. My parents' names are Dottie and Lyle. How about this one—can you remember the name of my family's restaurant?"

"Star of the Sea!"

During the drive, they'd stopped at dozens of restaurants, diners, and truck stops. She had told them about the Shelby family restaurant, founded by her parents. A now-famous destination on the peninsula, it was located on the beach at the edge of the dunes, where the sea and sand met in irregular stitches.

"That's right," she said. "Star of the Sea. I think you're going to like it."

"Can we go there now?" asked Flick. "I'm hungry."

"My sister is fixing breakfast at the house," Caroline reminded him. "You'll have plenty of chances to eat there. The whole Shelby clan works at the restaurant in some way or other." Her brother Austin was the finance guy, a CPA who kept the family books, and Georgia was the restaurant's general manager. "It's a true family business."

"Except you," said Flick.

"Except me," she admitted.

When she was little, Caroline hadn't realized how hard her parents had worked—the long hours, the tangled problems of launching and sustaining a restaurant. As she got older, she had tried to do her share, but she had never possessed the passion and focus it took to throw herself into the enterprise. In the Shelby family, she was the dreamer, always yearning for something that drew her far away.

"I did design the chefs' coats and servers' outfits a long time ago. They didn't like them, though. Too avant-garde."

"What's that mean?"

"Too awesome," she said.

"Are you going to work at the restaurant now?" Addie asked.

I don't know what the hell I'm going to do, Caroline thought.

"We'll see." She paused. "When I was a kid, I was always skeptical every time I heard a grown-up say, 'We'll see.' What does that even mean? See what? When? How will we see what I'm talking about if I don't even know what I'm talking about?"

No response. She didn't blame them for being as confused and out of their depth as she was. She sighed again. "Now *I* just said, 'We'll see.' Does that make me a grown-up?"

"You've always been a grown-up," Flick pointed out.

"Thanks a lot. You don't think I was ever a kid like you?"

"We'll see," he said.

"You're cheeky," she told him. "Now, pay attention. I want you to watch out the window for the mailbox. It says *Shelby* and it's decorated with seashells."

She slowed down as they passed undulating dunes on the west side and coastal forest on the east, with the fog snaking through like a serpent made of mist. Hand-lettered signs for fresh eggs and organic produce, U-pick cranberries and blueberries beckoned travelers. Battered mailboxes bore names both familiar and new to her—Gonzalez, Moore, Espy, Haruki, Ryerson.

"I see it," Flick exclaimed. "Is that where we're going?"

The seashell mailbox was a monstrosity, so ugly it had become a local landmark. She and her brothers and sisters had made it one year as a surprise for their parents. The five of them had mortared the base and mailbox with a mosaic of shells, sea glass, driftwood, and bones from a sea lion carcass on the beach. She, of course, had wanted to direct the design process, but the others had thrown themselves into it with no regard for aesthetics. When their mother saw it, she'd burst into tears, and to this day, Caroline wasn't fully convinced they were sentimental tears. Now, decades later, the mailbox was a silent sentinel to the past, evoking memories she was suddenly quite grateful for.

She turned into the lane that led to the Shelby family home. The driveway was paved with crushed oyster shells and edged by wind-sculpted shrubbery and a row of beach roses. Since she had left home right out of high school, she had dutifully visited a few times at Christmas, flying into Seattle or Portland, renting a car, and making the three-hour trek to the coast. That seemed to satisfy the family and also preserved her status as the official black sheep.

Every family needed a pet, her brother Jackson used to joke.

Today's arrival was different. This wasn't a visit. And now the black sheep had two lambs.

Nothing here, in the watery kingdom where she'd grown up, had changed. That was her first impression. The trees and structures were wind-sculpted and weather-beaten, anchored to the landscape by their spreading roots that clawed into the dunes. The home where she'd grown up was a big, unassuming saltbox, its clapboard siding painted iron gray, its trim white, its roof perpetually furred by moss and lichen.

The ordinary dwelling was made spectacular by the setting. Beyond the garden lay the dunes. The prelude to a kingdom. The shifting sands and blowing grasses stretched toward the sea, wild as a restless dream. There was no boardwalk here as there was in the main town of the peninsula, no network of pathways, just a tangle of waist-high beach grass entwined with sturdy small flowering plants—coastal strawberry and sea rocket, native lupine and beach pea. The occasional wind-harried cypress or cedar tree reared up, bowing eastward as if in perpetual flight away from the ocean.

"We made it," she said to the kids. "This used to be my whole world, once upon a time." She scanned the yard, with its gnarled apple trees and the big liquid-ambar with a wooden plank swing hanging from a high branch. There was a chicken coop and a garden surrounded by a deer fence. It really was a beautiful place—one she couldn't wait to leave.

"We're here?" Flick asked.

"We're here!" Addie said. She clutched Wonder Woman to her chest.

"Finally," Caroline assured them.

By the time she parked and unbuckled the kids, her parents had come out to the front porch to greet them.

"Welcome home," said her mother, rushing down the steps and crossing the yard, her arms open wide. Her long hair flew out behind her, and for a moment she looked ridiculously young in fitted jeans and a plaid cotton shirt, and the customary Blundstones she favored for gardening.

As she drew closer, Caroline could see the wispy lines fanning her mother's eyes, the slight thickening of her figure. But the smile and the outstretched arms were the same as always.

With the kids clinging like remoras to her legs, Caroline felt herself enclosed in Dottie Shelby's firm hug. Her mother smelled of hand soap and Jergens lotion, and her embrace was a sanctuary. "I'm so glad you got here a whole day early," she said, stepping back.

"I couldn't sleep, so we loaded up and started driving," Caroline said. "Hey, Dad."

He enveloped her in his assured, powerful embrace. It was the first time Caroline had felt truly safe since Angelique's death. Closing her eyes, she allowed herself to savor a moment of bliss, receding briefly into the role of cherished daughter.

Her parents were sturdy and good-looking, often cited in the local chamber of commerce brochures as the epitome of a couple who had built their dream out of hard work and dedication. They had met at culinary school in the Bay Area—Dottie, a peninsula girl, and Lyle, a California native. By the time the program ended, they had woven their dreams—and their lives—together.

"Well," Caroline said, "it's good to be back. Flick and Addie have come a long way to meet you."

Her mother went down on one knee and regarded the children at their level. "I'm glad you're here. My name's Dottie, and that's Lyle. You can call me Dottie, or Grammy Dot. That's what my other grandchildren call me."

By *other grandchildren,* was she implying something?

"You don't have to decide right now," she added.

Addie clutched Wonder Woman and stared at the ground. Flick regarded Dottie with sober contemplation. "My real name's Francis," he said.

"Oh! Do you prefer that to Flick?"

He shook his head. "When I was a baby, I couldn't say Francis, so I called myself Flick and it stuck. So I'm keeping it."

"Good plan. I bet you're hungry," she said. Dottie Shelby was the sort of person who saw others the way they wanted to be seen. She had a particular talent for finding the best in people, children and adults alike.

"We heard a rumor of pancakes," Caroline said.

"You heard exactly right. Come on in and let's eat. Dad will bring in your things. There's so much to do and see, but you don't have to do it all today," Mom nattered on. "You both look like you love to run and jump. Are you into running and jumping?"

Flick and Addie exchanged a glance, and Flick offered a slight nod. Mom didn't press but strode ahead with confidence.

The kids stuck close to Caroline as they all went inside. The old house welcomed her, as familiar as her mother's embrace. The foyer was bright with a mirror reflecting the light from the outside and a hall tree made of driftwood.

Every house had a smell. This one was a particular mix of baking, salt air, and the dry, tumbly aroma from a constantly running clothes dryer. At least it used to run constantly when Caroline and her siblings were young. Now there was probably far less laundry cycling through, but the fluffy smell lingered still.

The living room was filled with an eclectic mix of furniture, family pictures, a few antiques, and Mom's old upright piano.

"We all took lessons," she said, noting Flick's interest. "My brother Austin got really good at it." She steered them to the hall bathroom and somehow managed to change Addie out of her pee-smelling clothes and into clean ones. Then she supervised the washing of hands, still somewhat befuddled by the idea of having to supervise anything of the sort. Just a short time ago, she was on her own, living in the heart of New York City's fashion district.

There were artifacts everywhere—the pottery soap dish Jackson had brought home from preschool with his little handprint in the middle. Another family picture hung above the commode, this one of the older girls holding up a surfboard with Caroline and the boys seated on it. She still remembered the roars of laughter that had erupted as they'd struggled to stage the shot, getting dumped into the sand multiple times. She was eight or nine in the photo, wearing Virginia's hand-me-down swimsuit, which she'd rescued from looking like a hand-me-down by sewing a rumba ruffle to the back.

"I'm off to work," Dad called from the front hallway. "See you tonight, okay, C-Shell?"

"Sounds good," she said.

Next stop was the kitchen. Contrary to what people expected of a longtime restaurant family, the kitchen was small and plain, with a four-burner range, a roomy fridge, and the all-important dishwasher. Mom always said a fancy kitchen was no substitute for good cooking.

"I'm Virginia," said her sister, blowing them a floury kiss from her spot at the counter. "And you're about to have the best pancakes of your life."

Caroline gave them a nudge. "She's bossy sometimes."

"Not bossy," Virginia said with a sniff. "I just have better ideas than most people." She was the second eldest and most outgoing of the Shelbys. "I have a secret pancake recipe. But I tell it to everybody, so it's not really a secret." She pulled a couple of barstools over to the counter. "Have a seat, you two, and pay attention. You have to sift the dry ingredients together. See how the sifter works?" She demonstrated and gave them each a turn. "That makes everything nice and fluffy. And we use real buttermilk, not regular milk. It tastes kind of sour." She offered them a sample on a small spoon, but the kids shrank together and shook their heads in silence.

Watching her sister's ease with the children, Caroline felt a renewal of the doubts that had chased her across the country. Unlike Virginia and her mom, she didn't "get" kids. She never had. She'd always been vocal about being childless by choice. Possibly that made her boyfriendless as well, but that was the price she paid for clinging to her freedom. Yet here she was with two kids in tow, and she had no idea what to do with them.

She thought for a moment about the expression on Will Jensen's face when she'd told him, "They're mine."

And they were. Yet they weren't.

"The eggs are from our own hens. See how yellow the yolks are?" Virginia broke two of them into a glass bowl and whisked them together with the buttermilk and a bit of melted butter. Then she combined everything to make the batter. "The biggest secret of all is this awesome cast-iron griddle. It's a Griswold—they don't even make them anymore. This one is as smooth as glass. I have it on the perfect temperature. Help me out here."

She poured the batter and supervised as the kids dotted the pancakes with blueberries. A few minutes later, Caroline got the two of them situated on benches in the adjacent breakfast nook. Their eyes widened as she placed the first batch of pancakes on the table, bursting with berries and slathered in butter and warm maple syrup. The ultimate comfort food.

"Dig in, you two," she said. "Let's fill your bellies, and then I'll show you where you're going to be staying." Over their heads, she checked with her mother, who offered a nod of encouragement.

The children devoured their breakfast with gratifying speed. Caroline helped herself to coffee and a pancake fresh off the griddle. It was so good it nearly brought tears to her eyes. "Thanks, Virginia. That was delicious. It's been a long haul."

"You've all had quite an adventure," Mom said. "I want you to know, I'm so very sorry about your mother. You must miss her so much."

"She died," Addie said. "She's not coming back."

"It's a terrible thing. I wish we could help. All we can do is love you and keep you safe and help you remember your mom. If you feel sad and want to tell us about it, we can listen."

Caroline felt a surge of gratitude as she regarded her mother and sister. This was hardly the path she'd expected to find herself on, but here she was, in charge of two orphans, far from the life she'd been living in New York. Everything had changed in a split second—unforeseen, sending her scrambling. If she hadn't had this family to fall back on, she couldn't imagine what she would have done.

When they finished breakfast, her mother said, "Let's clear the table together, and then I'll take you to see your room."

Flick surveyed the table, his brow slightly quirked. Angelique had been an unconventional mother in many ways, and traditional chores had not been a thing with her.

"Let's take our dishes to the sink," Caroline said. "Then we'll wipe the table." Falling back into a family routine was easy for her, but she could tell the kids would need time to adjust.

They made short work of clearing up and then trooped upstairs, passing more family pictures on the landing. The room her mother had prepared for Flick and Addie was the one Caroline had once shared with Virginia. Georgia, the eldest, had the privilege of a room of her own, and she used to lord it over the others like an anointed queen. The boys shared another. All five of them had fought like littermates over the bathroom.

Her mother stood with the door held wide open. "I dug out a few choice toys from the old days," she said. "I hope you like Legos and stuffed animals. And books with actual pages that turn."

The children regarded the room with wide eyes. Compared to the walk-up in Hell's Kitchen, and later the apartment they'd shared with Caroline and their mother, the bedroom probably seemed as big as an airplane hangar.

A couple of old National Geographic maps still hung on the wall of her old room. The colors had faded and the dry paper was curled at the edges. She saw Addie studying them. "This is the United States," Caroline said. "Our whole big country. Here's New York, where we left last week. And we drove all the way here." She traced the route with her finger, pointing to the spot where Oysterville would be, were it significant enough to appear on the map.

"That was a super-long drive," Mom said. "I hope you two will be comfortable here."

Addie made a tentative study of the toys and books Caroline's mom had thoughtfully displayed. And Dottie's thoughtfulness didn't end with toys and books. She'd saved some of Caroline's early and most painstaking work. "Caroline made the coverlets and curtains all by herself when she was only twelve years old. She was always so good at making things. Do you like making things?" she asked the kids.

Flick offered a lost little shrug of his shoulders, then studied the floor.

The coverlets were known as crazy quilts. According to Lindy at the quilt shop, Caroline had taken *crazy* to a whole new level. The pieces were not even standard in shape, but free-form bursts of color stitched together and embroidered with whimsical designs. Now she ran her hand over the cloth, thinking about that girl who'd been so obsessed with art and design. There was never a time when she wasn't designing something. She'd felt so caged in here, knowing there was so much to experience and learn in the big wide world. Even after years in New York, she doubted that her family understood her hunger and need to be in the middle of everything in the hub of the design world.

Coming home felt like an embrace of safety.

Coming home felt like defeat.

Coming home was the last resort.

The sentiment was a sunken, hollowed-out spot inside her. Caroline realized it was wrong to let herself wallow this way. A better person would turn it into determination. But at the moment, as she drowned in exhaustion, it was the only possible way to feel.

Addie dragged Wonder Woman to the dormer window

between the two beds and gazed outside. A thick wisteria vine twisted down the side of the house, its purple blossoms nodding in the breeze. The yard below had fruit trees, gnarled with age, and a fire pit they used to sit around on clear evenings, toasting marshmallows and telling stories. Farther in the distance, past the dunes, was the flat sandy beach.

Caroline hunkered down beside the little girl. "Virginia and I used to stand here together on summer nights, watching people on the beach. You'll see—in the summer, it stays light ridiculously late, way past nine o'clock. So when we'd see kids still out playing on the beach, I thought it was totally unfair. It didn't seem right that Virginia and I had to go to bed while the rest of the world was out playing."

"And yet you survived," said her mother.

"True," Caroline agreed, straightening up. When she was older, the wisteria vine had been her secret escape route. She thought it best not to mention that.

"You're looking at the Pacific Ocean," she told the kids. "It's the biggest ocean in the world. Let's have a rest, and later we'll go check it out."

"I don't feel like resting," said Flick.

She felt like sleeping for a week. Not an option with two kids needing her. "Tell you what. Let's go to the beach and explore. And there's even more good news."

That always got their attention.

"No car ride today."

"Yay!"

"After all that driving, we need a little hike to stretch our legs." They trundled downstairs, and as they headed for the door, she turned to Virginia. "Thanks again for breakfast."

"You betcha." Virginia wiped down the counter. "I have questions."

"You betcha," Caroline echoed.

"Drinks tonight, after the little ones are in bed."

"You got it." Drinks and talking would be a good place to start. She led the children outside. The air was fresh and damp, smelling of the ocean and new growth. "You can play anywhere you want in the backyard," she told them. "Stay in bounds unless there's an adult with you." She walked with them through the orchard, showing them the berry frames and gardens, which were just getting started for the season. There was a chicken coop surrounded by wire fencing.

"Do chickens bite?" Addie asked, eyeing the birds.

"No, stupid, they don't have teeth," sneered Flick.

"Hey," Caroline said, hoping to fend off a squabble. "We talked about this. Even when you're tired and cranky, you can find a way to speak nicely to people. Or if not, you can zip your lips."

"Sorry," he muttered.

Caroline ruffled his hair. "Chickens don't bite," she said. "Sometimes they try to peck."

"Does it hurt?"

"You can't let them get away with it," Caroline said. "When I was little and it was my turn to gather eggs, I used to take a dish towel with me." She pantomimed with her hand. "I'd flap it like this, and they'd all go running away. I'll show you later how it's done."

Flick stopped to look at an acacia tree with a carved stone at the base. "That sign says *Wendell.*"

Caroline felt a bittersweet wave of emotion. "That's right, Wendell," she said. "He was our dog. We were all really sad when he died, so Grandpa Lyle's friend Wayne made a special stone with his name on it."

"Will Mama have a stone?"

She should have expected that. Though the children didn't know it, Angelique's remains had made the cross-country journey with them. The plain sealed container was stowed with the car's spare tire, and she had no idea what to do with it.

"Would you like one?" she asked.

Another shrug. His code for being at a loss. She rested her palm between his shoulder blades. He was so little and delicate. She'd been dwelling on the disaster her life had become, yet her troubles were nothing compared to the trauma these kids were going through. "You can let me know. There's no hurry."

A flicker of movement caught her eye. "Hey, check it out. There's a little creature living in the dunes. Be really still and watch. It's called a vole. See where it lives? It's like a little bird's nest."

They watched the tiny creature foraging in the grass.

"Can we pet it?"

"It's a wild animal. We can watch, but not touch, okay?"

"Looks like a mouse," Flick said.

The children had never known anything but the city. Their experience with wildlife was limited to messy pigeons and rats sneaking around the Dumpsters of the back alleys.

"This is going to be a whole new world for you," she said, watching their fascination as they squatted amid the buff-colored grasses and new green shoots to watch the vole, industriously padding its nest with bits of dried leaves and fluff. "So many birds and little creatures everywhere."

After a while, she led the way to the beach. It was the playground of her youth. There was never a time when she hadn't awakened to the muffled roar of the ocean and the deep, fecund aroma of salt air.

One of Caroline's earliest memories was of being lost amid the foredunes and hummocks when the grass was taller than she was. There had been a moment of disorientation, her heart jolting in panic. Then she recalled her father's advice. Don't walk in circles. Walk in a straight line. At least you'll end up somewhere.

Escaping from the tangled grasses, she'd found her family in the yard, probably gathered around the stone-built fire pit, or playing Frisbee with the dog. No one had remarked upon her absence. No one had come looking. From that early memory emerged a notion that had stuck with her ever since: as the middle child of five, she'd been invisible since birth.

Ultimately, her position in the birth order had actually worked out well for her. She was not as organized as Georgia and not as beautiful as Virginia. While everyone else was busy with the restaurant, Caroline was able to go her own way. She discovered that she actually liked disappearing. She often ended up at Lindy's fabric shop or the fiber arts and design center at the high school, pursuing the mad passion no one else in her family seemed to understand.

Now the children ran along the path, which ended abruptly at the edge of the vast sand flats.

"Watch your step going down," Caroline called. "It's a steep—Jesus."

Flick disappeared as though falling into a hole. Caroline broke into a run, reaching the edge of the escarpment and feeling the soft sandy bank collapsing underfoot. Flick lay at the bottom of the bank, half buried in sand, looking up at her.

"Hey," she said. "Are you all right?"

"Yes."

"You could have hurt yourself." She took Addie's hand and eased her down the bank amid a fall of loose sand.

"It was fun," Flick said, jumping up and brushing himself off. He looked around with wide-eyed wonder. The scenery here was ever-changing, yet changeless—the sand sculpted by wind and tide, the wrack line woven with kelp and shells, feathers and bones, small pieces of driftwood, and an unfortunate variety of litter.

Flocks of ghost-colored sanderlings rushed in a panic at the edge of the waves. Sandpipers probed the estuaries, and gulls chattered and swooped.

"It's so big," Addie whispered, regarding the scene with wide eyes.

"Isn't it?" Caroline plunked down onto the ground. "Take your shoes off. The sand feels wonderful. Have you ever been to a beach before?"

"Mama said she'd take us to Coney Island," said Flick. "She never did, though."

Caroline tried not to think about all the things they'd never get to do with their mother. "Well, you're here now." She jumped up. "I can't be at the beach and not do a cartwheel," she declared. "It's completely impossible. No matter what sort of mood I'm in, I have to do a cartwheel. There's something about these wide open spaces I can't resist."

With that, she spread her arms and executed a less-than-perfect cartwheel. "How's that?"

"I want to try!" Addie leaped into a crouch.

"That wasn't a cartwheel," Flick said.

"It takes practice. Pay attention now." Caroline drew a line in the sand with a stick. "You have to start in a lunge. It's like a warrior pose in yoga." She knew they practiced yoga at their school. "Put both hands down on the line and kick your feet over your head." She showed them another cartwheel. "And then you land in a lunge on the same line. Voilà!"

The kids made several attempts, and she helped them along. "Not bad for a couple of newbies. You'll have lots of time to practice. You know what else is fun? Running!" She took off, watching them over her shoulder. They eagerly followed and were soon running along the broad emptiness. They rushed toward a flock of birds and watched them burst into the sky in one huge motion. She led the way into the surf, letting the waves chase them, and they squealed as the cold water surged around their bare feet. For a few moments, they were just a couple of kids, and the sight of them running along the beach gave her a momentary sense of joy—and maybe hope.

Yet the feeling was tinged with sadness and uncertainty. She still had no answer to the question that had dogged her across the continent—now what?

After a while, she found a driftwood log, battered smooth by time and tide, with a twist that formed a natural bench. "Come here, you two, and have a seat." She tunneled her bare feet into the cool sand, finding a sand dollar and a broken nautilus shell. She made a simple mound. "In the summer, there are sand-sculpting contests. One year my family made a dragon as long as a truck."

Flick shaded his eyes and tilted his face toward the sky. "Is this where we live now?"

Oh, boy. Don't lie. "This is where we live for now. You have a nice room, and on Monday we'll get you enrolled in school. So yes. We live here now. I hope you're going to like it. It's where I lived my whole life when I was a kid."

"Did *you* like it?"

She looped her arms around her drawn-up knees. *Don't lie.* "I did," she said. "Once upon a time."

"Then why did you leave?"

"Oh, so many reasons. I wanted to explore the world," she said. "I went to New York to be a designer, but I always remembered this place, and even now, when I create something, there's a little bit of this beach in the design." She traced her finger around the whorls of the nautilus shell. "This is my favorite shape, in fact." She winced as she said it, because the motif had been tainted by the fiasco in New York that had ended her career.

A few fat raindrops spattered down on them. "Welcome to the Pacific Northwest," she said. "It rains a lot around here." She tucked the shell into her pocket. "Guess that's our signal to go inside," she said, tipping her face to the sky. "You're going to need raingear and some gum boots."

Somehow she muddled through the rest of the day. At bedtime, the kids were clingy, which was understandable. They were two little strangers in a world that probably felt to them like another planet.

Angelique had never been consistent about bedtime. Sometimes there would be a bath and a story. Other times the kids would doze off on the sofa and their mother would carry them to bed. The counselor had advised Caroline that they would do better with a regular bedtime routine. Even while on the road, she'd tried to stick to that. No matter where they were, she would start the process at seven.

A couple of nights during their trip, Caroline had felt like she was about to melt from exhaustion, but she'd forced herself to go through the routine in whatever motel or roadside inn they'd stopped at for the night.

On their first evening in Oysterville, she followed protocol. "Okay," she said, pointing to the kitchen clock. "What's that say?"

Flick eyed the clock, one of those silly cats with the pendulum tail. "Seven o'clock."

"Wow, telling time already," said Caroline's mother. "Impressive."

"He's super smart. So is Addie. What happens at seven o'clock?"

"Bath, bed, story, song," Addie said.

"We've been practicing every night," said Caroline. "We're getting pretty good at it, aren't we, guys?"

"I want to stay up," Flick said.

"I'll bet you do. But kids go to bed at seven. No exceptions." She was learning that they would always try to push. "Tonight there's one more seven o'clock job. You have to tell everyone good night."

They made the rounds, hesitant and dubious. Strangers in a strange land. They said good night to her parents, and to Virginia, who had moved to the apartment over the garage after her divorce.

Then they followed her up the stairs for a bath to scrub off the sand from the beach. "Can Dottie help you with your bath?"

Addie nodded. Flick thought for a moment. Then he said, "We have trust issues."

Caroline ruffled his hair. "Smarty-pants." She looked at her mother. "We've been meeting on Skype with a child psychologist. Flick and Addie are learning ways to talk about their feelings."

"I see." Mom went down to Flick's level again and looked him in the eye. "I realize you just met me, and you must have lots of feelings about the changes happening so fast in your life. It's amazing that you came all the way across the country to be here. I hope pretty soon I'll earn your trust."

Caroline's mom filled the tub and stepped away, watching from the doorway. There were questions during the bath.

"Why did we come here?"

Caroline soaped them up and gently washed their sweet, small bodies. "Because we couldn't stay at our place in New York anymore." Not after what went down there.

"We could get another place near my school," Flick pointed out.

"I couldn't afford it," Caroline admitted, tasting defeat, a bitter flavor on her tongue.

"On account of you got fired from your job."

"Pretty much." She saw her mother studying her and looked away, busying herself with the children. Fired. It happened all the time in her industry. Egos ran rampant, tempers boiled over, people stabbed one another in the back, designers were blackballed. Caroline had never believed it would happen to her, though. The job had been everything to her. It had defined her, and when it all unraveled, the sense of loss and despair had left her reeling. She wasn't just grossly unfit to raise two orphans. She was grossly unfit to do anything but flee to safety. What would define her now? Failure? Despair?

"You were getting money by fixing up clothes for people," Flick continued.

"You're very smart to remember that," she said, cupping his forehead as she rinsed off the shampoo. His hair was short, covering his head with tight whorls. Addie's was longer, a mass of corkscrew curls.

Through a painful process of trial and error, Caroline had figured out how to take care of it—lots of conditioner and a gentle combing with her fingers.

To her mother's questioning look, she said, "I took in piecework from vintage shops, repairing and repurposing old leather jackets. Not exactly sustainable."

"Mama was a model," Addie said.

Mom nodded. "Caroline told me your mama was super talented and a good, hard worker. And a fun mom."

Caroline had told her none of those things.

"Do we have to go to school?" asked Flick.

"Sure," she said, forcing brightness. "Every kid does, no matter where you live."

"We have wonderful schools here," Caroline's mom said. "I think you'll love it."

"Because what kid doesn't love school?" Caroline asked.

"Don't listen to her," Mom scolded. "She was a fantastic student. So creative."

"Let's not think about school tonight," Caroline said. "We'll get everything sorted on Monday. You'll meet your teachers and make lots of new friends."

"I would rather watch something," Flick said as she settled them into their beds for story time.

The daily battle. The kids were drawn to anything with a screen, like moths to a flame. Though Caroline didn't have a motherly bone in her body, she knew instinctively that too much watching numbed the mind. The child psychologist had also been clear on the rule—no more than an hour of screen time per day. This had come as unwelcome news to Flick and Addie. Apparently, Angelique had set no limits.

"I have something better than a screen," she told them. "It's better than anything, in fact."

Addie leaned in, her sweet face bright and eager. Flick rolled his eyes. He knew what was coming.

With an air of importance, she took out a book—one of her old favorites.

"That's just a book," said Flick.

"Exactly," said Caroline. "And a book is magic."

"A book is boring," he said, thrusting his chin up and pinning her with a challenging glare.

"A book is the opposite of boring." She ignored his dubious expression and settled between them on one of the beds. Then she dove right in. "'The night Max wore his wolf suit and made mischief of one kind and another . . .'"

"Why's he wearing a wolf suit?" asked Addie.

"Shush," Flick said, leaning in to study the whimsical pictures. "Just listen."

"They're in bed," Caroline said, coming downstairs to the kitchen. Her mom and Virginia were tidying up after dinner. "Finally. Somebody pour me a glass of wine, stat."

"Already done." Virginia indicated a tray of glasses.

"Bless you." Caroline grabbed one and took a bracing gulp of very good red wine. "How the hell did you do it?" she asked her mother. "Bath and bed, night in and night out. With five of us. We were a nightmare."

"A big family is not so different from a busy restaurant. It's all about dishes and laundry."

"The circle of life," Virginia said.

"Where's Fern?" asked Caroline. "With her dad this weekend?"

A curt nod. "She can't wait to see you and meet the kids. I tried to swap weekends with Dave, but he refused. He is on a mission to say no to my every request."

"Sounds like he's doing his job as an ex-husband," Caroline said.

"The one thing he's good at." Virginia had been divorced for a year. She'd had what everyone thought was a fine marriage to a lawyer, and a job as an investigator at his firm. Their eight-year-old daughter, Fern, was a bright-eyed Pippi Longstocking of a child.

In the Shelby family, Virginia was the "pretty one"—a designation people pretended not to espouse in this day and age. But they did. Virginia was adorable and perfectly proportioned. Virginia had a good hair day every day. Virginia had naturally fabulous eyebrows and flawless skin.

Yet when it came to love, she had either terrible judgment or terrible luck, depending on who was giving the opinion. "I've had my heart broken so many times, it's all scar tissue," she often said with a flair for drama. When she'd married Dave, an ambitious, newly minted attorney, the family all thought the drama would end. It did for a while, until the previous year, when his wandering eye stirred things up again.

Mom held open the back door. "Adult conversation awaits."

"Can I carry something?" Caroline offered.

"Just your emotional baggage," Virginia said, picking up an appetizer tray.

So it was going to be that kind of conversation, Caroline realized as she followed her sister out the door.

Their father had made a cheery blaze in the fire pit and they sat around in the Adirondack chairs, faces aglow in the golden light. "Wow," said Caroline. "We have a quorum."

Both her parents were present, along with Virginia and their brother Jackson. He was cheerfully single, a fisherman with a wild streak that lingered long past adolescence. Yet when it came to buying seafood for the restaurant, he was all business—a serious foodie and an advocate for sustainable fishing practices. Almost none of the seafood the restaurant served came from a radius larger than a hundred miles. It didn't need to, because the waters in the area yielded a bounty of cold-water fish and shellfish.

Their father lifted a glass of beer. "IPA from the Razor Clam Microbrewery, and the wine is a nice claret I've been saving for a special occasion."

He was a level 4 sommelier and managed the bar at the restaurant. When he called the wine "nice," it was almost always an understatement.

"A toast," said her mother. "Welcome back, Caroline. I'm sorry about the circumstances that brought you back, but it's wonderful to have you here."

They clinked glasses, sipped and savored. The claret was, as expected, extraordinary. "Oh, man," she said. "Thanks, Dad. Expensive wine is something I've never been able to indulge in."

"Looks like that's about to change." He gave her the dad smile—eyes crinkled, mouth a perfect bow of affection—the indulgent look she used to live for.

Lyle Shelby was the family's charming patriarch. He was the sun, blazing with passion and enthusiasm for life, and everyone else basked in his warmth. To win a word of praise was always the goal. He was so genuinely proud of his family that the worst punishment he ever doled out was disappointment. "We've missed you, C-Shell," he said, smiling across the fire as he called her by the old family nickname.

She took another sip. "I'm really grateful I had a place to bring these poor kids."

"They seem a little shell-shocked," her mom said.

"They are. But believe me, they're doing a lot better now." She cringed, still hearing the echoes of Flick's wailing cries for his mother and Addie's gasping sobs those first few nights.

Caroline looked around at her family, their faces so familiar and dear to her. Despite the passage of time, the feeling of security, of balance, was as powerful now as it had been throughout her youth. She clenched her jaw to stave off tears of utter relief. And then she remembered she didn't have to clench anymore.

She was home. She was safe.

Burning tears squeezed out on a wave of grief and stress, worry and uncertainty, fear and disappointment. And most of all, the utterly crushing knowledge that two little kids now belonged to her, and her alone.

She set down her wineglass and brushed off their concern. "Sorry," she said, using her shirttail to dab at her face. "I'm all right. Just exhausted. Running on fumes."

"Of course you are," said her mother. "You'll feel better tomorrow. Promise you'll sleep in and let me look after the little ones."

"I'd love to take you up on that," said Caroline. "Tomorrow, though, I want to make sure I'm up when they are. I've lost count of all the different places they've awakened." She tried to keep her voice steady as she added, "Poor kids. Their world's been turned upside down."

"It has," Mom agreed, "and they're lucky you were there to help."

Caroline shook her head. "I'm awful. I should have seen what was happening. I can't stop thinking about what I knew and what I didn't know and what I refused to see."

"Signs of domestic violence can be subtle," Virginia pointed out.

"It wasn't subtle. I saw bruises. And like an idiot, I let Angelique persuade me that it was nothing." She stared into the flames, searching for answers she would probably never find. With an effort, she pulled her gaze and her mind back to her family.

"So that was my first clue that something was wrong," she told them. "I never noticed signs of her drug use, either. I didn't see how horrible things would get, so quickly. Maybe I didn't want to probe deeper. And obviously I failed to ask the right questions."

"You're being really hard on yourself," Virginia observed. "One thing I've learned since I started this new job is that people guard their secrets."

Caroline pushed a stick into the fire, creating a flurry of sparks that climbed upward into the night. "You're probably right, but I feel incredibly guilty. I was so focused on myself and my career that I refused to see what was right in front of me. I'll never live down the idea that she was in danger and I didn't see it. How will I ever stop regretting that?"

Mom came in for a hug, and somehow a box of Kleenex materialized. "I know, baby," she said. "It must be overwhelming."

"*She* was the one who was overwhelmed. How could I have missed the signs?"

Virginia gave her shoulder a nudge. "What the hell have you been designing lately? Hair shirts?"

"At least Mick Taylor wouldn't rip off *that* design."

"I'm sorry that happened to you," Virginia said.

"It seems like such a small thing compared to everything else that happened. It ended my career, and I thought it was the worst thing in the world. But *this*. God. I'll never complain about work problems again."

"What happened to the guy who hit her?"

"Roman? I mean, I guess he was the one. No idea what became of him. And that sucks. Guys who hit women don't stop. He's probably hitting somebody else now. The police have his name, but everything happened so fast, I don't know what else to do at this point."

"Tell us how we can help," her mother said.

"You're already helping. Jesus. And just so you know, that was my first breakdown. I didn't want the kids to see me falling apart."

"We're proud of you for stepping up, C-Shell," her father said.

"They're so little." It was hard to speak around the lump in her throat. "What the hell am I going to do? I don't know the first thing about kids, much less kids who've been through this kind of trauma. I am completely unprepared." She paused. Crushed the Kleenex in her fist. "And scared."

"Trust me," Jackson said, "kids are scary even when you have time to prepare. That's why I've never had any."

Virginia elbowed him. "You'll change your mind after you grow up."

"Hey—"

"Go open another bottle of wine," said their dad. "We already killed the first one."

"How much do Addie and Flick know about what happened?" asked her mother. "You said you didn't think they'd been abused, but were they aware that something wasn't right?"

"Tough question. They've never mentioned seeing anyone hurt their mom, but that doesn't mean they didn't see anything. Joan, the therapist, told me to watch and listen. For what, I'm not sure. I keep going over and over that day in my mind, and I'm still confused. I can only imagine how those kids feel inside." Caroline still hadn't discovered what, if anything, Flick and Addie knew about the man who had hurt their mother. She and the social workers had tried to frame their questions carefully. *Did your mommy have visitors over to your apartment?*

No.

Maybe for a sleepover?

No.

Did anyone ever have breakfast at your place?

No.

As far as the children seemed to know, their mother went to work. They went to school and Nila looked after them. And their mom came home. Angelique had been a master at hiding things.

Caroline hugged her knees up to her chest. "Have you ever seen a dead body up close?"

"Oh, sweetie." Her mom shuddered visibly.

The memory made Caroline shudder, too, recalling the shock and horror that had enveloped her that day. She would never be able to un-see the scene in the apartment. "It's terrible in a really . . . special way. You look at this person and realize she's just gone. An empty shell. She'll never feel anything again. She'll never feel love or joy or sadness or anger. All her potential vanished. The things she might have done with her life—for the world, for her kids—are over. They'll never happen. That's what went through my head during the longest fifteen minutes of my life. That's about how long I waited for help to arrive. I had to set my phone on the table in order to use it, because my hand was shaking so hard. I could barely touch the numbers to call 911."

"That must have been so tough," her father said. "So you never knew about her drug use?"

"I didn't know a thing about it. Nothing. She seemed to be in a great place in her career and with her kids. Except . . . some guy was hitting her. The therapist I've been talking to online told me that it's not uncommon for a victim of violence to get hooked on drugs. Heroin completely eliminates pain—physical and emotional.

But I thought I knew her. How did I miss the fact that she was using drugs?"

"Addicts have a thousand ways to hide their addiction," Virginia pointed out. "As far as you know, she was new to using. Could be she had a bad mix. Or maybe she was in recovery and no one knew. And then this was a relapse. A lot of overdoses happen in relapse, because the addict loses her tolerance for the drug."

"That's what the EMTs said, and the police investigator agreed. So did the medical examiner. They said the signs can be subtle if you don't know what to look for. There were little details I didn't make sense of until it was too late. Like I noticed razor blades missing from my sewing kit, and I kept running out of foil. I had no idea those were dots to connect. My God, it was surreal."

"You told us on the phone that it's complicated," said Mom. "You weren't exaggerating."

In the swift exodus and journey west, Caroline had given her family a massively oversimplified explanation. With the kids present nearly every moment since the day of Angelique's death, she had not been able to go into detail about the suspected abuse, the overdose, their uncertain immigration status. She wanted to be absolutely truthful with them, answering their questions in simple, straightforward terms. But she was wary of giving them too much information before they were ready to hear it.

Now she tossed her tissue into the fire and watched it incinerate. "It's complicated on so many levels. I mentioned Angelique was Haitian. One thing I didn't tell you is that she was also undocumented. At first she had a visa. It's actually not that uncommon for high-fashion models to come on a temporary work visa and overstay. Or they come without a visa at all and work off the books. Angelique did it both ways. Her visa expired and she was working off the books. Turns out her agency was taking advantage of her, too."

"Does that mean the kids are also undocumented?" asked her father.

"I suppose so. She arrived in New York when Flick was one and Addie was an infant. See my dilemma? I don't know what on earth to do about it. I'm worried about asking too many questions about their status, because God knows what would happen if they were targeted for deportation now."

"They're little kids," Jackson said. "That would never happen."

"Don't be so sure," Virginia told him. "These days, anything can happen. When I worked at the law firm, one of the associates had a case where a nursing mother was separated from her baby. It was awful. Just heart-wrenching."

"Do you know of any friends or family Angelique might have had in Haiti?" asked Mom. "Anyone at all?"

Caroline shook her head. "There's no one. That's why I agreed to have my name on the guardian slip for the kids' school. It didn't seem like such a big deal at the time. Friends do it for each other all the time." She couldn't remember the precise moment she realized her life had changed irretrievably. Now she realized that moment had happened the day she'd casually agreed to be named the kids' guardian.

"And you're confident there's no other family."

"Yes, but even if they did have relatives there, the kids have no memory of Haiti. Angelique was an only child, raised by a single father who died when she was a teenager. She had it really rough." Caroline paused and decided not to get into exactly *how* rough it had been for Angelique in her native country. That would take all night. "She never knew her mother. Made it on her own as a model. She was discovered on a shoot in Haiti and eventually managed to get herself to New York. When I first met her, she was at the top of her game, constantly in demand, making gobs of money. That's how it looked to me, anyway. To everyone who knew her. As it turns out, her life in the city was rough, too, but I found that out too late." She shivered despite the heat from the fire.

"You did the right thing, coming here," said her mom.

"Did I? Flick and Addie still don't have a home. They don't have a family. All they have is a failed, unemployed designer who doesn't know the first thing about children—except how to avoid them."

"You're overwhelmed," Dad said. "You'll feel better after another glass of wine and a good night's sleep."

Leaning back, she felt the familiar ripple of ocean air on her face. She was still getting used to being home, the scents and sensations and flavors that were part of her blood and bone. Oh, she used to yearn to be away, certain her life was meant to be lived amid the bustle and excitement of the world's capitals. She looked around at her family's faces, so gentle in the kindly light of the fire. "I want you to know, I do appreciate this so much. It means the world to me to have a place to go while I sort out this situation."

"It's good to have you home," said her mother. "We'll do everything we can to help. You know that."

"Fern and I are not going to be staying in the guesthouse forever," Virginia said. "You can live there once I get my own place."

"The three of us don't need the guesthouse," Caroline said. "What I need is a plan."

"Well then, what's the next logical step?" asked her dad. His favorite question.

"For the first time in my life, I honestly don't know. That's why being responsible for these kids is so scary. How will I provide for them? What if something happens to one of them when I'm not paying attention?"

"Every parent's nightmare," Virginia said. "Welcome to the club."

"I didn't join the club. I got drafted."

"You're safe and sound here," said her father. "You can take all the time you need to figure things out." He reached over and gave her shoulder a squeeze. "You just got home, C-Shell. Give yourself a break."

She stared into the fire as if the answers might magically appear amid the sparks and the flames. "I've had three thousand miles to come up with an answer," she said. "I still don't know."

"Let's take this one small step at a time." Dad was always the voice of reason.

There was no rhyme or reason to this situation. She had no idea which step to take. But he was right. She was exhausted and needed to regroup.

"What are your options with the kids at this point?" asked Virginia.

"At the emergency hearing in New York, they said I had the option to surrender them to the state. The caseworker assured me it's not a horrible choice. They'd go immediately into temporary emergency foster care, although with no guarantee they'd stay together. She told me that they might grow up in the foster care system or they could be adopted. I couldn't imagine simply walking away from them, so I kept them with me."

"I don't blame you for stepping up," her mother said. "That was an incredible thing to do."

"I don't feel so incredible. I just couldn't stand the idea that they'd end up with strangers, and maybe even lose each other. Now that I'm in Washington State, I'll need to apply to be their permanent legal guardian."

"Is that what you want to do?"

"I . . . God, Mom. That's like making them my kids," she said.

"And?"

"It was never my plan. I never even wanted kids. I can't seem to find a serious boyfriend, let alone someone who makes me want to have his babies." She used to believe the one thing that would change her mind would be falling in love, falling so hard that she'd yearn to make a life with someone, make a family.

"You were with some great guys," Virginia said. "They looked great on your social media, anyway."

"Isn't that what social media is for?" Caroline *had* met some good guys. Just not *the* guy. There was Kerwyn—Welsh-born, ironic, and darkly handsome. When they first got together, she couldn't stop daydreaming about him and even found herself thinking she'd found something lasting. In time, though, she realized he rarely made her a priority. She'd been a mere convenience to him, an afterthought. And it wasn't enough for her. She wanted to be someone's whole world, an admittedly idealistic notion that had driven him away. After that, the pendulum swung the other way. Her next prospect, Brent, had been *too* into her. At first she'd enjoyed the attention, but after a while, she felt smothered and called an end to it. Most recently, she'd gone out with Miles, who was funny, charming, and good in bed—but they were moving through life at different speeds. She was in the fast lane, and he was in the no-go lane, drifting from job to job with very little purpose.

After three near misses, she couldn't help but think the problem might be with her. Did she not know how to be in love? How to stay that way, nurturing a relationship along in all its sustaining, exhilarating passion and delight?

Maybe she expected too much, dreaming of something that was ultimately unreachable. Long ago, there had been one moment when love was defined for her, and perhaps to the detriment of all future relationships, she could not forget that moment.

Ultimately she surrendered to reality. Her primary relationship was not with a man, but with her career. That was a relationship she could control. One that wouldn't be destroyed by someone else's priorities—or so she thought. Then Mick Taylor came along and ruined that for her, too.

"The New York fashion world isn't known to be a great dating pool," she told her family. "It hardly matters now. I'm single and in charge of two kids. Single and unemployed. Not exactly man-bait, you know?"

Virginia slid her a glance. "Actually, some guys are drawn to women with kids."

"Hey." She leaned across the arm of her chair. It was a relief to shift the topic away from the giant mess she was in. "You're seeing someone, aren't you?"

"If by *seeing* you mean dating, and if by *someone* you mean a few yummy men, then yes. I'm seeing several someones. And believe me, having a kid does not deter the right kind of guy."

"Well. That's good to know. Anyone special?"

Virginia shook her head. "For the time being, dipping my toe into the dating pool is a low-stakes game, because I'm completely unprepared for anything more. Meeting new guys is just a distraction. Something to do when Fern has to go to her dad and Amanda's."

"Jesus, you mean Dave's already with that woman? He couldn't wait until the ink dried on your divorce papers?" Caroline was outraged on her sister's behalf. "God, he sucks so bad. Why didn't I know about this?"

"Didn't seem very sisterly to pile my troubles on top of yours. And frankly, I hate the story I've been living. Turns out my 'perfect' husband pulled the oldest trick in the book. He took up with an associate at the law firm, plotted a slick exit, and brought my life to a screeching halt. She's awful, too—one of those phony Christians who claimed she was 'saving herself for marriage.'"

"I guess you should have asked *whose* marriage," Caroline said. "She ought to be ashamed, but apparently she's shameless, targeting a married man with a kid. Vee, I wish I'd been a better sister. You didn't do anything to deserve this, and I'm really sorry it's happening. What can I do?"

"I'll fill you in on all the gory details eventually." The flames painted her beautiful face with exhaustion. "Believe me, they *are* gory."

Caroline stabbed a dry stick into the fire. "Okay, it's official. I'm never going to look at a man. Ever."

"Famous last words."

"Speaking of last." She downed the rest of her wine. "I saw Will Jensen," she said. Not exactly a safe topic, but the wine was melting her reserve.

Virginia sat forward. "Already?"

"He was at the Bait & Switch early this morning when I rolled into town. Out running with a group of kids."

"He does that," she said with a nod. "High school coach. And?"

"And nothing." Yet a sudden strange flutter in her gut didn't feel like nothing. "The kids were having a meltdown, so I pulled over at the store, and he helped me out."

"And?" Virginia persisted.

He looked wonderful, Caroline thought. He looked like the reason she hadn't had a sustainable relationship with anyone in a decade. "You tell me. I saw him for like two minutes at six in the morning."

"He and Sierra moved to the old Jensen place on the bay."

"I'm sure you'll get a chance to catch up with Sierra," said Mom. "That will be nice. You girls used to be so close."

Nice—like hitting herself in the head with a hammer? She and Sierra had been best friends growing up. There had been a time when they'd harbored no secrets between them. When they'd shared everything, even—

"Will whipped the football team into fine shape," said Jackson. "Best thing that ever happened to the Peninsula Mariners." He looked at his watch. "And this Mariner is heading off to bed."

"Huh," Virginia teased. "I bet you have a hot date."

"I'm in the middle of reading a hot new novel."

"Jealous," Caroline said, standing up and giving him a hug. "I've gone to sleep every night reading *The Pout-Pout Fish* and *The Emperor's New Clothes*."

"Good choice for a designer," Virginia said.

"Really? Because the point is, the emperor is naked."

"Wait until you see what they've done to the town library," Mom said. "It's doubled in size. There's a story hour every day. Your kids will love that."

They're not my kids, thought Caroline.

Oh, but they were.

Caroline crawled into bed in the room that used to belong to Georgia. The settling sounds of the old wooden house and the murmur of the surf in the distance were the lullaby of her childhood.

There was a quality of sleep that happened only here at home. Surrounded by the cocoon of warmth imparted by a quilt softened by years, Caroline surrendered to a sense of utter security. Whether warranted or not, being here in the place where she had grown up felt safe—a feeling she had not experienced in a very long time. She slipped deeper into the crisp, sun-scented bed linens and released a sigh of relief.

This reprieve from worry was only temporary. She knew that. Her problems, like her new life, were just getting started. She had to make a new plan, not just for herself but now for the two children who had become her responsibility. She had no idea where to start.

Start here, she thought. Start now.

Her family had gathered around with soothing noises and gratifying reassurances. But coming back here felt like a step backward.

Later, she thought, tucking her arm around the freshly laundered pillowcase. I'll figure things out later. For the moment, she snuggled into the comfort of a familiar bed. Finally, she was about to get a good night's sleep. She was floating toward sweet oblivion when she heard a little *blip* of distress.

No, it was just her imagination.

Another blip, followed by a sniff.

Caroline blinked into the darkness. "Addie?" she whispered.

Two small silhouettes were framed in the doorway.

"We can't sleep."

Great.

"Of course you can sleep," she said. "You've been sleeping like champs at every hotel we stayed at."

"Because you were in the room with us," Flick said.

"I never realized my presence was a sleep aid."

"We're all alone here," Addie said, her small voice quavering. She clutched Wonder Woman to her chest.

Caroline gritted her teeth. At the same time, something different stirred inside her. She'd never been anyone's sleep aid before. "I thought you'd be excited to have a room all to yourself."

Silence for several beats.

"We don't want to be all by ourselves," Flick said.

She hadn't minded sharing the motel rooms with them. She'd grown used to their soft sighs and occasional whimpers. "Listen. I'm super tired, too tired to argue with you. So I'll make you a deal. You can sleep in here tonight because it's your first night. Starting tomorrow, you sleep in your bed all night every night."

The kids looked at each other. Then back at Caroline. With an elongated sigh, she lifted the blanket. They snuggled in like puppies, rustling a bit and then settling down, nestled close against her.

Caroline turned out the light.

Chapter 8

Fabric shops all had a peculiar, distinctive scent, subtle and evocative, a waft of nostalgia. When Caroline stepped through the door of Lindy's Fabric and Notions and took a breath, she recognized the aroma of dry goods and dye, sweet machine oil and tailor's chalk, and dried lavender and bergamot from the display of fine imported tea, one of Lindy's sidelines.

Familiarity washed over her as she took in her surroundings. Even the jangle of the little brass bell over the door awakened memories. The shop had been like a second home to Caroline while she was growing up. She'd spent countless hours here, learning the basics of sewing and design that had become her life's passion.

This was her first venture away from the children since Angelique's death, and she felt a tangible release of tension. Her mother had gathered Flick and Addie in like a hen clucking over a clutch of eggs, and she'd shooed Caroline off with a brisk flap of her apron. "Take a little time for yourself," she'd said. "I'm in charge now. Go have a look around town."

Caroline had seized on the opportunity. She needed it. Needed to be something other than a worrier. Needed to find her next logical step. So naturally the path led her to Lindy's.

"Hello, can I help you?" said the young woman behind the cutting table. She wore thick-framed glasses and an apron in a conversational birdcage print that managed to look very cool, and a name tag that read ECHO.

"I hope so," Caroline said, scanning the neat rows of fabric bolts. The shop was deserted other than a marmalade cat napping in the window display. "I'm an old friend of Lindy's. I used to work here. Is she around today?"

"There's a familiar face," called a voice from the workroom in the back of the shop.

Caroline felt herself light up with pleasure. "Lindy? Oh my gosh. It's so great to see you."

The older woman—she was about Caroline's mom's age—opened her arms as she bustled into the shop. "Miss Caroline Shelby, as I live and breathe. I heard a rumor that you were in town," she said as they hugged. She stepped back, beaming. "My star pupil. How nice to see you again."

Lindy had owned the shop for as long as Caroline could remember. She was a talented seamstress and quilter who had generously given Caroline access to the machines in her workroom, as well as basic lessons in sewing and patternmaking.

"This is Echo Sanders," Lindy said. "Another rising star."

Echo's cheeks reddened in a bashful blush. "We'll see," she said.

"My goodness, we go way back, don't we?" Lindy said.

Ever since she was old enough to thread a needle, Caroline had dreamed of designing and making clothes. Discovering, thanks to a trip to Portland with Lindy, that such a thing as design school existed. Lindy had given her a catalog from the Fashion Institute of Technology in New York, and Caroline was a goner. With relentless focus, she had conquered patternmaking, sample sewing, grading, and sizing.

"I'll always be grateful for all the time I spent here. You were such a fabulous teacher. I used to want to wrap the world in your vintage cotton prints."

"And it appears you're doing just that," Lindy said, then turned to Echo. "She's been working as a designer in New York."

Echo leaned her elbows on the cutting table. "That sounds like a dream come true."

"It's . . ." Caroline glanced away. "It's been quite a ride."

"I hope we get a chance to catch up soon," Lindy said.

"I'd like that. I don't know where to start." She sighed. "I've left New York. I'm looking for a way to get back on my feet."

Lindy's brow knit. "Back on your feet? Is everything all right?"

"It's a long story," Caroline said. "I lost a close friend in New York, and now I'm taking care of her kids—Flick and Addie. They're five and six years old."

"My goodness, Caroline. What happened? That is, if it's not prying . . ."

"Not at all." Caroline took a deep breath. "If I've learned anything through this, it's that keeping secrets can be toxic. Angelique died of an overdose. I didn't even know she had a drug problem. I'm pretty sure she was in an abusive relationship, too, and the biggest regret of my life is that I had my suspicions and didn't do anything."

"You weren't her keeper."

"I was her friend. I wish I'd known what to do. I mean, I asked questions, but obviously not the right questions to get a straight answer from her."

Lindy's expression changed. Her usual soft, professional facade hardened as she crossed her arms in front of her. "Let me guess. She said she tripped and fell. Bumped into a door. Banged herself on the subway."

"Something like that," Caroline agreed. "I thought she might be covering up, and I didn't force the issue. I should have pushed harder to make her tell me what was going on."

"You can't. That never works." Lindy's voice was firm.

Caroline faced her onetime mentor and teacher, a woman who had seemed as steady and grounded as the lighthouses along the coast. Lindy was married to a banker, known for his work with the Rotary Club. "Lindy?" she asked softly. There was a feeling she recognized. A *knowing*. It was the feeling she'd had about Angelique, but she'd dismissed it. "Are you all right? I don't mean to sound nosy, but—"

"No, ask away," Lindy said. "You said it yourself just a moment ago—secrets can be toxic. And to answer your question, yes. I'm all right now. But for years, I was married to a man who hit me."

Caroline pressed down on the cutting table to steady herself. She tried to reconcile her memories of Lindy and her scion-of-the-community husband. She'd scarcely known him. Mr. Bloom had always driven nice cars and worn bespoke suits. They had a gorgeous house with a swimming pool and endless ocean views. He'd attended church every Sunday. He'd seemed like the model citizen.

Caroline scrambled to take it all in. She'd known Lindy since she was a little girl, browsing through drawers of buttons and bolts of fabric. She had spent so many hours with her, nattering away, oblivious to a woman's secret pain. A moment ago, she would have said she knew this person well. She was fast learning that everyone had hidden facets. To realize Lindy had been suffering all that time filled her with guilt. "I'm sorry for the trouble you had with your husband," she said. "Are you all right now?"

Echo was listening intently. Lindy took a deep breath, and her expression softened. "I've been divorced for three years, and he moved away and I never have to see him again."

"Oh, Lindy. I'm glad you're not in that anymore."

"Yes, I . . . Well, life is different since the divorce. Mostly in a good way. I've put off any thought of retiring. Part of claiming my freedom also means having to provide for myself. I've had to simplify my life considerably, as you can imagine, but I'm safe and sound." She smiled across the table at Echo. "I won't ever get rich running this shop, but I've never been happier."

"I hope business is good."

"It could always be better. I'm getting by." Lindy's smile was wistful.

"Honestly, I'm still in shock," Caroline said. "I was as self-centered as any kid, and I had no idea you were going through such a horrible ordeal."

"No one knew for a very long time. There are still people in town who don't believe it. Because as I suppose you've gleaned by now, secrecy and shame are a big part of the syndrome." Lindy took out a tissue and dabbed at her eyes. "I feel so silly, getting emotional after all this time. It's just such a relief to talk about these things."

"Listen," Caroline said to her, "the last thing you should be feeling is silly. No one should have to suffer through something like that."

Lindy offered a wobbly smile. "I've always liked you, Caroline. You have a good heart."

It didn't feel that way. She'd been oblivious. "Is there anything I can do to help?" Caroline asked. "I mean, I know you're safe now, but if you need something . . ."

"The talking," Lydia said. "Just like this. It does help."

"Yes," Echo said, her voice barely audible. "The listening, too." She was staring down at the table. Her hands were tense on the cutting mat.

Lindy patted Caroline's arm. "Echo and I have something in common. We're both survivors."

"Oh, God. You too?" Caroline felt as if the curtains had been swept aside, revealing a hidden world she'd never imagined.

Echo lifted her gaze. "I walked away from a man who took everything from me. I'm still picking up the pieces. Lindy's been kind enough to give me a job here. I used to work sewing at a fabricator down in Astoria, making gloves and outerwear for the military. But they lost their government contract and laid everyone off. I guess they're moving all their fabrication work offshore like everyone else."

Caroline thought about her purpose coming into the shop, and now she dismissed the idea. "I'd love to talk to you more sometime," she said to both women. "That is, if it's not painful. There's so much I don't know about what my friend was facing. I owe it to her kids to understand."

Lindy neatened the supplies around the cash register. "Like I said, talking can help. Anytime, Caroline. And welcome home."

That night before bedtime, Caroline found a slender cord of Christmas lights in the basement. Crawling on hands and knees, she installed them along the upstairs hallway.

"Did I miss something?" asked Mom, arriving from the laundry room with a stack of folded clothes. "Are we putting up lights super early, or are these for the Easter Bunny?"

The children, watching from the doorway of their room, giggled softly.

"Neither," Caroline said. "I'm illuminating the route from the kids' room to mine." She looked over at Addie and Flick, freshly bathed and wearing their jammies. "You want to tell Grammy Dot the reason for this?"

"So we can find her in the night," said Flick.

Her mother rocked back on her heels. "That seems like a very good idea. I'd hate to lose my daughter in the night."

That drew a smile from Addie. Caroline took a few moments to show them how to follow the lights from their room, down the hall and to hers. "I'm not saying you should come and find me, but if you really, *really* need to, then the lights will show you the way."

"I have a request," said her mother. "While Caroline is finishing up, I would like to tuck you in. Would that be all right?"

The kids exchanged a glance. Caroline could tell they were drawn to her mother, but still unsure. They had tagged along with her all day as she went about her chores. Now they regarded her with sober, measuring expressions.

"She's a good tucker-inner," Caroline said.

"Okay," Flick said, "we'll give her a shot."

Chapter 9

On Sunday night, Caroline had a special treat for the children. "I'm going to read you another one of my oldest and best books," she announced. "My mom read it aloud to us, one chapter every night, and it became my favorite story. So I'm excited to share it with you."

She lay down on Addie's bed and the kids snuggled close. "It's a story about a boy and his dog," she said. "A classic."

"The pictures aren't in color," Addie observed.

"You can color them in your mind while I read." Caroline opened to chapter 1. She didn't remember the story so much as the feeling of being gathered with her siblings around their mother. Safety and comfort. That was what she wanted to give Addie and Flick. She didn't know how, and she didn't even know if it was possible, but snuggling together in the warm glow of a reading lamp seemed like a good place to start.

"'We called him Old Yeller,'" she read. "'The name had a sort of double meaning. One part meant that his short hair was a dingy yellow, a color that we called *yeller* in those days . . .'"

"Somebody scribbled in the book," Flick said.

"Yeah, that's weird." There was a thick black line through a sentence or two, as if the text had been redacted by a censor. "People shouldn't make marks in books. Anyway, let's keep going. We won't miss a few words."

By the time she got to the end of the chapter, the kids were thoroughly invested in Travis and Yeller, who had to look after Travis's mom and little brother while their father hit the trail to drive the cattle to market. Flick and Addie begged for more of the story, but she held firm at one chapter per night.

When she tried to tuck them in, Flick was restless, kicking at the covers, staring out the window, worrying the corner of his pillow.

"What's going on, buddy?" asked Caroline, setting down the book.

"I can't go to school tomorrow."

Oh, boy. "We've been talking all day about how much fun you're going to have with your new friends and teachers," she said.

"I don't feel good," he said. "I'm getting sick."

"I don't feel good, either," Addie piped up, patting her stomach.

She felt both their foreheads. "Cool as a cucumber," she said. "I think maybe you might be feeling nervous about starting school in the morning. You think that could be it?"

"Duh," Flick said softly.

"We won't know anybody," Addie said.

"It's always a bit scary to start something new," Caroline said, her own stomach twisting with nerves. "But once you start, you get over the new really quick."

"Nuh-uh," Addie objected.

"Fern goes to your school, and you know her." Caroline's niece, outgoing and guileless, had instantly embraced the elder cousin role.

"She's in third grade," Flick said.

"So will you be one day."

"Not tomorrow."

"True. Tomorrow, the teachers are going to make sure you settle right in," Caroline said. During the trip from New York, she had called ahead to explain the situation to the school principal and faculty. The school staff had sounded reassuring. "I've already talked to your teachers," she reminded them. "They're excited to meet you."

"Teachers have to like us," Flick pointed out. "Kids don't."

"Why wouldn't they like you?" Caroline asked. "You're awesome."

"They won't like us 'cause we're brown."

Caroline was taken aback. "What makes you say that?"

"'Cause they're white."

"I'm white and I like you," Caroline said. She didn't want to be one of those white people who pretended to be color-blind, knowing full well the world didn't work that way. "And some of the kids at your school are brown, too. And Asian and Latino and maybe even Kreyòl like you and your mama. You're going to make a lot of new friends. I know it seems hard. It *is* hard."

Addie's lower lip poked out. She grabbed her Wonder Woman doll and made her soar up and over the mound formed by her knees. "I wish I could fly away and never come back."

"You can't do that," Caroline said. "We need you here with us."

"Then I wish I had a superpower," she said.

"I think you do," Caroline pointed out. "Both of you do. You're super nice and super strong and super smart."

Flick sniffed. "All parents say that to their kids."

I'm not your parent.

"I don't know about that, and I wouldn't say it if I didn't mean it. I just know you're both going to be super in your new school."

Addie adjusted the doll's spangled top and carefully straightened the wispy cape. "How? How do you know?"

"I'm smart, too. I know stuff." She got up and went to the closet. "Tell you what. We can pick out your clothes for tomorrow and lay them out, so you can be super quick in the morning. What would you like to wear?"

"Doesn't matter," Flick said glumly. He chose a plain blue T-shirt, slightly worn but clean.

"Good choice," Caroline said. "Navy is a classic."

Addie selected a yellow one. "This is my favorite color."

"Then you should wear it, because it matches your personality—sunny and bright."

"Mama always got us new clothes for the first day of school."

Caroline's heart sank. She hadn't thought about getting them something new to wear. The list of things she didn't know about parenting was getting longer by the moment. "Tell you what. I'll iron your shirts and pants so they look brand-new, okay?"

This did not appear to impress them. Addie yawned and snuggled under the covers with her doll. Caroline tucked her in, then Flick.

"You're going to do all right," she said. "Get some rest and I'll see about blueberry pancakes in the morning." She gave them each a kiss, a gesture that was, day by day, starting to feel more natural. On her way out, she took the kids' shirts with her. She stood outside in the hallway, trying to force away the knot of anxiety in her gut. What would it be like for these kids to walk into their classrooms tomorrow, midyear, without seeing a single familiar face? Caroline really did wish she could give them a superpower—confidence to face all the changes in their lives. Maybe . . . She held out the T-shirts, feeling a tingle of inspiration as an idea formed.

Downstairs, her parents were cuddled together on the sofa, binge-watching some violent series or other. Caroline rolled back her shoulders, feeling a crick in her neck. "Kids are exhausting," she said.

"Gosh, we wouldn't know," her mother said.

"Hey, you had five kids by choice."

"Only because I couldn't talk her into six," her father said.

God.

"I need to sew something," she said.

"Now?"

"I'm going to repurpose some shirts so the kids have something special to wear to school tomorrow. Is there an old windbreaker I can cut up?"

Her mom got up. "I'm sure we can find whatever you need in the giveaway bin. Let me give you a hand."

"I don't want to interrupt your evening—"

"No worries. The zombie apocalypse will wait." She patted Dad on the shoulder. "Come find me if it gets too scary."

They went to the spare room off the kitchen. From Caroline's earliest memory, it had been a repository for their mother's many unfinished craft projects—printmaking, scrapbooking, crochet, painting on fabric, wood carving. Mom was irrepressibly creative, always starting something or other, but with five kids and the restaurant, she'd been too busy to finish anything.

Caroline had already set up her own sewing machine in the room. It was a prized possession, an industrial workhorse she'd gone into debt to acquire while in design school. Back in New York, she'd had to pay a moving company union wages just to get it from her apartment into Angelique's car, because the thing weighed a ton. Her father and brother had helped her haul it into the house.

"What are we making?" asked her mother.

"The kids just told me their mom buys them new clothes for the first day of school. So I'm going to make them something to wear tomorrow."

Mom gave her a hug. "Ah, Caroline. What a nice idea."

"They're worried about starting school in a strange new place."

"Of course they are." Mom rummaged in a box labeled DONATIONS. "What did you have in mind?"

"Something red that's light and slippery, like a windbreaker or some kind of lining."

"Will this work?" Mom held up a windbreaker with the Sustainable Seafoods logo—Jackson's company.

Caroline shook out the thin red ripstop garment. "It's perfect," she said.

"Great. Put me to work."

"Can you stencil a slogan on these shirts?"

"You bet. I can use the kit I got to make personalized workwear for the restaurant. Never finished that project, but I still have all the supplies."

As Caroline made a pattern and cut out the windbreaker fabric, she felt herself unbending, bit by bit. "This is my happy place," she said. "When I'm making something. Anything."

"You've always been that way," said Mom. "Remember Grammy's old treadle machine? You were about six years old when you learned how to use it."

"I loved that machine," Caroline said. "Everybody else was in the kitchen or garden, and I was in here making outfits for the dog."

"You were on your own path."

"I suppose. I always got the feeling I was doing something wrong."

"And I always thought you were the most creative of the lot. Look at you now. A designer from New York."

"*From* being the operative word. I can't go back."

"You will one day if you want," Mom said. "You'll return the conquering hero."

"Right." She focused on the task at hand, not wanting to think about her ruined career on top of everything else. Their silence was companionable. She caught her mother studying her. "What?"

"You're so passionate. It's inspiring to watch. Did you ever think of creating a sewing workshop, or . . . I'm not sure what you'd call it—an atelier?"

"That sounds a bit grand." Caroline brought up something she couldn't stop thinking of. "I heard there's an outfit down in Astoria that used to make garments for the military. They're going out of business. A woman I met at Lindy's said they're auctioning off machines and fixtures and so forth. The problem is, machines don't fabricate. People do. I'm only one person. One person with two kids, in fact." She sighed. "Suddenly my options seem to be very limited."

"I have a suggestion."

"You always do."

"Instead of regarding the children as a hindrance, why not see them as inspiration? Look what we're making right now." Mom held up the shirt. "Not bad, eh? Those kids are lucky to have you."

"Those kids are lost souls." They were the most innocent of victims, swept up in the hidden turmoil of their mother's life. "I failed Angelique. When I think of all the ways I could have helped and didn't, I want to throw up. What if I screw up her kids?"

"Listen, they are not meant to be your redemption, Caroline. Don't cast them in that role—it's not fair to Addie and Flick. They're meant to be children, and they have no other job than that."

Caroline flinched. "Ouch. And you're right. I'm just scared I'll miss the signals with them the way I did with Angelique. I don't know what they've seen or experienced. When I ask, they seem clueless. Flick says he never saw anyone being mean to his mom. And I believe him, because that's his truth. But what I've learned about domestic violence is that the secrecy and the shame are almost universal. The isolation and lack of support. I wish I'd done better by Angelique. I'm afraid I'm not the right person to look after her kids. I lie awake every night trying to figure out the right thing to do. I haven't slept soundly since the moment they landed with a thud in my life. There are times when I feel sure I can take care of them. That I can keep them safe and happy. Then there are other times when I have no idea what I'm doing, and I'm absolutely certain I'll ruin those poor kids. And it's not like ruining a design or a garment or a dinner entrée. These are two human beings. The stakes are too high for me to screw up." She carefully folded the new shirts. "Maybe I should contact social services. See if there's a family for them, one that would give them a better life. I mean, there might be a couple somewhere with the right skills. With job security." Could she do that? Surrender the children to a more qualified family? What would that look like?

Mom studied the neatly folded shirts. "What is your heart telling you?"

Caroline felt defensive even though her mother didn't seem to be criticizing her. "That I'm falling in love with these kids. But that's not going to put a roof over their heads or give them a secure future."

"You don't need to decide right now," said her mother. "Give yourself some time."

Caroline nodded. She needed to stop thinking about it for a bit. "I had a nice visit with Lindy Bloom and a woman named Echo who works at her shop. Did you know they're both domestic violence survivors?"

"Surv—what? Lindy?"

"I was shocked, too. Apparently she suffered for years and no one knew."

"Good lord. Quentin Bloom?"

"Is that his name—Quentin? I never knew. Always thought of him as Mr. Bloom. That's what Lindy called him, too—Mr. Bloom."

"Goodness. I did business at his bank for decades. I'd heard they split up, and he left the peninsula, but . . . Good lord," she said again.

"I'm learning that this syndrome is rampant. It crosses all boundaries—the fine upstanding banker and the trashy guy Echo was with. I need to learn more. Help more. I need a lot of things. I wish I could reach out to women who have been where Angelique was. Listen to them. Learn from them."

"Maybe you can. See if there's a local group."

"There's not. At least, none that I could find online."

"What about finding them in person? I think we're discovering that this problem is everywhere, even in our cozy little town. Even . . ."

"Mom, what are you saying? Do you know someone?"

Her mother hesitated, then said, "There's a young woman at the restaurant—Nadine. Georgia hired her last year when she showed up looking for work. She had a broken cheekbone and a restraining order against her boyfriend, and not much else. Zero job skills. Georgia started her in the back, washing dishes and sweeping."

"Do you think she'd be open to a conversation?" Caroline didn't know much about support groups. She'd always assumed they were meant for needy, distraught individuals who couldn't cope on their own. Now she realized just being able to speak openly in a safe place could make a world of difference.

"You never know until you ask," said her mother.

Caroline felt a spark of inspiration. That gut feeling when she knew something was right. She glanced over at her mother, and their gazes held as an idea took shape. "What if *I* started a group? A support group, right here in town? Do you think people would come?"

"Caroline, you've always been so full of ideas, it must be exhausting to be in your head."

"I just keep thinking about Angelique. Maybe if she'd had a safe place to talk, friends who were supportive, who listened and understood . . ." She saw her mother stifle a yawn. "Anyway, maybe it's crazy, but I'm going to look into it."

"It's a wonderful notion."

"Thanks for listening, Mom. You're the best."

A fleeting smile. "The older you get, the smarter I get, right?"

Chapter 10

Will finished off Monday morning practice with time sprints around the track that circled the football field. One of the athletes, a senior named Beau Cannon, showed major promise, and he was currently being recruited by several Division I colleges. Will had high hopes for the kid. Beau's single mom probably wouldn't be able to pay for college without a scholarship.

"Good work today," he said as they left the field together. "You're right at thirty-six seconds on the three hundred."

"I need to be under." Beau wiped his brow with the tail of his jersey.

"At the risk of sounding like a broken record—it's your start. You need to explode off the blocks. Run the first twenty meters like you're a scalded dog. That'll shave your time down to where it needs to be. Keep practicing your start and you'll get there."

Beau nodded. "Thanks, Coach. Will do."

The hunger in the boy's eyes looked familiar to Will. He remembered his own days as an athlete, attending DoD schools wherever his father happened to be stationed. He could still summon up the almost-painful feeling of striving, wanting to be the best, pushing himself to the limit. Despite the pain, it was also a kind of high that had filled him up, almost obliterating the sense that he didn't belong anywhere.

He'd just get settled into a school and then they'd move again. When he was twelve years old, his mother had died suddenly, leaving a gaping hole in his life, and exposing the yawning gulf between him and his father. Driven by grief, he had pushed himself harder still, but even the most extreme sports failed to fill the void.

In the navy, he pursued the toughest training courses he could find—BUD/S and SEAL training. The exercises were so grueling that there were days when his soul seemed to leave his body. He found survival mechanisms he never knew he possessed, and during active duty, they'd saved his life more than once. Serving in the navy had been his way of finding a place in the world—for a while.

"Do you miss it?" asked Beau. "Being on the SEAL team, I mean. Would you still be doing that if you hadn't been injured?"

"I don't think much about the what-if," Will said. "I always wanted to live here on the peninsula, and I always wanted to be a teacher. The plan just happened sooner than anticipated. Are you thinking about enlisting?"

"It'd be a big help to my mom," Beau said.

"Tell you what. Come by my office after sixth period and we'll talk."

Relief softened his eyes. "Thanks, Coach."

He watched Beau heading for the main building, seeing so much of himself in the kid—the eager yearning, the focus. But could he honestly recommend a stint in the military to anyone? It took a passion for service. Or maybe a complete lack of alternatives.

After the incident that had taken his eye, his path had changed almost overnight. He returned to his wife and to civilian life. Now here he was, the way he'd always planned, yet still wanting more. Wanting permanence. Wanting Sierra to find contentment. Wanting a family.

Life was good here. He'd always believed that. This place was part of his DNA, the one consistent element of his peripatetic childhood. As a navy kid, he'd been all over the world, and his grandparents' place in Oysterville, where he'd spent his summers, was the home of his heart. It was a boy's paradise, where he could explore the crystal-clear blue waters of Willapa Bay or brave the turbulent swells of the Pacific on the west side of the peninsula. He was filled with memories of riding horses and flying kites on the seemingly endless flats of shifting sand, hiking through mysterious forests, fishing for the freshest of seafood, or gathering the sweet, prized oysters for which the town was famous.

Slinging a towel around his neck, he checked the time and crossed the parking lot to his car. On the far side of the lot, he spotted Caroline Shelby walking toward the administration office with her two kids. He didn't feel the astonishment of seeing her the other day, a distant memory suddenly made flesh. Now he felt an instinctual urge to connect with her again.

Keep going, he told himself.

Go say hi, he told himself.

Pretend you don't see her, he told himself.

Ever since bumping into her the other morning, he'd been trying to stop speculating about Caroline Shelby. But school was a gossip mill, and people were already talking. The Shelbys' middle child was back in town with a couple of mixed-race kids in tow. He'd overheard the attendance clerk saying, with scolding conviction, that Caroline had always been an odd one—the purple hair, the crazy outfits. A misfit in the Shelby clan. People discussed those two little kids and wondered what she was up to now.

He wondered, too.

"It's that guy." The little boy with her pointed straight at Will.

She looked over his way, and he saw her stiffen when she recognized him.

"Hey there," he said, crossing the parking lot and falling in step with them. "First day of school?"

"That's right," she said, casting a nervous glance at the kids.

"Cool," he said. "What grades will you be in?"

The little boy—Frank? No, Flick—mumbled, "Kindergarten and first."

"I have it on good authority that the kindergarten and first grade teachers are the nicest."

"Oh?" Caroline offered a fleeting smile. "Where'd you hear that?"

"From their students," Will said. "Kids are tough critics. I should know. I'm a teacher, too."

Flick stared up at him. "You are?"

"Yep. I teach math to the big kids. I have to be extra nice because, like I said, students are tough critics."

"We're scared," Addie said.

She was so damn cute. She wore jeans and a bright yellow shirt, and little sneakers with curly laces. He read the words on the front of the shirt. "Hey, that says, 'Ask me about my superpower.'" He looked at Flick. "Your shirt says the same thing. So I'm asking. What about your superpower?"

The kids looked at each other, then up at Caroline.

"He asked," she said. The shadow of worry in her eyes eased slightly.

"Watch this." Addie unsnapped a side pocket of her shirt. She whipped out a thin red swath of fabric—a scarf?—and attached it to the back of her collar with snaps.

"Whoa," said Will. "Check it out. You have a cape."

"It's a superhero cape. Here's mine." Her brother took his out and snapped it on. "We can fly!" He took off running across the lawn in front of the admin building, the thin fabric flying out behind him. His sister followed, making a powerful whooshing sound as they zoomed around.

"I'm going to take a wild guess and say you made the shirts."

"Finished them up at midnight," she said. "My mom did the lettering on the front."

"Good work. They're really cool. Genius, in fact. How did you come up with the idea?"

"It's remarkable how inspired I can get in the middle of the kids' meltdowns. And how inventive I can be with old T-shirts and used windbreakers."

"Seriously? Those are made out of old clothes?"

"And a bit of ingenuity."

"Every kid is going to want one. What the hell, *I* want one."

That drew a smile from her. "Right."

He remembered that smile, like a light suddenly switching on. The still-familiar sense of easy friendship they'd shared long ago took him by surprise. Those days were over, he reminded himself. They belonged to a past that was gilded by nostalgia, something that could be remembered but never reclaimed.

"I ought to make one for myself," she said. "I think I'm more nervous than they are. Their school in New York was so diverse, like a mini UN. What if they feel out of place here?"

He wondered about their father. Where was the dad? Had she been married? He wanted to ask her that. He wanted to ask her a lot of things. Instead, he said, "Kids are adaptable. I bet they'll do all right." Lame. But he didn't know her anymore. He spoke in platitudes. "I'll let you get to it. I hope it goes well for your kids today."

Judging by all the swooping they were doing, he suspected they would be just fine.

"Flick got into a fight at recess and Addie wet her pants," Caroline said to Virginia. They were seated together on a bench at a playground near the restaurant, watching the children blow off steam after school.

Virginia gave her arm a pat. "First day of school is always hard. When Fern started kindergarten, she spent the whole day in the bathroom."

Caroline watched her niece flip herself over the monkey bars with supreme confidence. "And the next day?"

"I think we got it down to half a day. Eventually she settled in."

"Addie was too shy to ask where the bathroom was. The teacher had extra undies on hand, thank goodness."

"The sign of an experienced teacher," Virginia said. "Fern had Marybeth Smith, and she was terrific."

Caroline smoothed her hand over the packet of papers she'd been given to fill out for the school. Records requests, health forms, permission slips, enrollment histories. "God, I am so out of my depth here."

"You're new. Give yourself time."

She held out the bag of chips they were sharing—stale leftovers from Addie's uneaten lunch. "I thought the superhero shirts would give them confidence. Instead, Flick got in a fight over his, and Addie lost her cape. I found it in the bottom of her backpack."

"News flash," Virginia said. "It's not about the shirt. Kids get in trouble and lose stuff at school every day."

"I'm the one feeling lost."

"Welcome to parenthood. Trust me, everybody feels exactly that way at one time or other. And yet our kids survive. A year ago, I thought my divorce was going to turn me into a babbling idiot and Fern into a basket case. Now the two of us—we're doing okay." Her expression turned soft with affection as she watched her little girl scampering up the ladder to the tallest slide on the playground.

"You are," Caroline assured her. "I'm sorry I wasn't here for you during the whole Dave drama last year. I know it must've been awful, finding out he was cheating with someone at his firm."

"It was the most special kind of awful," Virginia agreed. "One of the sucky things about it is that, as bad as it felt, there was really nothing unique about my situation. My marriage failure story is the same as everyone else's. We got so busy, with both of us working and looking after Fern. *Too* busy, and we neglected each other. Then he took up with that young associate at his firm."

"I hope his nuts fall off."

"Right? And when I confronted him about Amanda, he tried denying it. Then he acted as if his cheating was my fault."

"*Damn.* I always thought you two were the standard everybody else had to live up to. You checked all the boxes—great careers, a nice house, perfect daughter . . . I thought you guys had it all."

"So did I. Until I realized how far apart we'd grown. I was the firm's investigator, for chrissake, and he took up with that woman right under my nose. It's remarkable how much you don't notice even when it's smack in front of you. And too easy to be so focused on other matters that you forget to pay attention to something that's crying out for attention."

Caroline thought about that. She wondered how many opportunities she'd missed with Angelique simply by failing to notice something important. "I'm sorry for what you went through, but I'm glad you and Fern are doing well." She felt a knot of guilt in her stomach. "You lost your marriage because you weren't paying attention. Flick and Addie lost their mom because *I* wasn't paying attention."

"It wasn't your job to parent their parent," Virginia pointed out.

"How did you get so smart?"

"It's funny how smart you can be in hindsight," said Virginia. "*And* after half a year of therapy. Uh-oh." Her tone and posture changed as her gaze tracked a woman hurrying toward them with purposeful strides.

"What's uh-oh?"

"Here comes Cindy Peters, president of the PTA. She's pretty much in charge of the whole school. You don't want to be on her bad side."

Cindy Peters had the perfect-mom look—coordinated crop pants and matte jersey top that complemented her yoga-sculpted figure, designer vegan sandals that matched her bag—and a gleam of determination in her eyes. "Excuse me," she called. "Are you Flick's mom?"

Caroline stuffed away the chip bag and brushed the crumbs from her hands. "Hi, yes, no, I—"

"Hi, Cindy," Virginia said easily. "This is my sister, Caroline."

Cindy flashed a toothpaste ad smile and stuck out her hand. "Great to meet you."

Caroline shook hands, sharing the crumbs she hadn't managed to brush away. "Virginia tells me you're the PTA president." She gestured at the pile of school forms. "I have my application here. I'll try to get to it soon."

"That's terrific." She took a familiar red cape from her bag. "My son Rutger says this belongs to Flick."

Oh, shit. Was that the kid Flick had fought with today? "Um, yes, actually—"

Cindy sat on the bench next to her. "In that case, we need to talk."

A half hour later, Flick and Addie were enjoying a playdate with Cindy's kids while Virginia and Caroline headed down the street to the fabric shop.

"Okay, you're my new hero," Virginia said. "That was so cool, and so unexpected when Cindy said all the other moms wanted to know where you got the shirts."

"You say 'other moms' as if I'm one of them."

Virginia sent her a level gaze. "You are. And you just made a deal to mass-produce the shirts for a PTA fundraiser."

"I don't even know what hit me."

"The promise of a big fat check from the fundraising committee, apparently."

Cindy Peters was a woman who got things done. The spring fundraiser was coming up, and the regular T-shirt vendor for the event had canceled the order because of a production delay. Cindy had offered Caroline a more-than-generous per-piece price, certain the snap-on cape would be a huge hit.

"It's not exactly a commission from Yves Saint Laurent," said Caroline. "But I'll take it, provided I can deliver the goods. It's completely insane, but that's pretty much been my life these days. It wouldn't suck to fabricate the shirts and make a little money to get back on my feet. Am I insane to think I can pull it off?"

Virginia found a parking spot near the fabric store. "Not insane at all. And trust me, it's empowering to get back on your feet. I mean, when I worked at Dave's law firm, it was a job, but it was secondary. Now that I'm back in charge of my own life and livelihood, the stakes are higher. Some things are harder. But I wouldn't trade the independence for anything. Well, maybe a better car." The door creaked as she opened it.

"I'm so damn scared," Caroline admitted. "I didn't sign up for this. One day I had a job as a fashion designer, and the next, I'm in charge of two little kids and an order for three hundred shirts."

"As Heidi Klum says"—Virginia affected a German accent—"'One day you are in, and the next day you are out.'"

"I'm out," Caroline said, still trying to get her head around this crazy new situation. "I'm so far out, I doubt I'll ever get back in."

Virginia strode down the sidewalk toward Lindy's shop. Caroline had filled her sister in about Lindy and Echo—the abuse, the need to talk. Virginia had not been surprised. In her job as an investigator, she had been privy to all sorts of secrets—dirty and otherwise.

"My little sister did not just say that," Virginia stoutly declared. "Where's the girl who fought and clawed her way to a fashion career in New York?"

"That girl? She grew up and realized there's no way to stop the top designer in New York from stealing her designs. No way to get back into the industry after being blackballed. And with two helpless little kids—"

"You're flooding."

"I'm drowning." Caroline sighed and slowed down, scanning the main street of the town, the shops and cafés gathered together like old familiar friends. "No, you're right. I need to regroup and sort myself out. Starting with these kids."

"Starting with a project that's going to help you *and* the kids." Virginia held open the door of the shop. A few customers were browsing, and Echo stood at the cutting table, measuring from a bolt of quilting fabric.

Lindy smiled and waved from behind the counter. “Welcome back!”

“Thanks,” Caroline said. “I’m here for supplies. Lots of supplies, as it turns out.”

“My sister got a big production order from the primary school,” Virginia said. “Check this out.” She showed off Flick’s superhero T-shirt, demonstrating the snap-on cape.

“That,” said Lindy, “is adorable. I love the slogan on the front. How can I help?”

“The PTA wants to produce them for a fundraiser,” Caroline said. “I can have the shirts printed wholesale, but the pocket and cape will need to be a custom cut-and-sew job. If I can get them made for a reasonable per-piece price, it could be a fresh start for me. So I wanted to talk about supplies, and maybe see about getting some help with assembling them.”

“Echo can sew like the wind,” Lindy said.

Over at the cutting table, Echo gave her customer the fabric. “She’s right. I can.”

Caroline thought about the up-front money she was getting from the PTA. She held up Flick’s shirt. “How would you feel about helping fabricate a few hundred superhero capes? I mean, it’s not military-grade outerwear and I’m not a government contractor, but—”

Echo’s face blazed with a smile. “I’d love to.”

"That's great. I'm going to need all the help I can get."

Echo rang up the other woman's purchase, then turned to Caroline. "Are you sure?" With nervous-looking hands, she snatched up a roll of trim and reeled in the excess. "I mean, if you're really sure . . . I could use the extra income, even if it's not a lot."

Caroline thought about Echo's situation. Abuse didn't end when the pummeling stopped. It took a person's self-confidence as well. "I'm really sure, and Lindy wouldn't say you're good unless you're really good. I promised Cindy—the PTA president—I'd see if I can get it done. It was an impulse, but I think we can make it work. I can't pay much to start . . ."

"I don't mind. I love to sew, and you're an amazing designer. We were looking at your stuff online. Amazing." Echo's posture changed. Her shoulders straightened and her eyes lit.

"Let's give it our best shot, then." Caroline felt more animated than she had in a long time. There was nothing like a design project to get her going, even something as simple as the kids' shirts. "Did you say the outfit in Astoria is getting rid of their machines?"

Lindy checked something on her phone and wrote on a slip of paper. "Here's the number."

"Cool," said Virginia. "I vote you go for it."

"I second that." Lindy beamed. "We had a lot of fun sewing together when you were a girl, didn't we?"

Caroline looked from Lindy to Echo. An older woman, calm now, and a younger one, tentative but eager. After what had happened to Angelique, she had been thinking a lot about the things women hid. Everything from the smallest slight or dismissal to outright physical abuse. Yet there was something indomitable about them—a sturdiness. It wasn't the sewing project that bolstered their spirits, she realized. It was something more. A sense of purpose, perhaps.

"I've been thinking about what you shared with me," she said. "I wish it hadn't happened to you."

"Thank you, Caroline," said Lindy. "Echo and I are two of the lucky ones."

She looked around the shop, empty now, save for the four of them. The space held the comfort of old memories. She wondered if it had been a refuge for Lindy. "What if there was a safe place to talk and listen?" she suggested.

"Her wheels never stop turning," Virginia said.

"I had this idea. Suppose there was a support group. I mean, it would take a bit of organizing, but . . . what if? I never examined or understood what was going on with Angelique until it was too late. I want to do better. If there's a way to help other women . . ."

"It's a fine idea," Lindy said. "I can't imagine how it would work, though."

"Watch me," Caroline said. "I bet I could organize something."

"If you do, I'm in," said Echo. "Lindy?"

"Of course. Your idea is a kind one. You have a big heart, Caroline."

"Do I?" She shook her head. "I feel as if I've been oblivious. I'm going to do it," she said decisively. "My sisters will help."

"We will," Virginia agreed. "I can't speak for Georgia, but I bet she'd want to be part of it."

"You let me know," Lindy said.

Caroline checked her watch. "We'd better get the kids."

Lindy walked to the door with her and gave her a quick hug. "I'm glad you're back. You used to be such a ball of energy around here, you and your friends. Have you seen Will Jensen yet? His grandmother was one of my best customers. Such an avid quilter. You and Will used to be inseparable."

"I've run into him a time or two," Caroline said, feeling a funny flutter in her stomach.

"Well, I'm sure he and Sierra are delighted you're back."

Caroline gritted her teeth. *I'm sure.*

Chapter 11

Sierra Jensen pulled up at Star of the Sea, knowing there would be a wait for a table at the popular, buzzy restaurant. But the cranberry scones with brown butter glaze were worth the wait. So were the buckwheat griddle cakes with bourbon-barrel-aged maple syrup. And the fried green tomato Benedict.

Every once in a while, Sierra allowed herself to splurge on calories, and she usually did so at the Shelby family's restaurant, which was housed in a weather-beaten clapboard building at the edge of the dunes. Thanks to its reputation for mind-blowing baked goods and the freshest local seafood, the place was now legendary up and down the coast, a favorite of locals as well as a destination for tourists.

Georgia Shelby Ryerson, the general manager, had come up with creative ways to make the waiting more pleasant. The front porch of the building, which faced Pioneer Park, featured a coffee bar with gathering tables and a strict ban on smoking and electronics. Instead, each of the tall tables was furnished with local and national papers, and patrons were invited to mingle and chat about the news of the day while sipping complimentary coffee from organic beans roasted in small batches on the peninsula.

As often happened, this week's photo shoot had run late the night before. Too exhausted for the long drive home, Sierra had stayed over in the city, grabbing a last-minute hotel deal at a place that was nicer than she could afford. Will worried when he knew she was out driving late at night. The coastal byways that veined the lowlands were twisty and deserted, and she preferred a nice room and a few hits of quality weed before bed to help her relax.

She missed life in the city. In the past, while Will was on deployment, she had lived and worked in Seattle and Portland. She'd gotten used to the bustle and traffic, the shopping and nightlife. After his discharge, they'd moved to Water's Edge, the remote, beautiful Jensen family property. It was a homecoming for them both—for her as a local girl who had lived on the peninsula from the age of fourteen, the year her father became pastor of Oceanside Congregational, and for Will, who'd spent his boyhood summers at the shore.

As a restless teenager, Sierra had yearned for a different life somewhere far from the humble string of beach towns. Settling down at Water's Edge, restoring the old place, and starting a family had been Will's dream. When they were first married, dizzy in love and full of plans, she'd shared that dream. Ten years later, she wasn't so certain.

Her frequent trips to the city should have been a happy compromise. But sometimes, maybe too often, she wasn't happy. She just felt . . . compromised.

And now her career was on shaky ground. Back when she was in her early twenties, she'd booked fashion shoots for luxury stores and high-end labels, loving the excitement and attention from stylists and photographers. As the years passed, she became a fanatic about staying thin, taking care of her skin and hair, but there were some things that couldn't be protected from the relentless march of time. She could no longer get away with telling people she was nineteen in order to book more jobs. Gradually she was being supplanted by the never-ending influx of young, willowy, fresh-faced teenagers. Never mind that they were often emaciated, coked-up minors clinging to their much older boyfriends. Never mind that they could barely find their way to the end of a runway without directions. All the experience and knowledge in the world didn't trump a size 2, five-ten teenager.

Even though Sierra could almost single-handedly style and set up a shoot in record time, she lacked the one asset the industry valued most: youthful innocence. These days, she found herself doing catalog shoots for discount stores or circulars that ended up in the recycle bin. Though the work was steady, the bookings through her agency lacked the prestige she'd enjoyed early in her career.

Have a baby, her well-meaning parents advised her, as if this might be the magic solution to her career frustration. They believed heart and soul in the importance of family. Her father preached it to his congregation every Sunday morning.

Fuck it, she thought, wishing she could sneak off somewhere to smoke a cigarette. But this was a small town and she was a preacher's daughter, married to the high school football coach, so it would be bad form to be seen smoking in public.

Besides, Will hated it. They were supposed to be trying for a baby. They *were* trying.

One of them was, anyway.

"Sierra? Oh my gosh. Hi!"

Sierra turned to see Caroline Shelby approaching her. She was so startled that for a moment she couldn't move. Caroline looked amazing, years younger than her actual age. Her dark hair was a tousled mop tipped in lavender, her jeans perfectly slouchy under a crisp, fitted white blouse. She wore purple-framed glasses and chunky jewelry, wedge ankle boots and a vintage bag. She was with two adorable mixed-race kids.

With a sudden rush of emotion, Sierra opened her arms. "Get over here, stranger. Holy shit. It's been forever."

"Forever and a day." Caroline hugged her.

Sierra sensed something tentative about the embrace, as if she were hugging a stranger. After all this time, they *were* strangers. But their coming-of-age years together had created a solid foundation. As young teenagers, they had been best friends, as close as sisters. Closer, Caroline used to joke. Sisters without the fighting. There had been a time when they'd known each other so well they could finish each other's sentences. The inside jokes, the nicknames, the secrets and shared heartbreaks of high school created a bond that felt different from the ones with friends Sierra had made since those days.

After high school, the two of them had drifted apart, a slow and natural seismic progression that sent Caroline to New York and the Fashion Institute of Technology and Sierra into the arms of the man she would eventually marry.

Now here they were again, back in the place they had both longed to leave.

"Join us at our table," Caroline said. "We've got a lot of catching up to do."

They crossed the bustling dining room, managed under the eagle eye of Caroline's sister, Georgia, and settled at a table by the window, which framed a view of the dunes, the distant cliffs, and the wild forested headlands to the south.

"Jesus Christ, you're a mom," Sierra said, feeling shell-shocked as she regarded the boy and girl.

"Flick and Addie," Caroline said, helping the little girl clamber into a booster seat. "Kids, this is my friend, Sierra."

The two of them offered timid waves. Flick, a boy with perfect café au lait skin and enormous dark eyes, said, "She's not our mom."

"Oh?" Sierra was tongue-tied. Then what the hell . . . ?

"Our mom died," the boy added.

"Oh my God." Sierra was mortified by the statement, its devastating simplicity and the blunt delivery by the little boy. She'd never been good at talking to kids. It just didn't come naturally to her. "Oh, shit. You guys. I'm so sorry."

"She said 'shit,'" Addie said. "That's a swear."

"You're right," Sierra admitted. "It was rude of me to swear." She sent a desperate look at Caroline.

"It's a long story," Caroline said. "Maybe another time . . ."

"Of course. Sure." Sierra didn't bother to mask her relief when a server with a name tag reading NADINE came with coffee and hot chocolate. The kids devoured their breakfast while Sierra could only pick at her scone, her appetite lost in a surge of nostalgia and a sense of things unfinished.

Nadine's hand wobbled as she poured, splashing coffee onto the table in front of Caroline. "Yikes," she said, blushing furiously. "Oh gosh, I'm so sorry."

"It's all right," Caroline said, using a napkin to sop up the spill before it dripped over the table edge.

Nadine went and got a rag. "I'm really, really sorry."

Sierra couldn't help but notice the waitress's arms. They were marked with an unfortunate constellation of garish tattoos. But the ink didn't quite mask the bruises. She traded a look with Caroline, and just for that split second, the two of them connected the way they used to in high school.

"Please, don't give it a thought," Caroline murmured as Nadine finished.

"Thanks," said the waitress. "Having an off day, I guess."

Sierra's mobile phone pinged, signaling a message. Shoot, she'd forgotten about an appointment to pick out coverings for the downstairs windows. "I have to go," she said. "Come up to the house one day soon, okay? Bring these two cuties and we'll catch up."

"Um, sure. The kids have a lot on their plates right now." Caroline glanced down at their nearly empty breakfast plates. "Figuratively speaking. Starting school and getting settled in."

A brush-off? Or the truth? Sierra couldn't quite tell. "Okay, I get it. And I have a better idea. How about you meet up with Will and me for drinks? There's a new place down by the docks called Salt. We haven't tried it yet, but I've heard good things."

There was a beat of hesitation. Sierra couldn't decipher the beat. She couldn't decipher the friend she used to know so well. Then Caroline smiled. "I'd love to."

"That's great. Let's make sure we have each other's digits." Sierra took out her phone.

"Is this yours?" Caroline turned her phone screen toward Sierra. "Because if it is, I already have it in my contacts."

"Holy crap," Sierra said. "I can't believe you kept me on the list for so long."

"You were the first kid in town to get her own cell phone. I was so jealous."

"I got the cell phone, you got the siblings."

"I would have traded all four of them for my own phone."

She sighed. "I never liked being an only child. And the preacher's daughter to boot. God, if you hadn't rescued me when I first moved to the peninsula, I would have shriveled up and blown away."

"Rescued you? I think it was more like I commandeered you to be the model for my sewing projects." Caroline smiled. "So many memories, huh?"

"Well, regardless. They say the friends you make when you're fourteen are the friends you'll keep forever."

Caroline's gaze cut away. "I'm sorry I've been so absent."

"Well, I'm glad you're back. It'll be like old times, you'll see. Damn, I forgot how much I like hanging out with you."

"I never forgot," murmured Caroline.

"Aw, Caroline. I want to hear everything. All your adventures in New York."

She swirled her spoon in her coffee cup. "It's a lot." She glanced at the kids. "Soon, okay?"

Sierra grabbed her bag. "It was nice to meet you guys," she said to the kids. As she left the restaurant, she saw Caroline gazing out the window, her face stiff with tension.

Chapter 12

Caroline stared at the message on her phone. The week after their icebreaker meeting, Sierra had invited her to bring the kids over for a visit. It was a simple invitation from a friend she hadn't seen in years. Should she go?

If she didn't, it would be awkward because it would seem as if she were avoiding them. If she went, it would seem weird because of their long and complicated history together.

Just go, she told herself. Get it over with.

We're not kids anymore, she reasoned. The past is the past. They could start fresh. Clean slate. A new dynamic, different from the inseparable trio they had been in their youth.

It was a brilliant spring day, the sun blazing deep into the shoreline and meadows, perfect weather for a visit to Water's Edge, a place where she'd found magic and joy and trouble, years ago.

"Come on, you yahoos," she said to Flick and Addie now that she'd made up her mind and accepted the invitation via text. "We're going to see some friends." She addressed the kids with a casual air she hoped didn't sound too forced. "On a nice day like this, you're going to want to play outside, so bring a jacket."

"Do we have to?" asked Flick.

"No. You could stay here and contemplate your navel if you want."

"What friends?" Addie asked.

"Sierra—you met her at the restaurant. And Will."

"Coach Jensen," said Flick. He lifted his shirt and stared at his belly button.

"Let's go. You haven't seen the Jensen place," she said. "I think you're going to love it."

"How do you know?"

"I used to go there when I was a kid and *I* loved it. There's a dock and an old barn and a really good climbing tree that's probably still there. Have you ever climbed a tree?"

"We're city kids," Flick said. "What do we know about trees?"

"I want to climb a tree!" Addie headed for the door. Flick followed more slowly.

She bundled the kids into the car. "It's a nice drive. They live up the road a ways."

"Why's it called Oysterville?" asked Addie.

"Because that's where the best oysters in the world come from."

"What's an oyster?" Addie frowned.

"It's a thing that grows at the bottom of the bay, in a shell. Most of the shells you see around here are oyster shells."

"You can find a pearl in an oyster shell," Flick said. "That's what Miss Liza told us."

"Your new teacher knows her stuff. Pearls are hard to find, though." She flashed on a memory of the seed pearls she'd used in her Chrysalis collection. Her stolen collection.

They were quiet as they drove up the peninsula. The morning mist lay softly in the dense thickets that lined the road. Springtime rose up out of the marshes, alive now with blue heron and wild irises and budding trees. She pointed out a porcupine rooting in the bracken. Chittering birds flitted through the forests of stunted pine. In a distant meadow, a herd of elk grazed.

Yet despite the beauty all around, she clamped her hands too tightly on the steering wheel. She couldn't stop thinking about the things she'd left behind. While living in New York, she believed she'd escaped the old feelings. But coming back brought everything to the surface.

With a nervous flick of her wrist, she switched on the radio and found a local music station.

"That's Lorde," Addie said, recognizing the song. "Mama liked Lorde."

Caroline glanced in the rearview mirror. Addie was holding Wonder Woman up to see out the window. "She did, didn't she? What else did your mama like?" She wanted the children to know Angelique, to hold the memories sweetly. They were so damned little. Would they remember her?

"Adele," Flick said. "And Bruno Mars."

"One of these days we should make a playlist of songs your mom liked, okay?"

Neither of them spoke. As the plaintive song drifted from the speakers, Caroline tried not to feel overwhelmed by sadness. "Hey, guess what? I'm going to be making superhero T-shirts for your school to sell. Isn't that cool?"

"You mean everybody's going to get one?" asked Flick.

"Everybody who wants one, yes." She paused. "Would that be all right with you?"

Silence.

"Are you shrugging your shoulders? I can't hear you shrug your shoulders."

"If everyone has a hero shirt, then we're all the same."

Oh, boy. "You and Addie had the very first ones. You're my inspiration. Is it cool that everybody wants to be like you?"

"I guess."

Caroline had been busy all week with dual projects—ordering the printed shirts and sourcing the cape fabric, thread, and snaps. She'd gone to the fabricator in Astoria and negotiated a deal to buy a serger and bar tack machine, a cutting machine, and a heat press. They'd thrown in tag piercers and some other gear she'd need to set up shop.

The only problem was, she didn't have a shop. She was going to need a large workspace for herself and Echo to get the shirts made using the industrial machines and cutting tables.

Finding a place for the support group meeting had been less challenging. There was a community room in an annex next to the police station, which was perfect. She could think of no better place for women who had been involved with violent men. She and her sisters—Georgia had embraced the project with both incredibly competent arms—had stayed up late every night, planning and organizing.

Staying busy helped keep panic at bay.

She reminded herself of that as she drove slowly through the small community of vintage houses, weathered picket fences, spectacular gardens, and oyster sheds. She turned at the mailbox with fading letters—WATER'S EDGE. Cypress sentinels lined the drive, and a weather-beaten picket fence, bearded with moss, bordered the lawn. The old painted house overlooked Willapa Bay, the preternaturally calm water mirroring a fringe of forested lowlands. There was a dock and an oyster barn, and another huge barn located across a meadow at the edge of a wooded area.

Oh, the adventures she'd had here, exploring and playing hide-and-seek, dipping a net into the water to see what came up. She remembered wearing old sneakers to keep from cutting her feet on oysters and barnacles in the bay. At certain times of the year, they could find salmon swimming through the forest on their muddy, migratory path. But the greatest adventure of all had been—

"Hey, guys!" Will strode toward her as she parked the car. "Welcome." He wore lived-in jeans that had faded in all the right places, a denim work shirt with the sleeves rolled back, a bandanna hanging from his back pocket, and a metal tape measure clipped to his belt. He was, as always, a man completely at home in his own skin.

She grabbed her bag from the passenger seat, ducking her head to hide a completely uncalled-for blush.

"We come bearing gifts," she said, getting out of the car and holding out a mason jar. Flick and Addie got out of the back seat and looked around. "My mom's strawberry jam. First batch of the season."

Will took it from her. "The first time I met you, you brought your mom's strawberry-rhubarb jam."

"Some things never change," she said, knowing it for the line it was. Nothing ever stayed the same. Yet she couldn't help being a little surprised that he remembered such a small detail from that day.

He hunkered down to Addie's level. "You were asleep in the back of Caroline's car the first time I met *you.* But the second time . . ." He gave a low whistle. "You turned into Supergirl."

"What did you do to your eye?" asked Addie, gazing steadily at him.

Caroline was mortified. "Addie—"

"It's fine," he said, not looking away from the little girl. "When I was in the navy, I was in an accident and I hurt my eye pretty bad. They had to replace it with an eye made out of acrylic. Sometimes I wear a patch over it like a pirate, but mostly I wear this one."

"Whoa," she whispered.

Caroline froze with shock. What the hell? He lost an eye?

Flick pressed close to his sister. "Which eye is it?"

"Which one do you think it is?" Will regarded them placidly, clearly unruffled by their curiosity.

"They look the same to me."

"They're supposed to."

With exquisite gentleness, Addie laid her hand on his left cheek. "This one," she said.

He nodded. "You're right. Some people, like you, can tell right away. Most don't notice."

I didn't notice, thought Caroline.

"What do you see when you look out that eye?" asked Flick.

"Enough with the questions," Caroline said. Jesus Christ, he'd lost an eye.

Will got to his feet. "If I close my other eye, all I see is a dense fog, the kind we have around here some mornings. Fortunately, the other eye sees just fine.

Come on inside. Let's go find Sierra and maybe have a taste of Dot's jam."

Like a pair of imprinted ducks, they followed him up the front steps.

Sierra was perfectly outfitted in pale blue cropped jeans and a crisp white top. "Welcome to our abode. I made cookies and lemonade."

Caroline hadn't seen Will and Sierra together since the weekend of their wedding a decade ago. One of them knew the reason for that. The other didn't.

Addie and Flick stuck close to Caroline as they stepped inside. The house was the same rambling Victorian that had seemed so grand to her long ago. Originally built by Will's ancestor, it had mullioned windows with wavy glass, carved woodwork, a fancy staircase, and a big bay window with a view of the water. The smell of newly finished wood and paint mingled with the warm scent of freshly baked cookies.

"This way to the kitchen," said Sierra. "Watch your step—it's a work in progress."

They made their way to a bright, open kitchen with new cabinets and countertops, and a breakfast nook with a view of the dock and oyster barn. "Have a cookie," said Sierra, offering a perfectly arranged tray of pecan sandies, black and whites, and oatmeal cranberry cookies with white chocolate chips.

Caroline gave the kids a nod. "When it comes to cookies, Sierra is a pro, because her dad is the pastor of a big church. After services, it's all about the cookies."

They looked mystified, and she wondered if she should be taking them to church. Would it help them adjust to their new life?

"She's right," Sierra said. "I know at least ten recipes by heart."

The kids climbed up to the table and helped themselves. "Thank you," Addie said, and nudged her brother.

He echoed his thanks. Caroline helped herself to a cookie. "Good lord, what did you put in these things, crack?"

"She's the cookie whisperer," Will said. He patted his midsection. "Fattening me up."

Caroline cut her glance away from his well-built form, which showed not an ounce of fat. She wandered over to the kitchen island, currently laden with sketches and swatches of material. "So tell me about this project."

"Will's obsessed," said Sierra. "In a good way. He did most of the work himself." She gave Caroline a quick tour of the space. "He removed a wall and put up new cabinets and countertops. Remember how old and poky the kitchen used to be?"

Caroline nodded, admiring the bright, clean space. It had been modernized, but still retained the charm of bygone days. "It's fantastic," she said. "After living in a tiny walk-up in New York, I feel surrounded by luxury." What she didn't say was that back in the city, living in a cramped apartment was a badge of honor for emerging designers. "It's all so wonderful, you guys. I'm really happy for you."

I'm really happy for you. One of the great empty phrases used by so many people to hide so many real feelings. Could you actually tie your happiness to someone else's?

Maybe, she thought, watching Flick finish off a second cookie, an expression of pure bliss on his face. One of the unexpected bonuses of having these kids was that when they were happy, their smiles lifted her heart.

Addie left the table and went to the back door, looking out at the sparkling waters of Willapa Bay. "Are there chickens?" she asked. "Grammy Dot has chickens."

"No chickens, but this morning, I spotted a robin's nest with three eggs in it," Will said. "Want to check it out?"

Addie turned back to look up at Caroline. "Can you come?" she asked softly.

The little girl was understandably tentative about new situations. By contrast, Flick tended to dive recklessly into the unknown. Both children held back from new people—a natural reaction, Joan had told her.

"Here's an idea," Caroline said. "We could all go."

Sierra glanced at her phone and swiftly replied to a message. "Sorry," she said. "Setting up a meeting." Then she tucked the phone in her back pocket, grabbing a wide-brimmed straw hat as they went out the back door.

Will strode ahead, his movements loose-limbed and easy, the way she remembered. Always the athlete, comfortable in his own body. The kids tumbled outside, following him across the lawn to a stand of gnarled old rhododendrons. "Let's be super quiet," he said to them. "The mama bird spends most of her time on the nest, and we don't want to disturb her. I need to lift you both up so you can see. Is that okay?"

It was cool of him to ask, Caroline observed. In her crash course on parenting a grieving child, she'd learned that kids, just like any adult, deserved to be asked before you touched them.

They both nodded assent, and in one swift movement, he scooped them both up at the same time, one on each arm.

Caroline must have made a sound, because Sierra nudged her. "I know, right? He likes to show off his Captain America arms."

He leaned in and said, "The nest is just there, in front of us. The mama bird's in it."

"I see her!" Addie said in a whisper. "Flick, do you see her?"

"Yep, she's cute." Flick leaned even closer.

In a sudden whir of wings, the bird shot from the bush, chittering in panic and disappearing amid the tall trees at the edge of the yard.

"You scared her, Flick," Addie accused.

"Did not! I—"

"Have a quick look at the eggs, and then we'll leave her alone," Will said. "Can you see all three eggs?"

"They're so little," Addie said. "And they're blue! How come they're blue?"

Will set them down on the lawn and stepped away from the rhododendron. "Sunscreen," he said. "The color keeps them from getting too warm." He grinned at their expressions. "Seriously, it's sunscreen, just like you wear in the summer to keep from getting burned. The blue eggs stay cooler. Come on. Let's give the mom a chance to come back." He backed farther away.

"*Will* she come again?" asked Addie. She slipped her hand into Will's.

"Sure," he said. "I've been watching her for a few days. She always comes back."

"What if she doesn't?" asked Flick.

"He just said she's gonna," Addie told him, her voice edged with annoyance. She looked around behind Will and stuck out her tongue at her brother.

"But what if she *doesn't*?" Flick persisted.

"In that case, the eggs won't hatch," said Will.

"Never? Not ever?"

"Nope. That's the way it works."

"It's sad," Addie said. "I want the mama bird to come back."

"Let's give her a little time," Will said easily.

"Our mama died," Addie whispered.

Caroline's heart melted. Will sank back down so they were face-to-face and gave both children a gentle look. "My mama died, too, when I was a boy. I think of her every day."

"She'll never come back," said Flick.

"That's right. It's really sad," Will admitted.

"Do you cry every day?" Addie asked him.

"No. Sometimes I still do, though." His honesty and matter-of-fact tone seemed to put them at ease. "I hope you'll tell me more about your mama sometime."

"Caroline's gonna get me some binoculars for bird-watching," Flick said.

"Lucky you. Come on down to the dock and I'll show you something else."

Addie beckoned to Caroline. "Are you coming?"

Caroline looked at Sierra. "Are we coming?"

Sierra was checking her phone again. "Oh, sure. There are some lawn chairs where we can sit and chat."

Will found a couple of life jackets for the kids and buckled them on.

"Why do we have to wear these?" asked Flick. "Are we going in a boat?"

"Not today, but when you're on the dock, you should have a vest in case you fall in."

He was so careful with the children. Caroline observed, watching them follow him to the weather-beaten dock, its planks bearded with moss. And they were quickly drawn to him; he was so naturally at ease. A small dinghy and an oystering scow were moored at the end. Will grabbed a rope and hauled in a float bag.

"What's that?" asked Addie.

"Yearling oysters," he said, taking one from the flat mesh bag. The kids leaned in, checking out the crusty outer shell. He took a stubby-bladed oyster knife from his belt and opened the shell with an expert twist, displaying the glistening inside. "Ever tried eating one?"

"*That's* the oyster?" Addie peered at it.

"It looks yuck," said Flick.

With exaggerated relish, Will slurped it down and wiped his mouth on his sleeve.

Predictably, they recoiled in horror.

"Kids don't usually like them until they get older," said Will.

He opened another and offered it to Sierra, who shook her head. "Not a fan. Never have been. You know that."

"That must mean you're still a kid," Caroline said.

"I tried my first oyster with you," Will told Caroline. "Remember?"

"Yep, and you loved it."

"She told me a saying—that eating an oyster is like kissing the sea on the lips."

"Double ew," said Flick.

Will held the shell out to Caroline. Touching it to her lower lip, she let the cool, briny morsel slip into her mouth. It was creamy and soft, almost buttery, salted by the ocean. Willapa oysters had a flavor all their own, tinged with a hint of sweetness compared to East Coast varieties. She laughed at the kids' expressions. "It's what's known as an acquired taste."

"This whole place was built a hundred years ago, all because people love eating oysters." Will gestured out at the bay. They walked farther out on the dock, and he showed them how to dip a small net down into the clear depths. Sunlight flashed on the water, and for a moment, time was swept away.

"All those hours we spent on the docks around here," Sierra said, seeming to read her thoughts.

Caroline could still feel the golden heat of the summer sun on her back as she lay belly down, mesmerized by the urchins and anemones and mussels clinging to the dock pilings. She could see them with knife-edged clarity through the shimmering water. She used to imagine patterns and designs swirling to watery life, leaving trails of sparkles that somehow wove their way into her imagination.

"I remember those days," she said.

"I was obsessed with hiding from the sun," Sierra said.

"I remember that, too." She eyed Sierra's wide-brimmed hat.

"You made me that great sun-safe gown, remember? I thought I was a queen, parading around in your creation."

"Should I be putting sunscreen on the kids?" Caroline asked. "It's early in the season, but—"

"Sunscreen is always a good idea, even for people with dark skin. Trust me. I've made a study of these things."

"Caroline, look!" Addie held up a whorled seashell. "It's just like your design!"

She took the nautilus shell in her hand. It was unoccupied, but still intact. "Other way around. I used this motif in my designs. It's my signature. You're very observant." She handed it back to Addie and looked away to hide a wave of frustration.

"What is it?" asked Sierra. "I bet your designs are beautiful."

"They are. They were, anyway, and I suppose that was the problem." Caroline didn't feel like talking about the demise of her career. "Long, boring story. It didn't work out."

A deep laugh burst from Will as he held out a Dungeness crab for the kids to inspect. Flick and Addie edged forward, then shrank away as the creature brandished its claws. Will slipped it back into the water and they leaned over to watch it swim to safety. Then Flick dipped the net and brought up something shiny from the depths.

Caroline exhaled in a long sigh as she and Sierra strolled back to the bank at the edge of the dock. "It's so beautiful here. We were lucky to grow up in such a magical place."

"We couldn't wait to leave," Sierra reminded her, motioning her over to a pair of gray wooden Adirondack chairs. "And now look at us. Back where we started from."

"For now," Caroline said.

"Forever," Sierra said. "Christ."

Caroline glanced over at her. Sierra was as gorgeous as ever, perfectly put together. Brilliant manicure, trendy nude lipstick, expertly blended makeup. Yet there was something different about her. Something indefinable. "You sound frustrated."

"Will is so happy here. We're trying to make it work."

It. Did she mean the marriage? Her career? Her life?

"After the accident—"

"What accident?" asked Caroline. "Oh, his eye, you mean."

"It happened while he was stationed overseas. He lost his eye and had to take a medical retirement. His grandparents had moved to assisted living, and Will started a new career as a teacher."

"I have about a hundred questions," Caroline admitted. "About everything. The accident?"

"He's never talked about the mission in detail, because you know the number one rule of Navy SEALs. Total secrecy. He was stationed in Diego Garcia, and it was a hostage rescue near Somalia. Some American aid workers were being held for ransom. Will was the only casualty—a shooting. He never said who shot him, just that it was too dark to see. And that's pretty much all I know."

"I'm sorry that happened," Caroline said, wincing as she imagined him being shot, injuring an eye.

"He was devastated, and the recovery was hard. When his grandparents gave him the house in a living will, he latched onto it. He's always loved this place, and now he's on a mission to fix it up. It's all part of his grand dream of a white picket fence, a family, small-town life . . ."

After the chaos in New York, that didn't sound so bad to Caroline. "What about *your* dream?"

Sierra shaded her eyes and looked out across the bay. "It's kind of hard to make myself a priority when my husband is the perfect one."

"What? Come on."

"You know I'm right. He's perfect. Spotless military record, local hero, teacher and coach, wonderful husband. And look at him." She gestured at the dock, where he was completely absorbed in the kids. "My dream?" She picked at a dry bit of wood on the chair arm. "I make a lot of trips to Seattle and Portland for work."

A loud wail erupted from Addie. Caroline was on her feet immediately, running to the dock. Since having the kids in her life, she had quickly learned the meaning of different cries. She was now keenly familiar with the uncomprehending-sadness cry. The I'm-bored whine. The pathetic bleats of hunger. This was none of the above. This was the *grand mal* pain cry.

By the time she reached Addie, Will had scooped the little girl into his arms and was striding toward Caroline. "She got a splinter in her knee," he said.

"Oh, that's a big one," Caroline said, inspecting the damage. Yikes. A full inch of the weathered gray wood from the old dock was embedded in Addie's tender flesh.

"It hurts," Addie howled, elongating each word. "Get it out!"

"I'll bet it does hurt." Will seemed unruffled as he carried her toward the house. Caroline took Flick's hand in hers and followed them inside. "When I was in the navy," Will said, "I learned how to deal with injuries like this. I'm pretty good at it."

"He's going to dig it out with a needle," Flick said.

"No!" Addie clung to Will's neck.

He placed her on the kitchen counter by the sink. "We won't use a needle. I have a better way."

"I'm scared of needles," Addie said.

"Pay attention, both of you. I'll show you how to make a proper field dressing." Will washed his hands at the sink and took a first aid kit from the cupboard.

Addie sniffled and whispered, "Still hurts."

"Yeah, I know," Will said. "Splinters are the worst. See this?" He held up a bottle. "It's cleansing solution and it doesn't hurt. I'll let you squirt some right on the sliver."

She took the bottle and dribbled the saline onto her knee. "Still hurts," she mumbled.

"Go ahead and use a lot," Will said. Then he helped her dry the area. "I have a secret splinter weapon," he said. "Duct tape. It'll feel like taking off an old Band-Aid." He kept up a stream of friendly patter as he covered the splinter with tape and then peeled it quickly away.

"Ouch!" Addie burst out.

"Here you go," he said, showing her the splinter stuck to the back of the tape. "You were brave."

"I wasn't brave. I cried." She gazed forlornly at the blood oozing from her knee.

"You let me fix you up even though you cried. I would call that brave." He finished up with antibiotic ointment and a Band-Aid. "All set," he said, lowering her down to the floor.

"Thank you," Caroline said. "Very impressive, Mr. Jensen." He was so self-assured with the kids. Where did that come from? And when would she ever feel even a fraction of his confidence?

Flick looked around the mudroom off the kitchen. "What are you building?" he asked, taking in the power tools and half-finished shelves.

"All kinds of stuff," Will said. "I'm always building, because we're remodeling. I'm putting shelves and cabinets in this room."

"I like tools," Flick said.

"You never told me that," Caroline said.

"You never asked."

"I like tools, too, buddy," Will said. "I bet I know something else you like. Otter Pops."

"Yeah!"

He went to the freezer and took out two of them, expertly snipping the tops and handing them over. Then he offered one to Caroline.

"No, thanks. You're good with kids of any age," she told him.

"That's because kids are awesome." He cut a glance at Sierra. "Right?"

He looked away quickly, so he missed Sierra's reaction—a physical shudder.

Really? Caroline wondered. Did that mean trouble in paradise?

Addie gave her treat a squeeze, and half of the frozen pop landed on the floor. "Oh, man," she said.

"It happens." Will got another one for her. He glanced again at Sierra, who was mopping up with a paper towel.

"How about you take them outside," she suggested.

"Keep your life jackets on if you go near the water," Caroline called as they scampered out the door.

"Hey, Mr. Will," Flick called from the yard. "Can we go have a look in the barn?"

"Sure," Will said. "Okay?" he asked Caroline.

She nodded. "Of course."

"I'll go with them." He headed outside. "Come on, you two."

Sierra crossed her arms and turned to Caroline, who was looking out the window at the kids following Will to the barn. "Right now, it's just a big empty space. He upgraded the electrical system to the barn because he had some idea about making it an indoor play area one day. See what I mean? He's perfect."

"Come on. Nobody's perfect."

"He wants to save the family home and have kids. Perfect, right?"

"I suppose that depends."

"On what?" Sierra paced back and forth as if caged. "If it's so perfect, why can't I want what he wants? Why can't I be happy with all this?"

Because maybe it's someone else's perfect, thought Caroline. "I'm not even going to try to answer that one," she said. Her goal in coming here with the kids today had been to try to normalize relations with Sierra and Will. She hoped they were making progress in that direction. Still, they were all different people now. Will was missing an eye. Sierra was missing her city life. And Caroline . . . She had been out of touch with her friends, but the palpable weight of their tension pressed hard. And she had no idea what to say.

"Let's finish the tour," Sierra said. "I'll show you the rest of our money pit."

Caroline made no comment as she followed Sierra upstairs. Reconnecting with her friend was uncomfortable, to say the least. They used to tell each other everything, but that used to mean confessing what you found in your mom's underwear drawer or that you sneaked a bottle of communion wine from church. This conversation was a new level of *everything.*

Sierra showed her a freshly painted guest room and a smaller bedroom filled with stacked and labeled moving boxes.

"This is supposed to be the baby's room," Sierra said. "Will wants kids so bad."

"You're telling me a lot about what he wants. What about you?"

She shrugged. "I keep thinking there's got to be

something wrong with me. He's wonderful, and I'm horrible. I feel like a fraud."

"There's nothing wrong with you," Caroline said. "It's just . . . relationships can be hard. God knows, you're looking at proof of that."

"So, no one special?" asked Sierra.

"No. I mean . . . I went out with guys. I fell in love a time or two. At least I think I did. And then . . ." She winced, remembering the soaring elation, followed by the sinking disappointment of the emotional roller coaster. "I wanted to find that one thing that would last. And you know what? I did. I did find it. But there was a twist—that one thing was not a guy. It was my career. Now I've left that behind. So it's kind of like a breakup I wasn't ready for."

"You'll figure something out. That project you're doing for the school—isn't that a start? You're one of the most clever, creative people I know."

"I appreciate the vote of confidence." She had poured all her energy, all her heart into the Chrysalis line, pinning her hopes and dreams like shiny beads to the gossamer fabrics. She wondered when the feeling of violation would fade. When she would find the confidence to begin anew.

"Well, *I* could use your help." Sierra opened a closet. "I outgrew the space in the master bedroom."

"Great, so now I'm a closet organizer."

"That's not what I meant. I've got a thing coming up," Sierra said. "Not a modeling gig, but a meeting about producing a high-end shoot. I need to dress like someone they'll take seriously."

"Now *that* I can help with," said Caroline. "Cool, elegant, or trendy?"

"Can I be all of the above?"

"You already are."

As they sorted through the clothes, old memories surfaced. They were kids again, best friends.

Caroline found a blouse in watered silk and paired it with a pencil skirt. They tried a few accessories, settling on a look with a bold arm cuff, shoes, and a bag.

"You're in your element," Sierra said.

"I've styled so many models." She paused. "My friend Angelique—Flick and Addie's mother—was one of the best runway models in New York. She came from Haiti and blasted to the top of her game. And then she died of an overdose."

"Oh, my sweet God above." Sierra shuddered. "I'm so sorry. Those poor kids."

"I'm constantly haunted by it. A few months before she died, I noticed she had some injuries. Bruises."

"You mean track marks? Needle marks?"

"No. Somebody hit her."

Sierra gasped. "That's horrible. But you know, it's a thing. I've seen it in the modeling world. Girls start so young. They don't know how to deal with the business, and they're so desperate to make it that they'll put up with anything."

Caroline looked at her. "Did it ever happen to you?"

"No," Sierra said swiftly. "God, no. I was hit on, but not hit. I knew how to handle myself."

"I'm not surprised. I wish more women could say that." She paused, hesitant to share an idea in its first stage. Then she realized her friendship with Sierra was coming into its own again. "My sisters and I are setting up a support group for survivors of domestic violence. Turns out it's more common than any of us knew. I think it'll help me deal with Flick and Addie."

"No kidding? That's good, Caroline. Really."

"After what happened to Angelique, I've been feeling so powerless. This is something. It might add up to a big fat nothing, but it feels right. There are women who need help, right here in our town. I can't go back and rescue Ange. But the more I learn about domestic violence and addiction, the better I'll be able to help Flick and Addie."

"Well. So it sounds like you're sticking around for a while."

"I don't know what else to do. God, I feel so stuck."

"Join the club." Sierra hung the outfit in the closet.

"I've missed you," she said. "I've missed having someone who gets me. Someone I can say anything to without worrying about being judged."

Wasn't that supposed to be the husband's role? Caroline wondered.

They went outside together. Will had hung a swing from the biggest tree in the yard, and the kids were taking turns on it.

"They're never going to leave," Caroline said.

He laughed briefly and gestured at the three of them. "Look at us. We got the band together again."

"What band?" asked Flick.

"We were never a band," Caroline said. "It's just a saying. When we were kids, the three of us spent our summers together. We were inseparable. Do you know what *inseparable* means?"

Addie shook her head.

"It means we were almost never apart. We got together every single day and had adventures."

"Speaking of adventures," Will said, "I need to pick up some things at the lumberyard."

"Can I go?" Flick piped up. He was clearly already hero-worshiping Will.

"Maybe another time," Caroline said.

"Definitely another time," Will agreed, then strode toward the pickup truck parked near the barn.

"We were quite a trio," Sierra mused. "I used to forget that you saw him first. Now I don't think of it at all."

Caroline threw her a sharp look.

"Tell me about when you were little," said Flick. "Did you play right here? And on the dock?"

"We did. It looks pretty much the same," Caroline said. "It's just the way I remember." Her gaze traced a path from the driveway to the front porch. "First time I ever came here, I was riding my bike. And Will, as I recall, was a frogman."

"What?" Flick leaned forward.

"It's true. When I met him, he was soaking wet, like a frogman."

"What's a frogman?"

"A guy who's at home on land and in the water—both. Do you know how to swim?"

Both children shook their heads.

Caroline and Sierra exchanged a glance. "You're peninsula kids now. We'll have you swimming by the start of summer."

Chapter 13

It was a welcome change to have a project—something other than kids and work and worry and uncertainty. There was a feeling of mission, too, something Caroline wished she had embraced long ago. She wanted to create a safe place for women like Echo Sanders and Lindy Bloom. And perhaps for the foolish girl she'd been long ago, the night before Sierra's wedding. Her commitment to the project was pathetically too little too late to be of any help at all to Angelique. Maybe, just maybe, it would help someone else, a woman like Lindy, who had suffered alone for so long with no one to turn to.

The notion of actually making a difference in someone's life was probably too idealistic. But lately

Caroline was feeling disillusioned, and doing something good would be good for her, regardless of the outcome. Sometimes she paused in the middle of whatever she was doing—reaching out to the local paper, reserving the meeting space, printing flyers—and pondered the changes in her life. Not so long ago, she'd been a New York designer on the cusp of a breakthrough. Now she was looking after two young children, reserving domain names for a new business enterprise, and researching domestic violence.

She laid into the project with a vengeance. She ticked things off her list. Assemble a team. Get the word out. She could do this.

"I need your help," she said to Sierra, regarding her across the table at Star of the Sea, where they'd met for coffee.

"Help with what?" Sierra asked.

"The Oysterville Sewing Circle." She grinned at her friend's expression. "That's what I'm calling my women's group—the one I told you about."

Virginia joined them, sliding into the booth. "What's up?"

"The Oysterville Sewing Circle," Sierra explained. "Caroline's on a mission."

"And you're going to help," Caroline declared.

"A sewing circle?" Virginia looked astounded. "I can't even sew on a button, and I'm not ashamed to admit it. Can such things be?"

"Well, it's not really about sewing, and it's not really a circle."

Virginia leaned back in her chair as realization dawned on her face. "The group, you mean. That's what you're calling it?"

"Yes. We're going to meet at the police station annex down in Long Beach."

"I want to be the first official member," Sierra declared.

Virginia stared at her. "Wait a minute. Do you mean . . . Jesus. Did Will—"

"God, no." Sierra waved away the unspoken question. "Will's a saint." Her voice held a bitter edge. "You both know that. I want to support you. It's a good thing you're doing."

"If we manage to get it done. Georgia's in, by the way," Virginia said.

"My God," Sierra said. "Then is Georgia . . . ?"

"Oh hell no." Virginia waved her hand. "Who would ever mess with Georgia? I appreciate you asking, though. To tell you the truth, I've learned that anyone can be sucked into domestic violence. It's a factor in so many of the cases I investigate for the county. It's not limited to women who are uneducated or poor or who had troubled childhoods. It *can* be women like you and me and Georgia—people with good families and resources and education."

"Yeah," Sierra said. "So creepy."

"Something happens—the guy needs to control and dominate because he feels inferior. Or he's reenacting something from his own past. A lot of times, he becomes a drunk. So we'd better be prepared to meet all kinds."

Caroline flashed on a memory of Angelique—regal and poised, commanding attention as she controlled a room full of high-powered fashion professionals with the slightest gesture or narrowing of her eyes. She simply had not looked like a victim—but as Virginia pointed out, women knew how to wear masks that made them seem put-together, successful, confident.

She opened a folder of printed material and showed them the flyer she'd designed. The logo was a stylized pincushion with needles and thread and the phrase *Mend Your Heart*, with contact information and a meeting schedule. "I wanted an innocuous-sounding name for the group, one that isn't likely to attract the kind of people who beat up their partners."

"And you picked sewing." Sierra smiled. "Of course you did."

"How many wife-beaters do you suppose are interested in sewing?" Caroline asked.

"Good point. Most men run from sewing."

"I'm glad you like the name. It's a tribute to the Helsingør Sewing Club, a little footnote in World War Two history. That's what a gang of resistance fighters called the fishing fleet in Denmark during the war to hide their real purpose from the Nazis. Right under the Germans' noses, they ferried boatloads of Jews from Denmark to Sweden. Said they were going to their sewing club."

"Cool," said Virginia. "I'm glad that you're doing this, Caroline. So proud of my sister."

"I had another idea. One of the biggest hurdles for survivors is finding work. And thanks to the PTA, I need help with every part of my fabrication operation. Because guess what? A school district in Seattle and another in Portland saw the superhero T-shirts and ordered some. Echo is already sewing for me. I can only offer minimum wage at this point, but if this works out, I'll need to hire more workers. And then I started thinking of other places that could employ women . . ."

"Georgia will be all over that," Virginia said. "She can train people in restaurant work."

Caroline thought about Nadine, the waitress. She'd reached out to her—a tentative overture. *I'm starting a women's group* . . . But Nadine had regarded her with a blank expression. Not everyone was going to embrace the idea. Maybe no one would. "So anyway, I'm going to book the police station annex for our first meeting. I need to make sure Mom's okay with me leaving the kids."

Not so long ago, she didn't have to check anything with anyone. And she'd liked it that way. Now she couldn't make a move without thinking of the children. They were the first thing she focused on when she woke up each day, and her last thought each night.

"Well then, let's get started," Virginia said.

Everyone pitched in. Caroline's mother used the restaurant menu printer to duplicate the flyer and a supply of business cards. Within days, they were placed all over town—the restaurant, the library, public restrooms, shops, schools, and churches. Caroline fielded a few calls—one from a shaky-voiced teenager who hung up on her. Another from a tourist staying in a bungalow near the dunes. There were a couple of emails. Maybe, she thought, just maybe this thing was going to work out. She hoped it would. One day the kids would be older and they'd have questions. She could only hope that she would have answers for them.

On the evening of the inaugural meeting, Caroline and Virginia arrived at the police station and parked in the annex lot. Sierra was already there, checking her makeup in her car mirror. Caroline posted a neatly lettered sign with an arrow directing people to the meeting room. The three of them brought in boxes of literature.

"Good choice of meeting space." Virginia looked around the plain, spare room. Folding chairs, a long service table, a bulletin board, and a sink and counter prep area. Beige walls, linoleum floors—a blank canvas.

"I think so," Caroline agreed. "Even the most persistent stalker is going to think twice before accosting someone here."

"Does that happen?" Sierra glanced at the door.

"According to things I've been reading, it's been known to. But right here next to the police station? I'm hoping our get-togethers will be blissfully uneventful." She looked at the clock, then checked her phone. "What if nobody comes?"

Sierra shrugged. "Then we'll go drinking and try again next week."

Virginia organized some pamphlets and a sign-in sheet on a table by the door. "Where's Georgia?"

"She said she was running late." Caroline checked her phone once more.

"And we're early."

"I'm worried. I created a dedicated email address for the group contact, and I got all excited when I heard from some people, but no one said they'd actually come."

"That's a bad habit of yours, worrying about things that haven't happened yet," Virginia said.

"Is it? Is it better to anticipate trouble and worry, or to wait for the trouble to happen and *then* deal with it?"

Virginia thought for a moment. "The latter," she said. "And that's something straight out of my divorce therapy. I loved my marriage. I was happy every day—until Dave dropped the bomb that he wanted a divorce. So I have to wonder, if I'd spent my time wondering and fretting about why he was such a workaholic, why he was so emotionally absent, why he was always boasting about Amanda at the firm—would I have been able to do something about it? Or was it better to be blissfully ignorant? Should I be glad he hid it from me?"

"He should have said something," Sierra said instantly, her voice sharp with vehemence. "Anything less is cheating. He knew that."

"Whoa, okay, I guess we know your opinion," Caroline said. She noticed the way Virginia was eyeing Sierra. A tiny unsettling question stirred in her mind, but she crushed it. "I still don't know if I should wait or worry."

The chairs were arranged in a loose circle. Flyers and name tags and pens set out. A whiteboard on which she'd written, *We believe you. We believe* in *you.* Then she wrote the mission statement under that.

Everything was ready. Caroline was ready. But nobody came.

Sierra glanced at the clock over the door. The hour was straight-up seven o'clock. "Okay, now you can worry."

Virginia nodded. "This is going to take time, Caroline. We just need to keep showing up, right?"

"Right." Caroline felt defeated. She'd hoped maybe one or two women would come. "And where's Georgia? Did she ditch us?"

"Maybe something came up with one of her kids," Virginia suggested.

"Maybe." Caroline sighed. She started halfheartedly packing up the flyers and other supplies. "I wonder if seven isn't a good meeting time. I suppose we need to do more outreach and try again next week. Or it could simply mean this was a bad idea."

At that moment, the door pushed open. "Who're you calling a bad idea?" Georgia demanded, bustling into the room. Behind her came Lindy Bloom, carrying a couple of trays. "Sorry we're late. Had to grab some things from the restaurant on the way."

With a flourish, she covered the table with a crisp linen drape. Everything about Georgia was assured and efficient, from her wash-and-wear jersey top and low-heeled sandals to her pixie crop haircut. She was excellent at many things, but her true passions were baking and running the show.

Now she showed a different side of leadership—strong but compassionate. "Well, don't just stand there," she said over her shoulder. "Give us a hand."

Caroline and the others broke into action. Virginia fetched the coffee service from Georgia's minivan. Caroline helped Lindy set out the trays of baked goods and savory bites—some of Georgia's most popular items from Star of the Sea.

Caroline stole an iced raisin bar and rolled her eyes, savoring the perfect balance of sweetness and spice. "No wonder Mom always liked you best," she said.

"Right." Georgia smiled. "The oldest always has to break the parents in. Remember that."

Caroline polished off the cookie. "Thanks for coming tonight. I wish some actual people would show up."

"What am I, chopped liver?" Lindy set down a stack of cocktail napkins and fanned them out with a twist of her fist.

"You know what I mean," Caroline said. "We plastered announcements all over town, but there are no takers."

"It's not like you to give up so quickly," Georgia said. "Honestly, Caroline, I'm super impressed. This project . . . It's going to be something special."

"You're all overachievers, the lot of you," Sierra declared. "I don't know how you do it all on top of kids and jobs and everything else."

"You make time for what's important, I guess," Georgia said.

The simple statement lit up an uncomfortable truth for Caroline. Her art and her career had consumed her entirely for nearly a decade. She wondered what she'd missed with those blinders on. As she helped her sisters transform the plain beige room into a welcoming meeting space, it occurred to her that maybe she should quit regarding her situation as a fiasco. Maybe she should view it as an opportunity instead.

Sierra helped Lindy with the coffee service. "So are you one of the organizers, too?" she asked.

The older woman lifted her brows in a flash of irony. "I plan to help out when I can," she said. "But no. Not an organizer. That honor belongs to Caroline. I'm a survivor."

With that, she scrawled her name and the word *survivor* on a tag and stuck it to her perfectly tailored blouse. Then she looked at Sierra. "Close your mouth, dear. You'll be catching flies. It's a long story, but if no one else shows up, you'll hear it all tonight."

"Oh, Lindy. I didn't know."

"Exactly. That was a huge factor in my situation—the secrecy." She handed Sierra a name tag. "You look beautiful as ever," she said. "I always loved it when you came to the shop to model things for Caroline."

Sierra stuck on the tag. "You were a wonderful mentor. I hope the shop's doing well."

"Well enough."

Caroline was thrilled with the support of her sisters and friends, but still disheartened by the low turnout. She was contemplating drowning her sorrows in lemon squares and espresso brownies when the door opened, and a woman slipped inside.

"Echo," she said. "Hey, I'm glad you came."

"You have no idea how tempting it was to spend the evening with a glass of wine and a trashy novel." Echo looked worn out as she helped herself to coffee. Then she noticed the spread of Georgia's goodies. "I take that back. This looks amazing."

Caroline felt a rush of gratitude—and sympathy. In addition to working at Lindy's, Echo drove a school bus in the morning. Caroline hoped the sewing gig would take some of the pressure off Echo. Of course, that meant *more* pressure for her. She'd had a good meeting about a small-business loan from a local bank, but setting up her own outfit was not going to be easy.

The door opened again, and to Caroline's astonishment, women began to arrive, most of them one by one, a couple with a friend or relative. Some of the visitors were furtive, avoiding eye contact, like shoplifters convinced they were about to get caught. Ever the preacher's daughter, Sierra greeted each arrival like a special guest. Nadine, who had rebuffed Caroline, showed up, still in her waitress outfit from the restaurant.

Caroline felt the unexpected heat of tears. These women, most of them total strangers, had come to the Sewing Circle. Please don't let me disappoint them, she thought.

Georgia nudged her. "Let's go ahead and start. If more people show up, I'll look after them."

Caroline swallowed hard to compose herself. "Welcome," she said, and composure failed her utterly. "Oh, for Pete's sake." She grabbed a tissue. "I didn't expect to get so emotional. My name is Caroline Shelby and this is the first meeting of the Oysterville Sewing Circle."

She took a deep breath, then blew it out. "Whew, sorry. Anyway, thanks for being here," she said. "Shall we begin?"

There was a murmured assent.

"Let's open with our mission statement. I stayed up way too late last night, trying to get the words right." She indicated the writing on the whiteboard. "'The Oysterville Sewing Circle was founded to provide a safe, supportive community for survivors of domestic violence and their friends and family members.' Okay, so it's not Shakespeare. Just want to be transparent. We're not a crisis agency—for that, you need to contact the numbers listed on the flyer. We're completely volunteer-run and self-supporting." She passed around a clipboard with a phone list. "I'm really grateful to those of you who showed up. You're welcome to share only what you're comfortable sharing, even if it's nothing at all. And please take care with other people's information."

She introduced her sisters and Sierra. "Bear with me," she said. "I'm new to this. I guess tonight we're all new." Then she paused as a young woman slipped in and hovered near the door, gave a curt nod, then took a seat.

"I'm Ilsa," she mumbled, staring at the floor.

Friendly murmurs rippled through the group.

"Thanks for coming," Caroline said, her heart pounding. Oh, she wanted this to go well. "Let's get started." She took a basket out from under her chair.

"This is a collection of mostly household items. The idea is to pick an object from the basket that has some kind of meaning to you and tell the group a brief story about it."

There were a few beats of hesitant silence. Caroline clutched the edge of her chair. Shoot. Was the ice-breaker activity too dorky? Too boring? Too threatening?

"I'll give it a shot," someone said. "I'm Amy." She wore a shapeless hoodie, sweatpants, and scuffed sneakers, and she looked to be in her twenties. Taking the basket, she returned to her seat and made a serious study of the contents. Caroline had gathered a collection of common items—kitchen tools, a paperweight, a ticket stub, the usual junk drawer detritus found in anyone's home.

"Okay, here's something." Amy held up a key chain with a flashlight attached. "A key chain doesn't seem very important, but to me, it's everything. I saw a notice about this meeting at the library, and I drove myself up from Ilwaco in order to check it out." Her voice was harsh, maybe from smoking or drinking or both. "That doesn't really sound like a big deal, and to most people, it's not. To me, it's everything. A year ago, I didn't even know how to drive. My goddamn husband wouldn't let me learn. See, if I could drive, I could get away from him, and then he wouldn't have nobody to beat up on. Best thing that happened to me was he got sent up for grand theft auto. Motherfucker's doing time in Walla Walla. First thing I did when he was gone, I took driving lessons. Hocked my wedding ring to pay for it—he would've flattened me for taking it off, but I have no regrets. I was determined. I learned to drive like a boss, and it was drive, drive, drive, for miles and miles, and I loved it. Felt like pure freedom. The day I got my license was a new beginning for me. I'm scared about what he'll do when he gets out, but for now I'm safe. I love to drive. It's, like, my favorite thing. I deliver pizzas, I drive for Uber, run errands for folks. Oh, and there's a dry cleaner down in Astoria that's got me doing pickups and deliveries. Ain't much of a living, but it keeps me on the road."

Silence fell over the group. Amy merely shrugged, placed the key chain in the basket, and passed it to the woman beside her. "Anyhoo, glad I came. Awesome cookies, by the way."

The next woman—Evelyn, calm and grandmotherly, the kind you'd see in church—sorted through the basket and picked out an empty checkbook register. "Ah, here we go," she said, her voice a soft contrast to Amy's rough speech. "This sparks something, for sure. The third time my husband put me in the hospital, the judge made a no-contact order against him. Now, I know the judge meant well, but it created a huge problem in my life. I had no job and no skills, I was raising my daughter, who needed medical treatment I couldn't afford. I went to court and begged the judge to undo the no-contact order, because my husband controlled all the money."

As she spoke, Evelyn twisted a gold wedding band around and around her finger. "I know how that must sound to you young, independent girls, but in my day, we didn't have options like you do. The judge looked at me and said, 'You're willing to be a punching bag for the sake of your daughter.'" She moved her hand to her wrist as if massaging an ache there. "Even though I pleaded, the judge left the no-contact order in place. But he was clearly troubled by it all. Later he introduced me to someone who showed me how to access benefits for my daughter and to lay claim to my husband's railroad pension. I'm still married to the man, though I've not seen him in years. I suppose one day there will be a divorce. For me, that would just be a formality. I've been free for a good while now."

Echo Sanders selected a spool of thread from the basket. "This was a no-brainer for me," she said, offering a flash of her bashful smile. "Sewing is my first love, and it's cool that this group calls itself a sewing circle." She spoke briefly, her gaze darting to the clock on the wall. She mentioned her gratitude at helping out with Caroline's new workshop. Then she brought up the idea of sacrifice. "I read somewhere that people lose their way when they forget their dreams. Do we? I hope it's not so. I've never forgotten my dreams. I know exactly what they are. My problem is, I'm too busy just trying to make ends meet. I'm not looking for pity. Just saying what's on my mind."

The next woman's name was Willow. She picked out a Quo Vadis planner, its creamy white pages blank. "Oh, this takes me back," she said. "I was an obsessive planner, had my life all mapped out to the last detail. That's the thing about life—it doesn't go according to plan. I married a man who subjected me to degrading tirades and episodes of rage that sent me cowering. There was a subtlety about it, though. The slow deterioration wasn't obvious, even to me. I couldn't see the situation clearly. The abuse eroded my independence and destroyed my self-confidence. By the time I found the fire to leave and start over, I was an empty shell."

She flipped through the blank pages. Her hands looked chapped and raw, ten years older than her smooth, round-cheeked face. "My ex denies everything. He gaslights me—makes me think *I'm* the crazy one, out to get him and imagining things. I've tried to tell people—friends and family—but I can't manage to convey the situation and they think I'm crazy, too. Some days I still question myself. He's successful, beloved by everyone who meets him. He's influential. Upstanding. Everything you think of when you think of a guy who runs a major hospital."

She turned to the calendar section of the planner and studied the grid for a moment. "I got a lot of bad advice from well-meaning people. My pastor suggested ways to mollify my husband, soften his anger. One friend said I should get better at sex."

A loud snort burst from Amy.

"Exactly. So I'm here in the hopes of finding someone who gets it." She looked around nervously; then her gaze darted to the floor. "I think—I hope—I might have found it."

Caroline grabbed Sierra's hand. They looked at each other and held on tight.

"I had to get a protective order as I was in the process of leaving," Willow continued, "and there was more gaslighting, even from the judge, because I simply couldn't explain what emotional abuse feels like. I was depressed, probably still am, but I can't afford to treat it. My self-confidence is in the dirt. The only job I dared to take was with a hotel laundry service. I don't know if I'll ever find my way back to who I was." She smoothed her reddened hand over the pages. "And I was somebody. A justice of the peace—can you believe it? Ironically, I'm authorized to perform marriages. I had other skills, too. I'm a business analyst and a patent lawyer. I wrote business plans for multimillion-dollar corporations and start-ups on a shoestring."

Caroline couldn't believe her ears. A lawyer. A judge. And now the woman was a hotel laundry worker?

Willow must have caught her expression. "Just because I'm educated doesn't mean I had some special warning that the charming, successful man I'd married was secretly a monster. My law degree didn't make me immune to the things that went on behind closed doors."

She snapped the book shut. "As the saying goes, a journey of a thousand miles begins with a single step." She looked around the circle. "So you're my first step."

Caroline didn't move a muscle. She felt heartsick and frustrated by the stories she was hearing. The losses caused by abuse mounted. Hearing the women speak was humbling. They came from every sort of diverse background, every stratum of society. The one common thread was that each had suffered at the hands of an intimate partner. A husband. A boyfriend. A girlfriend.

Economic hardship was part of nearly everyone's story. Women shackled themselves to abusers in order to survive, and they stayed trapped there, sometimes for years. Most people didn't have parents like Caroline's, offering a safe haven.

She had lived her life taking independence for granted. Now that she had children to look after, she could understand the compromises women were sometimes forced to make. She wanted to create something so successful that she could afford full-time help from Echo. And hiring Echo was only a small step. Caroline needed a bigger plan. She vowed to expand her business beyond superhero T-shirts. She wanted to create more opportunities for more women. Like Amy. Caroline was already paying a commercial driver to take her bagged and tagged garments to Seattle and Portland. Why not Amy, who loved to drive? And if the income stream ever permitted it, she'd hire Willow in a heartbeat, to help with the business side of things. Caroline knew design. Patternmaking and sample sewing, fit and sourcing. The business structure—not so much.

The latecomer named Ilsa rifled through the basket. "I don't see anything in here for me," she said. "I'm not even sure I belong in a group like this. I've never been married, haven't been in a long-term relationship. I'm here because I had . . ." Setting down the basket, she kept her eyes trained on the floor. "I don't even know what to call what happened to me. A bad date? A bad encounter?"

She absently rubbed the side of her neck with her hand. To Caroline, she looked very young, barely out of her teens. "It was a guy I'd just met for drinks, and he seemed kind of cute. I'm a web designer, and he was interested in my work. Good profile on a dating app. I was a little drunk," Ilsa went on. "I shouldn't have gotten in the car with him, but I was in no shape to drive. He offered to take me home. Then he wanted to make out, so we did that for a while, but I really wanted to go home. And . . . and he started forcing me, and I'm like, *no,* but it wasn't really a hard no. I didn't want to be awkward or dramatic. And he's like, 'Oh, you want it rough,' and he yanked off my blouse and tried to force me."

The young woman's words ignited a deep sense of outrage in Caroline, awakening an old but never-quite-forgotten memory. She didn't move, but felt her hands curl into fists.

"I—he . . . Somehow I managed to wriggle free. I shoved the door open and literally fell on the ground in the parking lot. Then I ran like hell to my own car. I don't even remember getting in. I remember him peeling out of the parking lot. I just sat there in my car with all the doors locked, shaking. Shaking so hard I thought my teeth would fall out. Finally I managed to get the key in the ignition. By then I was stone-cold sober. I'm sure I was in shock. God, it happened so fast . . ."

These things can catch you off guard, thought Caroline, feeling a prickle at the back of her neck.

"I should be grateful that I managed to get away," Ilsa said. "And I figured, that's that. It's over. It was a bad moment. I'm just going to forget it happened and move on."

Finally she looked up from the floor. "I can't forget. The whole incident took up maybe five minutes of my life, but I can't stop thinking about it. I go over and over it in my mind. Was I stupid to have one too many? Idiotic to get in his car? Was my skirt too short? My blouse too tight? Then I wonder if I should tell someone—my mom, a friend. But I couldn't bring myself to speak up. This is the first time I've said a single word about it. And here's the kicker. He keeps texting me, trying to get me to go out with him again. He's acting like we had a good time. He even sent me a dick pic. So I guess . . ." She hunched her shoulders. Rubbed her neck again. "That's why I'm not sure about being here." She stared down at her hands, picked at her nails. "Like, was I abused? Was it a sexual assault? Or just a really bad date?"

You were assaulted, Caroline told her with silent, fierce certainty. That's an absolute fact. She could scarcely imagine the trauma the girl must have felt. Except . . . maybe she could. A long-buried incident, never quite forgotten, nudged its way up from the past. The smell of salt water on his skin, Jägermeister on his breath. The weight of him, pinning her on the blanket. His husky voice in her ear. That, too, had been the briefest of encounters, but years later, it was burned into her memory. She was surprised by the vehemence she felt all the way down to the bottom of her gut. Now she realized that if the intimacy didn't feel right, it probably wasn't right.

"You're welcome here," Lindy Bloom said. "There's no prerequisite to join us."

When the basket came to Caroline, she took a moment to study the contents, even though she'd put the thing together. Ordinary objects. Things encountered every day. In her work, Caroline had made presentations to high-powered design professionals and creative directors, to the world-renowned designers themselves. Yet speaking to the group of women in Oysterville felt far more intimidating.

She took out a cockleshell, pinkish brown with ridges, a common find on the beaches in the area. "I'm drawn to this one," she said, holding the shell in her palm. "It reminds me of my old family nickname—C-Shell. I nearly forgot about that until I came back here. Now I've turned it into the name of the clothes I'm designing." She took a breath and looked around the room. "I have to tell you, I'm blown away by everything I've heard. And although I've never been in an abusive relationship, I have had an incident like the one Ilsa described."

Without even looking at her sisters, she could sense them sitting up as if someone had stuck a ramrod up their backs. "It was a long time ago, and I didn't speak up, either, but it still haunts me sometimes." She knew her sisters were going to be full of questions, and she'd answer them later. Maybe. Memories were powerful. They could haunt and torment and plague the soul with *what-ifs* and *should-haves*. She gripped the shell so tightly, she could feel its sharp edges biting into her.

"But that's not why I wanted to create a group like this. My life has been touched by domestic violence in a serious way. One of my closest friends was a victim. I wish I could tell you she's a survivor, but she didn't make it."

She took a deep breath, trying to gather her thoughts. She shut her eyes and the memories swept in, fresh as yesterday. "When I was a designer in New York, I worked with a beautiful model who I thought was at the top of her game in the fashion world. One day I noticed bruises on her. She brushed off my concern, and I didn't press her. I wish . . . I should have pushed harder, but I didn't know. I didn't realize . . . and then not long afterward, she came to me in a panic with her two kids. They needed a place to stay. I tried to help. I thought I was helping. Then one day I came home and found her dead of an overdose. I had no idea she was using drugs. I can't help but think it's related to her being abused. Now I'm taking care of her children and I'm overwhelmed. I'm trying my best to help them deal with what happened."

She knew she would forever be haunted by the promise she had made, sincerely and naively, to her friend. She was plagued by questions, doubts, uncertainty. Should she have called the police right away? Should she have pressed harder, bullied Angelique into opening up? Was there some other choice she could have made that might have changed the outcome?

"I miss my friend," she said, closing her eyes and picturing Angelique in all her glory. "She was more than beautiful. She had so much will and grit, maybe so much that the world looked past what was going on inside. I know I did. And now I've lost her, and everything happened so fast I haven't really mourned her. My worst fear is that I won't do right by her children."

Taking another steadying breath, she pressed the shell between her hands and continued talking to the group. "I'm grateful to be here and proud of my sisters and friends for helping me organize this. I've always known Georgia and Virginia were older and wiser than me, but I never realized how much wiser." The story had come out in a jumbled rush. Had she said too much? Did she sound like a blithering idiot?

When she looked around the circle, she saw only acceptance. "I'm hopeful that if I gain a better understanding of what happened to the children's mother, I might be able to help and protect them."

There was more talk. More eating of cookies. And at the end of the evening, every person present agreed to come the following week. As they were putting the room back together and boxing up supplies, Caroline felt a wave of hope. "It's a start," she murmured to no one in particular. "I'm glad we started."

Before going to bed that night, Caroline slipped into the children's room. Checking on them was a nightly habit now. Flick and Addie slept with sweet abandon, their breathing light and untroubled. Flick liked to sleep with the binoculars she'd bought him, his new prized possession. He claimed they helped him see the stars at night. Addie stuck with Wonder Woman, always.

Soft light from the hallway fell across their faces, and their utter vulnerability struck Caroline with an aching mixture of love and sadness.

Angelique, they're wonderful, she silently told her friend. *I wish you could see how fast they're growing, how much they're learning day by day. They miss you so much.* I *miss you.*

Their world is so different here. It's the world where I grew up. It was safe. *I never had to think about being safe, growing up. I just* was.

That's what I want to give them, Angelique. A childhood where safety is not just a goal, but a given.

PART THREE

For memory, we use our imagination. We take a few strands of real time and carry them with us, then like an oyster we create a pearl around them.

—John Banville

Chapter 14

The first time Caroline went to the old Jensen place, she was twelve going on thirteen. It was the very start of summer—three glorious months of no more teachers, no more books, no more homework, no more bells, no more dress code or walking in a straight line. The summer people were already arriving in their shiny cars with surfboards and picnic hampers, streaming from the cities to escape the heat and the traffic.

The wind in her face as she rode her bike down the shady lane felt like pure freedom, cool and sweet, flowing out endlessly behind her. The fat tires of her beach cruiser rattled over the dappled road, and she had to keep checking to make sure the jars of her mom's strawberry-rhubarb jam were nestled safely in the front basket.

Mom had sent her to deliver the homemade jam to old Mrs. Jensen as a thank-you, because Mrs. Jensen had made a nice donation to the town library, which was one of Mom's pet projects. Caroline was going to earn five bucks for making the delivery. If she had been a better person, like her perfect sister Georgia, she probably would have given the five to the library as well. But she wasn't Georgia. She wasn't perfect. She needed the money to buy fabric at Lindy's shop, the most special place on the whole peninsula. She had an awesome idea for a summer dress, her grandmother's old sewing machine was oiled up, and she couldn't wait to get started on it.

The Jensen place was a grand mansion, or apparently it had been back in the day. The house was covered with flaking greenish paint, with a wraparound porch and gabled windows. There was a railed walkway along the roofline overlooking Willapa Bay. In one of Caroline's treasured childhood books, *A Little Maid of Nantucket,* she'd learned that the rooftop lookouts were called widow's walks on account of women whose men went out whale hunting. Left behind, the wives used to walk around up there, watching for their men to come back. This made no sense at all to Caroline.

Why couldn't the women find something better to do? Like sew a gown, one of those fancy ones with hoop-skirts and layers of crinoline.

She parked her bike and took off her helmet, then picked up the basket and went to the front door. A scruffy brown dog scampered over, barking his head off. His feathery tail waved, indicating he was friendly.

"Hey there," she said, stooping down to give him a pet. He wore a red collar with a tag. "Duffy," she said, reading the tag. "Is that your name, boy?" He wriggled and bowed, then feinted away, picking up a dry stick.

She looked around, not seeing anyone else. The porch was furnished with white wicker chairs and a two-seater swing. There was a wrought iron table with a big aspidistra plant, and a boot scraper in the shape of a wiener dog. The chair cushions were covered in vile cabbage rose damask. Caroline had never understood why people liked damask. It always seemed so heavy and dull.

A historical society plaque was posted by the door: THE ARNE JENSEN HOUSE. 1881. In 1881, girls wore petticoats and boots that fastened at the ankle with a buttonhook. And corsets that looked brutal to wear but were also kind of awesome.

Caroline went up the steps, knocked on the door, and waited. Nothing. Cupping her hands around her eyes, she peered through the wavy old-fashioned glass into a foyer. She could see a hall tree and mirror, and a wooden staircase. Nobody home.

She knocked again, then turned and shaded her eyes, scanning the area. There was a giant barn with walls made of weather-beaten wood, its roof sagging like a sow's belly. In the distance were the docks and oystering sheds. Still nobody around, though.

Oh well. She left the basket by the door and propped Mom's thank-you note beside it.

"Hey."

Startled, Caroline swiftly turned. A boy stood on the gravel path leading in from the dock. Tall and skinny, he was dripping wet from head to toe, holding a mask, flippers, and a snorkel. He had blond hair slicked to his head like a seal's fur, freckles, and blue eyes that were framed by the imprint of the snorkel mask.

Her heart skipped a beat. Even dripping wet, he was totally cute. Lately she noticed boys in a new way. A way that made her chest feel warm and squishy.

"Hey," she said, wondering who this kid could be. She'd never seen him before.

"You looking for somebody?" the boy asked.

"Old Mrs. Jensen." She gestured at the basket. "I have a delivery for her."

"You mean my grandmother. She's not that old. Jeez."

She looked around at the fields and tidal flats, the big coastal cedars permanently bent like old men by the wind. "This is your grandparents' place?"

"Yep."

"Are you visiting, or . . . ?"

"For the summer."

One of the summer people, then. He didn't look so fancy in his swim trunks, his bare chest pale as a fish's belly.

He set down the snorkeling gear. "I'm Will Jensen."

"Caroline Shelby," she said. "I live in town. Year-round."

Like everyone on the peninsula, she had mixed feelings about summer people. They descended each season to soak up the sun and play in the surf, filling the campgrounds and beach motels, racing their bikes up and down the boardwalks, flying kites and shooting off illegal firecrackers almost every night. Her older sisters and their friends were obsessed with having summer boyfriends, which as far as Caroline could tell were boys they made out with and then never saw after Labor Day.

She glanced again at his snorkel gear. His legs were long and pale, and seemed made of equal parts muscle and goose bumps. "You like swimming?"

He nodded, and his bluish lips quirked up in a smile. “My granddad says I’m part fish. I didn’t see much around the dock, though.” He gestured over his shoulder. “Anemones and crabs, mostly. I wanted to watch the birds diving, but I got too cold.”

“Ever try a wet suit?”

“Nope.”

“You can stay in a lot longer if you wear a wet suit. They have ’em for sale at Swain’s store.” Being a local made her feel slightly superior, knowing her way around.

“I’ll keep that in mind.” He moved out of the shade and into a patch of sunlight. His eyes were as blue as her favorite color of gumball.

The squishy-warm feeling came back. “Do you have a bike?” she asked in sudden inspiration.

He shrugged his shoulders. “I think there’s an old beach cruiser in the barn.”

“Want to go for a ride?”

“Sure. I’ll go change.” He patted his thigh and Duffy followed him to the house.

While she waited, Caroline filled her lungs to the brim with the heady air of adventure. It seemed as palpable as the tang of brine on her tongue. As a general rule, she didn’t like boys. With two younger brothers, she was well aware of their shortcomings. Boys were noisy, and they smelled like hamsters, and they had an incomprehensible habit of wearing the same dirty shirt day in and day out until someone made them change.

This boy, though. Will Jensen. There was something interesting about him, and it wasn't just the freckles and blue eyes. For some reason, he didn't seem annoying like her brothers or the boys in her class. Not yet, anyway.

After a few minutes, he came clumping down the porch steps. His *Go Navy* T-shirt looked clean enough. His blond hair had a shampoo-ad shine now that it was dry. That hair was way too pretty, she thought. For a boy.

"The bike probably needs air in the tires," he said, leading the way to the barn.

She fell in step with him. "You like the navy?"

"My dad's in the navy, so I'd better like it. We've been stationed in Guam the past two years. Know where Guam is?"

"I'd be lying if I said I did. Sorry." She glanced away, feeling ignorant.

"That's okay. I probably wouldn't know either, except I live there. It's an island in Micronesia—in the South Pacific."

"Guam," she said, enjoying the shape of the word in her mouth. "What's it like?"

"Tropical. Like Hawaii, only with snakes."

"Sounds amazing. I'd put up with the snakes if it was like Hawaii, which I've never been to, but I bet it's beautiful. I've only ever lived here."

"I think right here is pretty awesome."

"In the summer," she agreed. "Ever visited in the winter?"

He shook his head. "Let me guess. Cold, dark, and wet."

"The worst." Every year her parents talked about closing the restaurant for a whole month in winter and taking the family someplace warm. All they did was talk, though. Then they'd start worrying about what to do about the dog. And the house. And the restaurant. And they'd worry about being able to afford a big trip with five kids, and the older girls missing school, and eventually they'd talk themselves out of leaving.

Will lifted the rusty latch of the barn door. The hinges creaked as he opened it. Sunshine poured through the cracks in the walls, creating long bars of light and shadow and illuminating ancient swags of spider webs. Dust motes swirled with movement. The tall, arched ceiling made the space feel huge, bigger than a church sanctuary.

"My granddad keeps saying we're going to clean this place out," Will said, "but we never get around to it.

I bet some of this stuff goes back to *his* grandfather, who built the place." He pointed out a carved wooden plaque that read JUSTINE. "That's from a ship that took the oysters down to San Francisco."

Caroline studied a wooden ship's figurehead of a woman's bare-breasted torso. "And is that Justine?"

He blushed so hard, his freckles disappeared. "Whatever. Give me a hand with this bike. I don't think anyone's used it since I was here last summer."

They extricated the bike from the clutter and wheeled it outside. She helped him pump up the tires, glad her dad had taught her how to do it so she didn't look like a klutz. He found a can of WD-40 and sprayed the chain, and everything seemed to work well enough.

"Better make sure there aren't any spiders in that helmet," she cautioned him.

He held it up to the sky to inspect it. She was grossed out, but not surprised, to see a shaggy-legged wolf spider clinging to the underside. She *was* surprised when he calmly picked it up and sent it on its way, then brushed off the cobwebs. Maybe after the snakes of Guam, he wasn't afraid of a mere spider. He clipped on the helmet. "Ready?"

She jumped on her bike and led the way down the main road. She went fast, showing off a little, raising both arms and calling out, "I love summer!" She was no match for the boy, though. He easily glided past her and took the lead. It was a long fast ride down the road to the south end of the peninsula. They passed the poky little golf course, where big-bellied men were drinking beer and hacking away with their clubs. The main town of Long Beach was crammed with traffic and people browsing through the shops. She and Will didn't talk much, although she pointed out some of the places visitors loved to explore—Marsh's Museum of Oddities, the go-kart track, the saltwater taffy factory, the shooting arcade.

"Let's ride the boardwalk," she said, turning toward the archway that framed a magnificent view of the beach, endlessly flat and dotted with people. They followed a scenic path through the dunes at the edge of the beach.

"That's our restaurant—Star of the Sea," she said, pointing out the big weathered building with its shaded decks and umbrella tables.

"Hey, we went there for razor clams the other night. I like that place."

"Almost everybody likes it," she said. "It's real busy in the summer, especially since there were some articles about it in the *New York Times* and *Condé Nast Traveler*. Oh, and a crew from the Travel Channel came out one time and filmed for a whole day just to make a half-hour show."

"Really? That sounds cool."

"I wanted to be on TV so bad. I even made a new outfit to wear and talked about it on camera, but that part all got cut out. They showed my parents because they're the owners, and then my sister Virginia on account of she's drop-dead gorgeous and she pretended to be a customer on the deck."

He was looking at her funny. She flushed. "I talk a lot, I know. Mom says it's because I'm the middle child, and when you're in the middle, you learn to speak up, or people forget about you."

"I doubt anybody'd forget about you," he said.

"Huh. You haven't seen my sisters and brothers. I got two of each. Do you have brothers and sisters?"

"Nope. Just me."

"Lucky you."

Dodging sun seekers and people with fishing gear and kites, they rode all the way to the fishing village of Ilwaco, its marina filled with charter boats and commercial vessels. "Ever been up to the lighthouses?" she asked. "There are two of them."

"Let's go," he said.

The twisty, hilly climb nearly did her in, but she didn't let on that her legs were about to give out. The ride took them up to a rocky headland with damp pathways leading through the dense forest to the lighthouses, North Head and Cape Disappointment.

At a viewpoint overlooking the place where the Columbia River surged into the Pacific Ocean, they stopped to rest near the first lighthouse—North Head. They peeled off their helmets and each took a long drink of water at the park fountain. Then they climbed out past the safety fence to the promontory, a rock-strewn perch with a view of the coastline as far as the eye could see.

"Awesome," said Will, staring down at the dizzying sight of waves crashing against the cliffs and rocks. Some of the breakers exploded hundreds of feet in the air.

"In the spring and fall, you can see the gray whales migrating," she said. "You should see it in a storm. The surf gets huge and there are giant thunderheads. Wind and fog like you wouldn't believe. It's super dangerous for boats around here. Does your dad work on a ship?"

"Sure. Next January we're moving from Guam to Coronado. That's in Southern California."

"Oh, California sounds nice."

They stood on a rocky outcropping, feeling the salt spray on their faces. "This is my spot," Caroline told him, gazing out at the seam where the ocean met the sky. "I mean, it doesn't personally belong to me, but I come here to think sometimes."

"It's a good one." He stared out at the blue horizon. Then he picked up a loose stone and hurled it far. She tracked it until it disappeared. He started walking along a trail that wound around the towering cliffs. She followed, trying to picture the place called Coronado. Whenever she thought of California, she envisioned the world of *Beverly Hills, 90210,* a boring show her sisters were obsessed with.

"California will be okay, I guess," he said. "I'll go to a regular school, not a DoD school."

"What's a DoD school?"

"Stands for Department of Defense. They have 'em on all the bases. Once we're stateside, I'll go to public school."

"Will your dad work on a different ship then?"

He shook his head. "Shore duty. He'll be working on base because it's just him and me now, so he can't go on deployment."

"Oh. Did your folks split up?" That's what happened to some of her friends. One or the other parent left, an idea that gave Caroline chills all through her body. The kids usually stayed with the mother, though.

"My mom's dead."

Caroline stumbled and nearly lurched into him. "That's terrible. That's . . ." Her mind was so crowded with questions, she didn't know where to begin. "What happened?"

"It was something called pulmonary edema. She had an undiagnosed heart defect." His voice was quiet and flat, which somehow made it sound worse than if he'd fallen apart crying.

"That's the worst thing I ever heard. When?"

"Just after New Year's last year. Dad was on shift, and I thought she overslept. She died in the night."

Caroline tried to picture what that must have been like, finding your mom dead one morning. "I don't . . . Gosh. That's horrible. I can't think of anything else to say."

"At least you're honest."

Her chest felt tight and a shiver went through her. "Oh, man," she said. "I feel really bad for you. Even just the thought of losing my mom scares the bejesus out of me. Without my mom, I'd be a total goner. I'd be like that fishing trawler that broke loose last winter and got sucked out by the tide and then smashed against the rocks right down there where the Columbia River flows into the ocean." She pointed, and they stopped to look down at the exploding waves.

"I thought you couldn't think of anything to say," he said.

"Guess I got over it. Anyway. If something happened to my mom, that's how I'd probably feel."

He was quiet for several moments, staring out at the view. The colors were amazing, from the summer blue of the sky to the deep indigo waters and the snow-white spray foaming on the cliffs where the waves broke. The crashing surf made a deep-throated roar, echoing through the rocky caverns under the cliff.

"Sorry," she said. "I hope that didn't make you feel worse."

"It didn't. And what you said about feeling lost and smashed on the rocks—that's about right," he said. "No. That's exactly right."

She stared at the seething surf exploding against the breakwater at the mouth of the river. "We learned in school that there've been thousands of shipwrecks here."

He turned and looked back at the cliff-top sentinel. "I thought the lighthouse was supposed to keep shipwrecks from happening."

"That only works if there's someone at the helm."

That summer, Caroline and Will fell into an easy friendship. Something inside her recognized that it was special, not like a passing acquaintance with a random kid in a beach volleyball game, but real and alive. It was different from the bond she felt with her school friends, the ones she saw all the time. This was separate, and it felt rare, somehow, maybe because they both knew it would end with the summer.

Sometimes she wasn't quite sure what to make of this boy. It was so easy to talk to him. The two of them got along in a way that seemed natural and effortless. He was kind of on the quiet side, and she was kind of a chatterbox, so maybe that was the reason they got along so well.

They made the most of each day, finding adventure at every turn. They both loved the smell of the sea, the quality of the salt air. She told him Long Beach had the best digging sand anywhere, not that she had dug in any other sand. There were sandcastle competitions, and people came from all over to build crazy sculptures of mermaids and towers, working all day on creations that would be swept away by the tide.

They went on hikes with his dog and hers—Duffy and Wendell. It was obvious that Duffy was the smarter of the two, obeying commands and easily finding his way through the forests and meadows and sand dunes. Wendell was playful and useless, but so ridiculously cute that everyone loved him.

"Wendell and I have the same birthday," Caroline said. "Well, we don't actually know his exact birthday, but they rescued him as a puppy the year I was born, so we assigned him my birthday."

"He gets around pretty well for an old dog," Will said.

"Wendell's not old," Caroline objected. "I guess maybe he is, but I try not to think about that. I can't imagine life without Wendell."

"Then don't," Will said. "And then one day he'll be gone and it'll be the worst thing ever and you'll get used to it."

She wondered if that was how he felt about losing his mom. She didn't ask, though. It was bad enough that he'd lost her. She shouldn't make him talk about it.

The beach in summer felt like her reward for getting through the dark, rain-soaked winters—glassy calms, the wild waves rearing up, all of it was part of her heart and soul. They went clamming, bringing their harvest home by the bucketful. They pooled their money to buy toffee apples and wispy cones of cotton candy. With Will, the season felt like a hidden passage to a special world. She imagined only the two of them could find it, slipping through an invisible gate and vanishing forever, like kids in an adventure novel.

Will was a super-strong swimmer, and fearless in the water, whether he was on a boogie board or in a kayak. She tried to keep up with him, but he was always waiting for her to catch up. She showed him the long string of beaches, each with its own special vibe, like the one called Klipsan, with the rollers that seemed to come from across the globe, maybe all the way from Guam, where he had lived with his dad.

She discovered that they both went to Oceanside Congregational Church, squirming impatiently through Sunday services and trying not to make eye contact because it gave them the giggles.

They couldn't wait to get back outside. Sometimes they'd join in with other kids, locals Caroline knew from school.

Will usually rode his bike down to her house and they'd go from there. They explored all her favorite places, including the marshy woods where sometimes, during the salmon run, the fish would actually swim across the pavement and through the forest during their migration. They discovered new wonders together, like the nest of blue heron they could perfectly observe from the widow's walk of his grandparents' house. She showed him how to sew on her grandmother's old treadle machine, even though he admitted he couldn't think of anything he needed to sew. In turn, he demonstrated his grandfather's power tools, and together, they made a purple martin house out of old lumber.

After they'd watched an old Bruce Lee movie, Will revealed that he'd been studying self-defense, because his dad believed every kid needed fight training.

"I've never been in a real fight in my life," she said. "Have you?"

He nodded. "There was a gang of bullies at my school in Guam. I came home with a split lip one day, and that's when my dad put me in Krav Maga."

"Never heard of that. How does it work?"

"The best self-defense is not to get into a fight at all. But if you can't avoid it, then the idea is to end it as fast as you can. You learn to keep your cool," he said. "Most people in a fight are mad, which only makes them more vulnerable. And don't fight the way your opponent wants you to—fight the way *you* know."

"Sounds like wishful thinking to me. I'm the middle of five kids. If somebody wants to fight, I wouldn't be able to stop it."

He walked a few paces away. "Rush me like you're going to attack."

"What? That's dumb."

"You wanted to know how it works. Don't worry about hurting me, 'cause I promise, you won't. And I won't hurt you because it's just a demo. Pretend I'm a bad guy and charge me."

Well, that was next to impossible, but she was challenged by the idea. She ran at him, trying to act like one of the characters in the movie. The moment she got close, Will made a quick move, and Caroline was on her back in the grass, looking up at the sky.

It took her a moment to catch her breath. "Hey!"

He went down on one knee and put his forearm on her neck. "If this was a real fight, I'd press down until you surrendered or passed out."

She stared up at his face. He smelled of mown grass and sweat, and his eyes were as blue as the sky above, and she was close enough to count the freckles on his nose. Flustered, she said, "I get it. Remind me never to attack you."

One day they saw Caroline's dad loading his surfboard and wet suit into the back of the pickup. "Hey, Mr. Shelby," said Will. "Where are you going?"

"Sunset Beach, just for a couple of hours. Are you a surfer, Will?"

"I wish. Maybe I'll learn once we move to Coronado," he said.

"Caroline's a pretty good surfer," said Dad.

"Yeah?" Will turned, looking at her in a new way. "I didn't know that."

"You didn't ask," she said. "I'm not that good. But I can get up."

"Tell you what. I'll load up some boards and wet suits for you guys, and we'll give it a go."

Will's eyes lit up like Christmas morning. "Cool," he said. "Thanks, Mr. Shelby."

Dad got the boards and suits. Will and Caroline piled into the club cab of the truck. At the last minute, her younger brothers tumbled out of the house, insisting on coming along. Caroline was annoyed, but Dad seemed delighted. "You all have to take turns," he said. "I can't take everyone into the surf at once."

"We'll take turns," Jackson said. "We'll be good, Dad. We will."

"Promise," Austin echoed.

Caroline caught Will's eye and shrugged. He merely grinned. He seemed to like the novelty of her big family, and he had a lot more patience with the boys than she did.

Her sisters were both in high school, and they worked at the restaurant. Next summer, Caroline was expected to do the same, starting out in the steamy, horrible dishwashing area with the big hand squirts, working her way up the ladder, as Mom put it. Dad called it paying your dues. Each of the Shelbys would start at the lowest level, and they'd be bumped up if they did a good job. Georgia, aka Miss Perfect, had lasted only a week in dishwashing and did so well that she was already in the front of the house at the hostess stand. Virginia, aka Miss Gorgeous, wasn't far behind.

Caroline wondered how long it would take to prove herself, bussing tables and washing dishes next year. She dreaded the prospect. Georgia and Virginia said they liked the energy, the noise, the ebb and flow of people coming and going. Caroline knew that the clatter and heat, the chef and foul-mouthed line cooks rushing around, and the constant demands of the customers would drive her nuts. She much preferred sketching or making things on her grandmother's old sewing machine. Most of all, she loved running around in the great outdoors, preferably with Will.

Dad drove them to the beach and parked the truck. Surfers were already floating out beyond the break, bobbing like buoys as they watched for a wave to ride. Several of them got up, black stick figures against the blue-green waves. Caroline could see Will checking out the scene, every muscle tense. Caroline wasn't very good at surfing, but sometimes she lucked out. Maybe today would be a lucky day.

"Wet suits are in the back of the pickup," her dad said. Even though it was a hot summer day, the water was never warm enough to surf without a wet suit. They zipped themselves into the neoprene and brought their boards down to the water. Dad was already paddling out, expertly dipping under the incoming waves. Jackson and Austin grabbed their boogie boards, which were easier to ride.

Caroline lugged her board to the surf. The water chilled her to the bone, but in a few seconds, the wet suit warmed her up. A wave rose, smacking her in the face. She laughed at the feel of the water and sunshine and fastened her ankle strap. Will was way ahead of her, as usual. She wasn't surprised when he took to surfing as if he was on a mission.

She knew he'd catch on pretty soon, because her dad was a really good surf instructor. He'd grown up in Southern California and he liked to say salt water ran in his blood. Thanks to him, all the Shelbys knew how to paddle out past the white water and find the gray-green curl of a wave. He used to stand in the surf for what seemed like hours, giving her board a shove at exactly the right moment and calling, "Attack position!"—her cue to pop up on the board and ride the wave to shore. His glee when she succeeded was almost as gratifying as the heady sensation of the ride itself.

Will kept struggling with the waves and the timing, long after the younger boys got tired and started building a fort out of driftwood. Dad said Will had a high center of gravity because he was tall, so it might take more practice to get his stance just right. He got knocked around by the rollers coming in, yet he never gave up.

"Timing is the hardest thing to get right," Dad told him. "And it's the one thing that makes all the difference. You want the wave underneath you just as it's about to break. So you need to figure out if you have to wait or to paddle fast."

Caroline was working on riding the curl, not just the white water. She watched the horizon for a swell to come to her, and got lucky a few times, finding that one glassy spot in the unbroken wave.

"Great work, C-Shell," Dad called to her. "You too, Will. You're doing all right."

"I'm gonna get it," he said.

And finally, in one sweet moment, he did. He spotted the right wave and paddled until Dad said, "Attack position!"

Will popped up, wobbled a bit, and rode the wave with a look of such glee that Caroline laughed aloud. He wiped out, then surfaced, punching the air in triumph. This was summer, she thought. She wished it could go on forever.

As the season waned toward its bittersweet end, Caroline felt a peculiar urgency to fill the days with everything she loved about summertime. Labor Day weekend reared up on the calendar, the last hurrah for so many on the peninsula—Will included. The Rotary picnic drew everyone to Sunset Beach. The moms showed up, toting wicker bags stuffed with egg salad sandwiches, bags of chips, trays of cookies, striped towels, and tubes of sunscreen. A local band was playing old dance songs from the eighties, and there was a volleyball game going on. Caroline and Will were lugging a picnic cooler from the boardwalk to the beach when a piercing whistle sounded. Will stopped walking and froze with a funny look on his face.

"My dad's here," he said, setting the cooler down.

She turned to see a tall man coming toward them. He wore a navy blazer and pleated flannels, his blond hair raked into gleaming comb furrows. His shoes shone in the sun. He had a clean-cut, square-jawed look and a perfect-posture stride that drew people's attention as he passed.

"Oh!" she said. "Is he coming to the beach with us?"

"I doubt it." Will wiped his hand on his shorts. "He's not dressed for the beach."

True, she observed. He looked out of place—but not uncomfortable—amid the people crossing from the parking lot to the beach.

"Howdy, son," said Mr. Jensen. "Your grandparents said I'd find you here."

"Hey, Dad."

They didn't touch or hug, but offered a mutual nod of greeting. "Are you coming to the picnic?" asked Will.

"Maybe later," said his father.

"This is Caroline," Will said.

"Caroline Shelby," she added, sticking out her hand, even though it felt totally phony. His grip was quick and hard, like a bite. "My dad brought surfboards and wet suits. We're going to go surfing, and you could come. That is, if you want." She felt herself getting all talky again, which she did when she was nervous. Something about Mr. Jensen made her nervous.

"Or you could come and watch. I can get up on a board now, Dad," said Will.

"Kind of pointless, if you ask me. The ocean is where I work, not play," said Mr. Jensen. "You kids run along now. I'm going to drop into the pub for a pint and a half."

"Okay," Will said. "See you later."

"Stay out of trouble, son."

"Sure thing."

Mr. Jensen made a brief saluting motion with his hand, then pivoted toward the main street. There were several bars and pubs where grown-ups sat around drinking, doing pull tabs and watching baseball on wide-screen TVs.

She studied Will's face. A peculiar sadness clouded his blue eyes. She wondered if he was remembering his mom, or if he was wishing his father would join in the fun on the beach. "Maybe he'll come back in a bit," she suggested, trying to cheer him up.

"Nah. He won't be back until the pub closes."

"I'm sorry," she said, not quite certain that was the right thing to say.

He stared at the retreating figure. "I'm not. If he'd stayed, he'd only spoil things."

She couldn't imagine someone spoiling a day at the beach. "How?"

"He'd probably drink too much and embarrass me."

"Oh." And again, "I'm sorry."

"It's my last day. I'm not gonna let anything ruin it. Let's go."

They brought the cooler to the picnic area, where her brothers were already decimating the platter of deviled eggs her mother had made. Her sisters and their friends were French-braiding their hair and arranging themselves on blankets where the boys would notice them. Her dad was already in his wet suit, waxing the boards.

"There's a good surf today," he said. "Want to have a go?"

"Sure," Will said. "I need all the practice I can get."

"Good attitude," Dad said.

Will grinned and in they went, surfing with the cluster of kids out beyond the break. As usual, Will kept at it, long after exhaustion and hunger drove Caroline to the barbecue area, where the Rotary volunteers were grilling for the crowd and drinking beers. After a while, Will showed up and devoured a burger with a look of bliss on his face.

Just before dark, his father came to collect him. She recognized that stride, only now it was punctuated with a slightly uneven swagger.

Dad came over and introduced himself. "Will's got a natural talent at surfing. He did really well this summer."

"Yep, well, we need to get a move on," said Mr. Jensen. "We're leaving first thing in the morning."

"Tell you what," said Dad. "I'll give you a ride up to your folks' place. I'm heading that way myself."

No, he wasn't, thought Caroline.

"No thanks," said Mr. Jensen. "I'm parked over there." He gestured vaguely.

"We'll get the car back to your place tomorrow. On a holiday weekend, the patrols are out in force and they love to write tickets," said Dad. "Can you give me a hand with the surfboards? Thanks, man."

Dad was totally smooth. He was an expert at dealing with people who'd had a few too many. He was a sommelier and had worked in bars his whole life, and he knew just what to do. Within a few minutes, the four kids were crammed into the club cab of the pickup, Dad at the wheel and Mr. Jensen in the front seat. Dad kept up a friendly conversation during the drive to Water's Edge. Will was totally silent the whole way. Caroline could feel him breathing next to her. They had to share a seat belt, and his leg pressed against hers, the muscles tense. When they parked in front of the old house, Will scrambled out of his seat as if he couldn't get away fast enough.

"Uh, thanks for the ride, Mr. Shelby," he said.

"No problem," said Dad. "None at all."

"Yeah, thanks for the lift." Mr. Jensen headed toward the house. "Let's go, son."

Caroline hung back, painfully aware that this was goodbye. And she didn't quite know how to say that. So she just said it. "Bye, Will."

He stiffened, as if the notion of goodbye had just struck him. "Okay," he said. "Guess I'll see you around."

"Guess so," she said. There were a hundred things she wanted to say to him, but he was already edging toward the house. Maybe she should offer to call him. But no, they didn't talk on the phone. It wasn't that kind of friendship. It was a "run around and play all day" kind of friendship. Trying to talk on the phone would only ruin things. Besides, there was no way to call Guam, was there?

There was always email over the computer, but in Caroline's family, there was only one computer and they all had the same email address—Shelbyfamily @willapa.net. She sure as heck didn't want her sisters seeing her notes to Will Jensen.

She hated this goodbye. It was rushed and weird. Not that she wanted to linger over it like Romeo and Juliet, but she kind of wanted to say a few things, like that she'd had fun. That she'd miss their adventures. That she'd think of him during the endless school year.

"Are you coming back next year?" she asked.

"Sure am."

"I'll be here," she said.

Chapter 15

Caroline was singing "The Winged Herald of the Day" with her mouth wide open when she saw Will Jensen again the next year. She was in her usual spot in church—the middle of a pew in the middle of the sanctuary—when she happened to look over while belting out, "Take up thy bed, to each He cries," and there he was, a row behind and across the aisle.

She nearly choked on the chorus. Her cheeks filled up with color, and she whipped her head back around.

Right after he left last summer, she had missed him so much that she wrote down all kinds of things she wanted to tell him, everything from what she had for dinner (tuna casserole made with her uncle's fresh catch and little English peas) to her schedule of classes (her favorite was something called domestic arts, which involved sewing). She never sent a single letter, though. For one thing, she didn't have his address in either Guam or Coronado. Oh, she could have asked his grandmother, but she was too bashful to do that.

She had to fight her sisters and brothers for computer time, and finally sat down and typed out an email one day. The modem kept squawking, and just at the crucial moment, it disconnected and the laboriously typed message disappeared like mist. After that, she gave up. Compared to long summer rambles and epic bike rides around the peninsula, email was a yawn.

After church, they met up at the cookie table. "Hey, stranger," said Will. "I'm back."

"Hey, yourself. You're back."

"Yep. For the whole summer," he said.

"Cool. Church is lame but the cookies are good. They're looking for a new pastor. Maybe they'll find one who isn't too boring."

She couldn't stop smiling, yet still she felt awkward. He looked so different—taller. Bigger in the shoulders, maybe. And his voice was totally different, kind of crackly and deep, a human computer modem. She wondered if she looked different to him. Probably not. She was still skinny and flat-chested, something her sisters liked to remind her of. She'd started wearing a bra anyway, hoping it would speed things up.

"Check out your crazy hair," he said.

Well, at least he was checking *something* out. "What about my hair?"

"It's pink. Duh."

"I was in a march for breast cancer awareness," she said, then blushed because she'd said *breast.* "Can you go to the beach tomorrow?" she asked, to change the subject. "There was a good surf report."

"Sure thing. My grandparents got me my own board."

The first Monday of summer was special, like a magical holiday, marking the first day kids didn't have to drag themselves out of bed, whine their way through breakfast, race for the bus as if it came at a different time every day, and sit through classes while their eyes turned to glass.

True to the weather prediction, the first Monday was a beach day, crowded with people welcoming summer. The hours went by like a series of snapshots—volleyball, kite flying, sandcastles, surfing. Caroline stayed in the water until she could barely stand up. She staggered ashore, peeled off her wet suit, and rinsed off at the outdoor showers. She put her wet suit in the back of the truck, pulled on a pair of shorts, and grabbed a sweatshirt.

"He's not going to notice you in that," Georgia said, taking the sweatshirt from her.

"What? I don't know what you're talking about."

"Right." Georgia adjusted the strap of her lime-green bikini. "That boy who came back for the summer. This outfit makes you look like his kid sister."

"So?" She glared down at her cutoffs and lace-up canvas sneakers.

"You're so obsessed with designing clothes, but you dress like a tomboy. Here, try this." With her customary bossy officiousness, Georgia traded the sweatshirt for a sheer blouse from her beach bag, rolled it up at the waist, and knotted the shirt tail under her chest, leaving her midriff bare above her cutoff shorts. "There. That's better. You've got those cute little abs."

"Jeez," said Caroline, feeling a blush come on. "Nobody cares about my cute little abs."

Her big sister tossed the sweatshirt back into the truck. "Huh. Tell that to Baby in *Dirty Dancing.*" Georgia and her friends were obsessed with the old movie. Songs from the soundtrack were on every mix CD they made. Even Caroline secretly loved the parts where Baby transformed from geek to goddess.

Will came up from the beach and peeled off his wet suit. He didn't seem to notice her abs, cute or otherwise. She handed him a can of root beer, which they both agreed was the best thing to drink after surfing. After a while, they joined in a game of volleyball, and she saw some of her friends checking him out.

"He's a total babe," said Rona Stevens, a girl in Caroline's class. Rona watched Will dive for a shot. "He looks just like Brendan Fraser. Only blond."

"What? No." It was so weird, having her friends check him out. A few of them already had boyfriends. Nearly all of them had boobs. Caroline had neither, and it didn't really bother her. Okay, so maybe it did, a little.

"He's a stone-cold fox," Rona declared. As captain of the cheerleading squad, Rona had been one of the most important girls in junior high—as far as she was concerned, anyway.

"What does that even mean? Jeez." Caroline shook her head. Several things confused her these days: The prospect of going to high school in September. The way she sometimes cried for no reason at all. How embarrassed she was that most of her friends already had their periods and wore bras. And how she got a funny feeling inside when she looked at Will Jensen. There was a part of her—a very big part—that just wanted to go back to being summer friends with him, the way they'd been the previous year.

At the end of the day, the sunset turned everything to pure gold, and people aimed their cameras to the horizon, trying to capture the brilliant image. The colors melded like spilled liquid as the sun sank lower. A group of kids sat together on the sand, goofing off and talking about their plans for the season.

"I have to work at the restaurant this summer," Caroline said mournfully. "My sisters both did it, and now it's my turn." She wrinkled her nose. "Bussing tables and washing dishes. Yuck. I made a big stink about it, but it's the family business and I have to do my part." She echoed the lecture her parents had given her when laying down the law.

"I got a job, too," Will said. "Part-time at Scoops."

"That's cool. I love their ice cream."

"Me too. Plus the owner said the tips can really add up. I'm saving my money to buy my own surfboard back home."

She wondered what his dad would say about that. Did Mr. Jensen still insist that the ocean was for work, not play? "So the surfing's good down there?"

"It is. I've been practicing."

"I could tell today. You're getting really good." She sighed, leaning back on her elbows and tracking the flight of a seagull across the water. He was good at everything. Probably even math. "Hey, ever seen a green flash when the sun sets?" she asked him.

"A green flash?" He frowned, shook his head.

"It's a thing you can sometimes see the moment the sun goes down. Not always, but on really clear days like today, the light separates out into different colors when it passes through the atmosphere." She grinned at his expression. "Sometimes I do pay attention in science class. Maybe if we watch tonight, we'll see it."

He hooked his arms around his knees and stared at the shimmering horizon. "If it works, it'd be a new one on me."

"Don't look straight at the sun until the last second," she said.

"If I wait, I might miss it."

"Nah, I'll tell you when to look. I always look for the green flash. There's a saying that once you see it, you'll never go wrong in matters of the heart."

He snorted. "I don't see how they're connected."

Was he more sarcastic than he'd been last year? "Whatever. It's just something people say. I still look for it, though. Just in case, you know?"

A bunch of other kids joined in, lying belly down on beach blankets and facing the endless horizon. Rona

Stevens managed to wedge herself in right next to Will, but he didn't seem to notice.

As the light deepened, Caroline elbowed him. "Okay, we can start looking now. It always seems to go fast toward the end."

Everyone looked at the shrinking orb. The moment before it sank out of sight, there was a subtle glimmer of green. "There!" Caroline said. "I saw it. Did you see?"

"I think so. Yeah, I saw the green."

"Cool. You'll never go wrong in matters of the heart, then."

"I don't know anything about that."

She felt silly and happy, just hanging out with him. "Me neither." They stood, gathering up towels and blankets, shaking out the sand and loading up the surfboards and boogie boards. Will was supposed to meet his grandfather in the beach parking lot. Caroline was getting a ride home with Georgia, who drove their dad's truck like a pro—according to Georgia.

"How's California?" she asked, trying to picture him like the kids in *90210.*

"Pretty good. Not as nice as here, though." He leaned his board next to the outdoor shower. With no hesitation at all, he peeled his shirt one-handed over his head and lifted his face to the spray.

She tried not to stare at his bare chest, and the way his swim trunks hung at the very edges of his hip bones. "And your dad likes his shore duty?"

He finished quickly and slung a towel around his neck. "Guess so. He's got a girlfriend now. I think he's going to marry her."

"Oh! So is that good news, or . . . ?"

"It's okay, I guess. Her name's Shasta and she works on base. She's pretty nice. A lot younger than Dad, which is kind of weird. I think she's only, like, fifteen years older than me."

Caroline tried to imagine her dad with someone other than Mom. It was impossible. There was no way she could picture someone coming into their house and taking charge of things. "Does she have other kids?"

"Nope. I overheard them talking about having another kid, which is why I think they're going to get married." He studied the color-drenched clouds blooming on the horizon. "Dad never talks about my mom. Sometimes it's like she never even existed."

Caroline hated dishwashing detail so much she felt like crying. The tubs of gloppy used dishes flowed into her area in a never-ending stream of greasy gray tubs, waiting for her to hose everything down with hot water. Her supervisor, Mike, was a total lazybones who spent more time in the loading area with his cigarettes than he did in the kitchen. Georgia and Virginia were waiting tables and seeming to love every minute of it. Yet Caroline knew that even if she got a promotion to hostessing or waitressing, she'd still hate it. Her four-hour morning shift seemed endless.

After just a couple of weeks, she sat down with her mother and said, "I can't take it anymore."

"Sweetie, you're just getting started."

"I want to help, Mom. You know I do. But dishwashing is killing my soul."

"Yikes. Sounds serious."

"Mom."

"All right. I'm sorry. I should know better than to argue with your feelings. What's on your mind, Miss Caroline?"

"I have a proposal to make. How about instead of the restaurant, I find a job doing something else?"

"You can't work anywhere but in a family business until you're fourteen."

"I'm almost fourteen. And Mrs. Bloom said she needs help in the fabric shop and she'd pay me under the table until I'm old enough. I love it there, Mom. Please."

"Oh, Caroline."

She held her breath. When Mom said, *Oh, Caroline,* like that, it meant she was softening.

"Can I just try? And if it doesn't work out, I'll come back to the restaurant. I promise."

"Your sisters love the restaurant. You'll be waiting tables before you know it."

"I love the restaurant, too. Just not working there. *Please.* Mrs. Bloom said I can get a discount on fabric, too. And you know how much fabric I buy."

"I do know. You've made some wonderful things, Caroline."

"I'll make even more wonderful things if you let me work at the shop." She still remembered walking into Lindy's for the first time. She'd been in third grade, and for some reason her mom had sent her there to get a card of buttons. Caroline had returned hours later, having spent her entire allowance on notions, thread, and fat quarters—precut pieces of cotton fabric. She had raced to her room with her treasures and immediately set to work fashioning an outfit for her American Girl doll. Even though her scissors were blunt and she sewed by hand rather than machine, the garment she'd made was a thing of beauty. Caroline was so proud of it that she'd taken it to Mrs. Bloom, who said unequivocally that it showed promise.

After that, Caroline found any excuse to go to the shop, captivated by the array of fabrics and the long metal drawers with patterns lined up like maps to El

Dorado. The hand-drawn illustrations on the envelopes haunted her dreams. All of her school notebooks were filled with drawings of clothes, everything from ball gowns to boleros.

Mom hesitated. "I'll give Lindy a call . . ."

Caroline threw her arms around her mother. "You're the best! You won't be sorry."

"No," said Mom, her face soft with understanding. "I won't be."

Caroline jumped on her bike and raced into town to tell Will the news. Behind the glass-front freezers at the ice cream parlor, he looked both ridiculous and cute in a white shirt with a button-down collar, striped apron, and goofy peaked paper hat. "My mom said okay! I don't have to wash dishes anymore. I can work at the fabric shop, right across the street."

"Sounds good," he said. "Hey, would you like to—"

"Hi, Will!" A cluster of girls burst into the shop, led by Rona Stevens.

Like to what? Caroline ground her teeth in irritation. He was just about to ask her . . . what? If she'd like to go to the movies? Hike to the top of the Willapa Hills? Get pizza? What?

She'd never know because the shop was now infested with cheerleaders. Rona and her friends were all about the short shorts and candy-colored lip gloss and giant hair bows that looked like an extra appendage. "We need ice cream. Screaming for it. Oh, hiya, Caroline."

"Hi, yourself." For some reason, Caroline always felt inadequate around Rona. She was famous for having made out with a high school junior—a guy who called himself Hakon, for some reason—at a Tolo dance last year. Supposedly Hakon was her boyfriend, but that didn't stop her from flirting with Will.

"What's the flavor du jour?" she asked, leaning toward the case until her boobs practically touched the glass.

"Cranberry crunch," Will said, seemingly oblivious to her boobs-first pose. "Want a taste?" He handed each of the cheerleaders a tiny plastic spoonful. He offered one to Caroline, but she shook her head.

"No, thanks. I know what I want."

"The usual?"

"Yep, you got it."

He dug out a scoop of sea salt caramel fudge and expertly seated it on a waffle cone. Caroline counted out her money and slid it across the counter. The other girls insisted on tasting all the flavors. Eventually, with an excess of giggling, they ordered their selections. Caroline was annoyed at how flirty they were being, but Will didn't seem to mind. Rona made a show of adding a hefty tip to the jar on the counter.

"We're heading to the go-kart track," she said to him. "Want to come after you're done here?"

He wiped the marble counter. "Can't. I promised my granddad a round of cribbage tonight."

"What's cribbage?" Rona cocked her head. "Sounds scary."

"It's his favorite game." Will grinned in friendly fashion. "Thanks, though. Maybe another time."

"Definitely another time." She flicked a dismissive glance over Caroline. "See you later, kids."

After they left, Caroline perched on a stool and watched him finish wiping up. "What's high school in California like?" she asked him.

He looked up briefly. "I went to a DoD school in Guam, so a regular public high school seems really different."

"In a good way? Or were there bullies like the ones you had to fight in Guam?"

"There are bullies everywhere, but none of them bothered me."

"Do you still study Krav Maga?"

"Yeah, my dad and I do it together. His girlfriend, Shasta, said we should have something we do as father and son. I went out for football and track at my new school." He studied her for a moment. "What's up? You nervous about starting high school?"

She nodded glumly. "I'm not really good at anything.

I make straight B's. I'm only medium-good at sports. I play second-chair clarinet—like *that's* a thing. Plus school starts a half hour earlier and I am *so* not a morning person." She licked the perimeter of her ice cream cone until she realized he was staring at her. "What?"

"You're better at surfing than anyone I know."

"You must not know many people."

"Come on. What's your superpower? My mom used to say everybody's got a superpower."

Caroline puffed up a little. "Okay, here's something. I'm really good at sewing. I can sew like the wind."

"Sewing, like with a needle and thread?"

"On a machine, too. My life's goal is to get an industrial single-needle machine. Mrs. Bloom lets me use hers. That's why I'm so excited about working at her shop. I get to use her machines." She jumped down off the stool and modeled her shorts. "Check it out. I made these from my own pattern."

"Cool." His gaze lingered on the shorts, and then his cheeks reddened.

"Anyway," Caroline said, feeling a blush of her own coming on, "how is this going to make high school any easier? Am I going to get through high school by sewing and surfing?"

"Probably not, but at least you'll be doing something you like."

Chapter 16

Working at the fabric shop was heaven compared to dishwashing hell. Caroline loved everything about it, even the nitpicky paperwork and the customers who messed up displays without buying anything.

"Here you go," Mrs. Bloom said at the end of the week. "Your first paycheck."

"Thank you." Caroline didn't even look at the amount. She would be willing to work here for free, truth be told. Mrs. Bloom was one of her favorite people, always happy to show her sewing techniques, from ways to improve fit to using the industrial machine and the serger. She was always totally cheerful with her customers, but every once in a while, a shadow would come over her, like maybe she thought of something bad or sad.

Just before closing time, Caroline saw her standing at the front counter, gazing out the window with a faraway look in her eyes. "Everything okay, Mrs. Bloom?"

"Oh! You startled me, Caroline."

"Sorry. I . . . Can you help me with something in the back? I already clocked out. I was working on a raincoat for Wendell."

"Wendell?"

"My dog. He's getting old, and he hates going out in the rain."

"That's very thoughtful of you," said Mrs. Bloom. "How can I help?"

"I'm having trouble with the fit." In the back room, Caroline showed her the project. For her dress form, she had a stuffed toy about the size of Wendell. "See, it's awful, and it's not going to stay on."

Mrs. Bloom studied the garment, and now the expression on her face was not faraway at all, but intensely curious. "Well," she said, "I always encourage you to experiment with design and construction."

"I know, but I worked and worked, and what's the point?" Caroline scowled at the coat, which buckled at all the wrong places. The fabric choice—a print with fire hydrants—now seemed cheesy.

Mrs. Bloom pinned a couple of seams. "I bet you figured out a few things."

"Yeah, like don't use a fabric with a one-way pattern."

"Then your effort wasn't wasted. The best way to learn is to fail." She locked the back door and they headed toward the front.

Caroline nodded. "I'm well on my way, then."

"Don't be afraid to fail. You just have to fail better every time," said Mrs. Bloom with a grin as she turned on the security system. "I have a book of new fall patterns coming tomorrow. Maybe you'd like to do up a few for displays."

"Are you kidding? I would *love* that." She looked around the shop, dim and quiet now. "I totally love making things," she said. "My mom says it's my *passion*."

"Moms are usually right about such things."

"Well, I have no idea why I like it so much. I just know that when I'm making something, I'm totally happy."

"That's lovely, Caroline. I like that sentiment."

"My mom says the secret to the restaurant's success is the family philosophy that fixing tasty food is a way to show love. So do you think it's the same as making things to wear?"

"A way to show love?" Mrs. Bloom's eyes softened and crinkled at the edges. "Another lovely sentiment. And I think you're absolutely right."

Caroline and Will almost never called each other on the phone. Some kids had mobile phones, the kind that fit in a pocket and flipped open, but Caroline didn't. And even if she did, she doubted she'd be any more inclined to call him. So instead of calling to see if he was home, she went to see him at Water's Edge.

She jumped off her bike and ran toward him. He was over by the barn, wearing a tool belt and pounding away at something. He and his grandfather were forever doing projects or fixing things around the place. "Whatcha doing?" she asked him.

"Skateboard ramp," he said. "Check it out." He jumped up, unbuckled the tool belt, and grabbed his board. "It's not done yet, but . . ." He skated the board along the driveway and popped up onto the homemade ramp. Almost immediately, he caught an edge and went flying, landing flat on his back.

Caroline bolted toward him and sank down to the ground. "Hey, are you okay?"

He slowly picked himself up. A livid road rash slashed across one elbow and one knee. "Dang," he said, inspecting the damage. "That hurts."

"We should go inside and clean it up."

He shook his head. "My grandmother would freak out because I'm not wearing a helmet and pads. I'll clean up with the hose." He wobbled a little, trying to stand up.

She stuck out her hand and he steadied himself as he climbed to his feet. Just for a second, he lurched into her, practically hugging her. He smelled of asphalt and grass and sweat, and she let go quickly, feeling flustered. "Helmet and pads. Maybe your grandmother's onto something."

He turned on the water at the spigot and hosed off the scrapes, wincing in pain. "Maybe," he said. "The ramp is pretty rad, though. I like making stuff. My granddad says I should live here when I'm grown, on account of I'm his only grandchild and he wants to keep it in the family."

"Here?" She shaded her eyes and squinted at the big painted house. "Are you gonna do it?"

"Maybe. It'd be cool, right?"

She didn't reply. She often dreamed of another life, far from the peninsula—Paris or Hong Kong or New York or Milan, someplace fashion designers worked. "I made something, too," she said after he'd rinsed off. "It's for you." She pulled it out of her backpack. "For Luau Night."

The event seemed to get bigger every year. It was one of the Booster Club's most popular summer fundraisers. Her parents chaired the event, a full-on night of Hawaiian music, tiki torches, hula dances, and traditional food. There was even a pig roast, which was gross, but people loved it. For the past twenty-four hours, guys had been tending the meat as it roasted in the ground. At the appointed hour, the feasting would begin at the beachfront park.

He held the garment out in front of him. "You made this?"

"Every stitch. And one for Duffy, too." She handed him the matching tiny shirt. "Wendell has one, too. Once I got started, I couldn't stop. The fabric's called modern barkcloth."

He looked clueless. Most people, especially most boys, didn't really care about fabric types.

"Okay, then," he said. "Well, thanks."

"No problem. Anyway," she said, "you don't have to wear it. Totally up to you."

He wore the shirt. Caroline couldn't believe he wore the shirt. He showed up at the luau with his grandparents, and he wore the shirt unbuttoned and floating open, over a *Go Navy* T-shirt and dark blue board shorts.

Tiki torches lined the walkway to the food pavilion, and hula music filled the air. Will joined a few of the older kids who worked at Scoops, and eventually made his way to the long tables skirted with fake grass. All the Shelbys pitched in, serving up fruity drinks, appetizers that her brothers proudly told everyone were called pu pu platters, and platters of grilled fish and veggies.

Most of the kids hadn't bothered to dress Hawaiian, but nearly all the adult guys wore aloha shirts and the women wore muumuus and sported flowers in their hair. Caroline had gone full native, as her sisters put it, wearing a lei of orchids around her neck and a string of kukui nuts around one ankle, and even coloring her hair jet black with temporary color. Ever since she was little, she'd loved any occasion to dress up like something other than who she was.

Other people noticed Will, too—namely, Rona Stevens. She wore a grass skirt and coconut bra and a crown of silk flowers. Even to Caroline, she looked amazing. She and her friends from the cheering squad were doing some approximation of hula dancing and were laughing at their efforts. Moving her hips from side to side in comical fashion, Rona sidled over to Will.

"Hey, surfer boy," she said. "You look cool in that shirt."

"Are you being sarcastic?" he asked her.

"Of course not." She planted herself in front of him, arms akimbo. "Do I look like I'm being sarcastic?"

"Guess not. Caroline made it." He spotted her and waved her over.

"No way. That's incredible." Rona reached out and gently touched the collar, her hand lingering there. "Good job, Caroline."

A big kid pushed into their midst. It was Rona's boyfriend, Hakon, who inserted himself between them and nudged Will on the shoulder.

"Jeez, Hakon," Rona exclaimed, stepping back. "What the hell?"

Caroline stopped breathing. Hakon was a big deal on the high school football team, and he had a reputation as a hothead.

"Nothing," said Hakon, keeping his eyes on Will. "Just wondering what's up with the kid in the pansy-ass shirt."

Will didn't flinch as he gazed calmly at the bigger boy. "It's a shirt, is all."

"Makes you look like a pansy."

"Gimme a break." Will tried to brush past him.

Hakon stood in his path, planting himself like an old-growth tree—wide and immovable. "Not so fast, pretty boy."

Will laughed—a genuine laugh. "You're kidding, right? 'Pretty boy'?"

"I'll mess you up, pretty boy," Hakon said.

"Come on," Rona said, taking hold of his arm. "Let's go get something to eat."

Hakon shook her off, the sudden movement both startling and disturbing.

Will dropped the good-humored facade. "Hey, I don't know you, man. I don't know why you're ticked off at me. Whatever it is, get over it. I'm going to walk away now."

Good for you, Caroline thought. He'd once told her the best defense is to not get in a fight at all.

Hakon didn't seem to get it, though. "Yeah? Gonna run to your mama?" Hakon feinted to one side, nudging Will's shoulder.

Caroline took in her breath with a gasp. Rona receded back into her group of friends, all her flirty confidence dissolving.

Will quickly stepped away. When Hakon followed him again, he said what was probably the one thing that would make Will forget his no-fighting rule. "Yeah, go run to your mama. She's probably giving hand jobs out behind the tav—"

Will struck like a bolt of lightning, so quick that Caroline nearly missed it. Hakon was suddenly flat on his back and Will was above him, forearm pressed against the bigger boy's neck. Hakon's face was bright red, and his eyes bulged with panic.

More kids came running, forming a small crowd. Caroline was close enough to hear Will say, "I'm going to walk away now. Don't be stupid." And with that, he got up and turned away, walking toward the banquet tables without looking back.

Hakon scrambled up, his face still the color of a tomato, his chest heaving. He made a move to follow, but then checked himself.

"Come on," Rona said. "Let it go."

He waved her away with a violent motion of his arm. At the same moment, he pivoted and walked in the opposite direction from Will.

For the third time, Caroline had to remind herself to breathe.

Mom woke Caroline and Virginia early one morning in late August. She almost never did this, because Virginia had been working dinner service and was allowed to sleep in. So when Mom came into their room and whispered their names, Caroline knew something was up.

The morning light through the dormer window made Mom look haggard and distressed. Georgia slipped in behind her and got into bed with Caroline.

"What's wrong?" Virginia asked, her voice raspy with dread.

"It's Wendell," said Mom. "He left us last night. Died in his sleep."

No.

Wendell.

Caroline felt as if everything inside her emptied out completely, an invisible pool of shock at her feet. And then, with the next breath she took in, she filled up with the worst hurt she'd ever felt. Pulling her knees up to her chest, she stretched her nightgown over them and hugged herself tight.

Wendell. Poor old Wendell. Her good, good boy Wendell. That dog had been part of her life every single day she'd been in the world, because her parents had rescued the little guy as a puppy a month before she was born.

And now he was gone. Forever. She'd never again hear his funny bark or feel his scruffy warm fur. She'd never feed him salmonberries from her hand or whisper her troubles into his little floppy ear.

Elsewhere in the house, she could hear her brothers wailing. Apparently Dad was breaking the news to them.

"What happened?" Virginia asked between hiccupping sobs. "Did he get sick?"

Georgia buried her face in her arms.

"He was following me around the yard yesterday," Caroline whispered, her throat on fire with grief. "He bothered the chickens, same as he always does."

Mom nodded and blew her nose in a tissue. "Dad heard him wheezing in the middle of the night, you know, how he started doing lately. Last night, the wheezing didn't stop, so we just held him close until he was gone."

"Why didn't you wake me?" Caroline said, pushing the words out past the tears. "I never got to say good-bye."

"Dad and I were too sad to do anything but hold him," Mom said. "We wanted to let him go in peace. I'm so, so sorry, my girls."

"Where is he?" Caroline demanded.

"He's on his bed in the laundry room, wrapped in his plaid blanket."

Caroline finally knew what a breaking heart felt like. It was the worst thing ever. The walls of the room felt heavy and close. She jumped out of bed and yanked on a pair of shorts and a T-shirt. "I'm going for a bike ride," she said.

"Be careful, sweetie," said Mom. "Wear your helmet."

On her way out the door, Caroline stopped at Wendell's bed. The unmoving pile of blankets with a swatch of fur peeking out shattered her into a million pieces.

She knelt down and put out her hand. The absence of warmth or response of any sort made the emptiness yawn wider. "Oh, Wendell," she said. "You'll always be my first best friend. Bye, my good, good boy."

She ran outside and jumped on her bike, riding as fast and hard as she could—so fast her breath came in great gasping sobs. She took the winding trail up to North Head lighthouse, pushing herself to the top in record time. This early in the morning, there were only a few hikers milling around.

She ditched her bike by the safety fence and slipped through to the other side, passing the coast guard warning sign. Skirting the eroding rocky slope, she made her way to an outcropping that reached toward the exploding shoreline. The surf was big today, the white waves throwing spray high into the air, and it suited her mood to just sit there and cry and think of all the ways she would miss Wendell. He was silly and full of mischief and completely useless for anything other than cuddling and entertainment. He had yucky breath and sandy paws, and when he was wet, he shook all over everything.

And he was the best dog in the world, the best dog that had ever lived, and she didn't know how she would go on without him.

She sat on the rock ledge for a long time, damp and shivering from the spray, folding all the memories she could into her heart. At some point, she heard the crunch of footsteps on the path.

Will sat down beside her and said, "I figured I'd find you here."

She couldn't even look at him. She could only stare out at the horizon, hazy with the morning fog and blurred by her tears.

"Your mom told me about Wendell," he said. "I'm sorry."

His very soft and very kind *I'm sorry* released another flood of tears, and she didn't even bother wiping them away. He put his hand on her shoulder. Then he scooted closer and slid his arm around her, and something burst inside her, causing her to melt into her grief. It all came out in a final rush of pain, lasting only seconds and then clearing like the marine layer before her.

She fell completely still for about three beats of her heart as her rational mind stepped in. Will Jensen had his arm around her, and it gave her the most amazing feeling, so amazing that she felt disloyal to Wendell, because the feeling was even stronger than her sadness.

She shifted a little and looped her hands around her drawn-up knees. "I never felt so sad about something in my life."

His arm slipped away, but he stayed close, his shoulder almost touching hers. He stared out at the horizon. The rearing waves boomed and shattered against the rocks. "Yeah," he said. "It sucks."

She dried her face on her sleeve. She'd done what her sisters called the "ugly cry"—the one that contorted her face and made it all red and blotchy. But Will didn't seem to notice, and she didn't care.

"When your mom died, it must have felt ten times worse," she said.

He didn't say anything for several moments. "Sad is sad."

She nodded, resting her chin on her knees. "I wish we could have them both back. I wish we could have them forever."

Something happened the day Wendell died. Something between Caroline and Will. They were the same together, running around, riding their bikes, spending long, lazy days at the beach, listening to music, and laughing at nothing. But that morning, when he found her alone and so sad, a seismic shift occurred. It felt as if she and Will knew each other in a different way.

They never discussed that moment together, but she thought about it constantly.

She went to bed each night thinking of him, and he was her first thought on waking in the morning. Every vision she had of her life included him. He talked about living at Water's Edge when he grew up, and she considered what that might be like, instead of Milan or Hong Kong.

She constantly pictured what he was doing at any given moment. She noticed things like the way he rolled his sleeves back when he wore his work uniform at the ice cream parlor. Or how he whistled tunelessly between his teeth when he was doing something like waxing his surfboard. Each time she saw him, she got butterflies in her stomach.

She didn't understand the feelings inside her. It was an entirely unfamiliar set of emotions, ones she didn't even have a name for. Not happiness or sadness, but a wild combination of everything and more. He seemed like somebody she had known all her life, and at the same time, he seemed like someone completely new to her.

It was all so confusing that she kept her thoughts entirely to herself. If she said something, he'd probably look at her with a quirked brow and tell her she was nuts.

On the last night of summer, after the Rotary picnic, she found him helping with the cleanup detail. Sunset had deepened into twilight, and the almost-full moon was on the rise. Will was hauling one of the recycling bins on a hand truck toward the beach parking lot.

"Hey," she said, falling in step with him. A flock of butterflies stirred in her stomach.

"Hey."

"So you're flying home tomorrow," she said unnecessarily.

"I am." He slid the bin off the hand truck and lined it up with the other ones. "Leaving first thing in the morning for the airport."

"Okay, then." She glanced around the parking lot. People were heading to their cars, parents carrying sleepy toddlers, kids dragging their beach toys and towels. "Is your dad giving you a ride home tonight?"

Will shook his head quickly. "I have my bike."

"Me too," she said. "Hey, we could ride as far as my house together. I mean, if that's—"

"Sure," he said. "Good idea. Let's go."

The moon, fully risen now, illuminated the deserted road, augmenting the light from their bike headlamps. Invisible frogs sang and fell silent in a constant chorus from the marshes. The ride to her house seemed way too fast, and even though she talked the whole time, she felt as if there was so much more to say. They stopped at the end of her driveway, marked by the homemade mailbox embedded with shells and sea glass.

She stopped there and got off her bike, and he did the same. Normally, Wendell would notice and come running down the drive, barking his fool head off. The silence now was a painful reminder of just how gone he was.

"Guess I'll see you when you come back next summer, right?" she asked Will, unclipping her helmet and hanging it on the handlebar. Her stomach was in knots. She already missed him.

"Right," he said. "I love coming here. Wish I could stay year-round."

"It's really different in the winter. Super dark. Storms nearly every day."

He hesitated, staring down at her, the moonlight soft on his face. "I can handle storms," he said quietly. Then he, too, took off his bike helmet.

She couldn't stop staring at his mouth. "Okay," she said, her voice soft with uncertainty.

"Okay," he repeated. "Guess it's goodbye for now." Then his hand touched hers and took hold. His other hand brushed the hair from her cheek.

She was startled into motionless shock. In a flash of movement, he bent and touched his lips to hers. It was brief and sweet and a bit clumsy, the way their heads didn't quite tilt at the same time. And the fireworks inside nearly knocked her over.

"Bye," he said, taking a step back. He took another step back and stumbled a little, then laughed at himself. "See you next year."

She was too dumbstruck to reply, so she just stood there like a statue as he put his helmet on and rode away into the night. She watched until the shadows swallowed him and the glow from his headlight disappeared.

Then she floated to the house, not feeling the ground beneath her feet.

Will Jensen had kissed her.

Will Jensen had kissed her.

Will Jensen had kissed her.

The world would never be the same.

And in that moment she knew, she just knew, that he would always be a part of her life, no matter what. They would always be friends, sharing everything, even if they were apart when he went away during the school year. He promised he would always come back, every summer. Their friendship would never change. Nothing—and no one—would come between them.

Chapter 17

At the start of the school year, while Caroline was fidgeting in church and contemplating the perils of the next grade, a miracle occurred. Not *that* kind of miracle, but the kind that made going back to school bearable.

Oceanside Congregational Church got a new pastor. *He* wasn't the miracle, either. His daughter, Sierra, was. Caroline took one look at Sierra Moore and knew they were going to be best friends. They were the same age, and according to the church bulletin that had arrived in the mail with a story about the new pastor and his family, Sierra was in her grade.

When Sierra and her parents stood to be introduced to the congregation, a palpable murmur rippled like a gust of fresh air through the rows of pews. Sierra was what Caroline's sisters would call drop-dead gorgeous. She had incredible red hair, pale skin, and ruby red lips. She had poise, too, regarding the sanctuary with a calm gaze and a slight smile. She was really tall, too, with model-perfect proportions—narrow hips and straight posture—and an actual sense of style. This was rare among the girls Caroline knew. Most of them stuck to cheap, trendy stuff from the discount stores. By contrast, Sierra was wearing a designer dress, low-heeled sandals that matched her belt—but not too perfectly—and a touch of makeup. *Makeup.* In *church.* It was like seeing a unicorn—thrilling and rare.

They were going to be best friends. Caroline just knew it.

She wasted no time getting to know the new girl. The moment services ended, she made a beeline to Sierra's side. Mr. and Mrs. Moore were standing near the coffee service, greeting parishioners like a pair of royals, which in a small town they kind of were. Sierra stood slightly apart, one hand resting on a perfect little clutch bag on a gold chain, the other holding a bottle of water. A few of the boys were already edging close, checking her out, but in that dorky boy way, shoving and punching one another and snickering. Like *that* was going to impress her.

"I'm Caroline," she said, elbowing past Kevin Pilcher, who was rolling up his shirt to demonstrate an armpit fart. "Don't mind those guys. They're idiots. I'm not. And we're going to be in the same grade. Probably even the same homeroom—*M* through *Z.* I really like your outfit." Stop babbling, Caroline told herself. Take a breath.

Sierra's gaze was guarded for about two seconds. Then she smiled. "Thanks. I like yours, too. That's a really cool skirt."

Caroline stood up a little straighter. "I made it."

A frown quirked Sierra's brow. "You mean, like, you sewed it?"

"Yep. I sew all the time, all kinds of things, mostly my own designs."

"No way."

"Way."

"That is seriously impressive. I love clothes so much, but I wouldn't know the first thing about making them."

"I'm still learning myself. Maybe one of these days we could design something together."

Sierra beamed, her expression brighter than the sun. "How about we do *everything* together?"

Caroline grinned at her. "It's a deal."

That was pretty much what they did, starting that very day. Caroline introduced Sierra to her friends and family, showing her the charms and foibles of small-town life. Sierra had grown up in Southern California, so moving to the Washington coast was a big change for her. Caroline was intrigued by Sierra's life—the only child, adored and indulged by attentive parents.

"Being a one-and-done is not all it's cracked up to be," Sierra often declared when Caroline expressed envy. "When I get in trouble, there's never anyone else to blame."

"If you don't have brothers and sisters," Caroline would point out, "there are fewer ways to get in trouble."

"But more people to blame," Sierra countered.

The first week of school was a whirlwind of trying to figure out schedules and lockers and extracurricular activities. Caroline, of course, picked Sewing Circle, which Lindy Bloom had organized. Rona Stevens tried to convince Sierra to try out for JV cheerleading. Apparently it was clear even to Rona that Sierra was the most important new student in school that year. Caroline held her breath, praying Sierra wouldn't go for it.

"I'm not really any good at jumps and gymnastics," Sierra confessed.

"There are tons of cheers that are mostly clapping and rhythm," Rona assured her.

"I don't know . . ."

"The bus trips are super fun. All the cutest boys are on the football team, too."

"I'll let you know," Sierra said, as smooth and diplomatic as her father at a Sunday social. "The outfits are really cute."

When Rona was out of earshot, Sierra muttered, "And by *really cute,* I mean yikes."

Caroline was delighted. "So it's a no on the cheerleading."

"I'm kind of into cute boys, though," Sierra said. And she didn't even blush when she said it.

"Well," said Caroline, "who isn't?"

"Do you have a boyfriend?" Sierra asked.

"What?" Caroline was taken aback. She thought about last summer's kiss—the moonlight, the hand brushing her hair from her cheek, the touch of his lips against hers . . . The whole thing had lasted maybe a few seconds, but ever since, she'd spent hours thinking about it. Too many hours.

"No," she said. "I mean, there are dances and stuff. I've hung out with boys at school, but they're just friends."

"Well, you're totally cute, and if you wanted a boyfriend, you'd have one," Sierra said.

"So . . ." It was on the tip of her tongue to tell Sierra about Will Jensen, but she didn't, mostly because she had no idea how to talk about that moment.

There was either way too much to tell or nothing at all to be said.

Saying nothing seemed safer.

Thanks to her friendship with Sierra, school was more fun than Caroline could have imagined. The peak event of the year was the annual spring banquet, an extravagant affair that gave students a chance to dress up and act like almost-grown-ups. This tradition dated back to who knew when; kids' parents all reminisced about the celebration. A volunteer committee worked for months to come up with the theme, the menu, and the music.

"'The Awesome Eighties'?" Sierra studied the flyer that accompanied the banquet tickets. "Seriously? Was there anything awesome about the eighties?"

"Um, blue eye shadow?" Caroline suggested. "Leg warmers? Disco music?"

"We have a design challenge, then," Sierra declared. "Our outfits need to be amazing."

"Don't worry. They will be. Let's watch some old movies and make a plan."

They went to the video store and checked out what Caroline's mom said were the classics—*Pretty in Pink*,

Sixteen Candles, Ferris Bueller's Day Off, Flashdance, Footloose, Say Anything . . . They watched them over a stormy weekend at Sierra's house, a preternaturally quiet and painfully neat home near the golf course. The girls were mesmerized by the dance tunes and torch songs, kids angsting about cars, parents, and detention.

Caroline was inspired by the bold fashions—miniskirts, huge belts, flashy jewelry, off-the-shoulder tops. She and Sierra planned and styled themselves for days in advance.

On the day of the banquet and dance, they got dressed at Caroline's house. Even though the Shelby house was ridiculously crowded, it was a better place to dress up. Sierra said her parents wouldn't approve of the skirt length, despite the colorful leggings.

"Big hair and bold makeup," Sierra said, crowding next to Caroline at the bathroom vanity. "Do we dare?"

Caroline laughed, tossing the teased ponytail that sprouted from her head. "We dare!"

Chapter 18

School finally ended for the year. Caroline knew the glorious Pacific Northwest summer would be a revelation to Sierra. The days stretched wonderfully long, with the light lingering on the horizon later and later each evening.

Caroline had convinced her parents once again that working at the fabric store was the perfect job for her. To reinforce her point, she applied her sewing skills to her mom's bottomless basket of mending she never got around to. Caroline hemmed jeans and altered blouses to fit perfectly. She replaced zippers in her brothers' favorite jackets, and even made a quilt to donate to the library auction. She left her parents no room to suggest that the restaurant would be a better choice for her.

Sierra was thrilled, too, because Caroline was working on her most challenging project to date—summer outfits for the two of them.

"I love this weather," Sierra exclaimed, bursting into the shop. "It's almost worth surviving that miserable winter." She spun around happily, admiring the array of colorful fabric bolts.

"It'll only get better from now until Labor Day," Caroline promised, reshelving bolts of quilt fabric. She was excited for her friend to experience her first summer on the peninsula. They were going to have such fun on the beach, and thanks to her job at the shop, she could go crazy making things. Sierra had turned out to be her biggest fan.

"Oh, she's right about that," Mrs. Bloom agreed, adjusting the reading glasses perched on her nose. "It's nice to see you, Sierra."

"Likewise." She executed a little curtsy, bumping into a roll of teal georgette, and it tumbled across the floor. "Oh my gosh, I'm sorry," she said, making a dive for it.

Mrs. Bloom grabbed the roll at the same time, and together, they set it on the counter. "It's fine," she said. "No harm done."

"Oh my gosh," Sierra said again. "What'd you do to your arm?"

Mrs. Bloom looked flustered as she quickly adjusted the sleeve of her sweater. "Oh, that. I banged it on the car door. I'm such a klutz, and I tend to bruise like a banana. Always have."

"Looks painful," Sierra said.

"I'm fine. Now, I need to tally up the till for the day. So if you girls want to work on your sewing in the back, go right ahead. I don't expect a rush of customers at this hour."

"Are you sure?" Caroline really wanted to finish the dress she was making for Sierra. She'd already finished her own, and it had turned out great. But Sierra's was going to be incredible if she got the fit just right. "I mean, if you don't need me for anything else, Mrs. Bloom."

"Go." She shooed them toward the workroom in the back of the shop. "Be creative. It does my heart good to see you girls doing so well with your sewing."

"She's the one," Sierra said loyally, nudging Caroline. "I can't wait to see the final look."

Caroline beamed with pride. As far as she was concerned, Sierra was the ideal dress model. Her patience for standing through fittings and adjustments was endless. She wasn't like Caroline's sisters, who sighed and fidgeted and made her rush through her work. Also, Sierra knew how to do makeup like a professional, and she had really good taste when it came to styling a look.

She subscribed to all the fashion magazines and studied them like the Dead Sea Scrolls.

The girls went to the small sewing studio at the back of the shop. Lindy happily shared the space with Caroline and other students who wanted to sew.

"Ooh, it's fantastic," Sierra said, inspecting the sundress on the dress form.

"We'll see. Let's get it on you."

Sierra eagerly shucked her skirt and blouse. Underneath, she wore a bikini bra and panties that would probably send her folks into a dead faint if they knew she had ordered them in secret from a lingerie catalog. She had an amazing figure, with perfect boobs—not melons so big they made her self-conscious, just the right size for her tall, slender frame. Her abs were defined by the yoga she rigorously practiced, and her hips had just the right amount of curve. She was obsessed with an Australian TV show, *Search for a Supermodel.* She recorded the show on the VCR and watched each episode again and again, practicing her signature walk and fierce expressions.

Though only six months younger than Sierra, Caroline was light-years behind. Her boobs had barely sprouted and her hips were so straight she could easily fit into her little brother's jeans. The only thing that marked her as a budding teenager was the least attractive thing about being a teenager—pimples. Yuck. Sierra, who was a genius with makeup, showed her how to cover up the spots, but Caroline was totally self-conscious, not even wanting to look in the mirror some days. Why couldn't she have been blessed, like Sierra was, with pretty, unblemished skin? And silky long hair, for that matter? Instead, she had an unruly mane scraped into a messy bun that did her no favors at all. Worse yet, she got braces this year. It was a trifecta of ugly.

She wasn't jealous of Sierra's looks, though. She was grateful to have a friend who loved fashion and looked like a model and had patience for fittings.

She helped Sierra slip the dress over her head. "Okay, lift your arms." She reached for a pincushion. "I need to fix the bodice."

"It feels amazing," Sierra said. She gamely raised her arms while Caroline made the adjustments. "I can't believe you designed this yourself, Caroline."

"Hold still," Caroline said around the pins in her mouth. She used them to make a tuck in the dress so it would mold perfectly to her body. Seeing the garment on her friend, she was totally excited, because she was pretty sure it was going to be the best thing she'd ever designed. "Okay," she said, "don't scratch yourself on these pins."

"It's cool you get to use all of Mrs. Bloom's gear," Sierra said, looking around the well-organized space: a wall of spools in every color of thread, original patterns hanging from clips, drawers of notions, jars of buttons and embellishments.

"Totally cool. My parents freaked out when I told them I want to work here for the summer again instead of the restaurant. They just don't get why I'm not obsessed with the restaurant the way my sisters are." She spoke in a joking tone, but the truth was, it bugged her that her parents didn't even try to understand how much she wanted to learn to design and make things. They seemed to think it was some passing fancy, like the time Virginia was dead set on getting a horse of her own. They had cured Virginia of the desire by having her work at Beachside Stables, taking care of the horses for tourists to ride on the beach. The plan worked. After a few weeks of cleaning stalls, picking hooves, and scraping horse sweat, Virginia was ready to hang up her spurs.

In Caroline's case, the plan backfired. Even though she started out working at the lowest level in Lindy Bloom's shop, sweeping the floor, shelving bolts of fabric, and filing patterns, she couldn't wait to get to the shop each day. Instead of getting sick of the chores, Caroline only wanted to do more. She felt happy every minute she was making things.

She finished marking the back seams of the dress with a flat piece of tailor's chalk. "Okay, I'll finish it up for you real quick."

"Cool." Sierra peeled off the dress and handed it over. Still in her underwear, she browsed through the samples hanging on a rolling rack. She was totally unselfconscious. Totally poised. Caroline had no idea what that must feel like.

She sat down at Mrs. Bloom's machine, which she coveted with every fiber of her being. This was the real deal. Not a home crafting machine like most women had stashed away in a closet somewhere, but an industrial wonder. She was saving up for one of her own, though even a secondhand machine cost the moon.

Feeling herself vibrate along with the hum of the motor, she finished altering the dress and then Sierra put it back on, smoothing her hands down the sheer cotton fabric, an unusual print of hand-drawn arrows. "It feels great," she said.

"The fit is just right," Caroline declared, positioning her in front of the cheval mirror. "Check it out."

Sierra put on her wedge sandals, which made her even taller, and studied her reflection. "Oh, Caroline . . ."

"Let's see," said Mrs. Bloom, joining them. "Oh, Caroline," she echoed, "that's really something. What a lovely, unusual dress. So beautifully cut and sewn. I thought the fabric choice was risky, but with that tonal wash and the lining . . . Wow. Good job."

"Thanks." Caroline beamed with pride.

"Is that a *Vogue* pattern?"

Caroline and Sierra exchanged a glance. Sierra twirled in front of the mirror and said, "No, ma'am. This is a Caroline Shelby original."

Mrs. Bloom inspected it further. "Wonderful work. Who knew I had a designer and a fit model right here in my shop?"

The girls couldn't stop grinning as they looked at each other. "Thanks, Mrs. Bloom," Caroline said.

Sierra fanned herself. "It's still really hot out. We should hit the beach."

Caroline glanced at Mrs. Bloom. "I need to stay and help close up."

"Nonsense." Mrs. Bloom made a shooing motion with her hands. "I'll close."

"Well, thank you." Caroline hesitated. "Um, would you like to come out to the beach for a bit?" Sometimes Mrs. Bloom seemed lonely, like she could use some fun in her life.

"It's nice of you to ask, but no. I need to run along and fix dinner for Mr. Bloom." She always called her husband Mr. Bloom, like he was her boss or something. He was a VIP at the bank, so maybe he liked being called Mr. Bloom.

"See you later, then," said Caroline.

"I imagine the two of you are looking forward to wearing your new things to the clambake tomorrow," she said.

"You bet," Caroline said. She'd made a cool outfit for herself, too. It was another original design—a wraparound utiliskirt with pockets and grommets for everything. She needed a lot of pockets because according to her mom, she was a magpie, collecting every shiny thing that caught her eye. It wasn't as dramatic as Sierra's dress, but it suited Caroline and would do just fine for the clambake.

The clambake was the official kickoff to summer, one of many celebrations that took place each year on the peninsula. There would be food and music and games on the beach—pure heaven. Some people said, only half joking, that if not for all the festivals, nothing would ever happen here. This one was sponsored by a coalition of local churches to benefit youth services.

When she thought of summer, Caroline's mind flitted automatically to Will Jensen. It seemed like forever since she'd seen him. It *was* forever. An entire school year had passed. She assumed he was coming to spend another summer with his grandparents, but she wasn't sure. The two of them didn't stay in touch during the school year. She didn't know why. Probably because they were summer best friends, and the rest of the time they lived totally different lives. She sometimes saw his grandparents in church, but she never asked them about Will. She didn't want to seem too eager. Or like she cared too much, which she totally did.

She was still amazed that he'd kissed her goodbye—a real, actual kiss, which was pretty much the best thing that had ever happened to her in her entire life. She thought about it all the time. So when she and Sierra ran into Mrs. Jensen walking Duffy on the boardwalk that day, she felt a guilty start, as if she'd been caught doing something wrong.

"Oh," she said, flustered. "Hi there, Mrs. J.!" She hastily introduced Sierra to Will's grandmother.

Mrs. Jensen offered a smile. "It's nice to see you, Caroline. I was just thinking of you."

Whoa. "You were?"

"We're going down to Portland to get Will from the airport tomorrow," she said.

Caroline's heart stuttered. *Tomorrow.*

"Um, that's, um, that's great, Mrs. J."

"I'm sure he's eager to see you again." Mrs. Jensen winked. "The two of you always have such a wonderful time when he comes for the summer."

We do? She swallowed hard. Oh my God, what had he told her?

"He'll be at the clambake, I imagine. He wouldn't want to miss that."

"Also great." Caroline was sure her face had turned a dozen shades of scarlet. "Well, see you around, Mrs. J.!" She scuttled away, veering off the boardwalk to the beach path through the abundant fountains of dune grasses.

"Who's Will?" Sierra followed close behind her.

Only the most important person in my life, thought Caroline. In the world, maybe. "Oh, just a kid I know," she said, adopting a casual tone. "That's his grandmother I just spoke to."

"So does he go to our school?" Sierra persisted.

"Nope. Comes here for the summer. You heard her say he's flying into Portland."

"How come you never mentioned him before?"

Good question, thought Caroline. She shrugged. "Dunno. His grandparents have a place up the road, and he doesn't really know anybody around here, so when he comes for the summer, we hang out sometimes."

"Is he cute? Because if he's cute, I'm going to be totally jealous of you."

Caroline's cheeks burned. She forged ahead to hide the blush. She didn't understand why she was so reluctant to tell her friend everything. It was as if Will belonged to a unique, private part of her that she didn't want to share with anyone else.

"So *is* he cute?" Sierra prodded.

"I don't know. Maybe, I guess. We don't—it's not like that." Liar. Why was she lying to her best friend?

"Not like what?"

"Not like it matters whether he's cute or not." Caroline veered off the boardwalk, kicked off her sandals, and jumped down the soft sandbank to the beach. The sand felt gloriously warm under her bare feet.

"Well, that's good to know," Sierra said.

"Why's it good?"

Sierra jumped, landing in the sand next to her. "Because that way, if I get a crush on him, I won't be stealing him from you."

"How come it's called a clambake if you bury the clams in the ground?" Sierra asked. "Wouldn't that make it a clam *burial*?" They were in the downstairs bathroom at Caroline's house, getting ready for the event. They had barricaded the door against Caroline's annoying brothers, and Sierra was expertly demonstrating the way to put on makeup so it didn't look like they were wearing makeup at all.

"The clams don't really bake—they steam." Caroline leaned toward the mirror and scowled at the lone pimple on her chin, which had appeared overnight like an evil mushroom in the dark. "See, the way it works is, somebody—usually my dad or someone from the restaurant—digs a big hole in the sand, and it's lined with stones and then hot coals, and a layer of seaweed. They put in the clams and corn on the cob and little red potatoes and cover it up and it all steams together until they dig it up and serve it."

"Sounds like a lot of trouble."

"I suppose it is, but people love it. And anyway, a clambake is more about the party than the clams. It'll be totally fun. You'll see."

"Good, because I could never eat a clam." Sierra shuddered. She stepped back and examined her silhouette in the mirror, perfectly draped in the sundress Caroline had designed.

Sierra never ate much of anything, Caroline had observed. She subsisted mostly on Popsicles and diet soda and the occasional rice cake.

"The corn and potatoes are my favorites," she said. "You'll like that part."

"I'll keep that in mind. Oh my gosh." Sierra twirled in front of the mirror. "This is the nicest dress. It's one of a kind, and it fits perfectly. You're a genius—do you realize that? Total frickin' genius."

Caroline couldn't suppress a grin. "Well, I don't know about that."

"I do. You designed and made every stitch of this all by yourself. And I feel amazing in it."

"It's easy to make you look amazing," Caroline pointed out. "That's pretty much how you look when you wake up in the morning."

"Oh, huh. Nope, Tyra Banks says it takes at least two hours of hair and makeup to turn a girl into a natural beauty."

"Right. Speaking of which, how's my makeup?" She was still getting used to wearing it and had a horror of looking *too* made up.

Sierra put her finger under Caroline's chin and tipped her face to the light. "You're adorable and you hardly need a thing. Just, maybe . . ." She grabbed a brush and did a little blending. "The skirt you made for yourself is just right, too. All those cool pockets and snaps." She tucked a lip gloss into one of the pockets. "Try to remember to put a bit of lip gloss on every hour."

"Okay." Caroline wished her plain white tank top had some curves, but she was still waiting for them.

Her sisters, in a rare moment of compassion, had told her they'd been late bloomers, too. But standing next to Sierra, she felt as if the blooming would never happen. "Ready?" she asked.

"Not for clams, but I'm totally down for the party. It's going to be so much fun—I just know it."

"Are you supposed to volunteer in the Oceanside Church booth?" Caroline asked.

Sierra pursed her lips. "I promised my parents I would. My dad wants me to help sign up more kids for church youth group."

"I'll pitch in," Caroline said. "Summer youth group isn't so bad. It's more about the youth than the church, that's for sure. Minimal churchy stuff. Some of the older kids sneak away after the meetings and make out. Both my older sisters have done it."

"Now that," Sierra said, "sounds better than clams."

"I overheard my parents say that more girls get pregnant thanks to church group than sex ed class."

Sierra snickered. "At least in sex ed they tell you how *not* to get pregnant. In church group, they just say you should wait. Like *that's* going to happen."

"Exactly." Caroline decided to brush her teeth and put fresh rubber bands on her braces. They were such a pain. The orthodontist swore it would all be worth it one day. She would never understand why braces had to happen in high school, when looks seemed to matter more than life itself.

"Have you ever made out with a boy?" asked Sierra.

Caroline's tiny rubber band went flying. "No," she said quickly. Yet her mind darted instantly to that moment last summer. That kiss. It wasn't a make-out-type kiss, though. It was goodbye. But she'd lived for a whole year on that goodbye. And here was her chance to explain Will to Sierra, since she'd failed to speak up yesterday.

Her mind emptied out once again. She couldn't. She simply couldn't. "What about you?" she asked.

Sierra swished her skirt as she gave herself a final once-over in the mirror. "Sure I have. Remember Trace Kramer?"

One of the star players of the Peninsula Mariners. "You made out with Trace Kramer?"

Sierra flipped her hair back. "Under the bleachers after a football game last fall."

"You never told me about that."

She shrugged. "I didn't really like it. Mainly because I didn't really like *him.* He was pushy and sweaty, and neither of us really knew what we were doing. I'm going to have a *real* boyfriend this summer."

"Yeah? Who do you have in mind?"

"Nobody yet. I'll know him when I see him."

"Right. Like when Lizzy Bennet met Mr. Darcy for the first time?" They had read *Pride and Prejudice* in English class this year, and Caroline still dreamed about it.

"They couldn't stand each other," Sierra pointed out.

"But they felt *something.*" Boy, did they ever.

"We'll see if Mr. Darcy appears," said Sierra, putting away the bin of hair spray and makeup.

"It's about time," declared Jackson when they unlocked the bathroom door. "You guys were in there forever." Jackson was eleven years old, and the only thing more annoying than him was Austin, who was nine and not only annoying but grubby. Both boys stood in the hallway outside the bathroom, holding a dripping wet burlap bag between them.

"What the heck . . . ?" asked Caroline.

The smelly wet bag brushed against her new skirt as the boys pushed their way into the bathroom. Sierra plastered herself against the wall to avoid touching whatever it was they had. "What's that horrible smell?" she asked.

They didn't answer as they set the bag—which was moving—in the tub.

"Mom!" Caroline yelled.

"Shut up," Jackson said.

Their mom usually ignored Caroline when she yelled, anyway. "What are you doing with that bag?" she demanded. "Oh my God."

Sierra gave a little scream and clung to Caroline's arm. "Is that a *rat*?"

"It's an otter," said Austin, jumping up and down. "A baby otter. We found it and we're keeping it."

"It stinks," Caroline said. "I'm not even telling Mom. She'll just follow her nose."

"Ew," Sierra said, leaning forward to peer at the little creature scrabbling at the edge of the tub. "It's kind of cute, though."

"Don't let its looks fool you," Caroline told her. "Otters are gross. They leave dead fish and poop everywhere."

"Let's name him Oscar," Jackson said. "Oscar the otter."

At that moment, the creature flung its oily body up and out of the tub. Its muscular tail slapped against Caroline's bare legs and dotted her skirt with dirty water and sand.

"He's getting away!" Austin yelled and made a dive for the scuttling critter.

"What's going on in there?" Their mother's voice rang down the hall.

Caroline grabbed Sierra's hand. "Let's get out of here before all hell breaks loose."

"Caroline?" Mom met them on their way out. "What are your brothers up to now?"

"Dunno," she said. "We're going to the clambake now. See you later!"

"Be careful," Mom called. "Don't forget to wear your helmets. Boys! What in the world . . . Get that thing out of my house!"

Caroline grabbed a pair of cutoff shorts from the clothesline, then made a beeline for the bikes. "Stupid brothers. Jeez." She tugged on the shorts and used the soiled skirt to scrub at the muddy streaks on her legs.

"Is your house always like that?" Sierra asked.

"Nope. Some days it's even worse." Caroline hopped on her bike. "That's why I always come over to *your* house."

The back door slammed open and the otter fled across the yard and into the dunes. The boys chased after it, and then Mom appeared, yelling at them to *get inside and clean this place up.*

"Your brothers are kind of nutty," Sierra observed.

"You think? Let's go." Caroline pedaled away from the drama. Her annoyance evaporated as they rode their bikes into town, savoring the feel of the sunshine on their bare arms and legs and the smells of new growth all around them.

They locked the bikes to a rack near the boardwalk and joined the stream of people heading to the beach. The weather was perfect, warm and golden, the light of early evening glimmering across the water.

The beach scene was everything Caroline loved about summer—music drifting from someone's car speakers, a volleyball game going on in the sand, kites sailing overhead, coolers filled with frosty cans of root beer and candy-colored soda, bowls of chips and dips set out on long tables, grown-ups standing around the clam pit, drinking and gossiping. She loved the clothes people put on for summer, too—white jeans and gold jewelry, fluttery swimsuit cover-ups and bare feet, toenails painted seashell pink. Looking around, she saw nothing as interesting as Sierra's outfit.

Caroline and Sierra helped out in the church booth, signing up kids for youth group. "We're getting a mad rush of boys," Caroline said as Sierra collected a stack of sign-up clipboards. "They're all checking you out."

"They can check all they want," she said breezily. "If my dad catches them . . ." She swiped her finger across her throat. "Dad's clueless, though," she added, watching her father passing out summer activities calendars. "Come on, let's escape while we can."

They left the booth and went to hang out with their friends. A group of them, led by Rona Stevens, got up the nerve to dance. "Come on," Sierra said, grabbing Caroline's hand. "Let's go for it."

Madonna's "Nothing Really Matters" broke the ice. The number loosened everyone up, and pretty soon they were all crowded together on the sand, laughing and bumping into one another and trying out new dance moves. Sierra was practically drowning in compliments on her new dress. Caroline basked in the reflected glow. A couple of high school girls even asked if she could make outfits for them.

After a while, they took a break for a cold drink. Zane Hardy, who had been Caroline's lab partner in biology last year, handed her a can. "Lemonade okay?" he asked.

"Sure, thanks." She took a sip, then pressed the chilled can to her neck. "I worked up a sweat out there."

"Yeah, I saw." Zane cleared his throat. "I mean, um, you're a good dancer."

"You think?" Caroline chuckled. "No way."

"Sure, you are. I always feel like such a dork when I dance."

She set down her can. "You're probably thinking too much. Forget you're dancing and have fun."

"New York City Boy" came through the speakers—

totally danceable. "Come on," she said, leading the way. "Nobody's gonna think you're a dork."

He balked, but only for a few seconds. Once they joined the crowd, everybody kind of mashed together, and by the end of the song, Zane was busting a move along with everyone else.

"See?" Caroline teased. "You're a New York City boy."

"And you're cool," he said. "We should hang out this summer."

Oh. Well. She didn't know if he was coming on to her or simply being friendly. There was only one way to find out. "Are you coming on to me or just being friendly?"

His cheeks turned bright red. "I don't . . . I'm not . . ."

She felt bad for making him stammer. Boys were such a combination of bravado and insecurity. She saw that trait in her brothers all the time. "Sorry. My mom says I'm blunt as a spoon."

At that moment, Sierra came over and grabbed Caroline's arm. "Oh, hey, Zane."

"Hiya," he said, his face still red.

"I need to borrow Caroline for a minute." She pivoted away, towing Caroline along behind her. "That kid is totally crushing on you," she said.

"Who? Zane?" Now Caroline felt a blush coming on.

"Of course Zane. I can tell. He's cute, too."

"I guess . . ." Was he? Longish hair parted on the side. Skinny jeans and a vintage T-shirt. He had a nice smile. That made him cute, she supposed.

"I need to show you something. So, remember how I said I'd know him when I see him?" asked Sierra.

"What? Who? Oh, yeah. Mr. Darcy."

Sierra pointed Caroline toward a lone figure down by the water's edge, tossing a Frisbee for a hyper little dog. "Well, I just saw him. Only I don't think he's called Darcy."

Caroline stared in the direction Sierra was pointing and felt a jolt of recognition shoot through her body.

He wasn't Darcy.

He was taller, of course. That was what boys did—they got taller every year. He was lean, but more muscular, too, his shoulders and legs silhouetted against the rushing waves. His shirtless torso glistened with salt water or sweat. The sunlight glinted gold on his hair, and his voice was deep and unfamiliar as he called out a familiar name. "Duffy! Here, boy!"

Caroline's stomach churned. It was Will Jensen. Will and his grandparents' dog, Duffy.

"Oh well, shoot," she stammered, "he's not—"

Sierra wasn't listening. When the Frisbee went flying past, she snatched it out of the air like a trained athlete. They'd been in gym class together all year, and Caroline had never seen her friend execute a move like that.

Now in possession of the Frisbee, Sierra laughed as the dog danced frantically around her. "What a cute little guy," she called out. "Can I throw it for him?"

"Sure," said Will, scooping up a T-shirt as he came toward them. His stare seemed to be glued to Sierra. Of course it was. She looked utterly, totally amazing in the dress Caroline had made for her. In the deepening light, she was almost too beautiful to be real, like a mermaid. No wonder Will couldn't look away, even as he yanked on a familiar *Go Navy* T-shirt over his head.

She flung the disc into the air, and Duffy scampered after it. "I'm Sierra," she said.

And I'm invisible, thought Caroline.

"Hi," he said. "I'm—"

"That's Will," Caroline interrupted, her voice a bit louder than she'd intended.

The moment she spoke up, his attention swiveled to her. His face lit with a grin that was suddenly familiar, despite the deep voice and big shoulders. "Hey, stranger," he said.

"Hey, yourself," she replied, her heart racing as if she'd just sprinted a hundred yards. "You're back." She had an insane fantasy in her mind that he would sweep her up like Rhett did Scarlett in *Gone with the Wind* and kiss her so hard she fainted.

"You guys know each other?" asked Sierra. "That's so cool." She snapped her fingers. "Your grandmother's Mrs. Jensen, right? We saw her yesterday. I should have recognized the dog."

Duffy came racing back with the Frisbee. Neither Will nor Sierra seemed to notice the dog, so Caroline flung the disc for him again. It caught the breeze and seemed to go for miles.

"Are you hungry?" Sierra asked Will.

"Always. How about you?"

"Starving," Sierra said.

She was never starving. She barely ate. Maybe meeting Will had whetted her appetite. Chattering away, she walked with him toward the food tables, now laden with steaming trays of clams, potatoes, and corn.

Caroline trailed along in their wake. Her stomach was in knots. Literally, it was. She knew she wouldn't be able to eat a single bite.

Right before her eyes, Sierra and Will seemed drawn to each other like magnets. Instant attraction, a high school Lizzy and Darcy.

Suddenly the magical summer Caroline had imagined wasn't so magical after all. She grabbed a piece of driftwood and stabbed it into the sand, furious at herself. She should have said something to Sierra. She should have just come out and admitted the truth. And the truth was, she'd had a crush on Will Jensen ever since she'd figured out what a crush was.

Now they were both lost to her—her best friend *and* her crush—and she'd been the one who had made it happen.

She glared at the beach scene—people playing and dancing, gathering at the booths, buying chances at the cakewalk and raffle. Summer at the beach—the season she looked forward to all year long.

And beyond it all, the great wild ocean stretched out to infinity.

PART FOUR

Appreciate the journey, and recognize your strength.

—See the Triumph

Chapter 19

Caroline was in the kids' room, going through their school backpacks and checking homework. She'd never pictured herself doing such a thing, and she felt like a fraud. Notes from teachers, permission slips, practice sheets—it was all new to her.

Sometimes, like at the present moment, it started to feel normal. It started to feel like her life. Not the life she'd imagined for herself, but something she never in her wildest dreams could have conceived of. Both Addie and Flick seemed to be settling in at school. They even seemed proud that the superpower shirts had become a thing. They were trendsetters, she liked to tell them.

The day was winding down. They'd had their supper and baths. Now Flick lay on his bed, absorbed in *Mike*

Mulligan and His Steam Shovel. Addie had found an old Barbie set in a carrying case that opened like a closet and was playing with the vintage dolls. Thanks to Caroline's mother, Barbie still lived in the case with her boyfriend, Ken. "She could be Wonder Woman's friend," Addie exclaimed. "They're the same size."

"Good idea," said Caroline. "They could even share clothes." She held up a tiny ball gown made of weird polyester calico. "I remember making this—a failed experiment. Sewing for Barbie is actually harder than sewing for grown-ups. But see, she has a lot of cool clothes and her own motor scooter. I got in trouble for making her a car."

"Why did you get in trouble?"

"I borrowed one of my dad's Italian leather shoes to make it. I stuck on the wheels with a hot glue gun, which seemed like a good idea at the time. But it ruined the shoes forever. Dad was so mad at me."

"Did he whack you?"

"What? Whack me? *No.*" Caroline felt a spike of awareness. "Is that what happens when someone's bad?"

Addie shrugged her shoulders, her typical reaction when Caroline brought up the topic. Neither she nor Flick had given any indication that they knew what was happening to their mother or who the abuser was, yet that didn't mean they hadn't seen anything.

"Well, I want you to know that whacking is never okay. Or hitting, smacking, punching, or shoving. Violence—hurting someone—is never, ever okay. You know that, right?"

Another shrug. Addie tried a denim skirt on Wonder Woman.

"Did anyone ever hit you? Or Flick? Or your mama?" These questions had been asked by emergency caseworkers in the whirlwind following Angelique's death, and the answer was always inconclusive.

Once again, no. Addie shook her head, and Flick pretended not to hear.

"I want you to know that we can talk about anything. It's important. And I promise I'll always listen," Caroline persisted. "Maybe you saw scary things."

She paused. No response.

"Maybe you heard yelling in a mean voice."

Still nothing.

"I want you to know that yelling is not okay, and you should never think it's your fault. There was nothing you could have done to stop what happened to your mama. I will do everything I can to help you feel safe. Can you talk to me about how you feel?"

The kids looked at each other and held their silence.

"I miss Mama," Addie said after a few moments. "I feel sad."

"So do I, and Flick does, too." Caroline drew Addie into a hug. "I wish I knew how to help you, baby," she whispered into the girl's soft hair. "You don't deserve what happened to you. Your mama didn't deserve it, either. You're safe now, and I'll always keep you safe."

After a few minutes, Flick grabbed the book they'd been reading together. "Read to us. Read *Old Yeller,*" he said.

"Good plan. I think we're on the last chapter." Caroline opened to the bookmarked page and started reading. She still remembered the warmth and safety of snuggling in bed with her sisters and brothers while their mother read to them. Yeller had been her favorite. He and Travis had adventures the way she and Wendell did. Poor Yeller had harrowing episodes—getting attacked by a bear, saving Travis from wild hogs, being bitten by a rabid wolf.

As she read the part about Yeller's festering bite, she could feel the kids coiling against her in dread. She recalled bracing herself, too, but her mom had read the reassuring final scene with a smile on her face. Just when it seemed all was lost, Yeller's eyes cleared. He stopped foaming at the mouth. He wagged his tail and whined a sweet greeting to Travis. He was all right. He and Travis were going to be just fine.

Except.

Caroline frowned as she heard herself reading the final scene. Wait. What? This was not the story she remembered. Right there in black and white, the book said Yeller had rabies and Travis shot him dead. With a sense of betrayal and disbelief, she kept reading, but it didn't get better. "Jesus H. Christ," she said, tears falling as she snapped the book shut and flung it aside. "What the hell kind of ending is that?"

"Did Yeller die?" Addie asked, her chin quivering.

"Travis shot him. Why did Travis shoot him?" Flick punched his pillow.

"That's not how it's supposed to end," Caroline said. "When my mom read it to me, the ending was totally different. It was totally happy."

"I don't want Yeller to be dead," Addie sobbed.

"It's just a story," Caroline said with an angry sleeve-swipe at her tearstained cheeks. "It didn't really happen."

"It's the saddest thing ever."

"I know," Caroline said. "I know. I'm sorry I read you such a sad story. The ending I remember was totally different. The *Old Yeller* my mom read us had a happy ending. Yeller got better and they kept his puppies, too."

"Then why's he dead now?" Addie asked.

Because my mom changed the ending.

It took Caroline another thirty minutes and repeat readings of *Go, Dog. Go!* to coax them to sleep. When they were finally settled, she grabbed the offensive book and went to confront her mother.

Her mom was in the living room, lost in a new novel from the library. Caroline dropped *Old Yeller* in her lap. "You changed the ending," she accused.

"What?"

"You read *Old Yeller* aloud to us and you changed the ending so that he got better and lived happily ever after."

"Did I?" Mom removed her reading glasses. "That was smart of me. I certainly didn't want the five of you up all night crying over a sad dog story."

"I lived my whole life thinking this was the best book ever because I thought it ended well for Yeller." She made a fist around the damp tissues in her hand. "And I just finished reading this to Addie and Flick, only I read them the real ending, thinking it was going to get better. And the goddamn kid shot his goddamn dog and that was that. It took forever to console them and get them to sleep, and it's a school night."

"Oh dear. You should have given them a happy ending."

Rain engulfed the peninsula in a sweep of wind and darkness. Caroline put the kids' lunches in their backpacks, shuddering at the blustery weather. Flick and Addie stared out the window, their expressions as gloomy as the weather.

"It's like this sometimes," she said.

"It's like this all the time," Flick grumbled.

"I hate the rain," Fern said, coming into the kitchen, flinging her backpack onto the floor. "I got soaked just coming in from the garage."

"Then you're going to love what I made for you," Caroline said. "New raincoats!"

"Yay!" Addie jumped down from the table. "You make the best things."

"It's a popover jacket," Caroline said, helping Addie put hers on. "Something I've been working on. I'll show you how it works." She had been inspired by the children, coming up with a unique design concept. The fleece jackets had a special pocket with a surprise inside—a rain fly and hood that covered them and their backpacks.

"It's cool!" Flick said. "I like how you make stuff." He offered a rare spontaneous hug.

Fern's face brightened as she examined her new coat. "I love it. Thanks, Aunt Caroline."

It had never occurred to Caroline to make children's rainwear, but the feeling of pleasure reminded her of something she'd nearly forgotten—designing clothes was a way of showing love. In all the turmoil over her career, she'd nearly lost that idea. The garments bore her signature flourish—the nautilus shell motif on the front pocket. She'd added the logo with a sense of defiance, determined to fight her way back into the business.

The three kids showed off their bright fleece jackets with their custom rain coverings.

"We need pictures," Virginia said, coming into the kitchen to admire the finished garments. "Caroline, these are really clever." She took out her phone and snapped a few pictures. "I hope you're prepared to get orders from all the other moms."

"That's the idea," Caroline said, herding the kids out the door to wait for the school bus at the end of the driveway. She handed her sister a printout of her designs and technical specifications for the jackets.

"Well, this is brilliant. Good for you." Virginia helped herself to coffee and sat down with the document. "I'm glad you're moving ahead with your design business."

"I've got to do something. It's not exactly the career I thought I wanted . . ."

"Welcome to the club," said Virginia. "Sometimes life shoves you off into the unknown, and it turns out to be amazing."

Caroline knew Virginia was talking about her divorce. "How are you doing?"

"Ups and downs," Virginia said. "More up than down lately. Fern and I have never been closer. Since I'm forced to share custody, my time with her is more precious than ever." Her expression softened. "And dating . . . it's actually fun, in a weird way. Don't you think dating's fun?"

"I've totally forgotten what dating is," Caroline admitted. "Been burning the midnight oil to get my workshop up and running. I have the machines from the factory in Astoria. I even have a couple of workers who were displaced when the place closed, and Lindy's friend Echo is on board. Am I completely mad?"

"No. You're motivated."

"Because nothing motivates me like the prospect of imminent failure." Caroline bustled around the kitchen, cleaning up after breakfast.

"You're starting to sound like yourself again," Virginia said.

"Jackson and I are taking Dad's truck down to Astoria this morning. I'll fill you in when I get back." With a flutter of nerves, she took out her own raincoat, an uninspired shell of a thing. A rain jacket didn't have to be boring. She was staking her whole enterprise on the idea.

"You're just so good," Virginia said, paging through the printouts of Caroline's designs, created in a fever of inspiration. "I thought you had it all. I thought you had your dream job."

"I thought so, too." Caroline stared out the window at the waterlogged landscape.

"You snagged a spot at a major fashion show in New York," Virginia said. "You were so excited."

"And it turned into a disaster. I'm scared of another disaster."

"If it was easy, everyone would be doing it."

"Well, I did solve one problem today. I found a space for the workshop." Currently everything was stowed in the garage. The garments were being fabricated there, but she knew she needed a better space.

"Yeah? Where's that?"

"The barn at the old Jensen place. Will and Sierra agreed to rent it to me, so I'm moving everything over there."

Chapter 20

Will helped Jackson Shelby unload the last of Caroline's sewing machines from the back of the pickup truck into the barn on his property. He was soaked in sweat from the job.

"Who knew sewing machines were so damn heavy?" Jackson asked, sucking down a bottle of water in one go.

"I warned you," said Caroline. She was sweaty, too, having done her share of lifting and moving. "These aren't your grandmother's sewing machines. They're industrial workhorses."

Sierra gave her a glass of sparkling water. "You're on the road to fame and fortune."

"Hope the floor holds up," Will said. "This place hasn't been used for anything but storage in years."

Caroline lifted her water glass. "You guys are so great to let me set up in your barn. Seriously, this is the coolest."

Will and Jackson brought the last machine into the space and Caroline showed them where to park it.

Jackson turned to Caroline. "You've always had nutty ideas."

"Who're you calling nutty, Mr. Liveaboard?"

He ruffled her hair. "Speaking of which, I'm outta here. I've got a date tonight."

"Oooh. Anyone we know?"

"Someone I met on a dating app."

"Sounds . . . promising?"

"We'll see."

"Thanks again, buddy." Will shook hands with him and Jackson took off.

Caroline turned in a slow circle, looking around the lofty space, lit by rays of sunshine through the high clerestory windows. "Not a cobweb in sight now."

"Will spent half a day getting the place ready," Sierra said. "It was a total cobweb factory in here."

He hoped he was the only one who could detect the bitter note in her voice. Lately there was no pleasing her.

"I owe you guys big-time," Caroline declared. "When your little Wills and Sierras come along, they'll get a lifetime supply of C-Shell apparel. That's a promise."

She turned to Will. "Sierra once told me you wanted to convert the barn into a play area for kids. I want you to know that when you need the space, I'll move out, pronto."

"It was just an idea," he said. He couldn't help shooting a look at Sierra. She was turned away, checking out the long cutting table in the center of the space. Mutual avoidance of the topic of babies had become their norm.

"I have to get going, too," Sierra said. "I have a meeting at my agency in Portland tomorrow, and I need to get some things ready. Pop in the house before you leave, okay?"

"Sure thing. Thanks again, Sierra."

"Get to work." Sierra made a shooing motion with her hands. "Do great things."

Caroline checked a sketch she'd made of the room layout. "She sounds like Marley at the bank where I got my small-business loan."

"Marley's a good guy," Will said. "I've had both of his kids as students. He's the one who started the special loan program to keep business and talent on the peninsula. Good job getting that loan, by the way," he added.

"Thanks. One of the perks of living in a small town. They know where to find me if I default." She looked up from her sketch. "Not that I intend to default. I promise, I won't miss a single rent payment."

"I'm not worried about the rent."

"I am. I mean, not worried, but I intend to make this work."

"You will. You've always been a go-getter, Caroline."

"Have I?" She smiled, and just for a second, she looked like she was about twelve years old again, the kid he'd met years ago at the start of their long and sometimes confusing friendship. "Give me a hand with this, will you?" She indicated a wide roll of white paper. "I need to hang it over the end of the cutting table."

They each took an end of the roll and lifted it into the brackets.

"Butcher paper?" he asked.

"Pattern paper. One of the tools of the trade." She sighed. "I wrote my career's death sentence on this paper."

"What? How's that?"

"It's a long story."

He looked at the boxes and equipment stacked around the room. "We've got a long way to go."

Her face lit again. That smile still got to him. "You're going to help me set up?"

"It's Sunday. I've got all day." He had plenty of chores to do around the house, but Sierra always said it was hard for her to concentrate when he was banging around.

They worked as a team, mounting rolls of fabric, organizing gear, moving furniture and equipment, checking electrical connections. And Caroline talked. She had always been a talker. She told him a bit about how the fashion industry worked, with independent designers doing contract projects for major companies. "I was always creating my own material after hours, nights and weekends, lunch hour, any time I could squeeze in some design and patternmaking. Finally, after more setbacks than I'm willing to bore you with, I got a shot at exhibiting an original collection. Behind my back, the big designer I was working for stole my designs and launched them under his label at a major show."

"Jesus. Some guy just stole your designs? How can he do that? Sounds totally illegal."

"Fun fact about the fashion industry—copying isn't illegal. Certain things can be copyrighted, like a textile print or a sculptural shape, but there's no prohibition against one designer copying another, stitch for stitch. And even if I wanted to fight back, there's no way I could afford to make a case for myself. When I confronted Mick Taylor—that's the guy who took credit for my designs—and his design director, they pointed out that I'd made some of my patterns in their atelier. Who knew they were keeping tabs on me? He could claim I created the designs while under contract to him, using his resources."

She unrolled a length of the paper, spreading it across the big table. "So that's how I went down in flames," she said. "It was horrible, like somebody assaulted me. I did try to fight back. I told every reporter and blogger I knew. Tried shaming Mick on social media. But my threat turned out to be as empty as my bank account. Unless a major media outlet picks up the story, no one pays attention."

He was quiet for several moments, trying to imagine her sense of betrayal and disappointment. "Damn, that sucks. Are you sure there's nothing else you can do?"

She shook her head. "Mick actually seemed slightly remorseful—not because he regretted or would even admit to appropriating my designs. No, I'm pretty sure the remorse had to do with the fact that I was so damned useful to him. I designed a ton of things for his label. He's going to have to find a replacement now."

"Sorry that happened to you," Will said. "I wish I could help."

"Are you kidding? You're totally helping by letting me set up here. He killed my chance to show a collection in New York. Out here, I'm so far off the radar, he wouldn't be able to find me. So you and Sierra are helping me restore my sanity."

"Along with the local economy," he said.

"Well, I don't know about that. But I'm going to give it my best shot. I've got two people coming to work for me. And two interns from the high school vo-tech program—did Sierra tell you?"

"That's great, Caroline." He liked her energy and focus; he always had. "Tell you what. I'll install these overhead work lamps for you." He gestured at a stack of boxes that had been delivered.

"You don't need to do that. I can call an electrician—"

"Or you can let me help," he said.

"I—yes. I can. And thank you." Surprise and delight lit her face. "I'm impressed that you know how to install light fixtures. Electrical things have always scared me."

"I learned a lot, restoring the old house," he said.

"It's really beautiful, Will. I can see the love you put into the place."

"Yeah?" He buckled on his tool belt.

"Definitely."

"It's always been my happy place," he said.

"I remember that. You and your granddad were forever making things."

"Remember her?" He extracted an old cobwebbed icon from a pile of junk.

"Justine! That old ship's figurehead."

He dusted off the piece. His grandfather had saved it from a shipwreck at the mouth of the Columbia. It was a classic pose, a sturdy Valkyrie with a bare chest, tangled hair, mouth open as if shouting at the waves. "I used to be obsessed with her boobs."

"She still looks fierce. I like her."

Grabbing a ladder, he hoisted the carving high on the wall overlooking the workspace. "How's this?"

"Perfect. My fabricators are gonna love it. We're all about fierce women in this shop."

"Right. It's cool what you're doing with the women's group."

"Thanks. I'm learning a lot from those ladies." She gazed at him, her head tilted slightly to one side, and touched a finger to her lower lip, a gesture he remembered from way back when. Then she seemed to shift gears and turned away, but not before he saw her cheeks turn red.

Like a butterfly in a garden, she went from machine to machine, making adjustments and testing connections. "Life's funny sometimes, isn't it?" she said.

"Life's funny all the time." He found some hardware to mount the figurehead like a hunting trophy.

"True. I was thinking about how I ended up back here, the last place I thought I'd be. And it turns out, it's probably exactly where I belong."

"Are you sure about that? You're not going to miss the city?" His thoughts shifted to Sierra, her frequent laments about Seattle and Portland.

"Don't get me wrong—I love the city," Caroline said. "But my life is where it makes the most sense. And right now that's here." She picked up a small half-finished garment—a jacket with lightning bolts and attached mittens—and studied it for several seconds. "I thought these kids were the end of my career. I thought it would be too much to juggle them and all the things I wanted to do with my designs."

"And here you are, doing it. I'm surprised there was ever a doubt."

"Ha. Two kids, remember. Now I realize that Flick and Addie aren't in my way. They're my inspiration. These days, it's impossible to imagine my life without them." She glanced over at him. "Yes, you're hearing this from the original 'I'm never going to settle down and have kids' Caroline Shelby. They kind of grew on me. They kind of stole my heart." She set aside the garment and started unpacking a box of tall spools of different-colored thread. Now he saw what the pegboard was for. She placed each spool carefully, organizing them by color.

He felt a rush of affection for her, embracing this new plan for the sake of two orphans. "That's good," he said. "I'm glad it worked out that way." It was on the tip of his tongue to take the confession further. To say he thought Sierra would come around, too. That she'd embrace the small-town life and the idea of having a family. But as time went on, he was coming to realize that she might never get there. That was a discussion to have with Sierra, not Caroline. He knew better than to bring it up now. But there was this old connection with Caroline, something that had been present between them from the start. It was incredible that he could still feel it after all these years. It was as if the attraction had been slumbering underground, invisible but never gone.

"I always knew I'd end up here," he said. "Just not so soon. I was planning on serving in the navy a lot longer."

She paused in her sorting and turned to him. "I'm sorry about your accident." Then she put a hand to her lips. "I shouldn't bring it up. Sierra said you don't talk about it."

Sierra was right. He didn't. "Actually, I should," he said. "It's supposed to be good for me to talk about it. Good for my mental health."

"I'm good for your mental health, then," she said with a grin. "Who knew?"

You've always been good for my mental health, he thought. She'd been the first person he'd told about losing his mother. His dad, teachers, and counselors had all tried to get him to talk about it, but he'd never said much until he met Caroline. He remembered that day so clearly—the bike ride, the sunshine, the waves erupting against the cliff. The funny girl who made him want to talk about the unspeakable.

"It was an extraction," he said. "A hostage rescue operation."

"Sierra told me that part. She said the hostages were aid workers."

"Ever heard of Djibouti?" It was pronounced *Jabooty.* He grinned at her expression. "Don't worry. No one has. I hadn't either, until the call came for a mission there. It's in Africa, between Ethiopia and Somalia. Not known as a hot spot of unrest, but some American aid workers were kidnapped there while in transit. A group called Al Shabab was holding them for ransom."

That had been his last operation, though he hadn't known it at the time. He'd attained the rank of lieutenant commander in the Naval Special Warfare Development Group, aka SEAL Team 6. In a split second, he'd become medically retired Lt. Cdr. (SEAL) Willem Jensen.

Caroline set aside her box of sorting. Her full, quiet attention felt like a gift, the way it had the first summer they'd met as kids, when he'd told her about losing his mom.

He remembered being in the team compound when the call came in. It was one of those you hate to hear—participation was voluntary, meaning extra risky. Nobody had opted out, though. It was precisely what they had trained for.

"To get them out, it had to be a quick insert. We'd go in by helo and fast rope, extract the hostages, and disappear. Usually there'd be plenty of rehearsals, only that night, the time window was almost nonexistent. We made a plan but there wasn't time to test it."

He remembered a new moon, a night of perfect darkness, ideal for the operation. "Thanks to an informant, we found the workers—two nurses and an aide. Two of them were in rough shape, dazed and sick with fever. The op went as planned—until the bandits opened fire, which we expected based on the intelligence."

Caroline winced. "You got shot."

"Not just then. So far the kidnappers were the only casualties. The team dropped nine of them in a matter of seconds." He could still hear the staccato sound of the fight. Sometimes he heard it in his dreams. "The extraction went as planned. Until it didn't."

Caroline stood looking at him, her face soft with wonder. She seemed to be listening with her whole body. "What happened?"

Here was the part he never talked about. The part that haunted him. "We had the hostages. I was bringing up the rear, running through the bush toward the helo. We thought all the bandits were down, but deep in the bush, I noticed a flare of movement in my night vision—never a good sign. I slowed down to try for some facial recognition. I had to check it out, because one guy with a big firearm could take us all out. And . . . there was this kid."

"A kid—like a boy?"

Will could still picture the scene through his night-vision goggles: A little boy, peering through the parted grass. A little boy with an AK-47. His eyes were bright and vacant, probably from chewing *khat*, a kind of speed, his hands nervous on the trigger and the grip.

"A scared little kid. He was maybe ten years old, I thought. High on this stuff the natives chew. Draped in ammo and pointing an AK-47 at me."

"Oh my God. I can't even imagine what that was like," she said.

"This is what a SEAL trains for. Months and years of practice drills every day—to confront and eliminate a threat without hesitation."

"Let me guess," she said softly. "You hesitated."

Training and instinct had dictated that Will should eliminate the threat. But something deeper had stopped him—this was a child. A *child.*

Will nodded. "And he opened fire."

The body armor had protected him from mortal wounds, but his goggles flew off on impact. When his face was hit, it felt as if half his head had been blown off.

"One of my team members took him out. I later learned the boy's name was Hamza. He was fourteen years old."

Caroline exhaled slowly and softly. She came around the side of the cutting table and stood in front of him, briefly touching his forearm and then taking her hand away. "I'm sorry that happened. What a horrible choice to have to make—to shoot a child or be shot. I understand why you hesitated."

He'd faced a board of inquiry over the incident. His team had vouched for him, thank God. He realized that other than responding to the inquiry, he'd never told anyone the details of the incident. Not his dad or his grandparents or even Sierra. Only Caroline, whom he'd met when they were kids, no older than Hamza, perched on a rocky outcropping above Cape Disappointment.

"Thanks. I'm . . . I guess it'll always be with me," he said.

"Now you're a teacher," she said. "I'm connecting the dots."

He went back to work. "Not sure about connecting the dots. I'm not that deep. My life changed in a split second. I just did the next logical thing."

"You know how the saying goes—life is what happens to you when you're making other plans."

The silence between them was a companionable one. Every now and then, Will would glance over at her and catch her looking at him. They'd immediately look away from each other. It was a tentative dance, reestablishing a friendship that had been dormant for years.

Although he tried to deny it, he felt drawn to her in a way that was absolutely and completely forbidden. It was impossible to lie to himself about this. But he could lie to everyone else. And he fully intended to do so.

"I wasn't sure what to do with these storage boxes," she said, startling him away from thoughts he shouldn't be having.

"What's that?"

"These boxes over here." She indicated a few by the door. "I wasn't sure what to do with them."

"Let's have a look." There were bankers boxes crammed with receipts and records. Another box contained college textbooks. "I'll ask Sierra about these," he said. "During my last deployment, she was working on getting an MBA." The box at the bottom was oblong and unexpectedly heavy, its once-glossy white surface covered in cobwebs and dust. He lifted the lid to reveal a cellophane window in an oval shape. "Damn. Haven't seen that in a while."

Caroline leaned forward to have a look. "Is this . . . ?"

"Sierra's wedding dress. The one you made for her."

"Wow. Never thought I'd see that again."

He set the box with the others on a hand truck. He studied her with heightened awareness. She stood close enough for him to catch the herbal smell of her hair. The not-unpleasant scent of her sweat. He fixated on the damp bow of her lips. "I never thought I'd see *you* again."

"Will—"

"I mean that, Caroline. We broke apart and here we are again. Sierra and I . . ."

"Stop," she said. "Just stop."

PART FIVE

Sometimes when I look at you, I feel
I'm gazing at a distant star. It's dazzling, but the light is
from tens of thousands of years ago. Maybe the star
doesn't even exist any more. Yet sometimes that light
seems more real to me than anything.

—Haruki Murakami,
South of the Border, West of the Sun

Chapter 21

"I have news," Caroline said to Sierra, ambushing her in the school parking lot after seventh period. "I'm freaking out."

"Did Zane Hardy finally ask you to senior prom?" Sierra asked. "You shouldn't have worried. I knew he would."

"Screw the prom," Caroline said. "That's not what I'm talking about. We've got to go to my house. My mom said I got an important-looking envelope in the mail."

"Ooh." They hurried to Sierra's car, a shiny daffodil-yellow Volkswagen bug. "Let's go."

College letters had been rolling in, and Sierra already had her options—UW in Seattle, Lewis & Clark College in Oregon, and UC San Diego. Her decision to go to San Diego was no coincidence. That was where Will Jensen had fast-tracked to his junior year. Her crush on him, dating back to the first summer they'd met, had continued unabated. Each subsequent summer, their romance had burned like a bonfire on the beach. Caroline had watched from the sidelines, trying not to remember that, for one crazy, magic, irretrievable, impossible moment, he'd been hers.

By now she knew it was silly. When you were fourteen, no one belonged to you, not even yourself. You were like a lump of unformed clay, still trying to figure out who you were or what you would become.

Through each summer, the three of them had been inseparable, coming of age in the golden sunshine. Will got his license first, being a year older, and he drove around in his granddad's old Grand Marquis, sometimes getting the unwieldy sedan stuck in the soft sand at the entrance to the beach, other times making it to the hard-packed tidal flats for illicit drag racing. He usually won the races, not because the car was so awesome, but because he knew how to handle it. Together they had won and lost kite-flying competitions, dominated at Ultimate Frisbee, tried their first weed, and gotten drunk for the first time.

Caroline was always the sidekick, the funny friend, tagging along on their summer adventures, sometimes with a boy who liked her, sometimes not. Sierra and Will were nuts for each other, the golden couple, the kind that gave teenagers a good name. When people saw them in church together, looking deceptively clean-cut and well-behaved, they nodded approval, never knowing the pair had probably been humping in the deserted parsonage the night before. Caroline made her peace with the situation. Will Jensen had never been hers, not even for a moment. Well, maybe just for a moment—a vanished slice of time. That first kiss. The only kiss. He'd never mentioned it. He'd probably forgotten.

Sierra parked at the Shelby house and they raced inside, finding the stack of mail her mom had left on the kitchen counter. She grabbed a business-size envelope with the return address she'd been waiting for ever since sending in her portfolio and samples last winter. She was picturing a fat packet of information, like the one she'd received from the Art Institute of Seattle, her backup school. A simple letter was a bad sign.

"Wait," said Sierra before Caroline ripped into it. "We need to do the laying on of hands." It was a ritual they went through for good luck. Sierra's dad would probably scold their pagan ways, but the girls did it anyway, just in case it worked. They pressed their hands on the envelope and closed their eyes.

"I wish I may, I wish I might," Caroline murmured. Then she opened the envelope and slid the pages out. "I can't look," she said, shrinking away as a feeling of dread knotted her stomach. "This letter is going to make me or break me, and I'm scared to know. I can't look," she repeated.

"Yes, you can. Caroline, you have to. You *have* to."

She made herself look. And there it was, on FIT letterhead, in black and white: *Dear Caroline, Congratulations! You've been . . .* She let out a scream. "I'm in!"

"You're in!" Sierra grabbed her hands and they danced around the room.

Caroline's heart nearly burst with happiness. This was it. The dream. The goal. The start of the life she'd always wanted—New York City, studying design at one of the best schools in the country. When she stopped hyperventilating, she read the rest of the letter and discovered that she had been accepted early, a privilege extended only to students who showed exceptional promise. "I can't believe it," she said.

"I can." Sierra beamed at her. "When it comes to making clothes, you're amazing. You totally deserve this, Caroline. You totally earned it. Let's go find your mom."

The school year dragged on, and among Caroline and her friends, rampant senioritis took over. No one wanted to sit through class, no one wanted to study for exams. Everyone was eager for their lives beyond high school to begin.

As Sierra had predicted, Zane asked Caroline to prom. Sierra's date was Bucky O'Malley, who was gay and easily the best dancer in the senior class. Caroline designed and made their dresses, and they were the envy of the school.

Summer came at last, and so did Will Jensen, all big shoulders, blond hair, and blue eyes. Sometimes when Caroline looked at him, she could still see that skinny kid, dripping wet with his mask and snorkel. His flashing grin never changed. When the three of them met up at their favorite beach spot, he gave her and Sierra each a friendly hug, though he kept hold of Sierra longer—as expected.

"Hey, strangers," he said to them.

"Hey, yourself," Caroline said.

"I've missed you like crazy," Sierra told him. "How long can you stay?"

"This is probably my last full summer here. I have to start classes the minute summer's over. I'm fast-tracking in order to finish my degree early."

Caroline suspected his dad wanted him to finish early. She didn't ask, though. Will and his father were complicated. He wanted a career in the navy, like his dad. He'd been in ROTC in high school and now college. Yet no matter what he achieved, it never seemed to be enough for his father.

"What about you two?" he asked.

Caroline would be working full time at Lindy Bloom's shop, saving every penny she could for New York. Sierra had a part-time gig at the visitors bureau, greeting tourists and helping organize community events. She was amazing at it—pretty and personable, the face of Long Beach Peninsula. Last spring, she'd won a statewide scholarship pageant. The program had sent her to the famed Dallas Apparel & Accessories Market to explore the world of modeling. She'd returned even more stylish and polished than ever.

"Do you have a summer job?" Caroline asked Will.

"Sort of. I'm training with the county surf rescue team down in Seaview."

"Ooh, the Jet Ski guys," said Sierra. "Yikes, they go out in anything. Promise you won't drown."

He flashed his trademark grin. "Drowning is not an option."

"It looks really scary," Caroline said.

"It *is* scary," he said. "Surf rescue, technical and cliff rescue—that's why you train for it."

"No, *you* train for it." Sierra shuddered. "I worry about you."

"It's good preparation for BUD/S training," he said.

"You're starting to speak in acronyms like a navy guy," Caroline said. "Translation, please."

"Basic Underwater Demolition/SEAL training. Starts with indoctrination, and then there are three phases. Eight weeks of physical conditioning, eight weeks on diving and water skills, nine weeks of land warfare. Then you graduate and the real training starts. Assuming, that is, that you make it."

"You will," Sierra said. "I know you, Will. You'd never give up."

"I hope you're right. I used to watch the training on a courtyard in Coronado called the Grinder. I saw bigger, stronger guys than me reduced to tears."

"So let me get this straight," Caroline said. "You're going to spend seven months learning to be part frog, part trained killer, and then go to the most dangerous places in the world, fighting and rescuing people."

"You're oversimplifying, but okay, it's kind of like that."

"Well, it all sounds completely terrifying and hard," she said.

"That's how moving to New York and being a designer sounds to me," he joked.

"I wish you were coming to San Diego with me, Caroline," Sierra said. "We'd never have to break up the band. There are design schools all over Southern California."

"Aw." Caroline gave her a nudge. "That's tempting. It would be . . . safe, wouldn't it? Like, too safe. I'm ready for something totally different."

"I'm ready to take a swim." Will peeled off his shirt and dropped it on the sand, then ran into the surf. He was chiseled to the last inch of his shadow, and already tan from California.

"God, he's amazing," Sierra said, untying the wrap skirt she wore over her bikini.

Caroline didn't answer. She took her time shrugging out of the oversize baseball shirt that belonged to one of her brothers. The whole world knew Will Jensen was amazing, for chrissake.

"Let's go, you." Sierra grabbed her hand. "Let's run. Let's run so fast we can't stop."

Both girls let out loud whoops as they raced into the curling waves. Their whoops turned to screams as they hit the cold, heavy surf, but they persevered, as they did each summer, knowing the only way to deal with the chilly water was total immersion.

They surfaced in a circle of three, shuddering from the cold and laughing. "I'm dying," Sierra said through chattering teeth. "Literally, dying."

"I don't think you mean literally," Caroline said. "It feels *good.*"

"Summer never felt so good," Will agreed.

Caroline dove beneath the surface, hearing with preternatural sharpness the shifting sand and the shush of the waves. When she emerged, Sierra was already swimming for shore.

"She didn't last long," Will observed.

"Nobody does."

"You do," he pointed out.

"I'm a freak. Just ask my brothers and sisters."

"So we're both freaks." He held her gaze for a few seconds, then backstroked away.

Every once in a while, Caroline's imagination played tricks on her. She'd see him looking at her in a certain way, maybe studying her mouth or her eyes and holding her gaze for a few seconds too long. Just for a moment, she thought about confessing that she had feelings for him, romantic feelings, but the moment passed, and she chickened out. Did he ever wonder about what would have happened if he hadn't gone crazy over Sierra, if he'd chosen Caroline instead? It was the silliest of notions, and she was always quick to thrust it aside.

Sierra was his perfect match, not only in looks, but in temperament. Unlike Caroline, Sierra didn't have some grand plan for her life that would send her haring off to New York City. Sierra was all about being in a relationship. Being a couple. Making a life that revolved around family. No wonder Will preferred her.

Caroline contented herself with being the third wheel. Boyfriends came and went, mainly to balance things out so she didn't feel abandoned. Also to hide her yearning.

Summer ended, and with it, the days of their childhood. It was time for a new chapter for all of them. Will was leaving, and on their last night together, they made a bonfire on the beach, sharing bottles of beer illicitly acquired from the restaurant.

"On the last night of the last summer before the real world starts, I propose a toast," said Caroline. "Wherever we go, we'll stay friends."

"Just like we are now," Sierra agreed, taking a sip of her beer.

They all came in for a group hug. Will's arms were strong as they pulled her and Sierra close. He smelled of salt air, and warm sand clung to his skin. She felt the craziest mixture of happy and sad, excited and scared, anxious and determined all at once.

"Friends, no matter what," Sierra reiterated.

"Yes," Caroline agreed. "No matter what."

Like continental drift, their movement away from one another was both imperceptible and inevitable. There was a reason for the term *drifted apart,* Caroline learned. *One of these days* turned into *none of these days. Let's get together for sure* actually meant *never—how does never work for you?*

Will went into the service, completing the grueling training to join the elite Navy SEALs, like his father before him. Sierra got her degree and moved from San Diego to the L.A. area. Caroline finished school and turned her tiny apartment into a crowded atelier, the entire space dominated by the tools of her trade—her prized single-needle machine, rolls of pattern paper and muslin, racks of samples and experimental garments. She made the rare visit home to Oysterville, but it never seemed to coincide with a visit from Sierra. Their friendship still existed, but it lay in the background, like their old snapshots preserved in albums they never looked at.

The drift was a natural progression, and as the seasons and then the years passed, the busyness of life simply took over. They were linked together on social media, but no one seemed to have time to spend bonding online.

When Sierra's number appeared on Caroline's phone one day, she did a double take. She was in the middle of a fitting for a piece from a major designer. His design director had hired her to do some patternmaking and sample sewing. Caroline wanted to perfect the piece, because if the director was happy with Caroline's work, she'd likely hire her to do some actual design.

Although ignoring the call was agony, she let it go to voice mail. Fit models charged a hundred bucks an hour or more, and she didn't want to get in trouble for keeping her model too long. The moment the fitting was over, though, she rushed outside and returned the call.

"Caroline!" Sierra sounded slightly breathless. "I need you."

"What?"

"We need to get the band back together, that's what." She spoke as if no time at all had passed.

"Where are you?"

"In L.A. I have news. I'm getting married."

Married.

Lots of her friends had been getting married, the news trickling in through online and family networks. And now this. Now Sierra.

"Wow," she said. "Um, congratulations!"

"I want you to make my dress. And be my maid of honor," Sierra said.

"Of course." There was no hesitation. And it wasn't until the call ended that Caroline realized she'd never even asked if the groom was Will.

And it was. The natural progression continued. Sierra flew to New York for the design and fitting of the dress. The nuptials took place in Oysterville, and it was the wedding of the year, uniting Pastor Moore's daughter and her naval officer. The bustling preparations swept through the town. There would be a sword arch of Will's groomsmen in full dress uniform and a reception catered by Star of the Sea. There was a dazzling ring from Tiffany, an ultra-modern swoop of platinum and diamonds designed by Paloma Picasso.

When she saw Will for the first time in years, Caroline steeled herself. His familiar "Hey, stranger" was accompanied by the briefest of hugs. Now they *were* strangers.

The rehearsal dinner was a beach party flowing with champagne and excitement. Guests had been encouraged to bring swimsuits for a midnight plunge. The SEAL team groomsmen looked as though they came from a special breeding program, one that selected for square jaws, perfect posture, massive shoulders, and piercing eyes.

Thumping music from someone's car speakers filled the air. Stoked with driftwood logs, the flames of a beach bonfire climbed high. Champagne shifted to tequila shots and the music got louder. People grabbed partners and danced in a circle around Sierra and Will, who looked blissfully happy, surrounded by dozens of friends. So many from Southern California, Caroline observed. She didn't know most of them. She barely knew Sierra and Will these days. Yet she recognized their joy, which soared like a pair of fireworks.

A couple of times, she caught Will looking at her with a question in his eyes, but didn't know what to make of that look. Too much time had passed. This was what they all knew would happen. What they all expected. *Wanted.* She wasn't jealous. No way. She certainly didn't want to be married, not now. Maybe not ever. An amazing design career in New York City, not a husband, was what beckoned her.

The moon came up, illuminating the breaking waves along the shore.

"I can't stop looking at the navy guys," Rona Stevens said to Caroline in a stage whisper. "If I drink any more, I can't be responsible for my actions."

"That's all of us tonight," Caroline admitted, taking another tequila shot from a tray that was being passed around. It was her fourth or fifth shot. She'd lost count. "Let's jump in the water and cool off."

"The Navy SEALs are in the water," Rona pointed out.

"Exactly," said Caroline. She wasn't much of a drinker, but tonight she wanted to go somewhere else in her head. She wanted to go to a place where she could be unambiguously happy for her two best friends. She untied her silk sarong—one of her original creations—and let it drop. "Are you with me?"

"I'm in." Rona shucked her skirt and top. Five years after high school, she still had her cheerleader body, thanks to her job as a trainer at the local gym. She'd been voted "The Girl Most Likely to Succeed," professing her intention to study sports medicine and work for an NFL team, but she'd never left the peninsula and still dated Hakon off and on again. She looked fantastic in a trendy one-piece maillot, though. "We're going to freeze our asses off," she warned Caroline.

"The navy guys will warm us up." Caroline grabbed her hand and they ran headlong into the breaking waves, where people were already splashing and shrieking. The cold shock took her breath away, but she powered through it, diving under the water into blackness. By the time she surfaced, Rona was already fully flirting with one of the SEALs. Two others surfaced on either side of Caroline like a pair of trained orcas.

"Damn," said one of them. "The weekend just got about a thousand percent better. What's your name, darlin'?"

"I'm Caroline. You're Matt, right? And Lars?"

"Beauty and brains," said Matt, who had glorious teeth and large, beautiful hands. "Matt Campion, at your service."

She hiccupped. "Right. So I'm a genius because I listened to the introductions?"

"You're a genius because you're smoking hot."

A wave sloshed over her head and she lost her balance and was pulled under. In a split second, a pair of iron-hard arms scooped her up, and she found herself looking into Matt's smiling eyes.

"My first rescue of the night," he said, then glanced at Lars. "Take a hike, man. This one's mine."

"I am, am I?" She wound her hands around his neck and hung on while he carried her out of the water. "Yikes, now I'm freezing," she said through chattering teeth.

"Let's do something about that," he said.

A few moments later, she was lying with him on a thick tattersall blanket some distance from the bonfire. The firelit bodies, dancing to the thumping rhythm, looked vaguely tribal. Matt handed her an airline-size bottle. "Jägermeister," he said. "It'll warm you up."

She drank down the shot, a curious mixture of citrus, licorice, and spices. "Ooh, now I'm dizzy," she confessed.

He rolled closer to her and drew her into his arms. "I know what you mean, darlin'."

"No, I mean—"

He stopped her with a deep kiss that tasted of salt water and liquor, his thighs hard and damp against hers, his erection apparent. The swiftness and surprise took her breath away, and she pressed her hands against his chest. He made a throaty sound as his muscular tongue searched deeper and his hands found the straps of her bikini top.

She turned her head to the side, ducking his mouth. "Whoa, slow down, big fella," she said. The Jäger and the tequila seemed to evaporate in an instant. "I'm not really into this."

"Hell yeah, you are," he said with a chuckle. "Hold still, gorgeous. I've got something for you." He put her hand on his erection. "Ah, that's nice."

"Oh, for Pete's sake." She took back her hand. "Knock it off."

"It's okay," he murmured, pressing her shoulders against the blanket. "I have protection."

"Protection?" A sharp, incredulous laugh escaped her. "What the hell—did you really think we were going to—"

"That's right, little lady. It's your lucky night."

Little lady? Seriously? Caroline squirmed beneath him, trying to put some distance between them. He was massive and rock hard, immovable. She was confused. Embarrassed. She felt something else as well—a quiver of alarm. "Enough already," she said. "Get off me. I mean it."

"So do I," he said, his voice rich and warm. "You are the sweetest handful I've held in a long time."

She managed to free one hand. She shoved it against his shoulder. "Dude, listen to me. It's late and we both had too much to drink. I'm not into this, so get the hell off me." She pushed harder.

"Oh, so you like it rough, do you?" he asked. "In that case, you and I are gonna get along just fine."

"What? *No.* What part of *no* do you not understand?"

"I understand what your sweet body's telling me, and I'm not hearing *no.*" He grabbed her wrist and pinned her to the blanket, a predator toying with its prey.

"Then you'd better listen closer," she told him, her teeth chattering.

"Closer," he said. "*Yeah.*" His hips ground down on her. He went in for a kiss. She turned her head away and his warm mouth slid along her cheek.

Now what? Should she yell for help, hoping she could be heard above the loud music? If she did that, would the stupid drama ruin the evening for Sierra and Will? He was just a big, dumb, drunk guy, after all. No need to make a federal case out of it.

He lifted himself up, but before she could roll out from under him, he shifted so he was on top of her once again.

"Let me go, damn it," she said through gritted teeth. Then she drew breath to yell, even though she knew she'd be humiliating herself by overreacting. She didn't even know what to yell. *No*? *Help*? Maybe just a scream—

"Dude, I meant what I said. Don't force me to make a scene and ruin our friends' wedding."

"C'mon, baby. We'll make a scene together. You're gonna love it." He pinned her wrists and his mouth ground down on hers before she could turn her head again, stealing her breath, closing off her airway. Now she couldn't scream. She couldn't breathe. She felt trapped by inertia and terror and foolishness and indecision. She managed to wrench her mouth away from his for a split second.

"*Stop,*" she said, and then he kissed her again, a brutal invasion of teeth and tongue. She bit his tongue. It was like a tough, undigestible cut of meat.

"Shit," he said, "you're a wild one." He didn't kiss her again but covered her mouth with his hand. Panic shot through her. She was trapped. The loud music and crashing waves drowned out her muffled voice. His free hand groped at her swimsuit.

This could not be happening, she thought. And yet it was, engulfing and smothering her with a sense of powerlessness. A moment later, she couldn't breathe. Couldn't think—

The hard weight of him lifted suddenly, as if plucked by a steam shovel.

Dizzy with panic, Caroline gulped in air.

He let out a yell. "What the fuck—"

"She said stop." Will's voice cut through the night.

"Fuck off, Jensen, we're just having a little fun." Matt scrambled backward, then lunged. Their silhouettes clashed like two stags in rut.

Caroline gasped, her entire body buzzing with shock. She crab-walked to the edge of the blanket and jumped up, wrapping herself in a towel. Her bikini top was gone.

Will made a Krav Maga move she remembered from long ago, and she heard a noise like a bag of liquid hitting concrete.

"*Fuck,*" said Matt. "Goddamn, Jensen, I think you broke my fucking nose."

Will pivoted and walked away. "Let's go." He grabbed Caroline by the arm and strode toward the parking lot.

Clutching the towel, she nearly stumbled, trying to keep up. She was too mortified to say anything except "Hey, I can take care of myself."

"Yeah, I could see that. What the hell were you doing?" Will demanded. "Jesus, look at you."

She bristled, holding the towel closer. "What, like that was my fault?"

He yanked open the door to his car—his grandfather's Grand Marquis. "Get in."

Her top was missing. She was barefoot, too. She got into the car.

He wheeled out of the parking lot. At the same time, he groped behind the seat and found a jacket. "Put that on if you're cold."

She was shivering uncontrollably.

Then she realized it wasn't from the cold. "D-did you really break that guy's nose?"

"He'll be okay. But shit, Caroline, he's on my goddamn *team.*" He careened into the driveway of her parents' house, the crushed shells crackling under the tires.

"Well, he sucks," she said. "I didn't ask for him to—I didn't want—"

"Then what the hell were you thinking, parading around in your bikini, doing shots?"

"Don't you dare blame *my* clothes for that jerk's behavior."

"He was looking at you like a lamb chop all night."

"How do you know how he was *looking* at me?" she demanded.

He threw the car into park and leaned over, pinning her against the seat, his face inches from hers, his whiskey-sweet breath on her face. "That's what guys like him do."

She gasped in horror and shoved at his chest as hard as she could. "Get the hell away from me!"

He drew back immediately, also looking horrified. "Okay, yeah. I know. I'm sorry. I just . . . Jesus, Caroline. I didn't mean to—"

She couldn't even hear him, because she started wheezing in a panic that suddenly roared through her like a forest fire. The latent terror of being pinned down and groped made it impossible to breathe. Her heart hammered against her chest, loud and frightening.

"Hey, hey . . ." Gentle hands cupped her shoulders. "Caroline, hey, listen, it's over. It's okay. I'm sorry for what happened." His touch was tender, his words finally penetrating her panic. "I'm sorry I yelled at you. I was scared about what might have happened if I hadn't noticed you'd wandered off. It's over now," he said again. "I'm here. I'm here, okay?"

She collapsed against his chest, pressing her cheek to his heart and clinging to him. The solid comfort of his embrace felt like a seawall, keeping fear at bay. He was right. Some drunk guy had come on to her, and Will had intervened, and she didn't need to be afraid anymore. The panic ebbed, and she stopped trembling.

"You all right now?" he asked.

"I was so scared," she said in a small voice.

"I know, baby," he whispered, his breath warm against her hair. "I know. It's over now."

With aching tenderness, he cupped her face between his hands and stared down into her eyes, placing a feather-light kiss on her forehead. And then something else caught fire, not with panic but with a mindless, long-buried, unstoppable desire. Caroline wasn't sure who made the first move, but suddenly she was planting a terrible, irresistible, illicit kiss on his mouth.

Time stopped.

Everything stopped.

It was a deep, thirsty kiss, born of years of yearning, and it was like an out-of-body experience. The world fell away, just for a moment. A blazing moment of sweetness. The taste of him. His smell. His hands on her bare skin. Then they broke apart as if burned.

She stared at him. He stared back.

"Caroline, my God. This is—this was . . . Shit. I've been wanting this forever, to—"

"Don't you dare say anything more. Don't you fucking dare."

He froze. "Yeah, okay. We both had too much to drink. It's just . . . You're right. Damn. I'm sorry, Caroline. I'm so damn sorry."

The generalized *I'm sorry* left her wondering, For what? She groped blindly for the door handle and leaped out of the car, filled with an insane jumble of guilt and excitement and horrible shame.

Caroline woke the next morning with a hangover—not from the drinking, but from the lingering fallout of her kiss with Will Jensen.

Her best friend's soon-to-be husband. How the hell had it happened? *Why* had it happened? What on earth was she going to do now?

Forget it, that's what, she told herself stoutly. Pretend it never happened. And hope like hell Will does the same.

Their thoughts were in sync. Without exchanging a word, they avoided eye contact as she and her co-groomsman—*not* Matt Campion, thank God—led the wedding party down the aisle, where Will, in full dress uniform, awaited his bride. She quickly stepped aside, taking her place as maid of honor. The unfortunate placement put her in a direct line of sight with Will, but she studiously avoided his gaze.

It was almost as if she had dreamed the whole thing. Maybe she had. And maybe Will had been so drunk he didn't remember that moment. The friendship-destroying moment that complicated everything between them.

She glared instead at Matt, sullen and cowardly, his black eye and swollen nose barely covered by poorly applied concealer. He hadn't said a word. No apology. No admission of wrongdoing. What the hell gave some guys the idea that forcing women was okay?

When Sierra walked down the aisle, she was a fairytale princess, an utter romantic triumph in the dress Caroline had made for her. Gasps of wonder and sobs of emotion drifted from the congregation. Caroline felt as cold as a stone. She didn't allow herself to feel a thing—not jealousy, not shame, not disappointment, not regret. Not happiness, either, but she forced herself to pretend.

At the conclusion of the ceremony, she hung back, letting everyone else hug and congratulate the happy couple. As she stood apart from the joyous celebration, her mind was filled with flashbacks of the three of them growing up together, the golden summers, the three musketeers, sharing adventures, sharing everything, promising they'd be friends forever.

At the reception, no one seemed to notice that she didn't dance with the groom. She left without saying goodbye, the tires of her rental car spitting crushed oyster shells in her wake. Glancing in the rearview mirror, she saw the broad silhouette of a man, watching her go.

PART SIX

Sometimes good things fall apart so better things can fall together.

—Marilyn Monroe

Chapter 22

"I have a brilliant idea," Sierra said, wandering into Caroline's workshop and admiring the ready garments—beautiful rainwear, bagged and tagged for sale. Each piece featured the signature nautilus shell on the sleeve. And each piece represented hours of work and stress. Amy, from the Sewing Circle, had eagerly agreed to make the deliveries to the boutiques that had agreed to sell the goods, in Long Beach, Astoria, Portland, and Seattle.

"What's your brilliant idea?"

"Let's get hammered."

Caroline pushed away from her workstation, which she'd hastily cobbled together with an old door and two file cabinets. She and Ilsa, a web designer, had been setting up her e-commerce website. "What? Hammered? Nobody does that anymore." She peered at her friend and at Ilsa. "Do they? Do you?"

"Nah," said Ilsa. "I used to, but not anymore. Not since . . . well, you know." Caroline knew Ilsa was referring to the groping incident she'd related at the Sewing Circle meeting. "I'm going to call it a day. You two have fun."

"I don't usually drink," Sierra said. "Too many calories. But tonight is special."

After Ilsa left, Caroline looked at her friend. Her pretty, troubled friend. "Are you celebrating something? Or lamenting something?"

"Both," Sierra said. "That's what makes it so special. That's why I need to drink. Come over to my place."

Caroline hesitated. She was in an uncomfortable spot with Sierra and Will. She was friends with each of them, friends with both of them. And there were secrets between them all.

"Come on," Sierra cajoled. "I need some girlfriend time."

"I'll come up for a bit. I won't get hammered, though. I have to drive."

"Well, at least have a couple of shots with me, for old times' sake."

Doing shots was not Caroline's friend. Whether Sierra realized it or not, having too much to drink years before had caused the breakdown of their friendship.

"What about Will?" she asked. "Will he join the festivities?"

"He won't be home for hours." Sierra dismissed the notion with a wave of her hand. "He's got a committee meeting, and then he's going to the lumber supply to pick up a load of boards for the oyster shed. My busy, busy husband."

"On a Friday night?"

"Perfect time to do it," Sierra said. "Otherwise he'd have to spend it with me."

Caroline tried not to read too much into the comment as she stepped into the foyer. Water's Edge was a beautiful home, so lovingly restored. Yet Sierra didn't seem happy at all. "I'll have two shots with you—one for the celebration and one for the lamentation."

"Fair enough." Sierra led the way back to the kitchen.

Caroline looked around in wonder. "It's finished."

"Pretty much. Will and Kurt added all the finishing touches last weekend."

"Oh, Sierra. It's fantastic." She took a moment to check out the airy, light-filled space. The house's old-world charm was on display even though it had been fully modernized. "Did you design it yourself?"

She lined up a bottle of tequila, salt, lime, and shot glasses. "Me? Heck, no. We have a kitchen designer, Padma Sen. She's really good. Has a huge crush on Will. Just like everyone else."

Caroline cut the lime into wedges, keeping her focus on the sharp knife blade. "Everyone else?"

"It's like I told you—Will is incredible. I married a unicorn." She poured two generous shots.

"You say that like it's a bad thing."

"It's a thing."

They tapped glasses, licked the salt, and downed the shots, chasing them with lime wedges. Caroline savored the salty, tart flavors along with the heady burn of alcohol.

"Now then," she said, "assuming you can still speak after that—what are we toasting?"

Sierra settled onto one of the country chic barstools. "I got a job offer from Nordstrom."

"That's . . . great?" Caroline couldn't quite read her friend's expression.

"I used to get tons of modeling gigs there. Now I've aged out of the role."

"Unfortunately, I've seen too much of that in the industry. So they want you back?"

"As a producer, not a model. And not just *a* producer—*the* producer. As in, the entire shoot will be managed by yours truly."

"Holy crap, that is great. Seriously—great." A producer was tasked with supervising catalog and website shoots, everything from scouting locations to planning the travel and managing the scouts, stylists, set designers—the whole process. She studied Sierra's face again. "Is this the good news or the bad news?"

"It's the dilemma. I'll be away half the time. Maybe more. It'll be like Will's navy deployment, only in reverse. I'll be the one leaving. And instead of defending our nation, I'll be on tropical beach shoots in the winter and mountain resorts in the summer."

"It sounds amazing, except for the separation part."

"How am I supposed to have a marriage if I'm gone all the time?"

Caroline poured two more shots. "Can't help you there."

"I'm so screwed. When we were young, I was the one who wanted the relationship, the husband, the marriage. But then . . . my priorities changed. He went away on deployment, and I discovered my own life. It's not fair to either of us. I changed into a different person. I'm not the girl he married. And I feel so guilty about that."

"Listen, everybody changes."

"God. You're as bad as Will."

"What does he think of your plan?"

"He keeps saying it's up to me. That we'll make it work. But he's wrong. No matter what I decide, one of us gets shafted. If I take the job, he loses his wife. If I decline the opportunity, I lose out on the future I really want."

"No room for compromise?"

Sierra was quiet for several moments. Then she downed her second shot. "Will would hate it if he knew I was drinking. We're supposed to be trying for a baby. I'm horrible."

"Stop it."

"I can't. I know I'm horrible. You know how the women at the Sewing Circle meetings talk about trying so desperately to escape their monster husbands? Well, here's me, also desperate. I'm desperate to escape my *perfect* husband. So in this case, *I'm* the monster."

Caroline grabbed her second shot and threw it back with a vengeance. "Christ, Sierra. Why are you telling me this stuff?"

"Because you're my friend."

"For something like this, you need more than a friend. You need a therapist. Or a marriage counselor. Some kind of professional. And I'm not one, not even close. And coming to me for relationship advice? Like asking the plumber to accessorize your outfit."

Sierra helped herself to another drink. "For what it's worth, I did see a counselor and laid it all out for her, the whole story. The only result was that I came away feeling even worse than I already do. Why would I put myself—and Will—through a painful session like that? No thank you."

"I'm so sorry. Maybe it wasn't the right counselor for you. I don't know. I wish you had someone better than me to help you figure things out."

Sierra sighed. "Everything seemed so easy when we were young."

Speak for yourself, thought Caroline.

"It was all so crystal clear. Remember the summer you introduced me to Will for the very first time? I remember it like yesterday. I looked at him and just knew he would be my everything. God, I wish I could find that feeling again. It was so powerful. I thought it would last forever. And now here we are. I'm trapped by his perfection."

"Not to be too obnoxious," Caroline said, feeling the effects of the tequila, "but that's not exactly the worst problem to have."

"I had an abortion," Sierra blurted out.

Every small hair on Caroline's body prickled to attention. "What?" She gaped at her friend. "I mean, I heard what you said, but . . . Jesus. What happened? When? Are you all right?"

Sierra pressed her hands down on the countertop, the sleek new stone gleaming. "It was last year. I got pregnant. I thought I wanted . . . Will wants kids so badly. But I couldn't do it. I tried so hard to want the same things he did. I knew he would be so happy. But I . . . I didn't tell him, and I ended it in secret. I'm a terrible person."

It was shocking, but Caroline refused to judge someone else's private decision. "I hope he was understanding about it when you finally told him."

"He still doesn't know."

Caroline nearly fell off her stool.

"He doesn't know I was pregnant and he doesn't know I terminated it. You're the only one I've ever told."

"Holy shit," Caroline said. "Listen, this is really big, Sierra. Like I said, I'm no relationship expert, but I want . . ." What did she want? For the two of them to be happy, yes, yet she wasn't sure what that meant. Sierra's confession festered inside her, unspoken. The truth needed to come out, but it wasn't hers to disclose—not to Will. Not to anyone. She couldn't bear the thought of being around him, carrying this secret. "You should tell him. You *need* to tell him. He's your husband, for chrissake."

"It would break his heart. It would break our marriage."

Caroline did not consider herself to be someone who knew how an intimate relationship worked. She'd never had much success in that department. But she was pretty sure a marriage plagued by a secret that big was already broken.

PART SEVEN

So often the end of a love affair is death by a thousand cuts, so often its survival is life by a thousand stitches.

—Robert Brault

Chapter 23

Standing at the kitchen counter, Will stared at the divorce decree, which had arrived in the day's mail along with the Northern Tool + Equipment clearance catalog and the *Peninsula Tattler.*

The page was sectioned into vertical columns like a divided highway, like his life and Sierra's had been split in two once the inevitable decision had steamrolled over them with breathtaking finality.

It had taken fifteen years to build a life together.

It had taken a mere three months to dismantle it. And after all was said and done, the settlement was just a formality. The life he'd dreamed of, planned for, built with his own hands and the sweat of his brow, was gone even more quickly. In an instant. In the time it took for a phone to ring, for a plus sign to appear on a home pregnancy stick, for a tear to fall down someone's cheek.

The mediator—they had decided not to be contentious about it—told them they were lucky and smart to avoid a huge battle over their assets. There was no need for a battle. The fight had gone out of them both some time ago, slipping away unnoticed until it had irretrievably disappeared. In the end, being starkly honest, he and Sierra were forced to agree that they had the same goal—to end their marriage.

Will didn't linger over the multipage document. He knew what was in it. The decree summed up their marriage in crisp, objective terms—how they would divvy up the cars, the Tiffany ring and other jewelry, the property, the pensions, the policies. A clean business transaction. It didn't address the blurry details of all the ways he and Sierra had grown apart—his deployments, her loneliness, his accident, her ambivalence, his dream, her deception. Those things were all like a trickle of water through a crack in a rock, seemingly harmless. But when a deep freeze came along, the water cracked the rock into pieces.

That final deep freeze turned out to be the most frank and painful conversation they'd ever had. She told him she didn't want kids.

Despite a churning disappointment, he had tried to be understanding. I'm married to you. I made a commitment, a vow. If you've changed your mind, I'll make my peace with it.

That's not what I want, she'd responded, her flood of tears seemingly endless. I tried so hard to want what you want. I couldn't. I simply couldn't. Could. Not. She told him then that, last year, in the middle of a major catalog shoot, she'd terminated an early, unexpected pregnancy.

After that, there were no words that could have saved them.

He believed absolutely that a woman had a right to choose. His wife had a right to choose. But he also knew that Sierra's choice meant something more than changing her mind about having children. It was an acknowledgment that she didn't want to be married to him anymore. Didn't want the future they'd envisioned when they were both too naively young to know that life didn't always go according to plan.

"Fair enough," he said, recognizing the irony of the statement. Then he dropped the papers into a drawer filled with all the detritus of the past three months. "Fair enough."

Sometimes, going about his business in town, he encountered his ex-in-laws. While he was married,

Sierra's parents had not hesitated to treat him like family, including him in holidays and traditions, even reaching out to his own unreachable father. These days, when they saw Will, they ducked their heads and avoided eye contact as if they were the guilty ones. Did they know about Sierra's choice? Or did they think the breakup was caused by something else? Did they think it was his fault? Did they think he'd cheated? Cheating was almost always a factor in a divorce. Will and Sierra were an exception. They had diverged. Wandered away from each other and stopped wondering why. They'd lost each other in the weeds of everyday living. They'd stopped talking about the things that mattered. They'd stopped dreaming their dreams together.

He went outside to tackle the day's project—replacing some dry rot under the soffit of the garage.

Ladder, crowbar, Sawzall, chop saw. He climbed the ladder and stabbed the crowbar into the soft, rotten wood. A couple of wasps shot out of the gaping hole—a bad sign. And a bad sound—a low, steady, ominous hum. The sound of anger.

He yanked out another portion of the soffit, releasing a storm cloud of wasps. They streamed from a huge dirty-paper hive, their fury rising to a deafening crescendo.

"Fuck," he said, feeling the burn of a sting on his neck. "Just . . . *fuck*."

He swatted at the gathering storm as more stings darted into him. He didn't panic, though. Once you get shot in the face by a terrorist, not much else rattles you.

The hive was half detached. He made one more swing with the crowbar and missed. The motion took him off balance and he went over backward, arms wheeling, hands swiping at empty air. Every bit of air left him when he landed flat on his back. He lay motionless, unable to draw breath for several seconds. And the furious humming went on.

The hive hung from a few spirals of fiber. The wasps encircled it. Maybe they circled his head like birds over a downed cartoon character.

After a few seconds, he managed to take in some air. Did a mental check for injuries. Everything seemed to be in working order. He glared up at the hanging hive, the hovering wasps. When dealing with venomous insects, you were supposed to call a professional. Wear protective gear. Use appropriate pesticides. There were rules.

"Fuck it," he said, and levered himself up. He went and got a lighter and a can of WD-40. *Warning: Do not expose to open flame.* He aimed a stream at the hive and lit it. The homemade flamethrower roared.

The hive exploded into flames, the flaky dry material disintegrating, the insects roasting. The whole thing drifted to the ground like remnants of the *Hindenburg.* It lay in the dry grass, igniting the brush, flames licking the side of the old garage. Will grabbed a shovel and flung loose dirt on the fire until it went out.

Looking around at the mess he'd made, he inventoried several livid stings. Then with one more *fuck it,* he peeled down to his skivvies and made for the dock, hitting the deep water with a satisfying splash. He floated on his back, gazing up at the sky while the salt water flooded over him, cooling the stings.

It was weird, being on his own. A new situation for him, now that he thought about it. He'd lived in college dorms. Then with his training unit and team in the navy. With Sierra after they married. On base during deployments. He'd never actually lived all on his own like this.

After Sierra left, friends and colleagues had rushed to him, offering comfort and companionship—one of the perks of living in a small community. The women especially had been attentive. An unattached guy, gainfully employed, was back on the market. He'd never consumed so much mac and cheese, so many Bundt cakes. He'd even gone on dates, mainly to distract himself from the fact that his heart was broken.

It really was, he reflected. And a broken heart was a lot worse than a fall from a ladder and a few dozen wasp stings.

A heartbreak can turn the world on its head.

A heartbreak can lay you out.

A heartbreak can change the shape of your dreams.

The clinic on Monday after school was crowded with sniffling children. That was how it seemed to Caroline, anyway.

There were a lot of things about raising children she didn't understand, and one of them was that kids got sick all the time. They traded germs and viruses like baseball cards, passing them from one to another in an endless circuit. Today, though, both kids were sniffle-free, which was a good thing, because they were due for booster shots.

"I'll tell you what. If you're good at the doctor, I'll take you for ice cream."

"Ice cream is not as good as a shot is bad," Flick said.

He was getting so smart.

"Fine, then tell me something that's as good as a shot is bad."

"A dog," Flick said.

"What?"

"I want a dog. Like Ribsy in the book you read us."

"Oh, Flick."

"A dog! Let's get a dog!" Addie jumped up and down.

Although the children didn't know it, Caroline had already talked to her parents about getting a dog for the kids. They were on board, even excited. Ever since she'd arrived, they'd been urging her to live with them on a permanent basis. The house was so big, they'd said. Way too much house for them. It was a house meant for kids and dogs.

Caroline couldn't deny that the arrangement was helping her beyond measure. To have a place to live, loving people to look after the children while she was reorganizing her life, was a gift, to be sure. Yet in the back of her mind, she also couldn't deny that she regarded this as a temporary arrangement. She refused to be that boomerang adult child who came running home to lick her wounds after a setback.

She had plans. She was making a go of it. If her line of apparel succeeded, she could move to the city once again, make a name for herself, and resume the life she'd envisioned so long ago—only this time on her terms.

Getting a dog felt permanent. It was another line on the anchor embedded so deeply into the yielding ocean floor of home. Another knot in the apron strings.

An assistant called their name, and the three of them stepped into a small exam room.

Addie went first. The little girl sat on the paper-covered table, staring ahead with admirable stoicism. With her free arm, she hugged Caroline tight and clutched Wonder Woman in her hand. The nurse introduced herself as Connie. She managed the syringe with a clever sleight of hand, practically concealing it.

"You're going to feel a quick pinch," she said. "Can you hold still for me?"

Addie nodded. Then she looked at the needle and went completely slack, collapsing on the table like a dropped marionette. Wonder Woman hit the floor.

Caroline gasped. "Addie! What the—"

"Fainted," the nurse murmured. She quickly laid Addie on the table and checked her breathing and pulse. The nurse was preparing to shine a scope into the little girl's eyes when Addie blinked and sat up, glancing around in confusion.

"You fainted," Flick said, seeming delighted. "That was cool."

"I've never seen anyone faint before," said Caroline. The sight of Addie going down, even for mere seconds, had rattled her. It was frightening to see how utterly vulnerable a little child was.

"Fairly common," the nurse told her. "We'll keep an eye on her. So she hasn't done this before?"

"Did I get the shot?" Addie asked, blinking.

The nurse checked her pulse and pupils. "Not yet. You're doing really well. Let's try again."

Addie's chin trembled. "Okay," she whispered.

"I'll hold you tight." Caroline slid her arms around the little girl, and her heart warmed with sympathy and affection. "I'm proud of you, Addie. Let's look at each other while Miss Connie does the shot. She's super quick."

The needle darted in. Addie yelped but held still, and within a split second, it was done. Then it was Flick's turn, and he made a horrible face but endured the shot.

"You were brave," she told Flick. "I'm proud of you."

He watched the nurse expertly apply a cowboy Band-Aid.

The nurse inspected a rash under Flick's arm. "You've got a bit of dermatitis. You can get some cream from the pharmacy next door," she said, writing down the name of it.

"Thanks," said Caroline. Her kid had dermatitis. Jeez. "We'll do that right away."

The nurse stepped out. Caroline helped the kids straighten their clothing.

"Mama was chicken," Flick said. "She was scared all the time."

Caroline froze. "What do you mean? Scared of what?"

The little boy shrugged. "Of everything. She was scared to talk."

"To talk? About what?"

"She just was. She'd tell us, 'Don't talk, don't say anything.' "

"Flick, do you know why?"

He stared off into the distance for a moment. "She was just a scaredy-cat."

"Now, I don't happen to agree with you. Your mama was very brave. Let me tell you about the first time I met her."

Both children came to attention. Despite their confusion, they were hungry for stories about their mother. Caroline was determined to keep Angelique alive in their memories. "I was just getting started, and I had one of those rolling racks with my very best designs to show. Some guy grabbed my bag and ran off—and guess who stopped him?"

"Mama," Addie whispered. "*Maman.*"

Caroline nodded, remembering the extraordinary moment. "I had no idea who she was at the time. She was walking toward the venue with a group of models, and when I yelled out, she took off after the guy. She was as tall and fast as Wonder Woman. She caught up with the guy and grabbed hold of my bag. He was so scared, he dropped it and kept running. And that was the moment your mom became one of my best friends in the world."

"You're making that up," Flick said.

"Nope. It happened just like I said. I'm not making it up." Caroline touched his cheek. "And that's the mama I want you to remember."

In the pharmacy, she picked up the lotion and stood waiting while a pair of women huddled behind the counter, ignoring her. "He's so hot," one of them said.

"So freakin' hot. I have such a mad crush on him."

"He's the high school football coach," the first woman said. "Did you know that?"

"No. God, that makes him hotter. Is he dating anyone?"

"Honey, he's dating *everyone.*" She fanned herself with a pharmacy bag. Then she filed it on a rack marked *J* and finally turned to Caroline. "Can I help you?"

She flushed, wondering if it was true, if Will Jensen was dating *everyone.*

"Will!" Flick piped up. "Hey, Coach Will!" He and Addie rushed to see him as he entered the shop.

Caroline's flush grew warmer. She ran into Will all the time, but for some reason, she was surprised to see him whenever it happened. Particularly looking the way he did now, his face alarmingly rashy and swollen.

She peered at him. "Are you all right?"

"Yeah. Does it look bad?"

"You're all swollen."

"You should see the other guy. And by *other guy*, I mean wasp nest."

Addie and Flick studied him with wide-eyed, sober expressions.

"Oh. A wasp nest? Yikes."

"I'll be fine," he said. "I need to pick up a prescription for the swelling." He turned to the kids and hunkered down close. "It's gonna take a lot of medicine to get me back to my usual beautiful self."

Addie put forth a hesitant hand, gently touching his chin. "Does it hurt?"

"Not anymore."

"We got shots and I fainted," Addie said.

He regarded her solemnly. "Wow. But you're okay now."

"I got germatitis," Flick said.

"Dermatitis." Caroline patted her bag with the lotion. "These kids are a new adventure every day."

"We were good at the doctor, so we're getting a dog," Flick announced.

"I said 'we'll see,'" Caroline corrected him.

"That's code for a reluctant yes," Will said. "Trust me, I know these things."

Both kids rounded on her. "Yes means yes," Addie said.

"And 'we'll see' means we'll see. How about we go to the shelter and see if there's a dog that might work for us? Because we might not—"

"We will! We will!" Flick danced a little jig.

"See what you started?" she asked Will.

"I know. I'm awesome."

"Come with us," she said, an impulse taking hold. "I need a second opinion." There were quite a few moments, she realized, when she wished she had a partner in this parenting gig. Her sister Virginia often said as much. She didn't miss her cheating ex, but she did miss having someone to talk to about Fern.

"Yes! Come with us, come come come." Flick danced around him.

Caroline sent Will a pleading look. "The pet rescue place?"

"I'll meet you there," Will said. "Let's hope my ugly mug doesn't scare the critters."

Outside the Peninsula Pet Rescue Society, Caroline tried to temper the kids' expectations. "Listen, we might not find the right dog today. Sometimes you have to keep coming back until you find the best match."

"Did you check out other kids before you picked us?" asked Flick.

"What? *No.*" Christ, she thought. "Why would you even think such a thing?"

"Sometimes you gotta take what you get." He ducked his head, but she caught his mischievous grin.

"Cheeky," she said.

As soon as Will arrived, they all went in together. Flick and Addie were nearly beside themselves as Caroline filled out an adoption form on a clipboard.

"Be still," she said to Flick. "I need to finish this before we can visit the dogs."

"When we adopt our dog, does that mean we get to keep him forever?" asked Addie.

"Sure," said Caroline. "Forever and ever. That's why we need to find just the right match."

"We're not gonna be the foster family?" Addie asked.

"No, if we find the right dog, we'll be its forever family." Caroline felt Will watching her. She focused on filling in all the blanks.

"Rutger Peters said we're foster kids and you could give us back anytime," Flick said.

Caroline stopped writing. She glanced at Will, then back at Flick. "That's not so. I'm your guardian. That's the same as a parent. I'm going to keep you with me, safe and sound, forever."

Will watched her thoughtfully. She could tell his prescription was already kicking in, easing the swollen wasp stings, and he looked ridiculously sweet.

"But it's not the same as adopting," Flick stated.

The statement was like a punch to the gut. Here they were getting ready to adopt a dog, and yet her kids were still foster children. "It's . . . Okay, it's the same," she said, fumbling a bit. "Trust me, there will be no givebacks. That's a promise. Do you trust me?"

"Are we the right kids for you?" Addie asked.

"You're the perfect kids for me," Caroline said. "What a silly question."

Flick said, "Can we go see the dogs now?"

She caught Will's eye over the kids' heads. "Welcome to my world," she muttered.

"I like your world just fine. Come on. I want to see the dogs, too."

The inner sanctum of the shelter was a gauntlet of wagging tails, pleading eyes, and "look at me" yips and yaps. There were scruffy coats and smooth, big dogs and small ones, gray-muzzled seniors and agitated pups.

A volunteer introduced them to a few dogs, and they narrowed the choices to a friendly chocolate lab mix with one blind eye and a small black-and-white dog that was cautious and shy, bowing low with her tail quivering. "She was abused," the volunteer told Caroline and Will. "But she's come a long way, thanks to 4-H students who have been working with her every day. We think she'd be a wonderful pet for your family, Mr. and Mrs.—"

"Oh," Caroline said, startled. "We're not a fam—I mean, Will's just a friend who came along . . ." She fumbled with her words, feeling a flush rise to her cheeks.

Will touched her arm. "How about we take both dogs out to the play yard with the kids and see how they get along?"

A few minutes later, Flick and Addie were in heaven. They petted the dogs and tossed balls and toys for them, the kids wriggling and wagging every bit as excitedly as the dogs. Caroline stood watching with Will, and her heart swelled with affection.

"You're having a moment." Will touched her shoulder.

She let herself lean into him, just for a second. "I love seeing them like this."

"I bet it feels great. What's better than making a child happy?"

"That's the question that keeps me awake at night. How can I make them happy? How can I keep them that way? I'm so scared of screwing this up."

"It's called being human, Caroline. Parenting's not an exact science. You're good with them, and they're crazy about you. Sure, you'll make mistakes. You'll also get it right a lot of the time." He gestured at the happy tangle of kids and dogs in the yard. "Like now."

"Thanks. God, I hope you're right." She paused, sent him a quick glance. "I've been thinking of adopting them. Making it legal and official. Am I nuts?"

He bumped against her, a teasing nudge. "Yeah, I've always liked that about you."

"Seriously, am I?"

"No, you're awesome. You took in these kids and made them your own and gave them a life after the worst possible thing happened to them. And that makes you awesome, not nuts."

She didn't realize she'd been holding her breath until it came out as a sigh of relief. "You have no idea how much I needed to hear that. These kids . . . God. They're the best, hardest thing I've ever done. I wake up every day, scared I'm going to screw up, but somehow we seem to be making it."

They stood together in silence. Kids and dogs at play were the embodiment of pure joy. Sure, they got rashes and fainted at the doctor. They made messes and noise all day, every day, it seemed. But the rewards of seeing them grow were beyond anything she'd ever imagined.

"So how are *you* doing?" Caroline eyed Will. "And you know what I'm asking."

"I'm good. Getting used to my new reality."

"I wish I knew how I could be a better friend."

"We've always been friends," he said quietly.

Usually after a breakup, the couple's friends went their separate ways, staying loyal to one or the other of the riven pair. Caroline felt torn between both of them. Sierra had relocated to the city. She was constantly on the move in her new job. Caroline had called her many times. Sent text messages and emails. The responses were brief, almost dismissive. Then she sent a note that summed it up: *I'm reinventing my life and I'm doing great. For the time being, it's easier for me if I don't bring along anything from the past. Hope you understand.*

Caroline stopped calling her.

Will was a different story. She saw him often, since the rainwear workshop was on his property. A couple of times, she'd been working when a woman came to see him. A date. He was dating. He was back on the market. And that of course made her think about the way things had been when they were young.

She remembered a time when she'd had feelings so powerful she thought she would explode, but she had kept them hidden.

Was she doing that now?

"I can listen," she stated.

He held a long silence. "Hell, don't I know it."

"What's that supposed to mean?"

"Sierra ended a pregnancy. She said she told you."

Caroline looked away, seared by a sense of guilt. "It's none of my business. I wish she hadn't said anything."

"She told you before she told me."

"She knew it would hurt you."

"It's a huge thing to keep from your spouse," he said.

"I'm sorry. I really don't know what to say."

"Most people don't. Hell, half the time, *I* don't."

There were so many other things Caroline wanted to talk to him about. She hesitated, though, uncertain about who they were to each other after all that had happened. Their friendship was different in ways she couldn't quite get her head around. She wished . . .

"Have you made a decision?" The shelter manager came out and watched the kids and dogs playing together. The brown one fetched a stick tirelessly. The black-and-white one nestled sweetly in Flick's lap.

"Oh, boy." Caroline glanced at Will. "This is going to be hard."

"Blackie is really nice," Addie said. "But so is Brownie."

Flick nodded. "We can't choose."

Shit, thought Caroline. Two dogs?

"We have to pick one," she said. She, too, was completely torn. Both dogs were lovely and either one would make the kids happy.

"I have an idea," Will said. He hunkered down and the chocolate lab mix scurried over, trying to climb his chest and lick his face. "I need a dog, too," Will continued. "Suppose I take this one home and you guys take the other."

"Yay!" Addie jumped in the air. "We can visit him, right?"

"Sure you can. Any time you want."

"Will, that's incredible," Caroline said. She felt the sweetest sense of relief. "Are you sure?"

"It's fine." He rubbed the ecstatic dog behind the ears. "I've been wanting a dog for a long time. Sierra never did, though. So I figure there's no reason to put it off any longer."

Chapter 24

"Why's it called 'homecoming' if we're already home?" asked Flick, craning his neck to check out the scene.

"Everybody comes together to welcome back people who went to high school here."

"Is Sierra coming back?"

The town always went all out for homecoming. Corsages of giant mums, a special performance with alumni band members, and of course the all-important homecoming court—king, queen, and courtiers. Sierra had been homecoming queen their senior year. She'd been paired with Bucky O'Malley, the head cheerleader, because he was the only one who came close to her in good looks. Caroline had never been a member of the court, but she'd made Sierra's faux-ermine cloak for the halftime show.

"Sierra won't be back this year. You've probably never gone to a homecoming game," Caroline said. "It's like a regular football game, only with lots more people."

There was a rally in the parking lot of the stadium, crowded with people in letterman jackets and school colors. The smell of rain was heavy in the air, but everyone seemed to be ignoring it. Star of the Sea had a booth, and they stopped by for a snack—gourmet corn dogs and cookies with the Peninsula Mariners team logo. The sounds and smells stirred waves of nostalgia—the rivalries, the romances, the regrets. The ridiculously big dreams that too often came crashing down with the onset of adulthood. Caroline spotted people she hadn't seen since high school, greeting several of them and garnering raised eyebrows of inquiry as they noticed her kids.

One of the inquisitive looks came from Zane Hardy, her onetime lab partner. He looked the same—cool glasses, shaggy hair parted on the side, skinny jeans, vintage tee layered under a buffalo plaid shirt. Only now he had a little boy in tow who looked so much like Zane it was almost comical. She smiled at him but kept going. Sometimes the best part of nostalgia was wondering *what if . . .0*

She and the children found seats in the bleachers, and they were soon swept up in the excitement, stomping their feet as the alumni band blared an opening number and watching the cheerleaders in utter fascination. "Caroline, they do cartwheels almost as good as you," Addie said.

Caroline gave her a hug. "Right, kiddo."

With much fanfare, the players burst through the paper banner at the locker-room tunnel.

"I see Will!" Flick jumped up and down, pointing. "Hey, Will! Can we go say hi?"

"Not right now," Caroline said, although privately, she had the same thought. It was great seeing him in his element, in charge of a team bent on winning. He was an energetic presence, talking earnestly to his assistant and players. After the kickoff, he seemed wound tight as a drum as he paced the sidelines, clipboard in hand. He was chewing gum, which caused his jaw to bulge rhythmically.

". . . still dating half the town," said a woman's voice a couple of rows back.

Caroline whipped a glance behind her. She recognized Lanie Cannon, an attractive, available single mom. Lanie worked at the local grocery. Single women seemed to be everywhere these days. And they were all after Will Jensen.

". . . should just ask him out."

"I couldn't."

"Didn't he help your older boy get into college last year?"

Caroline leaned back to eavesdrop.

"Totally," said Lanie. "Beau got an athletic scholarship to UW thanks to Will. I won't have to go to the poorhouse paying for tuition. A couple of years ago, I couldn't afford Beau's athletic fees, and someone mysteriously paid them. I think it was Will."

Of course it was Will, Caroline thought.

"Well, there you have it. Tell him you want to make him dinner as a proper thank-you."

"So obvious."

"He's a guy. You need to be obvious."

"I wouldn't mind if *he* was more obvious," Lanie said. "I've heard he never goes past first base. Or maybe the first down, in football speak."

"He's the local coach. Probably trying to avoid gossip. Or—hey—waiting for the right girl to come along. Maybe you should—"

"Can I get a foam finger?" asked Addie, pointing to a concessionaire hawking swag.

Caroline tried ignoring her. One thing she'd learned about kids—they all liked everything for about five minutes. After that, the thing was forgotten and, worse, discarded and left for her to pick up. She couldn't help mulling over what she'd heard the women discussing. And she couldn't help thinking back to a secret she'd held enshrined in her heart for far too long—the night she'd lost herself, for only a single illicit moment, in Will Jensen's arms.

"Can I?" Addie persisted. "Please?"

"No," Caroline said. The overheard conversation had irritated her. "Finish your hot dog."

"Aww . . ."

When the halftime show started, so did the rain. Umbrellas sprouted like mushrooms in the gloom. "Gear up, you guys," Caroline said.

The kids pulled their rain flies out of the pockets of their popover jackets and put them on. Caroline donned a prototype of her latest design for C-Shell Rainwear—the stadium coat. Her seat cushion transformed into a lightweight raincoat in a cool print. She shook it out and put it on, and when she looked down at the field, she spotted Will looking directly at her.

Their gazes held for a moment; then he lifted his arm and beckoned her.

"Hey, is he waving at you?" asked the woman behind her. "I think he is!"

"Let's go find Will," Caroline said, taking Addie's hand. "Watch your step."

They were halfway down the narrow concrete steps when someone tapped Caroline on the shoulder. “Excuse me.” It was Lanie Cannon, brushing the rain from her eyes.

Good lord, was she looking for a catfight?

“Yes?” Caroline was not going to let her by.

“I was just noticing . . . Did you just turn your seat cushion into a raincoat?”

Oh.

“I did, actually,” said Caroline.

“That’s genius. And super cute. I’ve sat on more cold, wet benches than I can count. Where’d you get it? If you don’t mind my asking.”

“Caroline made it,” Addie piped up.

Caroline nodded and indicated the nautilus shell logo on her jacket. “On my website. They have them at Swain’s store, too.”

“Cool. Thanks!”

She saw Flick making a beeline for Will. “Gotta go.”

There were perks to being single, Will discovered. People felt sorry for him. They fixed food and brought it over, the way some folks did after a death in the family. They sent text messages and emails with funny pictures and video clips. They invited him places.

He was grateful for the attention. But sometimes all it did was remind him of what he'd lost—a wife, a carefully planned future, a dream. He looked around and saw couples being couples, functioning with seemingly little effort, sharing the daily joys of living. Yeah, so probably there were hidden issues. But knowing this didn't keep him from feeling the glaring hole in the middle of his world.

At the annual homecoming game, during halftime, Caroline joined him just as he was about to head into the locker room for the team pep talk. Despite the chilly rain, despite the fact that his team was down by seven points, he'd greeted her with a grin and a wave.

She had invited him to Thanksgiving dinner at her family's place, and he'd gladly accepted.

It was a start, he thought, as he got ready for what promised to be an epic feast.

A start of what?

Maybe something. Maybe nothing.

Since the divorce, he'd sensed a shift in his relationship with Caroline. It was subtle, and sometimes he wondered if he was imagining things, but he felt drawn to her in a different way. When he saw her coming and going from her shop, he noticed things that used to be filtered out by the fact that he was married. To her best friend. Now he noticed the way her eyes lit up when she smiled, and the curve of her butt in the snug jeans she liked to wear, the fullness of her lips and the sound of her laughter.

Armed with a big bouquet and a box of fancy chocolates—five pounds, enough to feed a crowd—he showed up at the Shelby house on a dark, rainy, muddy afternoon. The entire house held the warm aromas of a classic family Thanksgiving—roasting turkey and sage, baking rolls, sweet cinnamon and apples.

"Thanks for taking in a stray," he said to Dottie as she greeted him at the door. "I was going to bring a pie, but I figured that would be like bringing coals to Newcastle."

"You'd be right." Georgia took his rain jacket and hung it up. "There's no competing with my maple pecan pie or Mom's brown sugar pumpkin."

"You're never going to get rid of me."

The Shelby clan surrounded him, amoeba-like, enclosing him in a kind of warmth that was gratifying, but that also filled him with yearning. There were two sets of grandparents present. Georgia came with a husband and two kids. Virginia was there with her daughter, Fern, and a guy she was dating. Both of the brothers had brought dates as well. Will was relieved to see he wasn't the only non–family member. The presence of the others made him seem slightly less pathetic.

With Dottie directing and everyone pitching in, a mind-blowing buffet materialized, tables were set, conversation flowed, and the football games came on TV.

Lyle proposed a toast, pouring what Will knew was probably an exceptional white wine. There was local apple cider for the kids. Glasses clinked all around. Then everyone loaded their plates and savored the incredible feast.

"Are you having a good Thanksgiving?" Will asked Flick as they indulged in too much dessert.

"Uh-huh."

"What was Thanksgiving like with your mom?" he asked. He could feel Caroline's attention drilling into him.

Flick shrugged his shoulders. "I don't remember."

"Maybe you had people over or went to someone's house," Caroline suggested. She locked eyes with Will over Flick's head.

"Nah," he said. "Can I have more pumpkin pie?"

A series of chords burst from the piano. Austin was at the keyboard, and he started off with "All Star" by Smash Mouth. Then "Shut Up and Dance" came around, and there was a bit of actual dancing. Will grabbed Caroline and they laughed their way through the number, bumping into the other couples and the little cousins. The music ended with the ultimate earworm, "Sweet Caroline."

"That's my song," she exclaimed during the intro. "It's the most awful song, and I love it!"

Watching everyone laughing and singing around the piano filled Will with a feeling he hadn't experienced in a long time—the gentle, inclusive embrace of a real family. Sure, he knew he was idealizing things; families were messy and often problematic. But they also had moments of soaring joy and a sense that the world was right. He focused on Caroline, her smile and dancing eyes, the natural curve of her arms as she hugged her kids in close, and the loneliness inside him roared.

Chapter 25

On the one-year anniversary of the Oysterville Sewing Circle, the meeting room was packed. Caroline and her sisters put out a sheet cake decorated with a needle and thread and the message *Mend Your Heart.* The same phrase, along with the help line phone number, was featured on the little pocket sewing kits Lindy had made to give out. There was a core of regular attendees—Caroline never missed a meeting—and several who came and went. Most had heartbreaking stories to tell. A few were truly inspirational or even transformational. The insights into women who survived violent relationships were life-changing for Caroline.

Some women showed up and said nothing and were never seen again.

One of the lessons, maybe the hardest one for her, was to accept that there were limits to what she could do. The failures were painful to watch. Not everyone could boast of a happy ending. More than once, a member who seemed to be on a path to safety ended up returning to her abuser. Some fell into other abusive relationships, struggled with drugs and alcohol, or sank deeper into poverty and despair.

To Caroline's surprise, Rona Stevens, whom she'd known since high school, attended a couple of meetings. Though she still had her varsity cheerleader looks, her posture had eroded to rounded shoulders, downcast eyes, and an attitude of defeat. She vacillated between breakups and makeups with Hakon, the school jock. And he was still awful. He didn't hit her, Rona was quick to point out. Living with him was stressful, though. He controlled every aspect of her life, from how many calories she ate to the way she folded and stacked the bath towels. He had become a toxic, insidious voice in her head, convincing her she was worthless.

"He totally stalks me," she'd confessed at her first meeting, saying they were on a break. "When we first moved in together, I thought it was sweet how he'd come home unexpectedly with flowers or a bottle of wine. After a while, I realized he was checking up on me. He checks the mileage on the odometer. He monitors my phone. He bugs me about the way I dress and wear my hair." A look of exhaustion had swept over her face. "Sometimes I just want to be by myself, and he accuses me of not loving him. That might be the one thing he's right about."

She'd stared at her knees, seeming to shrink into herself. "I don't know what I'm going to do. Probably nothing."

"This is something," Virginia had softly pointed out.

After two meetings, Rona had gone back to him. The occurrence was all too common. Some women changed their minds, recanted their stories, and went back to their violent partners.

The failures only made Caroline and her sisters more determined than ever to sustain the group. There was no way to save them all, but Caroline had to believe change was possible. She had to believe the Sewing Circle was a lifeline for some of these women. The anniversary meeting was a chance for this reminder. They started off as they always did, with a reading of the mission statement and someone saying, "Shall we begin?"

"I came to this group after I'd hit the lowest point in my life," said Amy. "I was climbing out of a hole so deep I thought I'd never see the light again. At first I didn't want to talk about what had happened to me.

Didn't want to hear what happened to others. Now I can't imagine life without this group. But I do have to imagine life without you guys."

There was a palpable, collective held breath in the room.

"I'm moving away," Amy said.

The collective breath turned into sighs of disappointment. "Is everything all right?" someone asked.

"Bolton is getting out of prison, but that's not why I'm leaving," Amy explained. "I've been training to be a long-haul trucker, and I just got a job. A legit job. Even though I'll miss everyone, I couldn't be happier."

"We'll miss you, too," Echo said. "Change is good. If we all stayed the same all the time, we'd just be stuck, right?"

"That's really cool, Amy," said Nadine. "I'm getting better at setting boundaries. It's made me a better mom, that's for sure. My kids were getting rude and demanding—no surprise, given what they saw. I've changed and they've taken note. Most of the time, anyway."

"I want to be brave again," said Yvonne, a relative newcomer to the group. "I used to dare to do so much. I lost all that when I lost myself in a relationship with an abusive man, and I'm sick of being afraid. The truth is, I'm lonely. Like, really lonely. I quit trusting myself to know what love is supposed to be. But I do know. See, there's a guy . . ." She looked down at her hands twisting in her lap. Then she seemed to realize what she was doing and lifted her head high. "He knows what I went through. He's been super patient and understanding. I'm pretty sure I've loved him for a long time. I want to find the courage to tell him. What do you think?" She looked around the group. "Am I crazy?"

"What's the worst thing that will happen if you tell this guy how you feel?" asked Georgia.

"He'll say he doesn't feel the same way about me, and then he'll feel terrible and I'll feel awkward, and—" She stopped. "Yeah, so the world won't come to an end."

"And what's the *best* thing that could happen if you tell him?" asked Georgia.

The mechanical hum of industrial machines filled the air. After all the hard work and struggle, it was sweet music to Caroline's ears—the sound of her garments being made. She was designing like never before—the stadium seat jacket. Another jacket that lit up in the dark. A smart signal jacket that responded to a cyclist's hand signals. Everything the workshop produced was beautiful, because she supervised every stitch.

The barn had been transformed into a pleasant space that felt safe and productive. No one was getting rich, but sales were steady and the operation was at least solvent. There had been write-ups in the press and on fashion blogs. Following a successful outing at a trade show, they were shipping garments to indie boutiques every week, and she'd hired two trainees and an intern.

The Oysterville Sewing Circle offered more than she'd ever imagined, yielding surprising dividends—the mostly untapped talents of the women themselves. Sometimes it seemed like a kind of magic. If something needed doing, there was a good chance one of the women here could do it or knew someone who could. Echo was becoming a skilled patternmaker and sample sewer, and she had connected Caroline with laid-off workers from her former factory. Ilsa ran the website and was an expert at flawless, bright product shots. Economic survival was one of the most crucial elements for these women, and it was gratifying to be able to help. Caroline and her sisters had secured a grant to fund training and job programs throughout the county. A few other local businesses were now involved, and there was a pilot program at the high school.

One of her best moves had been bringing on Willow from the Sewing Circle. Caroline now had an LLC and a solid business plan, expertly crafted by Willow. C-Shell Rainwear was getting a reputation for garments that were ethically sourced and made with love and skill. One of the girls had machine-quilted a wall hanging with that message: *Made with Love and Skill.* It became the company motto and was proudly hung under the Justine figurehead.

Sometimes, when the work seemed overwhelming and the balance sheet looked totally unbalanced, Caroline would panic and call herself crazy for trying to make her enterprise work. Other times, like now, when everyone was hard and happily at work, it felt exactly right. Amy arrived with her trainee to pick up a shipment, and they started loading bagged and tagged garments into the back of the van.

There was so much noise and activity that Caroline almost didn't hear the *ping* that signaled an incoming email message.

She went to her computer and checked the mail. She blinked and sat down slowly. Maybe she made a sound, because Echo stopped what she was doing and came over to her makeshift desk.

"What's up?" she asked. "You have an *oh shit* expression on your face."

"More like a *holy shit* expression." She sat back and stared at the screen. It was a photo of Catherine Willoughby from *Vogue* Celebrity Style, an obsessively followed media feature. The compelling, doe-eyed actress, currently starring in a smash-hit superhero movie, was wearing a C-Shell raincoat.

"Holy shit," Caroline said again, mesmerized by the surreal idea that one of the most famous women in the world was wearing her coat. It was one of her best and most expensive designs, a fantasy of frosted white with a clear hem filled with silk flower blossoms. "'Cat's go-to coat on a rainy day is the April Showers anorak from C-Shell Rainwear. Check it out at c-shellrainwear.com, where one percent of profits go to the Sisterhood Against Domestic Violence.'"

"Well, well, well." Echo beamed at Caroline. "You've got an A-list star wearing one of your designs. She's got, like, forty-five million followers on Instagram. How cool is that? And how cool that they posted about the Sisterhood Against Domestic Violence."

Willow had set up the affiliation, and Caroline was quickly discovering that her platform had grown larger than any of them had ever anticipated. She only wished Angelique could be around to see what they'd created.

Amy came over with her intern and her digital inventory monitor. She was spending her last two weeks on the job training her replacement before moving to

Reno to train as a long-haul truck driver. To Caroline, she looked like a different person, carrying herself with swagger, not shame. With confidence, not fear. "What's up, buttercup?" she asked.

Echo grinned at Amy. "We're looking at *Vogue* Celebrity Style."

"My fave." Amy referenced her skater hoodie and combat boots.

"Cat Willoughby is wearing one of our coats." Echo turned the monitor so Amy could see.

"No shit. Isn't she the lightning-bolt girl in that new movie? Hey, that's fantastic. Now everyone's going to want one. You're hitting the big time, Caroline."

"I'm stunned," Caroline agreed. "It's a really beautiful coat, isn't it?"

"Absolutely," Echo said. "I worked on that one. Made all the clear hems with the brilliant silk flowers. I knew that would be a hit."

Caroline tapped her keyboard, forwarding the news to Willow, who usually worked from home.

"Speaking of hits . . ." Ilsa, who was now running the website, came over. "We just had our biggest hour of all time. Check it out." Her tablet showed orders coming in, one after another. "*Ka-ching, ka-ching,*" she said. "The April Showers in white is already sold out. We have back orders."

"Here's why." Echo showed her the picture in *Vogue.* "We've got a big day tomorrow, eh?"

"Do we ever."

Caroline pushed back from the desk. "Look at the time. You girls go home for the day. I'll close up."

After they'd left, Caroline stared at the photo for a few minutes more.

She knew the value of an influential celebrity endorsement. She knew the value of a mention in *Vogue.* Designers stalked the media in search of publicity. Though she lacked the funds for a campaign, she'd sent samples to Daria and Orson Maynard in New York, hoping to get her garments into the right hands. The process usually involved huge sponsorship fees, which she couldn't afford.

Finally, somehow, her coat had ended up on a major star. She couldn't stop staring at the beautiful photo, a candid shot of Cat, who had paired the anorak with high neoprene boots. She was strolling past a wrought iron fence, and she looked as fresh as the springtime.

Ordinarily, Caroline worked late after everyone had gone for the day. This was her design time, when there was music drifting through the barn and a vision in her mind. The brush with celebrity inspired her, so she noodled with a design she'd been thinking about. It was a trench with a capelet that could convert to a hood. "You'd look amazing in this, Cat Willoughby," she murmured, clicking on the digitized illustration. "Blue serge? Maybe dotted swiss is due for a comeback . . ."

"I like the way you think." Will stepped into the shop. His adopted dog, whom he'd named Fisher, trotted at his heels. He was in his teaching outfit—chinos, a long-sleeved shirt, striped tie. "I've always been a fan of dotted swiss."

She snorted. "You don't even know what that is."

"It's due for a comeback." He unknotted his tie and leaned his hip against the counter.

"How was school?" she asked. When they ran into each other, coming and going, they tended to linger, shoot the breeze.

Like old friends, she told herself.

But the truth was, since his divorce, things were different between them. She did not examine this too closely. Evidently Will didn't either. He dated women. Lots of different women. He was a regular man-about-town these days. She even teased him about it sometimes.

"School was amazing," he said. "I'm amazing. I gave a group of sophomores a tour of the calculus and showed them how it will actually be useful to them later in life. Let me tell you, they were riveted."

She grinned. "As am I."

"How are things at the C-Shell Sewing Works?"

"Ha! So much more amazing than calculus. And I mean that. Check it out." She clicked to the window showing the photo from Celebrity Style. "Cat Willoughby is wearing one of my coats. It was posted about an hour ago, and the website already sold out."

"Hey, that's fantastic. All the kids at school are nuts for that movie she's in. Way to go, Caroline."

"Thanks. It's a shot in the arm, for sure. We're going to have to work overtime to fill orders. I don't have the infrastructure here to make things fast. I'm trying not to panic."

"Don't panic." He gestured around the shop. "Look what you've done so far. You can handle anything."

She couldn't help smiling. "I like the way you think. And honestly, I couldn't have done it without you charging me a pittance to rent this place. But I—"

Another email *ping* sounded. She glanced at the subject line and couldn't suppress a gasp.

"More news?" he asked.

She opened the message. "Oh my God. Eau Sauvage wants a meeting."

"Oh-So Vage? Never heard of it."

"*Eau Sauvage* is French for *wild water*. It's a high-end fashion label. Massively successful."

"I assume wanting a meeting is the start of something big."

She gripped the edge of the desk and looked up at him. There was a part of her—the biggest, most impulsive part of her—that wanted to leap up and throw her arms around him. Down, girl. He probably had a date tonight. He always had a date.

"It could be huge for me," she said. "Complicated, though. I hope it's not a be-careful-what-you-wish-for situation."

"What do you wish for?"

She leaned back in her chair. "Being discovered by a big label *used* to be my greatest wish. Since I came back here, though, since the kids . . ." She pictured herself back in New York, going to meetings, living a dream that didn't quite fit anymore. "I'll listen to what they have to say. They might just steal my designs the way Mick Taylor did."

"Man, I hope not. What ever happened to that guy, anyway?"

"He's still going strong," she said. She shut down her computer and grabbed her bag, suddenly eager to see Addie and Flick and hear about their day. They'd changed her perspective. They'd changed her life. "I try not to think about him because it makes me crazy. I still have revenge fantasies."

"You ought to change channels, have a different kind of fantasy." Will winked at her. *Winked.*

"Fuck off," she said, certain he was teasing.

"Here's a question: If this thing suddenly happened for you, for real, what would that look like?"

Her stomach churned. "I'd be back in New York in a New York minute. I admit it wouldn't be easy with the kids, but it wouldn't be impossible either. They might even go back to their same school."

"You'd leave here, then."

"I might. I'm getting way ahead of myself, though." She paused. "Why do you ask?"

"Just curious. I shouldn't have asked about your plans. I have a way of screwing up people's plans."

She kind of wished he would screw hers up. "Knock it off. Quit feeling sorry for yourself."

And there it was. That smile. The smile she had fallen in love with, once upon a time.

Caroline designated Cat Willoughby her new best friend, because after the *Vogue* feature, her rainwear became a trend—and not just for the garments. The Sisterhood Against Domestic Violence invited her to Atlanta to tell the story of the Oysterville Sewing Circle.

"You're going away?" Flick asked as she was packing

her bag. Blackie scampered around the room, wrestling with a knotted rope.

"To talk to a group about our domestic violence program. It's just for the weekend. I'll be back Sunday night."

Addie brought Wonder Woman over to the bed. "I don't want you to go."

Caroline stopped what she was doing. In the whirlwind of all the attention, she realized she had never spent a night apart from the children since they came into her care. Every time she woke to the fact that she was important to these kids was a small epiphany. "Oh, baby. It's just for two nights, and you'll be with Grammy Dot and Lyle."

"It's not the same." Flick glowered at her.

"I think you can handle it, though."

"We're just getting to the good part in *Ramona,*" Addie said. Caroline was reading the book to them, a chapter a night.

They'd been doing so well lately that sometimes Caroline forgot how absolutely vital it was for them to feel secure. "Tell you what. We can do a video call and I'll read to you."

"It's not the same," Flick repeated.

"Why do you have to go?" Addie asked.

Caroline had discovered the one thing that always worked with these children—honesty. "Because it's important," she said. "Because your mama's life was important. The most terrible thing in the world happened to her and she died. There's nothing we can do to change that. But there's this organization that can help other families dealing with violence, and they want to hear our story and what we're doing about it now. If we keep talking about it and teaching people that violence is never okay, maybe we can help others."

Both were quiet. She let them think about it. She still didn't know what Angelique's children had seen, what they'd heard. She wondered if Angelique had coached them to keep silent, possibly because she feared being separated from them thanks to her immigration status. Had they seen her injuries? Overheard arguments? Maybe one day they would open up to her. She wouldn't push or nag them for answers.

"Why d'you gotta go?" Flick asked, echoing his sister.

"When the organization called, I asked them the same thing. And we talked about the group I started up and the job-training program we have. But mostly we talked about you. And how you were left all alone and how important it was to keep you safe. They want to hear about that. It could help people."

"It can't help us," Flick pointed out. "It can't help our mama."

"I know. But you like helping others, right?"

He thought for a moment. Reached down and scratched Blackie behind the ears. "Yeah," he said. "I guess."

Caroline sat on the bed and opened her arms. "Come here, you two."

They clambered up, and Blackie jumped into Flick's lap. She gathered them all into her arms. They filled her to the brim, and she rested her lips on their sweet warm heads. "I'll be back before you know it. Okay?"

"Yeah," Flick said.

"Okay, Mom," Addie whispered.

"She's not Mom," Flick said.

"She's not Mama," Addie told him. "But she's our *mom*."

The words burned into Caroline's heart. "Addie, you're so nice. Why are you so nice?"

The little girl shrugged her shoulders. "Guess I'm just a good person."

"You are. Both of you are. And Blackie, too. She's a good girl. And I feel so lucky to have you all." Caroline hesitated, then decided this was the moment to bring up something she'd been thinking about for a long time. "You can call me Mom or Caroline or anything that makes you happy. There's something I've been wanting to ask you two. When your mama died, I became your guardian. That means I'm responsible for giving you a home and keeping you safe. I love being your guardian. But lately I've been thinking . . . How would you feel if I adopted you?"

They were silent for a few moments.

"You mean the way we adopted Blackie?" asked Flick.

"Yes, like that. Nothing will change. I'll still be responsible for you in every way. But if I adopt you, I'll become your legal parent. I won't ever replace your mama. No one will. But it means you'll have a parent again, forever and ever."

"Forever and ever until the end of time?" asked Addie.

"Yes. What do you think?"

"I think yes," Addie said.

Flick stayed silent. His arms tightened around Caroline. He sniffed, and her shirt was warm and damp. "Okay," he said in his raspy whisper. "Okay."

Chapter 26

Caroline heard a car door slam and glanced at the time on her computer. Everyone had gone for the day, and she'd just called her parents to let them know she would be working late—extremely late. The proposal from Eau Sauvage was a huge opportunity. They wanted to do a pop-up rollout of her designs in a limited run, and when it caught on, it would expand from there. Prior to the scheduled meetings with the marketing team, she had to craft an irresistible presentation. This would make her preparations for the ill-fated Chrysalis line look like child's play.

She got up from her desk, massaging a crick in her neck, and wandered outside. To her surprise, there was Will in jeans and a striped shirt with the sleeves rolled back. As always, she had to work to disguise her reaction to seeing him.

"I thought you had a date tonight," she said.

"I did, but I bailed."

Caroline couldn't escape a reality she'd been running from for a long time. She still had a crush on Will Jensen. No, it was worse than that. It wasn't a crush. It was much more, a yearning so powerful it kept her awake at night, plagued by restless cravings. It distracted her all day, filled her with equal measures of joy and guilt.

He was off-limits. Her best friend's ex.

He probably didn't even feel the same way about her as she felt about him. Except sometimes she thought maybe he did. Every so often she'd see him looking at her in a certain way, his eyes alight. And she'd think maybe . . .

"Why?" she asked.

"What's that?" He stuck his hands in his pockets.

Oh, God. She even loved the way he stuck his hands in his pockets.

"Why did you bail?"

He paused. Checked her out with a warm, slow, up-and-down look. She wished she were wearing something nicer than work clothes—ankle jeans and a stylized white smock she'd designed, her homemade homage to houses like Chanel, where the workers dressed in lab coats.

"Come on inside. I'll tell you over a beer."

She glanced over her shoulder. "Thanks. I could use a break. I already told my mom I might be pulling an all-nighter."

"Big project?"

"The biggest. I'll tell you over that beer. God, I hope I haven't bitten off more than I can chew."

He gave her a nudge, the way he used to when they were kids. "You don't chew beer."

She rolled her eyes and followed him into the house. Fisher greeted them with swirls of ecstasy. Since Sierra had left, Water's Edge hadn't really changed. She had walked away with nothing but her clothes and personal things. To Caroline, she'd explained, "It was never my house. I picked out furniture and finishes and paint colors as if my life depended on it, but really, it was just to make Will happy. To make our life look happy, I suppose. But in the end, it wasn't enough."

The place was still beautiful. How could it not be, given Sierra's sense of style? Caroline noticed more of Will's things—a framed team picture on the wall, sports gear in the mudroom.

She was struck by a curious notion. She was totally excited about her plans. And there was only one person she really wanted to tell—Will. But first—

She climbed up on one of the kitchen barstools and took a big gulp of beer. "Beer is always a good idea," she said. "Coats my nerves with happiness. Now, you bailed on your date . . . why?"

"I realized I was wasting her time and mine. This past year, dating has just been a distraction for me." He paused, looked at Caroline with an expression she hadn't seen before. "Gets in the way of what I really want."

"Which is . . . ?"

"To be with someone longer than a night or a weekend. It's been fun, but now I'm over the just-divorced phase."

"Now, that," she said, "is going to break a lot of hearts on the Long Beach Peninsula."

"Nah."

"You say. I've been watching, Will. Women love you. Everyone's been talking about the hot young coach who's back on the market."

"Everyone, eh?" He chuckled. "Who are these women who love me?"

"It's a small town. I hear stuff. So you're going to quit dating and do what?"

"I'm going to quit dating and fall in love again."

She was so startled to hear the words come out of his mouth that she inhaled too quickly at the exact moment she was swallowing a mouthful of beer. The result was not pretty. Choking and trying to catch her breath, she grabbed a tea towel and held it to her mouth.

"Easy," he said, patting her on the back. "You okay?"

She nodded and waved him off, then went to the sink and washed up. "I'm fine. Got all choked up, is all."

"Not exactly the reaction I was looking for," he said.

What reaction were you looking for? She didn't let herself ask. "I'll try to finish my beer without spewing again."

"You're not dating, either," he said.

"How do you know? Are you keeping track?"

"No," he said quickly. Then, "Yes. Yeah, I have been."

She sat down again. Took a cautious sip of her beer. Tried not to stare at his face, but couldn't help herself. He had the lips. He had the eyes. "Why?"

Holding her gaze with his, he took the beer bottle from her hand and set it gently on the counter. "Caroline. You know damn well why."

Caroline's eyes flew open. She awoke with a leap of panic—a "what have I done?" swirling through her mind. No, she thought, clinging to a thread of denial. I did not do that.

I did not just sleep with Will.

A gentle, peaceful, ridiculously sweet snore came from the slumbering man next to her.

Oh my God, I did, she thought. I did just sleep with Will.

And oh my God, it was the best thing ever.

She held herself motionless. Hardly breathing. Heart hammering, threatening to give her away. Then inch by inch she edged toward the side of the bed. It was still dark, the middle of the night. She still had plausible deniability on her side. She could sneak out now, drive home, slink into her bed like a truant teenager, and pretend this night had never happened.

Except of course it had.

She'd slept with her best friend's ex-husband.

And before sleeping with him, she'd had the best sex of her life. The kind of sex she'd been wanting ever since she knew what sex was. The kind that left her glassy-eyed, helpless, weightless, terrified, and . . . unbearably smitten.

She had no excuse. No alcohol to blame, no sexual predator who had driven her into the safe arms of a man she trusted, a man she had loved as long as life.

This was bad. This had to stop.

A large warm hand tunneled under the covers and slowly, assuredly, made its way up her bare leg. "You're awake," murmured a deep voice.

"How do you know? I haven't moved a muscle."

"I can feel you breathing." The hand circled the top of her thigh. "I can hear you thinking."

"Yeah? What am I thinking?"

"Same thing I am."

One touch of his hand nearly undid her. "I'm not breathing," she said. "I'm frozen with mortification."

"Cool." In one easy movement, he covered her and started nuzzling her neck. "Then I won't have to chase you around the bed. Don't move. I'll do all the work."

"I . . ."

"All. The. Work." His lips. His tongue. His knowing hands.

She practically melted into the mattress. The large, comfy, pillow-top mattress on his bed. She was in Will Jensen's bed. Sierra's bed. And the things they'd done to each other . . .

"Knock it off." She scooted away from him and clutched the covers against her chest. "It's after midnight. I need to go."

"You already called your mom and said you were

pulling an all-nighter." He touched her bare shoulder, drawing swirls on her skin. "She said she'd look after the kids."

Caroline burned under his touch. "We can't do this, Will."

"Too late. We already did, and it was awesome, and I never want to stop."

"Are you kidding me? It's insane. You're my best friend's ex."

"*Ex* being the operative term." He sat up and leaned against the headboard, which was upholstered in luxurious fabric, probably chosen by Sierra. "Look, at our age, everybody has an ex."

"Not like this. It's a problem, Will. She was my best friend, and she used to be married to you."

"Almost everybody was married to someone else. We all have a past."

"Not a past like we have."

"Oh, baby, we're just getting started. And you don't get to say how this goes."

"And you do?"

"Yeah. Yeah, I do." His hands again. Fingers tracing, swirling. Glint of moonlight on his incredible chest.

She shoved a pillow at him. "This is a terrible idea."

He was quiet for a few minutes. "Listen, Sierra and

I grew apart. We got a divorce. It happens. And now this. Now *we're* happening. You and me."

She scooted even farther from him. She was glad for the darkness in the room, because she was certain her face was a mask of panic, wonder, and confusion. "We're not. We can't."

"Damn, Caroline. What the hell are you afraid of?"

Everything. Mostly, she was afraid of wanting this too much, of falling for him and being utterly incapable of picking herself up after whatever inevitable disaster awaited them.

"Talk to me," he said. "I'm not used to you not talking. You talk all the time. I love that about you."

Was that the same as *I love you*?

She drew her knees up to her chest, overwhelmed. "I'm afraid of . . . God, where do I begin? What about my kids? And by *my kids*, I mean it's about to be official. I've submitted a petition to adopt them."

"That's fantastic, Caroline."

"I told them, too. They're going to be my kids. *My kids.*"

"I love Addie and Flick, too," Will said. "We get along great. Listen, you're making this more complicated than it is." He moved the covers aside and hovered over her. His lips, his hair falling forward, his muscular frame impossible to resist. "I'm all in."

As Caroline drove with Virginia to the weekly meeting of the Sewing Circle, it was hard not babbling on and on about Will. Despite her trepidation, their love affair burned like a wind-driven forest fire, dangerous and impossible to curb. The sex turned her into a blithering idiot, but sometimes, sex was the smallest part of her passion. Sometimes, lying with him on the dock, looking up at the stars, and talking endlessly about life and dreams and fears and plans was everything she desired.

Their years-long friendship was no longer a friendship. It had exploded, then melded into a different shape entirely.

She wanted to say something. She wanted to shout it to the world. She couldn't, though. Not yet. Maybe not ever. "Are we going to have a crowd tonight?" she asked, noting the nearly full parking lot.

"Looks that way." Virginia parked and they got out. "Ready?"

Caroline nodded.

She went inside and was nearly blown back against the wall by a loud "Surprise!"

What the hell? The room was decked with pink and blue garlands and balloons. On the snack table was a large sheet cake, and overhead was a banner that read

Congratulations! It's a boy! And a girl! Pictures of Addie and Flick were stuck to the rolling whiteboard, which was covered with scrawled messages, hearts, and flowers.

"You guys," Caroline said, falling against Virginia. "A baby shower?"

"A kid shower," Georgia said, greeting her with a hug. "It's never too late to celebrate having kids."

Her mom was there with chilled champagne. "Don't worry, the children are with your father. I wanted to be here. I hope you don't mind that I told everyone that the family court approved your adoption petition."

"It's provisional," Caroline pointed out. There had been extensive pre-adoption studies and home visits. She would be subjected to a placement period and post-adoption follow-ups as well.

"The waiting period is standard," Virginia said. "Face it, Caroline. You're committed. And we have the cake to prove it."

Caroline nearly came undone. "I need a tissue," she said. "And a piece of that damn cake."

Her sisters brought her to a chair in the circle and served the cake. It was one of Georgia's most requested—organic lemon with lemon cream icing, decadent and delicious. It tasted like happiness. It tasted like love. "You got me," Caroline said, savoring the first bite. "I can't believe you did this."

"We couldn't let you miss out on a shower," Echo said, cutting and serving the cake on pink and blue paper plates.

"We're really happy for you, Caroline," Ilsa said. "How does it feel, being a mom?"

"Different," she said. "I'm not sure why. The adoption is really just a formality. It feels different, though. It's hard to explain."

"Not really," Georgia said. "I can explain it."

Of course she could. Georgia was a know-it-all. "Yeah?"

"You're a mom."

The reality of it took her breath away. Georgia was right. Caroline had a son. A daughter. She had been transformed, not by a court document, but by two incredible little human beings who had come into her life uninvited and set up permanent residence in her heart.

"Yes, that's it," she said after a long pause. "I'm a mom."

Chapter 27

Sierra reveled in finally having a job that didn't depend on her looking like an emaciated seventeen-year-old. She was on the road more often than not, going from shoot to shoot, in charge of a crew that didn't dare tell her to "sweeten up the lips" or "relax your forehead—you're turning into your mother." Or "give me your most fuckable look."

She didn't miss that at all.

She didn't miss her old life.

She didn't miss her marriage.

She did miss Will, though. Her perfect, perfect husband, whose heart she had trampled on, whose dreams she had shattered.

People said she should be grateful and proud that the two of them had managed to uncouple without undue drama. Without leaving scorched earth in their wake. She didn't feel grateful, though. Or proud. She just felt . . . empty.

But in a good way. In a way that made her feel untethered, open to any possibility.

The current possibility involved sitting on a deck overlooking a ridiculously scenic beach while sipping a cosmo and reading *Cosmo.* The shoot had been a whirlwind, and at last, it was quitting time. She tasted the lovely, sugary drink, which would have been kryptonite to her back in her days in front of the camera. And then she pictured the models in their shared rooms, chugging Diet Dr Pepper and smoking cigarettes, studying their pores and wrinkles in mercilessly magnifying mirrors.

No, she didn't miss that.

She paged past the requisite "How to Make Him Make Out with You" article. Instructions not necessary. For the first time since high school, she was available, and guys were eager. She'd discovered that she was good at dating, good at having fun with no complications.

Her phone chimed with a notification, and she glanced at it in annoyance. After rushing around all day, she just wanted some downtime. Then she saw a picture pop up. *Caroline would like to FaceTime.*

Fine, Caroline she could handle. Sierra swiped up. "Hey, stranger."

"Sierra, hi." Caroline's face appeared. Behind her was a familiar sandy expanse, the waves crawling in at low tide.

"This is a beach-to-beach call." Sierra panned her phone so Caroline could see.

"That's gorgeous. Where are you?"

"Descanso Beach on Catalina Island. Having a my-job-does-not-suck moment."

"I'm glad, Sierra. Your posts on Instagram look so good. I'm happy for you." Caroline paused. Her face in the phone screen did not exactly look happy.

"Everything all right? I've been following the photo stream for C-Shell and saw your news about getting a pop-up with Eau Sauvage. Way to go, Caroline. That company made a smart move."

"Thanks. I hope it works out. So . . . yeah."

Sierra took a sip of her cocktail and cast about for something to say. Since she'd been gone, their friendship had begun to fade back to the occasional thumbs-up on social media or a quick comment on a post. It just wasn't the same as a genuine, face-to-face friendship. Sometimes Sierra thought that might have been an early sign of her breakup with Will. When he was in the navy, he was gone for months and months, and the unavoidable separation had been the start of the long, slow drifting apart.

She considered asking about the kids, but to her secret shame, she didn't actually care that much.

"How are the girls in the Sewing Circle?" she asked.

"Oh! Mostly good." Caroline gave her a quick rundown on a few of the women from the group—uplifting successes, disheartening backslides. Sierra hated to hear that a woman would go back into her abusive relationship or take up a new one, but it happened.

"And Will?" Sierra asked the question lightly, aiming for a casual tone. She wanted to be a hundred percent done with the past, but a part of her still clung to him. "Who's he dating these days?"

Caroline's jaw dropped, and Sierra laughed. "What, you don't think I hear things? Remember, my mom's the town gossip. She always makes sure I get all the scoop on my ex. Sometimes I think she took the divorce harder than I did."

"Oh, um, yeah." Caroline's eyes darted away, then returned. "Sierra, the reason I called . . . I wanted to let you know about something that happened."

Sierra felt a slight ping of awareness. "Everything okay?"

"Yes! Absolutely. I mean, nobody's sick or hurt or . . . Ah, shit. I'm calling to let you know that Will and I are together."

Well, of course they were, Sierra thought. They'd been together every summer from the beginning of time. The three of them had been inseparable. Big whoop. "And?" she asked.

"I mean, *together* together," Caroline said. "Damn it, I'm not explaining this well at all. The thing that happened is . . . we're in love. It's that kind of together."

Wait. What? Sierra frowned at the screen, then lifted the frown with her eyebrows. "You're in love," she said, trying not to choke on the words. She tried to picture the two of them—together. In love. It was like trying to picture a chimera—something that didn't actually exist. The image wouldn't form. It was always Will and Sierra and Caroline. Not Will and Caroline in love.

"I wanted to tell you before you heard it somewhere else," Caroline said. "I didn't want you to be caught by surprise."

Surprise? It was more like shock. Like a fist to the solar plexus.

She took a drink. "I don't know what to say." She took another drink. "Congratulations for banging my ex?"

Caroline winced visibly. "I didn't plan it, Sierra. But when it started happening, I realized it was real, and it's not going to stop. I mean, we . . . It's not a fling. We're getting serious."

"Serious."

"Like it could be permanent."

Permanent. Her best friend and her ex. Which left Sierra with . . . nothing. "What the hell do you want from me?" she asked. "My goddamn blessing?"

"No. I mean, *no.* You're entitled to feel however you feel about the situation. I wanted to tell you myself. We were friends once, as close as sisters," Caroline said. "And when I moved back, we got there again. I wish . . . I don't want to lose that, Sierra."

"Too late," Sierra said. "It's already gone."

She ended the call, freezing Caroline, open-mouthed, on the screen. Glaring out at the sinking sun, she gulped at her drink. Now it tasted as bitter as regret.

And that, Sierra knew, was on her. She had chafed with discontent in Oysterville. She'd panicked about the pregnancy, regarding it as a tether that would hold her there forever, when all she wanted was . . . everything else. Freedom and independence. A job that didn't suck. The world.

This, she thought, flinging the rest of the drink over the balcony railing.

Chapter 28

Caroline went to New York City with a heart full of hope, convinced that she was finally getting back on her feet. Back in the game. Back on track. As she and Willow got off the train at Penn Station and made their way to the Ace Hotel, she felt a whir of excitement.

The hotel let them check in early. Willow wanted a nap. Caroline was too restless to sit still. "I'm going for a little walk," she said, eager to reconnect with the place that had been her home for years. She went to the neighborhood she used to know like the back of her hand—the shops and bodegas, tiny groceries, modern buildings shoulder to shoulder with old brick and stone warehouses, newsstands, and street carts filling the air with a smoky, oniony scent.

Unexpectedly, the city felt strange to her, disorienting. It wasn't just the fact that she'd taken a red-eye and was operating on minimal sleep. It was that she was preoccupied with what she'd left behind in Oysterville. The kids—*her* kids, or soon to be hers—were back there. Will was back there. Her family. Lindy and the Sewing Circle, and C-Shell. Everything she cared about. In one short year, her entire world had shifted.

And yet she cared about this, too. She had a lifelong passion for design, and her workshop created things that were beautiful and useful. The operation itself empowered the women who worked there, fostering their self-respect and optimism.

How could she want both things at the same time? How could she want the love and joy of a family along with the fulfillment of a calling that fed her soul?

She passed the kids' old school, its play yard surrounded by a chain-link fence and crowded with running, laughing children. She wondered if Addie and Flick ever thought about their life here, what memories they held of Angelique. Caroline made a conscious effort to talk to them each day about their mother. She had thousands of pictures on a photo stream of Angelique, one of the most photographed models in the business. Yet despite the vast collection of shots in every variety, there would always be something mysterious and unattainable about her—secrets and hidden pain, unanswered questions.

Maybe that was why she'd attended church at Saint Kilda's, a couple of blocks from the school. Maybe it felt safe to her. Maybe there was a sympathetic pastor. It started raining, and Caroline put up the hood of her jacket, one of her own designs. She stood in front of the old Gothic Revival church, thinking about her friend and wishing she could talk to her, just one more time, even. Umbrellas popped up and pedestrians hurried by, but Caroline stood still, reading the schedule of services posted near the door.

A woman brushed past her and went up the steps. Then she paused and came back down to Caroline. "You looking for the NA meeting?"

Flustered, Caroline frowned. "No, I'm . . . A friend of mine used to attend church here."

The woman shrugged. "Oh, well. Just in case—there's one at ten and another at noon. In the basement fellowship hall."

"Wait." As an idea took hold, Caroline followed the woman up the steps. "Maybe . . . My friend's name was Angelique. She, um, she died last year. Of an overdose."

The woman stepped inside the foyer. It was dim and close, and smelled of old stone and fresh flowers. "Angelique?"

"Did you know her?" Caroline paused. "I mean, I guess you can't really say . . . But she was my friend, and I'm raising her two little kids now."

The woman was in her forties or fifties. She was slender and well dressed, and had tired eyes. "Come on in. It's an open meeting."

An hour later, Caroline sat in the nearly empty meeting room with a woman named Jody and a man she never thought she'd see again—Roman Blake. Jody had been Angelique's sponsor in NA.

"I thought it was you," Caroline said to Roman as they put together the puzzle pieces Angelique had left scattered behind her. "She refused to say who was hitting her, and I thought . . ."

"Understandable, I guess," Roman said. "We weren't good together. We fought a lot. But I cared about her. I cared about her staying clean."

She flashed on a memory. "I saw you fighting," she said, remembering Roman reaching for Angelique and Angelique batting him away. "It was at Terminus, that club a lot of us used to go to."

He steepled his fingers together, staring down at his large, strong hands. "I remember that night. We weren't fighting. Or maybe . . . we were always fighting. Both of us addicts, both messed up." He looked up at her. "But the heart wants what it wants."

Jody vouched for him. "Everyone in the program knows it's a bad idea to hook up, but it happens."

"Yeah," Roman said. "I'm so damned sorry. Not sorry I loved her. Sorry I didn't love her enough to walk away."

Caroline used to think he was brutish and mean, with his big muscles and tattoos. But maybe she should have looked past that rough exterior. "So that night?"

"She . . . I figured out that she was using again, and I was trying to get her back into the program."

"Did Angelique ever mention other guys? Boyfriends?" Caroline asked.

"When I met her, she said she wasn't seeing anyone. Said she was too busy with her kids and her career. Said one of her exes went to rehab, and I got the impression she couldn't stay away from him—or keep him away," said Roman.

"Angelique was my friend," Caroline said. "She died in my home. I wish I knew how it happened. I feel so guilty not knowing that she was struggling with addiction. God, how could I not know?"

"With a high-functioning addict, you can set aside what you think of when you think of an addict," Jody said. "You won't find them pushing shopping carts along the sidewalk, sleeping in recycled clothing bins, shooting up in alleyways. In fact, some of them seem incredibly successful. Maybe because they have to work overtime to keep up appearances and feed their habit."

A new picture of Angelique emerged. She was able to hide her demons from everyone—even herself. For a while, at least. Unfortunately, maintaining her facade came at a great price. It was dangerous. She was trying to stay clean for the sake of her kids, but something pushed her back into using. Caroline again remembered razor blades missing from her sewing box and running out of foil. One time, she'd noticed tiny orange caps in the trash but never paused to wonder where they came from. Now they were puzzle pieces, falling into place.

"I wish I could have helped," she said, her voice rough with tears. "So her kids are doing really well. She never told me who their father was. Did she ever tell you?"

They didn't know any more about the situation than she did—Angelique had Flick at seventeen and Addie at eighteen, when she lived in Haiti. There were still so many unanswered questions, but the new glimpses into Angelique's secret life filled in a few blanks.

After leaving the church, she walked a few blocks to her former apartment building. She tried the door code in case it might be the same.

It was the same. She looked around the foyer. There was the clanking radiator that used to steam and overheat the place in winter. The usual litter of junk mail on the floor. The pervasive smell of soup. The day she'd found Angelique dead came rushing back at her—the urgent phone call from the school. The dropped Con Ed bill marked with the tread of a shoe. The unlocked door, the preternatural stillness of the apartment when Caroline stepped inside.

The next day, as the elevator in the Eau Sauvage headquarters whisked them skyward, Caroline felt giddy. "I used to fantasize about this moment," she said to Willow. "I even had it all planned out in my head—discussing my work with a major firm, making a plan for a partnership. Now that it's actually happening, I'm either nervous as hell or insane from sleep deprivation."

"It's going to be fabulous," Willow assured her. "Look at us." She gestured at their images in the polished elevator mirror. They both wore C-Shell jackets, which were beaded with raindrops. "*We're* fabulous."

She had sent off her samples, hopes, and dreams to the offices of Eau Sauvage. All that was left was to meet the team and discuss the launch. The conference room was filled with creative energy as the marketing team laid out their plans. They wanted to know about the journey that had brought her to this point. She talked about Oysterville and her struggle to launch her designs, and then she explained the Sewing Circle.

"We love your story," said one of the marketing experts. "A woman-owned business, helping other women."

She glanced at Willow and felt an unexpected surge of emotion. "Those women helped me just as much. I could never have done this without them."

There was a presentation of her designs on a big screen in the conference room. When a picture came up showing the nautilus shell detail, someone—a junior associate—said, "You used to work for Mick Taylor, isn't that right?"

Her stomach knotted. "I did contract work for his design house, yes. Why do you ask?"

The associate, a young woman with cat's-eye glasses and three smartphones, said, "It's just . . ."

Jeanine, the product developer who was running the meeting, stepped in. "We're going to need to remove the shell logo," she said. "We're launching a line of

Mick Taylor bags, and the nautilus shell is too similar. It's a minor detail. Just to avoid confusion."

Caroline had heard the expression *a head full of steam* before, but she'd never actually experienced it until this moment, as she stared at a series of pictures of couture handbags featuring her logo. The pressure built as her thoughts raced. It was not enough that Mick had stolen her designs and accused her of copying him. Apparently he'd appropriated her logo as well. The sense of violation washed over her, as fresh as it had been the first time. She forced herself to take a breath. Looked at Willow, who was scratching notes on a yellow legal pad. Like Jeanine said, it was a small detail. But it was her logo. *Her* logo. A part of her identity. Her brand. And they wanted her to change it.

"We have some ideas," the junior associate said, clicking to the next slide. "It's totally up to you, of course, but here's an inspiration board."

Caroline could feel the color draining from her face. It took all her self-restraint not to go ballistic, trash the deal, and walk out. Somehow she managed to hold her tongue. Willow was the consummate professional, telling the group they'd be in touch about the final details.

Caroline managed to contain herself until she and Willow left the building together. Then she blasted out her anger. "He took my career away, and now this?" she fumed.

"That sucks," Willow agreed. "Is keeping the logo a deal-breaker for you?"

"I wish I could say yes, but this is still a huge opportunity for me. For *us.* When I look at the bigger picture, I have to think of Flick and Addie. They depend on me. And then all of us who work at C-Shell—we need our jobs. And then I think about all the effort I poured into this enterprise. My precarious bank balance. The truth is, I need this opportunity more than I need to keep a little detail on my garments. If I have to change the logo, it wouldn't be the end of the world."

Willow regarded her thoughtfully. "This is how it starts. We settle. We make compromises. We let them whittle away, bit by bit, and don't really notice the erosion, or we rationalize it away. We tell ourselves it's for the greater good."

Caroline heard echoes of Willow's story coming through. Although it was about a marriage, not a job, there were similarities—letting a man chip away at things that were rightfully hers. Accepting injustice because a fight seemed too hard. Shrinking from confrontation instead of standing up for oneself. These were all matters she'd heard at the Oysterville Sewing

Circle. Now she had to ask herself—what had she learned, really?

"I'll meet you back at the hotel," she said.

Caroline walked into the Mick Taylor headquarters. It felt strange, being back here, where she had spent so many hours creating designs. She used to feel a sense of wonder, even a sort of reverence, that she had a coveted job here.

Now she felt the clean, sharp edge of anger as she climbed the main stairs, strode past his bullshit mission statement written, Basquiat-style, on a long wall, passed by a protesting receptionist, and found Mick in his sleek glass-walled office. A small team was in the adjacent conference room, having a meeting with the design director.

Mick looked up from his computer screen and regarded her with a slight frown. "Do you need something?"

She couldn't tell whether or not his ignorance was feigned. "Caroline Shelby. You know, the one whose designs you stole."

He gave a small shake of his head. "Sorry, what?"

Rilla Stein came into the office. Caroline's onetime mentor didn't even acknowledge her. She leaned over and muttered something to Mick. Something that sounded like "I'll call security."

"Ah, now I recall," Mick said, offering his charming favorite-uncle grin. He dismissed Rilla with a wave. "Go back to your meeting," he said. "I got this."

Rilla hesitated, her gaze darting at Caroline. "You're sure?"

He nodded. "Close the door behind you."

After she left, he regarded Caroline with a long, measuring gaze. "Hey, I thought we put that trouble to rest."

"I thought you were going to quit stealing from me, but you're using my nautilus logo on a line of bags for Eau Sauvage," Caroline snapped. "Who'd you steal *those* from? Need anything else, Mick? Some ideas for your next fall collection, maybe? My firstborn child?"

He seemed startled by her, maybe because she was not the cowed and powerless young designer who had fled New York with her tail between her legs. His expression hardened and he leaned forward in his chair. "The people at Eau Sauvage know you used to work for me. They know you were laughed out of the business because you copied my designs."

"And yet I'm making a deal with them." He blinked, and she could tell she'd startled him again. "Say what you will," she added. "And so will I. I'll tell them the truth."

"You should leave now," said Mick. "And it'll be easier if you'd also walk away from whatever you think you have going on with Eau Sauvage." Once again, he offered her his mild-mannered smile, a smile she now knew concealed a pit viper. With a relaxed air, he leaned back and crossed his ankles on the desk.

As she regarded his posture, something niggled at her. A memory flitted through her mind and disappeared. Then it flitted back, hardening into sickening suspicion. "You came to my apartment the day Angelique died."

"No idea what you're talking about," he said. "And now it really is time for you to leave."

Caroline stood her ground. "She died of an overdose in my home."

Mick got up and came out from behind the desk. "A tragedy that has nothing to do with me." He strode to the door and gestured for her to exit. "Find your way out. *Now.*"

She noticed tiny beads of sweat on his brow and upper lip. She noticed his hand-tailored untucked shirt and his ultracool couture half boots from the Apiary Shoe Company. The tread on all their shoes had a honeycomb design. On the day Angelique died, Caroline had seen a piece of mail with the imprint of that distinctive shoe tread, a detail only someone in the fashion world might recognize. "You were the one who abused her," she said, her voice low and trembling from the stunning realization. "After you got out of rehab. I saw what you did to her."

He took a step toward her, his eyes like shards of ice, and she felt a moment of panic. She flashed on Angelique's bruises. He grabbed the door handle. Those hands, thought Caroline. Were those the hands that had battered her friend? Was that the anger that had sent Angelique fleeing in the night?

"Get the fuck out." The low command dug into her nerves.

"Oh, I will," she said. "I'm going to make a report."

"To whom? About what? You're a liar, bitter against your employer. Who are they going to believe? Jesus, the whole city knows me. I'm Mick fucking Taylor."

He was too close now, crowding her against the door. "And I'm your worst nightmare. I said that before, but then I walked away. I'm not going to walk away this time."

He smiled—the mild-mannered smile of the Mick Taylor everyone knew and loved. "You do not want to fuck with me," he continued in a friendly, conversational tone. "Try it, and you'll be so fucking sorry—"

"What are you going to do?" she demanded. "Hit me, too?"

Daria greeted Caroline with a "Shhh—the baby's asleep," followed by a hug and a pantomimed squeal. "Oh my gosh, it's wonderful to see you," she said. "I can't wait to catch up!"

"You look amazing. Motherhood agrees with you," Caroline said. Daria wore a Chrysalis tunic, one of the prototypes from Caroline's ruined collection. The shimmery fabric encased her now-slender figure like a cocoon, and the nautilus shell detail on the shoulder concealed a fastener for nursing access.

"I love it," Daria said. "I'm exhausted all the time, but I couldn't be happier." She brought Caroline over to the tiny kitchen bar, which was cluttered with teething toys, packets of wipes, boxes of organic baby snack food, and stacks of unopened mail. "I have bottled water or . . . bottled water. Sorry, Layton's out of town and I haven't been to the store."

"In that case, bottled water."

"At least it's the bubbly kind." Daria poured while Caroline gave her some little gifts for the baby.

"A rain fly jacket and her own superhero T-shirt." Caroline held up the shirt. "She'll grow into it soon enough."

"These are wonderful. I wish I had a superpower of my own—the ability to clean the house while I sleep." She lifted her glass of bubbly water. "To you, my friend. I've been following C-Shell Rainwear online. No surprise that it's fabulous. That piece that ran in *Vogue*—Cat Willoughby. Come *on*."

"Yeah, that was such a lucky break. Now we're scrambling to get the garments made as fast as they're being ordered." She told her about the deal with Eau Sauvage, earning a quiet high five from her friend.

"Take *that,* Mick Taylor," said Daria. "You know, I never worked for him again after what he did to you."

"Funny you should bring him up," Caroline said. "He has a collaboration with Eau Sauvage, too. Bags he claims he designed, but who knows? One of the things about laboring in obscurity and being under the radar is that he thought I was gone. And he can't steal what he can't see."

"Now suddenly you're in the spotlight again. I bet it's making him completely mental. That's the best revenge."

"I don't want revenge. But here's the thing. There's something else I discovered about Mick Taylor. Something a lot worse. He's the one who was abusing Angelique, and I'm pretty sure he had something to do with her drug use."

Daria's jaw dropped. "Mick? Seriously? I don't know, Caroline. He's a dick for stealing designs, but hitting a woman? Angelique, of all people?"

"That's why I didn't realize it until now. We all assumed it was Roman or some other guy she refused to talk about. But guess what? I went to see Roman and figured out some things." She explained about the meetings at the church and what she'd learned from Angelique's sponsor.

"God, that's so sad. I feel horrible for not figuring it out. How do you know Mick was with her that day?"

"It was the smallest thing. His shoes."

Daria frowned.

"He was wearing shoes from Apiary. They're, like, a thousand dollars a pair. The day Angelique died, someone in Apiary shoes was in my building—I saw the tread marks on my mail and on the stairs going up. At the time, I didn't think anything of it, but today I saw him in those shoes, and I thought about the fact that no one in my building ever wore thousand-dollar shoes. And then I remembered that Mick had been to rehab. He denied everything, of course. Even tried to gaslight me. He said I'd be regarded as a liar, trying to spread rumors about my former employer."

"Did you tell the police?"

"I called them and made a report. But since I didn't witness anything directly, they're limited as to what they can do. No victim, no crime. And it's Mick Taylor. 'Mick fucking Taylor,' as he called himself as he was throwing me out of his office. He can afford any legal team in the city."

"He's a nightmare, and you're right—worse than I thought. But what can we do?"

Caroline told her about the Sewing Circle and the things she'd learned. "Guys who abuse women don't stop at just one. It's a habit, ingrained, especially in a guy with so much power and status, a guy who's been getting away with it probably for decades."

"So you're saying there are other women?"

"With Angelique gone, he's torturing someone else. Other models. Other designers. Interns and assistants. If I can find someone, talk to her, maybe it'll start something."

"I don't know, Caroline. Sounds like a long shot."

"It does. But maybe I have a superpower, too—knowing how to organize a group of women."

Chapter 29

Will missed Caroline like hell, and she'd only been gone a few days. Christ, he missed her when they were apart a few *hours*. It was bad. And it was so, so good. In the aftermath of the long, sad failure of his marriage, Caroline was doing the impossible. She was making him feel that kind of soaring, head-in-the-clouds love a teenager felt, but this was better, because he knew exactly what it was and what it wasn't.

It was the kind of genuine, deep relationship he'd craved all his life, maybe without even knowing how much he needed it.

It wasn't a crush. It wasn't what his grandma used to call a passing fancy.

No, this was as real as the ground beneath his feet.

It wasn't going to go away. It was going to get stronger and deeper, day by day. Knowing this was sweet relief, because after Sierra had left, he'd had his doubts that he would ever find a love like this, or that it even existed outside of starry-eyed books and movies.

Looking back over the years, he marveled at the long and twisty road their story had taken. He remembered every moment with Caroline, beginning when they were kids. The memories were as bright as the sunrise and gilded with happiness. Sometimes he looked back over those days and wondered why he hadn't seen it, the fact that he had loved this girl beginning with the very first day they'd met.

After the incident in Africa, a trauma counselor had said—in a different context altogether—that things happen in their own time. Could be that was the reason the love of his life had been right in front of him for decades, and he simply hadn't recognized it.

Her trip to New York solidified something he'd been thinking all along. When she sent him a text message saying she was back, he left his assistant coach in charge of practice and went straight to her parents' house. She came outside as he was getting out of his car and flew into his arms.

"Hey," he said, his heart filling up as he inhaled the scent of her hair. A second later, he realized she was crying. "Hey, what's the matter? Didn't the meeting in New York go well?"

"It did. And it didn't," she said. "Long story."

"I've got all day. Get in." He held the car door open for her. As he backed out of the driveway, he saw her mother in the window.

"She's a lifesaver," Caroline said. "I don't know what I'd do without her, watching the kids and giving us a place to live."

He drove to the main town of Long Beach, where shops and businesses were closing for the day, and headed south to the wooded trails and cliff-top lighthouses. As he parked in the deserted coast guard lot, she smiled and murmured, "Our spot."

"We came here together the first day we met, remember?"

They hiked out to the rocky escarpment at the tip of Cape Disappointment and sat watching the waves. The sky was overcast, the ocean an impenetrable iron gray. "It was strange being back in the city," she said. "I spent nearly half my life there, but in a way, it felt like I was starting all over again. The deal with Eau Sauvage is moving ahead, so that's all good. Willow was awesome in the meeting. I also met up with some people who knew Angelique."

He put his arm around her and let her talk. She'd uncovered some hard truths about the kids' mother, including the fact that the guy beating up on her was Mick Taylor, the same one who'd stolen Caroline's designs. "It's like he's got this horrible hidden side, so my friend Daria and I reached out to women who've worked with him or are working with him now. Models and interns and assistants." She looped her arms around her knees and stared straight ahead at the horizon. "I tried to convince them that it was safe to speak out, that it's not okay the way he treats people."

Will studied her profile. She was so beautiful to him, somehow both determined and vulnerable at the same time. "Let me guess. Nobody spoke up."

She nodded, letting out a sigh. "This business is hard at every level, but especially for women who are desperate to establish themselves. They worked all their lives to get to New York, and there I was, a stranger, telling them to point the finger at a guy who can end their careers the way he ended mine. I was naive, thinking they might come forward. They're not going to throw themselves under the bus for my sake. They have bills to pay. Some probably have kids. No one can afford to rock the boat. Before all this happened, I probably would have been the same way. Remember, I'm the one who walked away after he stole my designs. And now I'm asking them to stand and fight?"

"You're being too hard on yourself."

"I'm being realistic. You know, I've been following the #MeToo movement along with everybody else. And wouldn't we all like to march and speak out? But guess what? This is real life, and our bills are real, and we need real jobs."

He couldn't argue with that. It was idealistic and certainly current to point the finger and call out men and incidents that exploited and even harmed them. It all sounded good on social media and the news, but protests didn't pay the bills. He'd seen it in the military and in education as well—women staying silent rather than risking their careers.

"How can I help?" he asked her simply.

She turned to him and there was that smile, the one that lit her face. "You're already helping."

Caroline gave each of the kids a kiss on the head and sent them down the driveway to wait for the school bus. It was their first day without their cousin Fern, because Virginia had bought a cottage on the south end of the peninsula, moving ahead in her post-divorce life.

"When did kissing my kids goodbye start seeming so normal?" she asked her mother, who was making a second pot of coffee.

"You're a natural."

"Nah. But you're a good teacher. Seriously, Mom, I don't know how to thank you and Dad. Now that Virginia's gone—"

"Do you want to move to the garage apartment?"

"That's really nice, but what I want is to be on my own again. Supporting myself *and* the kids."

"I have no doubt you'll do that," her mother said, handing her a mug of fresh coffee. "There's no hurry. We love being able to help with the kids." She paused. "Take all the time you need. It's probably premature to say this, but you and Will are getting really close."

Please don't say how close, Caroline thought.

"I'm happy for you," Mom said. "He's a good guy, and you're . . . different around him. In a good way."

"Am I?"

"He lights you up, Caroline. It's really nice to see."

Caroline looked out the window at the wind-harried dunes. "Is it weird that we're together? Me and Sierra's ex? I ran into her mother the other day, and she all but accused me of breaking them up. She said if I hadn't come back, they'd still be together."

"Sierra's mother probably misses her desperately, and she's grieving. She knows as well as you and I do that your coming back didn't end Sierra's marriage."

"The timing must seem incredibly suspicious. Honestly, this was the last thing I expected." And the thing was this—Caroline was so in love with Will Jensen that she couldn't see straight. But lately she wondered if he was already regretting their newfound love. She came with two kids, a struggling business enterprise, and a complicated adoption proceeding. So much baggage to bring to a new relationship.

She opened her laptop and checked her email queue. It was a mile long these days. This morning brought a series of attached documents from the social worker who was helping her with the adoption. Feeling a twinge of apprehension, she opened a document with IMPORTANT in the subject line.

The words on the screen blurred before Caroline's eyes. Everything inside her turned to liquid and drained away on a wave of horror. She must have made a sound, because her mother dropped everything and came over to the table.

"What's the matter?"

Caroline managed to catch her breath. "There's . . . Mom, there's a problem with the adoption."

"What do you mean, a problem? The hearing is on the calendar, and we've got the party all planned. What could possibly go wrong at this point? My God, you're white as a ghost, Caroline. Is it their immigration status?"

Caroline nearly came undone as she tried to find her voice. "The children's father hasn't relinquished his parental rights."

Chapter 30

Caroline stepped out of the car in front of the Pacific County courthouse, trying to keep her knees from wobbling. The domed 1910 building faced the bay with brooding symmetry, its blocky shape dominating the surrounding gardens and crammed parking lot. More cars lined the road, and there were several news vans topped with gear, the crews rolling out cables and cameras.

What should have been a simple case of adoption had become notorious. Caroline had barely slept for days as she braced herself for the confrontation.

Flick and Addie got out of the back seat, and Virginia went to park the car. The nightmare that had begun with the paternal rights claim had extended to her home, her heart, her dreams.

Caroline hadn't been able to afford a lawyer, so her parents had put up a retainer to an attorney who specialized in family law. Because everyone knew Caroline was going to need all the help she could get.

Theresa Bond, the lawyer, had advised Caroline to bring the children to the hearing. Caroline had tried to explain the situation to the children in a way they could understand. But they didn't understand. "Mama always said we don't have a father," Flick insisted.

"I don't want a father," Addie had stated. "I just want you."

Now Caroline took both their hands. She hoped they didn't notice how cold hers were. She was utterly terrified. She'd promised these children repeatedly that she would keep them safe. And now that promise was in jeopardy.

Judges almost never terminated the rights of a natural parent against that parent's will. Almost never.

She clung to the *almost.*

A gleaming SUV with blackened windows silently docked itself at the curb. Out stepped a couple of men with briefcases, followed by Rilla Stein and Mick Taylor. Cameras flashed and journalists called out questions. It was bizarre, seeing them here at the far edge of the country, uncomfortable transplants from New York.

Mick Taylor was the children's father. An expedited DNA test had verified the claim. Caroline was still in shock. The children had been born in Haiti, so she'd assumed the father was there. Yet now, she couldn't help but notice Flick's nose was very slightly aquiline, and maybe Addie's eyes were a certain shade of flecked green. According to the documents filed by Mick's legal team, Angelique had never told Mick the children were his.

Caroline had nothing to say to him or any member of his entourage as they surged past, dogged by reporters and photographers. Mick had found her Achilles' heel. The one thing that could take her down. Although custody cases usually ground slowly through the system, Mick's powerful legal team had won an injunction against Caroline's adoption petition.

Addie made a small, almost inaudible sound. The little girl was staring at Mick, and a small trickle of pee tracked down her leg.

"Oh, sweetie," Caroline whispered. "Let's go inside, okay?"

With both kids in tow, she threw her bag on the security scanner and quickly found a restroom. "We'll get you cleaned up," she said, taking off Addie's undies, shoes, and socks. She rinsed the things in the sink and dried them under the hot hand dryer. As she helped

Addie get dressed again, she looked into the little girl's eyes.

"Are you all right?" she asked. "Did something upset you?"

Addie kept her eyes downcast.

"Sweetheart, can you say what it is?"

Addie shook her head. "I don't want to go out there."

Caroline's heart nearly burst. The sight of Mick had frightened the little girl. "I'll keep hold of your hand. You can sit right in between Grammy Dot and Grandpa Lyle. We'll never let you go." She prayed it wasn't an empty promise.

She and the kids stepped out into the courthouse lobby, and she was stunned by the size of the crowd waiting to enter the courtroom. Her parents, sisters, and brothers, of course. A contingent from the Sewing Circle. Restaurant people. Neighbors who had known her all her life.

And Will. In a perfectly tailored suit that showed off his flawless military posture.

Caroline tried to hold it together as she joined her lawyer and they entered the courthouse. The interior rotunda was grand and intimidating, with twin winding staircases and a huge stained-glass dome glaring from high above the mosaic-tiled floor. She was numb with fear as they made their way to the courtroom. She caught Will's eye as they passed, but the moment was quickly gone. When she'd first heard the news, Will had held her in his arms and let her vent. *He doesn't want the kids,* she'd raged. *He wants revenge.*

She had not realized what she'd set in motion the day she'd confronted Mick in New York.

Her friends and family filled the courtroom. Addie and Flick went with her parents, and she and her lawyer took a seat at the table. She darted a glance at the other side. There was Mick, with a fresh haircut and conservative suit, flanked by a team of lawyers and the ever-present Rilla, anxious as a mouse sniffing the air.

Everyone rose as the judge entered. Theresa had said she couldn't predict what Judge Rudolph would make of the situation. He had a reputation for being impatient and conservative, which might or might not work in Caroline's favor. He had not been the presiding judge in the initial adoption proceeding, and that, Theresa admitted, was not ideal.

"I'm not fond of surprises," the judge said. "And I don't like sloppiness, particularly in a case like this involving young children. This adoption was presented as a clean and unencumbered case. And now we have Mr. Taylor, seeking to assert his parental rights to Francis and Adeline Baptiste. Is that correct, Mr. Taylor?"

Mick glanced at his lawyer, then said, "It is. Yes, that's correct."

"And on the other hand, we have Ms. Shelby, the children's guardian, who wishes to become their adoptive parent?" Rudolph looked at Caroline.

"Yes, Your Honor. I've been their full-time guardian since their mother passed away last year, and—"

"I've read your statement," he said with a wave of his hand. "I'm going to assign a guardian ad litem to be the children's advocate, because the heart of the matter is the well-being of the children. I'll hear from both sides, but I'm not likely to render a decision today."

Mick scribbled a note to his lawyer in a rapid, impatient swipe of the pen.

One of his lawyers stood and folded her hands demurely. She wore Mrs. Claus–style wire glasses and her white hair was neatly coiffed. Her smile was sweet and just a little naive. Caroline had no doubt she had the instincts of a barracuda.

"As the DNA test shows unequivocally, Your Honor, Michael Taylor is the natural father of Adeline and Francis, and he has *not* relinquished his parental rights. This man founded a fashion empire, and he has the resources and the heart to give them a safe and happy home."

Theresa got to her feet. "Your Honor, Mr. Taylor has never acknowledged the children's existence or given these children support of any kind—"

"Because the mother kept them from him," said one of Mick's lawyers. "Sadly, Angelique Baptiste was a terrible addict. She was also an undocumented alien, as are the children. Their status is questionable—"

"Your Honor." Theresa shot up again. "The very fact that Mr. Taylor would allow his representative to speak this way in front of the children indicates how little regard he has for their well-being."

Caroline's mother was already leaving the courtroom with the children. She paused at the door, spoke briefly with the bailiff, and headed outside.

When asked why he never offered to support the children, Mick claimed he had never met them and didn't know their ages. He claimed Angelique was promiscuous, with a reputation for taking up with multiple partners.

"Given these claims," Theresa interjected, "how would Mr. Taylor guess he's the father?"

Mick's lawyer was clearly prepared for this. "He saw their picture in a feature article boasting about

Ms. Shelby's newfound career success. The resemblance is quite remarkable, don't you think?"

Caroline felt as if she might explode. She'd set this in motion when Orson had published a piece, complete with photos, about C-Shell and her life on the peninsula.

She was burning to point the finger at Mick and expose him as a violent, abusive man. Her lawyer wouldn't go there. They had nothing but hearsay. The judge was required to rule on the facts, and Mick's team would rip the story to shreds.

Theresa did have access to several indisputable facts, however. "Based on the date of Francis's birth, we know that Angelique was seventeen when her son was born. This means she was sixteen when Mr. Taylor impregnated her. And just seventeen when he fathered her second child. The age of consent in Haiti is eighteen, so Mr. Taylor committed statutory rape."

"Your Honor, this is character assassination," said Mick's grandmotherly lawyer. With mild-mannered sweetness, the woman explained that, during a high-fashion shoot on a Haitian beach, Angelique had told Mick she was nineteen, and they fell in love and had an affair. But Angelique had an unfortunately promiscuous nature. When she arrived in New York City with her young children, everyone thought the father was someone back in her native Haiti.

It wasn't enough to destroy Angelique's reputation. Caroline soon learned the reason Rilla Stein had come. "Ms. Shelby was employed under contract to Mr. Taylor," Rilla explained to the judge. "The association ended badly when she copied his designs and tried to pass them off as her own."

The words thundered in Caroline's ears. She felt a wave of nausea.

Across the aisle, Mick portrayed himself as the wounded but magnanimous victor. Caroline saw herself depicted as a petty, vengeful underling who had copied designs from her former boss and sought to punish him by absconding with his children.

"There are some troubling aspects to this situation," said the judge. "However, the state has a duty to honor the natural parent . . ."

The gavel came up. Hovered. Theresa's phone screen lit with a silent alert. She quickly stood. "A moment, Your Honor. My colleague is here with additional information."

"Did you not hear me, Ms. Bond? I don't like surprises."

"It's—I do understand, and I apologize." Theresa spoke slowly, as if trying to cause a delay. "I can't apologize enough."

Mick's attorney clearly recognized the ploy. The grandmotherly one also stood. "Please, Your Honor, this is simply a—"

The door at the rear of the courtroom swished open, offering a glimpse of eager reporters and curiosity seekers. Willow slipped inside and hurried over to Theresa, handing her a folder. With an impatient gesture of his hand, the judge took the folder from the clerk and scanned the documents. A moment later, he regarded the attorneys with a face made of stone. "In my chambers at once," he said. "We'll take a half-hour recess."

Caroline teetered on the verge of a panic attack. She slipped out a side door of the courtroom and took refuge in a nearby conference room, dim and close and full of shadows. Turning toward the window, she pressed her hands against her midsection and tried to regulate her breathing. She was going to lose her kids. The judge was going to give them to the man who beat their mother. Already she was plotting ways to flee with Addie and Flick, to go into hiding, to—

Someone else came into the conference room. She turned and found herself face-to-face with Mick.

A rod of cold steel stiffened her spine. She glared at him. "What do you want?"

"The judge called a recess," Mick said. "Figured I'd wait here."

"That's not what I mean," she snapped. "I mean, what do you want? What's your ask? You don't want these kids."

"I warned you back in New York—walk away from Eau Sauvage. Admit you lied when you accused me of hitting Angelique."

"Forget it. I don't bargain with bullies."

"Then you'd better introduce those kids to their new daddy."

A chill crawled over her skin. "Seriously—what will make you go away?"

"Everything all right in here?" Will appeared in the doorway, his gaze locked onto Caroline.

"Who are you?" Mick blustered with bravado. "This is a private conversation. Get the hell out."

"Oh, buddy." Will spoke softly. His stance was relaxed, yet his voice thrummed with menace. "You do not want to fuck with me."

Caroline had no doubt that Will could go full-on Navy SEAL in the blink of an eye.

Which would be gratifying. But not helpful.

"Mick is going to surrender his parental rights," she said, fixing him with an unwavering stare.

He glared back at her. "I told you what I want. Take it or leave it."

She felt a spike of panic. If she allowed the tentative deal with Eau Sauvage to fall apart, C-Shell Rainwear would sink like a stone. Far worse, if she failed to report the part about him being an abuser, it would betray everything the Oysterville Sewing Circle stood for—believing women, making them feel seen and heard.

He narrowed his eyes and repeated, "Take it or leave it."

He wanted her to surrender *her* reputation to save his. He wanted to destroy her integrity along with everything she had built—her business, her livelihood, the chance to help the women who had helped her build C-Shell. He wanted to strip her of everything, the way he had before, when he'd stolen her designs. He was suggesting that the way to keep the children was to excuse the actions of a violent sexual predator who had victimized Angelique and set off the chain of events that had led to her death.

Go fuck yourself. That was what she wanted to say to him. To this smug, sexist, misogynistic man.

This man who had violated her by taking her power from her.

Then she thought of Addie, peeing herself at the very sight of Mick. She could speak out and risk losing the children, or make a deal right here and now. It was a horrible, wrenching dilemma, choosing safety while bottling up what she knew to be true.

She looked at Will, then back at Mick. "Get your lawyers in here. We're settling this now."

Caroline couldn't breathe. Will brought her outside the courthouse, finding a private area facing Willapa Bay and its surrounding marshes, spiked with forested atolls and abandoned docks. She pressed herself against the pale yellow stone of the building, trying to catch her breath.

"I have to settle," she said to Will, nearly choking on her own words. "I have to do whatever it takes to protect my kids."

He put his arms around her and she pressed her cheek against his chest. "Easy, baby. You're not going to lose them," he murmured.

"My lawyer said no judge would ever take away the rights of the natural parent just because he steals designs and he's unethical. She said bringing up the abuse would work against me because it's nothing more than hearsay." Her throat was clogged with bitterness.

"We'll fix this," Will said. "We'll find a way."

"What way? The judge has to rule on the facts. In order to make Mick back off, I have to annihilate my own career and deny what I know he did to Angelique. But when it comes to Flick and Addie, I'm willing to throw myself under a speeding bus."

"The guy isn't interested in those kids," Will said.

"You're absolutely right. Mick Taylor doesn't want to be a parent. That was never his goal. I ought to call his bluff. I could say, 'Take them, they're yours, good luck.'" She pulled back and looked up at Will, drawing strength from his steady gaze. "There's no way I'd ever do that to my kids. I'd never use my children to make a deal. Because in every way that matters, they're *my* children. My family. They're not bargaining chips on the negotiating table."

If her business, her career, her reputation had to go down in flames, so be it. The old Caroline would never tear down everything she'd built, the idealized trust and belief. But she wasn't that person anymore. She was a mother.

There were few things, she'd learned, more precious than one's integrity, but one of them was surely the need to love and protect a child.

Leaving Will's embrace, she found her mother with Addie and Flick in the courthouse garden. Gathering them into her arms, she held them close.

"You're my kids. You're mine forever," she told them. "You're safe. You'll always, always be safe."

"Can we go home now?" asked Flick.

Virginia rushed over to her. "Caroline—you need to come back to the courtroom."

Caroline couldn't look at anyone as she approached the long table where Theresa and now Willow sat. We had a deal, she thought, her pulse leaping into overdrive. Our lawyers were supposed to make a deal.

A third attorney joined them at the table. To Caroline's shock, it was Aisha Franklin, an advocacy lawyer she'd met at the meeting in Atlanta.

"What's going on?" Caroline whispered, wavering between hope and fear.

Willow touched her arm. "Be still. You'll find out soon enough."

There was a wave of silence as the judge returned to the bench. Aisha handed a dossier to Theresa, who approached him along with Mick's lawyer.

"Your Honor, I would like to submit this exhibit reciting facts pertinent to this proceeding. These are sworn statements made under oath." She placed one of the dossiers in front of Mick's attorney and gave the other to the clerk for the judge. "These are from individuals who have direct knowledge of Michael Taylor's history of violence toward women. There were witnesses who saw him treating Angelique Baptiste in an abusive manner. And there are also others who suffered abuse from him."

"Your Honor," Mick's lawyer said, "you yourself said you don't like surprises."

Caroline clutched Willow's arm. "Isn't it too late to submit these statements?"

"This is a hearing, not a trial," Willow reminded her in a low whisper. "It's up to the judge."

There was a stir in the back of the courtroom. The judge picked up his gavel and barked an order at the bailiff. Several women entered through the double doors. Caroline recognized models and junior designers she'd met in New York, the ones she and Daria had asked to come forward. They'd demurred, afraid and vulnerable, and Caroline had given up trying to convince them. Now they were here, appearing like a tidal wave through open floodgates.

Despite the judge's hammering gavel and shouted dismissal, a babble arose in the room.

"This is bullshit," Mick said, coming up out of his seat as if on fire. "A goddamn witch hunt."

His lawyers and entourage surrounded him, clearly trying to minimize the damage by hustling him away.

"The hunt is over," Willow said to Mick as he passed by. "We've found the witch."

Caroline turned to Willow and Aisha. "What just happened?"

"It's still happening. Let's go."

Mick's accusers had gathered in the domed entryway and on the courthouse steps, talking to the media and pointing the finger at Mick. Holding up cell phone pictures and giving interviews. Women's voices echoed off the marble walls, and the historic rotunda echoed with the powerful sound of triumph. They spoke of pressure and intimidation, of coercion and threats, economic abuse.

Caroline grabbed Willow's arm to steady herself. Humility and relief nearly overwhelmed her, washing away the agonizing bitterness of staying silent. "How did everyone get here?" she asked. "Did you know about this?"

"I've made it my mission since our trip to New York. Even though they were reluctant to talk about their experience, we persisted and finally persuaded these six. Your friend Daria was instrumental. She said that now that she has a daughter, she can't let something like this go. And the Sisterhood in Atlanta funded us.

The sworn statements are powerful, Caroline. Affidavits. Pictures and videos. At least two women are filing criminal charges. Mick's got much bigger problems than claiming custody. I don't think you need to worry about him being willing to sign away his paternal rights now."

Caroline couldn't believe it. She should, though, because one thing she had learned from the Sewing Circle was the power in a group of women determined to tell the truth.

"Thank you," she said. "That sounds so inadequate—"

"Don't thank us. You started this, Caroline. Now go find your kids."

Chapter 31

Caroline sat propped against a bank of pillows in Will's bed, poring over the lengthy investigative article that had come out in the national press with the headline THE TAKEDOWN OF A FASHION EMPIRE.

Early-morning sunlight tracked across the floor. Will had gone to let the dog out for a run, and now he returned with two mugs of coffee. There was nothing quite like the sight of a shirtless man bearing coffee first thing in the morning.

"Bless you," she whispered, warming her hands around the cup and taking her first sip.

He settled in next to her. "How is it?"

"Delicious," she said, taking another sip.

"The article, I mean."

She turned the magazine so he could see. The main image was a dramatic shot of the neo-Gothic courthouse surrounded by six harshly lit, glowering models, looking like a predator's worst nightmare. The exposé had been written by Becky Barrow. Caroline had met her as Orson Maynard's intern. Now she was a star reporter, making a name for herself by exposing exploitation in the fashion industry.

Caroline laid the magazine open so they could both look. "Hard to read," she said. "It's horrible to think about what he did, what he got away with for so long. I'm glad it's over now, but I hate that it happened. And to so many."

In addition to the women who had shown up at the courthouse, there were others, more than she'd imagined—models and assistants and interns and underlings who were initially dazzled by Mick's affable manner and talent, and later in private discovered his violent nature. They described his abuse in painstaking detail. They stepped out of the shadows with stories of wild parties, bullying, sexual assault.

Mick Taylor was swept out to sea like so many other men who had used their status and power to prey upon women. And like those men, he would soon be washed into the depths of obscurity. Initially he'd attempted to shrug off the accusations. Then, with a non-apology to "those who may feel wronged by me," he headed to rehab in Sedona. As the storm against him gathered force, he was deserted by all his famous friends. His brand collapsed like a house of cards in the wind. The mounting evidence made it clear that he was facing a barrage of civil suits from his victims, along with criminal charges and prison time. As Willow had predicted, he had willingly surrendered his paternal rights to Addie and Flick.

During their interview for the exposé, Becky had asked Caroline how it felt to bring him down. "I didn't bring him down," Caroline was quoted as saying. "The truth brought him down." It felt strange, seeing her own words framed as a pull quote on the page.

"It's an exoneration for you," Will pointed out as he finished reading the article.

"I don't care about being exonerated," Caroline said. "I just want to be done. I just want to move on with my life, be a mom to these kids and try to get my business back on its feet."

He set her coffee mug on the nightstand and folded the paper. "And I just want to marry you," he said, pulling her into his arms.

She pushed back and gaped at him. "Stop it."

"Not exactly the answer I'm hoping for."

"Will." She studied his face, every line and angle and plane familiar and beloved and longed for. "Don't you dare kid around."

"Me? A kidder?" He touched his hand to his heart. "Caroline Shelby, I love everything about you. The way you laugh at my stupid jokes and the way you cry when something touches your heart. The way you talk all the time without stopping and still manage to listen. The way you create designs out of nothing but imagination. The way you take joy in Addie and Flick even though you say you're scared. You're all I think about. You're everything I want. You and your kids and your little dog, too. And sweet Jesus, I mean that from the bottom of my heart."

Her own heart nearly exploded. She was too overwhelmed to speak. If she said yes, it would change the course of her life. She pictured herself here at Water's Edge, in this house that was filled with hand-carved woodwork and ancient family treasures. She pictured Addie and Flick playing with the dogs, following Will around, finding the adventures that awaited them in the woods, the bay and the seashore, the lighthouses and little villages strung along the peninsula.

She pictured forever with him. The wild excitement felt like a panic attack.

"You're not saying anything," he pointed out.

"Give me a minute, okay?"

"Yes, sure." He let go of her and opened the top drawer of his nightstand. "Just so you know, I have a ring."

"*What?*" She couldn't breathe.

He opened a small box, revealing a band of figured gold set with a square-cut diamond. "It was my grandmother's," he said. "I've been saving it for you."

Once again, she was uncharacteristically at a loss for words. She couldn't speak, nor could she take her eyes off him as she took in the moment, heartbeat by heartbeat. He was the person who had defined love for her, decades before, when she was too young to understand its power. It was the best feeling in the world, raw and powerful, beautiful and devastating, a rush of blood to the head. He had unknowingly set the standard for what she understood love was supposed to be like.

Every relationship she'd had afterward was measured against the love she imagined she would have had with Will—if only. She knew she was idealizing something that had never existed. If it had actually happened, life would have interfered. It might not have lasted. It might have worn thin.

"Caroline?" A crease appeared on his brow. "If the ring's too old-fashioned, I could—"

"Hush," she managed to say. "The ring is perfect."

She'd barely glanced at it. "Just listen. There's something I need to tell you." She took both his hands between both of hers. "Will Jensen, I've loved you for as long as life. I didn't even know how to talk about love until I talked to you. I was thirteen years old when I fell in love with you. It was the truest love I'd ever felt. I've been waiting for this day since I first laid eyes on you. But I never thought it was meant to be. So I've spent half my life teaching myself *not* to love you. Not to want something I could never have."

"That was then. Everything's different now. This is about you, Caroline. You and me. And if I'm not mistaken, you just admitted you're in love with me."

"Since the beginning of time."

Somehow the ring slipped onto her finger. And Will asked, "Why didn't you say anything?"

"I was afraid. I didn't know if I could—if we could go from being friends to being a couple."

"Yeah?" He gently traced his finger along her collarbone, following it with his lips. "We're doing okay in that department."

She could barely think straight when he touched her like this. "Uh-huh . . ."

"So now?"

"Oh, Will. Now it's all yes. Yes to all of this. Forever yes."

Epilogue

"The flower girl is missing."

Georgia's worried statement cut through the babble in the bride's getting-ready room adjacent to the restaurant.

Caroline swiveled around on her stool at the vanity, dropping an eyelash curler and probably creating a dark smudge across her cheek. "What? Where's Addie? How could she be missing?"

"I don't know—maybe with a hundred wedding guests arriving in the pouring rain, she wandered away and no one noticed."

"Oh my gosh, Addie." Caroline rushed for the door.

Georgia planted herself in the doorway. "Oh no you don't. I've got a search party looking for her right now. You need to finish getting ready."

"I can't even finish breathing until I know where Addie went. What if she wanders out into traffic? Is she lost in the dunes? On the beach, for chrissake? What if she's wet and scared somewhere?"

Virginia raised the window blind and gestured out at the parking lot. "It's like a dragnet out there. Look at them all."

The tux-clad brothers and ushers fanned out across the parking lot in all directions. The raised black umbrellas looked like a Magritte painting. A vast white pavilion was set up in the event area of Star of the Sea, sheltering the rows of chairs from the thick drizzle that persisted as the guests arrived for the ceremony.

"She's probably at the banquet table, sampling the wedding cake," Virginia added.

Georgia brought Caroline back to the vanity. "Sit," she commanded. "Let Ilsa do her thing."

Ilsa had a deft hand with makeup. And with Caroline as well. Instead of attacking her with foundation and highlighter, she took Caroline's hands. "Breathe," she said. "It's going to be a beautiful day."

"Fern, get over here," Virginia said. "I need to do your hair."

Caroline's niece could barely sit still. She spun around on a stool. "You look like a princess, Aunt Caroline. A legit princess."

Caroline's gown was dead simple—a gorgeous swath of watered silk that spilled from a stylized nautilus shell cutaway in back. The design was her own, but it had been constructed and sewn by Echo Sanders, now one of her best friends.

"Found her," Will called from the doorway. He held Addie in his arms. Flick stood beside him. "She was in the back seat of the car, sound asleep." He placed a kiss on the little girl's nose. "Just like you were the first time I saw you."

"Don't look at the bride," Fern shrieked. "It's bad luck if you see the bride!"

"Not looking," Will said, handing Addie to Georgia.

Caroline looked, though, and she nearly melted with love for him. He looked like every dream she'd ever had of the man she adored, and she couldn't wait to be his wife.

Watching Will leave the room, Addie clutched her doll and yawned. "I needed to find Wonder Woman," she said.

"That was a dumb thing to do," Flick said.

"Hey," Caroline warned.

"Sorry," he said quickly. He was growing so tall and confident. Today, in his tux and suspenders, he was beyond cute.

"Come here, you two," she said, opening her arms to them. "I have something for each of us." She took out Angelique's cowrie shell bracelet. She'd carefully separated the triple strands to make three bracelets. "Your mama gave me these on a very important day. They're made of shells from the beach in Haiti. She used to make them to sell when she was a little girl. We can each wear one to remind us of your mother and how much we love and miss her." She fastened one bracelet on each of them.

Then she gathered the children in for a hug. *Thank you, Angelique.* She sent the thought out into the universe. *Thank you.*

"She'll never leave us," she whispered. "She lives in our hearts, okay?"

"That makes me sad," Addie said, examining the bean-shaped shells of her bracelet. "This is supposed to be a happy day."

"It sure is," Caroline said. "If you see people crying, like Grammy Dot or me or . . . just anyone, it's because we're really happy." With that, she looked around the room, strewn with makeup and hair products and bouquets and filled with women who meant the world to her—not just her sisters and mother, but the friends she'd made in the Oysterville Sewing Circle. They had all played a part in her journey. Even Sierra had reached out in a conciliatory gesture. There was a card from her, mailed from Sharm El Sheikh. Her name now appeared on the masthead of a major fashion magazine.

Georgia bustled over and took charge of them both, shepherding them to their places. The music swelled, and each member of the wedding party went down the aisle. Will and Willow, who was the officiant, waited under a driftwood arch.

Then Caroline found herself completely alone for a moment, about to take the biggest step of her life. She dwelled on all the things that had brought her to this moment—the devastating losses and dizzying triumphs and everything in between.

She didn't hurry down the aisle but paced herself. She wanted to take in the warmth of the smiling faces turned in her direction. She felt so connected here, in a way she never had before, with the family she'd created in the aftermath of tragedy, the friends she'd made by reaching out and opening her heart.

She made her way to the end of the aisle and stood before Will. The whole world was in his face.

The music trailed softly away. A waiting silence descended. Will took both of Caroline's hands in his.

Willow looked from one to the other. "Shall we begin?"

Author's Note

Although this is a work of fiction, the issue of domestic violence is entirely real, and it can happen to anyone, regardless of age, gender, race, level of education, or income. I will be donating a portion of the proceeds from my royalties from this book to a nonprofit in my home county that provides safe, supportive, longer-term affordable housing for survivors of domestic violence.

If you need help, or if someone you know is in need, please reach out. In the United States, you can contact the National Domestic Violence Hotline: www.thehotline.org, 1-800-799-SAFE (7233), or TTY 1-800-787-3224. See also the Partnership Against Domestic Violence: www.padv.org.

Please note that these are not crisis response resources. If you need immediate assistance, contact your local authorities without delay.

Know that you're not alone. Know that it's real and it's not your fault. And trust that you'll be believed and supported.

Acknowledgments

Researching the subject matter for this book led me down a dark path, into the secret lives of women dealing with domestic violence. I cannot overstate the traumatic, toxic, and far-reaching effects of this syndrome. This novel illuminates only a glimpse of the issue, but my hope is that survivors everywhere will find a way to reach for safety. To all the women who shared their stories with me—thank you from the bottom of my heart for your candor, your bravery, and your determination to survive.

Thanks to my editor, Rachel Kahan, and the remarkable team of professionals at William Morrow—Liate Stehlik, Jennifer Hart, Tavia Kowalchuk, Lauren Truskowski, Alivia Lopez, Karen Hansen—for their enthusiasm for this book. Meg Ruley and Annelise Robey of the Jane Rotrosen Agency are, as always, pillars of strength and humor. For guiding me and my readers through the social media labyrinth, I am eternally grateful for Cindy Peters, Ashley Hayes, and Elizabeth Wiggs.

Thanks to Laura Cherkas for thorough and thoughtful copy editing and to Marilyn Rowe for proofreading.

My husband, Jerry Gundersen, is a real-life designer and a source of inspiration in more ways than words can express.

About the Author

Susan Wiggs's life is all about family, friends . . . and fiction. She lives at the water's edge on an island in Puget Sound, and in good weather, she commutes to her writers' group in a twenty-one-foot motorboat. She's been featured in the national media, including NPR, PRI, and *USA Today;* has given programs for the U.S. embassies in Buenos Aires and Montevideo; and is a popular speaker locally, nationally, internationally, and on the high seas.

From the very start, Susan's writings have illuminated the everyday dramas of ordinary people facing extraordinary circumstances. Her books celebrate the power of love, the timeless bonds of family, and the fascinating nuances of human nature. Today she is an internationally bestselling, award-winning author, with millions of copies of her books in print in numerous countries and languages. According to *Publishers Weekly,* Wiggs writes with "refreshingly honest emotion," and the Salem *Statesman Journal* adds that she is "one of our best observers of stories of the heart [who] knows how to capture emotion on virtually every page of every book." *Booklist* characterizes her books as "real and true and unforgettable."

Her novels have appeared in the #1 spot on the *New York Times* bestseller list and have captured readers' hearts around the globe, with translations into more than twenty languages in thirty countries. She is a three-time winner of the RITA Award. Her recent novel *The Apple Orchard* is currently being made into a film, and the Lakeshore Chronicles have been optioned for adaptation into a series.

The author is a former teacher, a Harvard graduate, an avid hiker, an amateur photographer, a good skier, and a terrible golfer, yet her favorite form of exercise is curling up with a good book.

Visit Susan Wiggs's website at

www.susanwiggs.com

Social Media:

https://www.facebook.com/susanwiggs

https://www.pinterest.com/beachwriter1

https://twitter.com/susanwiggs

http://www.goodreads.com/SusanWiggs

https://www.instagram.com/susan_wiggs_

Susan's Amazon page:
https://www.amazon.com/Susan-Wiggs/e/B000AQ1FJO

Susan's Amazon page in the UK:
https://www.amazon.co.uk/Susan-Wiggs/e/B000AQ1FJO